THE IRON TRIANGLE

A Novel of the Vietnam War

By

Douglas L. Edwards

Table of Contents

DISCLAIMER

This is a work of fiction. Names, characters, places and events are the product of my imagination. The events described in this novel are composites of events experienced by the author and of purely imaginary events. Any resemblance to actual persons, living or dead, is entirely coincidental.

If you were a combat infantryman in Vietnam, you will see yourself in some of the narrative. This is not a coincidence. We all shared a common story in Vietnam, and we all have stories to tell. We fought in a war as we were asked to do. We didn't want to be there, but felt it was our duty. We returned home and were hated for our service. We were shunned.

Our stories should be told.

Welcome home, brothers.

Prologue

He moved through the jungle as if he were born to it. He didn't fight it as some did, but used its dense lushness to conceal and hide him. There were no snapping branches or thudding footfalls to mark his progress, only the gentle rustle of leaves as they lightly brushed against his fatigues. He moved with a slow, deliberate, fluid grace, gliding over and under and around the natural obstructions placed before him.

It was his favorite time of the day, early morning, when it was still cool and damp from the previous night. Soon, as noon approached, the sun would begin to scorch and bake the earth and torture anyone unfortunate enough to be out and unprotected from it. But now, the grass and leaves still glistened with dew and dampened his trousers as it brushed him in a gentle caress.

He stopped and dropped to one knee. He checked his compass and stared at the wall of vegetation that surrounded him. He listened to the hum and buzz of insects and checked the ground for anything that shouldn't be. Satisfied that everything looked as it should, he slowly rose and started off again.

Ahead, a tangled mass of vines and branches hung chest-high across his path. He approached it cautiously, looking for the telltale glint of wires. He bent low at the waist and passed under it. As he straightened up, he saw and heard nothing. The bullet struck him with an impact that sent him reeling back into a tree. The pain was immediate and excruciating, but it passed quickly. In a stupor, he slowly slid down the length of the tree until he sat in the muddy earth. He touched his shoulder with his fingers and felt the warm, sticky ooze of blood from his shattered collarbone.

He slowly rose above the trees. He never felt the second bullet hit his neck, almost severing his head. He was gone from himself by then. His body slumped over. He lay on his side and stared down at the scene unfolding with no particular emotion. He continued to float free toward the light. His time had come and he was not afraid. He was going home.

Chapter 1

The Day Before

"I can't remember how many people I've killed. I've tried; but somewhere along the way, I've lost count. That doesn't seem right. It would seem to be an easy question to answer. Ask any average twenty-year-old, and I'm sure they could provide an accurate answer. I guess it depends on who you're asking and where they are."

Alfie, the platoon dog, looked up at him with a dull, uncomprehending stare.

"I'm sure you're right, Alf, but it still isn't right. Remembering someone's death at least provides a measure of dignity to it. But then again, maybe it's better to just go numb."

Don Holt sat on a rusted lawn chair between the third- and fourth-platoon barracks. It was mid-afternoon, and the day's worst heat had passed. He was wearing a pair of cut-off fatigue pants and nothing else. His body glistened with a thin sheen of sweat that made his sunburned skin gleam a deep burnished red.

Alfie lay shaded beneath the chair.

Don swirled the contents of his nearly empty beer can before swallowing the last tepid remains. "Everything has changed. I'm not even in control of my own life anymore. I made a mistake in coming back. I feel like I screwed up big time, Alf." He scratched the mongrel's head, and Alfie moaned softly and moved to make his ears more accessible. "What do you say? About time we head in and grab a couple of cold beers. I'm tired of thinking. Nothing I can do will change things."

Don pushed himself away from the chair and slowly got up. As he neared the barracks, he stopped to admire the sign hanging over the door.

The sign announced the occupants as members of Company D, 2nd Battalion, 27th Infantry Regiment, 25th Infantry Division. On the sign was a black square bordered in gold with a finely detailed wolf's head in the middle, the battalion crest of the "Wolfhounds". Beneath the wolf's head were the words Nec Aspire Terrant, the regiment's motto: "No Fear on Earth".

As you entered the barracks, it would be easy to think you were in an all-boys camp if it weren't for all the weapons casually scattered about. The fourth-platoon boys had smooth skin and short hair, and barely looked their average age of nineteen. Most didn't even shave on a regular basis. But their looks were deceiving. Each, regardless of how innocent they appeared, possessed the necessary training and weapons to kill. More importantly, and certainly more frightening, some had the desire to kill.

They occupied themselves with cleaning their weapons and assembling their gear in anticipation of the evening's inevitable inspection. They were to return to the field tomorrow after a brief three-day stand-down, and Sergeant Camp never missed an inspection the night before a mission.

Staff Sergeant Wendell Camp sat in the rear of the barracks. The sergeant's quarters was a small area partitioned from the main room with sheets of burned plywood, the universal military paneling of Vietnam. He was with "Doc" White, the company medic, and "Mad Dog" Jaxon, the fourth platoon's medic. They were drinking beer and relaxing.

"Any word on where we're going?" asked Mad Dog.

"Somewhere in the Triangle. Don't know where exactly," said Camp.

He referred to the Iron Triangle, the name given to a vast expanse of thick, triple-canopied jungle northwest of Saigon and just north of the Base Camp. The Wolfhounds routinely operated in the Iron Triangle; it was one of their three areas of operation. The other two were the Hobo Woods and the Boi Loi Woods.

"Jesus Christ! We just came from there," Mad Dog exploded. "That will be three fucking months back-to-back in that shit hole." He threw his empty beer can across the floor. "2nd Battalion lost 34 guys last month. The fourth platoon lost 8 guys. There's not one fucking squad that has more than six guys left. There are no VC in there anymore, all are fucking NVA. We've been chasing these motherfuckers since Tet. This is all bullshit. How can they expect us to do that?"

"I'll let you know the next time they ask my opinion," Camp said.

"I'm serious, Wendy; they can't do this. They can't keep sending us up to that place month after month. It's not fair." Mad Dog looked from Camp to White for confirmation. "Anyway, it's the 1st Division's turn. They're supposed to switch with us. Right?"

"Hey, Mad Dog, calm down. What can I tell you? We're going and that's it." Camp said.

"He's right," Doc White agreed. "Nothing we can do about it. Maybe it will be the plantation. That's not as bad."

At that moment, they noticed Don. He walked in and held the door open for Alfie.

Mad Dog reached into the ice chest and pulled out a cold, wet can of Black Label beer and handed it to him. "Guess where they're sending us?"

"Yeah, I heard you guys. If we're not leaving Vietnam, I'm not interested."

"Back to the Triangle! Can you believe that?"

"One jungle is the same as the next. Half the time, they don't even tell us where we are."

"That's not the fucking point. Some places are genuinely worse than others."

Mad Dog looked to Doc White for a reaction.

"Anywhere in the Triangle is fucked up, but there's no reason to get all excited. It's not like we got a choice. Long as you come out in one piece, you're that much closer to going home."

"Well, I fucking care!"

Don shrugged and walked over to sit on a footlocker. He reached out for a battered aluminum bowl, then poured a generous measure of beer. Alfie rose slowly and, with great dignity, walked to his dish. With loud slurping, he quickly emptied the bowl, arched his back and emitted a loud belch, looking at Don for approval. Don reached down and scratched his head behind his ear, causing Alfie to rhythmically kick the air with his leg.

"Jesus, that dog is disgusting."

Alfie raised his tail and farted in Camp's general direction.

"All he wants is to drink, eat and fuck."

"Sounds like you, Wendy."

"That's probably why you dislike him; he exhibits all your worst traits."

"I remember when he first showed up. He was filthy and all cut up. We gave him a bath and Doc stitched him up. Stayed under my bunk 'til he was feeling better, and he's been here ever since."

Don picked absently at Alfie's matted orange fur.

"I don't like going back there either."

"Where? What the fuck are you talking about?"

"The Triangle. Isn't that what we were talking about? I'd rather the Boi Loi Woods; easier walking, no tunnels."

"It's the same fucking jungle. No one fucking place is worse than the other. They all suck."

"You haven't noticed how different things are now. All we fight are NVA, and there are fucking thousands of them up there. And they don't run anymore. They got beaucoup ammo, mortars and rockets up the ass and they use them. We don't fight little firefights anymore; we fight battles that last for days. They're killing us by the dozen. Mad Dog's right. We lose thirty to forty guys each time we go out. We have five guys left in the fourth squad. Five fucking guys!"

"I know, I know. It's been different after Tet. They stand and fight now."

"We should have bridge security. We're due to have security at the Phen Loi bridge," added Mad Dog.

"What fucking Phen Loi Bridge? Are you making that name up?" asked Camp.

"That bridge we guarded a few months back, the one on the river," said Mad Dog.

"I don't know what the name is, but I do know the gooks guard it now. It's their job."

"Fucking ARVNs get the soft jobs and we fight their war."

"That's enough. You assholes are making my head hurt. Go get your shit together and get cleaned up, I want to talk to Don in private."

Don pulled out two cold beers and handed one to Camp. "What did I do now?"

"The Lieutenant wants to speak with you tomorrow morning."

"Why? I thought we were leaving tomorrow?"

"I'll find out for sure later this afternoon, but I think we're getting an extra day. We're getting replacements. A bunch of them are coming in tomorrow morning. They'll need to get outfitted and squared away. Can't do that in the field. Also, the Lieutenant is talking about giving you your stripes back. I won't be going out, not at first. The Platoon Sergeant is short and wants off the line. So they're sending me to advanced NCO school for two weeks. If I make it through, I'll get another stripe and come back as Platoon Sergeant."

Don jumped up and grabbed Camp's hand. "Wendy, that is great news. You deserve it, brother. I really mean that. Fucking great news."

"The plan is he'll make you an Acting Jack and you'll have fourth squad. When I get back, everything will then be official. I'll be Platoon Sergeant and you'll be the squad leader."

"I know you have something to do with this. Thanks, pal. You're the best."

"When you volunteered to come back, you got a thirty-day leave and you took a few extra days. That's why you got busted. Right?"

"Yeah."

"Well, the Lieutenant told me he didn't think that was all that bad considering you volunteered for a second tour. He also said you could use the extra pay." Camp studied Don before continuing. "All this was what, two months ago? You got anything you want to tell me?"

"No. I took an extra few days. Seven, I think. I thought, 'What are they going to do? Send me to Vietnam? Fuck 'em.' They fined me a few weeks' pay and I was busted by some dipshit Lieutenant at Fort Dix."

"The Lieutenant said you need the extra pay now that you are married."

"Oh, that. Yeah. Look, Wendy, I was going to tell you, but the time was never right."

"We're supposed to be friends, and you fucking get married and don't say a word to me. Who'd you marry? Janet?"

"Of course it was Janet. It's a really long and complicated story. I just didn't know what to say or how to tell you."

"We got time now. Grab me another beer and start talking."

"Uh, where do I start with this? I got home, and the first thing I did was call Janet, and her fucking father answered. He wanted to see me, asked if we could meet somewhere. I said sure, all the time dreading meeting this prick. He never liked me, always thought

Janet could do better than me. So anyway, we meet at this old-time bar near their house; the kind with dark wood and big overstuffed booths in red leather. I walk in and he's sitting in the back. I sit down, and he just stares at me; no 'welcome home' or anything. He just stares with his dead fish eyes.

"The waiter comes over, I order a scotch on the rocks and just stare back at him. He lights a cigarette and says, 'Look, I wanted to talk to you before you see Janet.' I jump in and ask, 'Is everything okay?' He says Janet's fine, but there's a problem. He tells me Janet was going out with some friends during my first tour. I thought, fine. I didn't expect her to sit at home alone all year. He says one night, she's talking to this guy and apparently he slipped something in her drink. Next thing she remembers, she's in a cab going home. She gets home and she has some bruises on her wrists and blood in her underwear. Right away, she knows what happened, but doesn't remember how it happened. The blood part; she was a virgin. She doesn't know what to do, and a month later she doesn't get her period. She panics and tells her mother. They go to the doctor and confirm she's pregnant. This happens just a couple months before I get home.

"I'm just sitting there, listening, not saying a word. Next, he says, 'You're going back to Vietnam, and there's a very good chance you won't be returning home. I actually figured it out; your chances of surviving a second year of combat are only about thirty percent.' Oh wait, I forgot to mention, he's some big-deal actuary who figures out how long people are going to live for an insurance company. Makes a shitload of money. Thirty grand, I think. Anyway, he pulls out all these papers from his briefcase and spreads them on the table. He runs his finger along the lines. 'Thirty percent, maybe thirty-four. I can be more precise if I can ask you some questions.'

I'm looking at him and going, 'No, thirty percent is fine. Let's go with that.'

"We order more drinks and he is still studying his papers. He says, 'I would like you and Janet to get married. You know how people are and how they gossip. Once married, the baby will have your name and her reputation will be intact. She can live at home, and her mother and grandmother can help out. And if things go as I predict, she'll be a war widow and can start her life again.' I'm stunned. This guy is just so matter-of-fact about everything. So I say, 'Janet is okay with this? Did you even discuss this with her?' He says, 'We did, and she is.'

"'A lot of this is based on me getting killed over there. You do know I plan to do my best to see that doesn't happen. What happens then?' He looks at me and says, 'We'll deal with that outcome if and when you return. You have to understand my figures have always proven highly accurate. It's my job to be accurate.' I tell him I need to speak with Janet before I can make any decision.

"So later that night, I'm sitting with Janet on her front porch and she's barely looking at me. For a long time, we sit in silence. Finally, I say to her that we should get married. I tell her that I love her and I know she doesn't feel the same, but maybe love will come. She buries her face in my shoulder and is crying, and I'm crying. We go inside and tell her parents, and now everyone is crying. For the next thirty days, I barely see her. It was all about planning the wedding. When I do see her, it's mostly family shit, meeting her relatives and her friends, shit like that. The wedding is small, maybe twenty to twenty-five people. Nice church, and a nice party afterwards. I had nobody there. And that's how I got married."

"I know that your father's dead, but what about your mother?"

"Who the fuck knows? She couldn't be bothered to come."

"Look, I have to ask. Did you have a honeymoon? Did you get to fuck her?"

"That's complicated, too. We did go somewhere for a few days, a sort-of honeymoon, but it was really awkward. Both of us were uncomfortable. It was just weird. She was throwing up a lot, so it wasn't very romantic. I mean, we fooled around some. But it really wasn't... you know. It was kind of fucked up."

"Wow! Quite a fucking story. And you're okay with everything? It's kind of hard to believe. Her first time up at bat, and she hits a home run?"

"What can I say? She must be a fertile little bunny. There's no reason for her to lie about this."

"I'm still pissed that you didn't tell me, but now, I sort of understand."

"You're just pissed about the way things worked out. I know you always hoped we would be together, but you should have put a ring on my finger before I went on leave. No ring; no commitment."

"Don't be a fucking homo. What about the guy? The guy at the bar?"

"Oh, him. He wasn't hard to find. I asked around, and a bartender pointed him out. Seems like he had a reputation for doing shit like that."

"And what did you do?

"Me? I did nothing. Didn't have to. I heard he got mugged one night. Somebody took a bat to him. He got the shit beat out of him, got his arms and legs broken. His nose and jaw, too. He was some sort of big high-school jock. Not anymore. He got fucked up big time."

"They know who did it?" Camp asked.

"No. He was a real prick. Could have been any number of people. Made the newspapers though. I made sure Janet's father saw it."

"Remind me not to get on your bad side."

"Wendy, I told you. It could have been anyone."

"But you're not saying you didn't do it."

"And I'm not saying I did. It's like what the Buddhists say, 'Karma will rip you a new asshole.' He got exactly what was coming to him."

"I never heard the Buddhists put it exactly that way."

9

"I'm paraphrasing, you ignorant redneck."

"I wonder why they didn't kill him. I know I would have."

"I guess whoever did it had their reasons. He's going to walk with a limp for the rest of his life. He'll remember what he did everyday when he wakes up."

"Hey, by the way, where's your wedding ring?"

"I got it here on my dog tags." Don wriggled his dog tag chain in front of Camp.

"Well fuck me, I never noticed."

They got up walked slowly through the barracks, passing the men as they were getting dressed for chow.

"I have a briefing at the CP. We'll meet up at chow."

"Later, 'gator."

Camp gave Don a wave and headed toward the CP.

Chapter 2

Preparation

Don walked past a few cots to where the Wilson brothers were sitting. They weren't brothers, but everybody called them that. He sat next to PFC Richard Wilson, a tall, slender, caramel-colored, regal-looking black man who was cleaning his M79 grenade launcher. PFC Eugene Wilson was a skinny kid with a receding hairline and a large, bushy cavalryman's mustache. Eugene was of average height and was called 'Little Wilson'. Richard, standing at over six feet, was naturally called 'Big Wilson'. Big and Little Wilson were unlikely friends. Their backgrounds were different. Little Wilson came from Washington State, and Big Wilson called a sleepy little town in the Mississippi Delta home.

Little Wilson was loading magazines. "So, we still going out tomorrow? What did Camp say?"

"Haven't spoken to him. Hey, make sure there's eighteen in the mag and one in the chamber."

"Yeah, yeah, yeah, I know. No more than eighteen in the magazine. Sounds like some old Sergeant's tale."

"It's what I was always told to do starting way back in basic. If you put 20 in the magazine, the spring can jam."

"So what did Sergeant Camp say, then?" asked Big Wilson.

"Nothing. He's at the briefing now. I guess we'll find out after chow. You guys got all your shit together? Gene, how many mags you carrying?"

"I think I got 16 packed already and I'll throw in four bandoleers, plus one in the rifle. Is that enough?"

"Sounds about right. You can't have enough ammo and water. Pack all you can carry."

At that point, Gene looked up. "Where's Alfie?"

"Probably went to clean up. He likes to look good for the ladies. I heard he has a little bitch over by the Signal Corp. Either that, or he's over by the mess tent seeing what he can scrounge up. Cookie always saves him something nice."

"Where's the briefing at?" Gene asked.

"At the Command Post, I would imagine."

"I try to steer clear of that place. You go anywhere near the CP and you're bound to get pulled in for some shit detail. Filling sandbags for the REMFs, raking the dirt around the officer's hooches, or burning shit. Why can't they leave us alone when we come back in? Why do they always have to fuck with us? I mean, we only get three days back. Scumbags. Just leave us the fuck alone."

"You ever notice how the REMFs make themselves scarce when we're back?" Big Wilson said.

He was referring to the Rear Echelon Mother Fuckers—the clerks, cooks, mechanics and supply guys. In Vietnam, nine out of ten guys worked in some form of support job. Only one in ten participated in actual combat.

"I think they're afraid of us savages," Little Wilson added.

"I know they stay away from the EM Club. I wonder who does the shit work when we're not here?"

"They hire gooks to burn shit, and they have hooch maids to do their laundry and clean their barracks. Those bastards sleep on real mattresses with sheets and pillows. Not these mildewed World War Two cots they give us. Those fuckers would shit their pants if they ever had to go out to the field. Did you know some of them are 11Bs?"

"It's up to the First Sergeant who goes where, and he's the

biggest fag of them all. Even if you're classified 11 Bravo, Infantry, he can change your assignment. He probably checks their assholes personally. He gotta make sure they are regulation-tight."

"Man, you don't think that's true, do you?"

"It's Vietnam. Nothing, and I mean nothing, would surprise me anymore."

Don got up and shut his eyes tightly from the pain in his knees.

Little Wilson grimaced when he saw Don's face. "You okay?"

"Must be going to rain. Knees get a little stiff if I sit too long. Gotta get back out in the jungle. That's where we belong, not sitting around here like a bunch of REMFs. Going to throw on some clothes and head over to chow. Hey, by the way, where's everyone else?"

Gene scratched his chin. "Let's see. Nick's with the Spanish guys, Elderidge is with the brothers, and I don't know where Kelly is."

"If you see them, just tell them to get back here for inspection. Until we're told otherwise, we leave tomorrow."

Confirmation as to where and when they were going came at the Mess Hall during dinner. The first indication was the meal itself: roast beef, mashed potatoes, corn and string beans. The traditional pre-mission meal was always steak and baked potatoes. The confirmation came from Little Wilson when Don sat down at the rough wooden picnic table.

"We're going out, day after tomorrow, to the Iron Triangle."

"Where did you hear that?"

"Got it straight from Cookie. He got it right from the CP clerks. The cooks got to know so that they can prepare the meals. That's what he told me. We're leaving Monday."

"That's great. The clerks know and the cooks know and I guarantee, by tomorrow, the gooks will know."

"How's that?"

"In the CP, they got Vietnamese secretaries working. The Mess

Hall got Vietnamese KPs. The REMFs got hooch maids. These gooks listen to every word they hear. By tonight, they'll be back in their village, telling the local VC Cadre Officer what they heard. The info gets passed up their chain of command, and bingo. They know when we're leaving and where we're going. How many open fields are there in the Triangle? Space's big enough to land... eight slicks? Not many. So they leave a squad at each field. Maybe they'll even take a couple of shots at us, drop in a few mortars before they take off. Everyone knows where we are going but us. We're the last to know. And that, my friend, is bullshit!"

"But how do they pass the word on?"

"They pass it on by radio. How do you think they communicate?"

"The gooks got radios?"

"What are you, brain-dead? Of course they got radios. You think they use drums, like in a Tarzan movie?"

"I just never thought of them using radios like modern people, that's all."

Don looked up and saw Camp coming over to their table. "We know already. Iron Triangle. We leave on Monday."

Camp looked stunned. "How the hell do you know? I was just told not more than ten minutes ago."

"The clerks at the CP told the cooks, who told Wilson. The CP secretaries told the hooch maids, who told the shit burners, and they told the KPs. Alfie overheard them and told me. And before you ask, Alfie is bilingual and understands gook, so he translated it to me."

"This is bullshit. It's no wonder we land hot every time we go out. Every LZ's been hot ever since Tet."

"Eugene says the gooks pass the message using drums. Like in the Tarzan movies."

"None of these useless pricks know how to keep their mouths shut."

"They're told not to talk around the gooks, but they all do. Well, I do know some shit that you don't. Tomorrow, we're getting a new Lieutenant and brand-spanking-new replacements. A whole truckload just for us, the fourth platoon."

They finished their dinner, talking just to pass the time. When they emptied their trays in the garbage cans out back, they saw Alfie eating a large plate of roast-beef fat and potatoes.

"See, I told you Cookie takes care of him."

"Want to go to the EM Club and grab a few beers?"

The Wilsons were going to catch a movie and then turn in. Don was going to write a letter and turn in early himself. As Camp started to walk to club, he heard Don ask: "So what about the other stuff? Your school and training?"

"I'm surprised you're asking me. Go ask your dog. I'm sure he knows everything by now."

Camp sat in the Enlisted Men's Club, slumped over a small formica table. He took a long pull of Black Label beer and wiped his mouth on his sleeve. Lumbering across the room was Doc White, balancing a plate in one hand and two cans of Black Label in the other. He stopped and blinked myopically several times before seeing Camp's waving arm. As White got closer, Camp pushed out a chair from under the table.

He flopped down, straining the cheap plastic chair to its limits. He set his plate down and pushed a beer toward Camp. "You look like you could use a refill."

"Sure can, Doc. What is that slop you're eating?"

White examined the dripping, oozing mess covering his plate; and pointed out a thin slab of steak half-covered by baked beans. A gummy cube of corn bread balanced precariously on the edge of the plate. "I'd rather eat this shit than Cookie's mystery beast."

He started to saw at the meat ineffectively, finally picking it up and folding it in half. He bit a large chunk off. His hands and face were soon covered in barbecue sauce. He finally stuffed the last of the meat into his mouth. He pushed his plate away without touching the rest of his food, and picked up his beer.

Toward the front of the bar, Nick Mercado, the fourth-squad RTO, was dancing to the Box Tops' "The Letter".

"Look at these guys, Doc. They're like kids at a high-school dance."

"They're excited, Wendy. They got another day's reprieve, another full day with no one shooting at them."

"Don's acting a little squirrelly, all moody and moping around. Problems with his girlfriend or something. You should talk to him."

White ignored the suggestion and lit a cigarette. "None of my business."

"You shouldn't talk to him because it's none of your business? You're the company medic; it is your business. If his performance is off, then it affects all of us."

"Hey, Wendy, you okay with your divorce? You haven't talked about it."

Camp looked at him with narrowed eyes. "Fuck you, Doc. Fuck you."

"I've made my point. Like I said, none of my business."

It was times like this when White wished he didn't know the details of anyone's personal life. The more you knew about someone, the more that person became real. The more real someone became, the more it hurt when that person was killed or wounded. It was enough that he treated their wounds. He didn't have to like them or know anything about them. For a lot of guys, he didn't even know their first name or where they were from or anything else about them; and that was just fine. It was a cold way to be, but it was the only way if you wanted to keep sane.

With Camp, Holt and Mad Dog, it was different. He became friends with them not even wanting to. It just happened. Of all the guys he could have been friends with, he had to pick these three lunatics. Camp was on his third tour; and Holt, his second. For those two, the odds were stacked against them. Holt enjoyed walking point, and point men didn't last long. Neither did medics, especially medics like Mad Dog. The "Dog" was fearless. He would go anywhere and do anything to get a wounded guy back to safety. It was stupid. He took too many chances. Jaxon was warned repeatedly, but he just wouldn't listen. As much as White lectured Mad Dog about safety, he was just as bad.

White looked up from his beer and saw Jaxon and Holt walk into the club. He nudged Camp and pointed in their direction. Camp snapped out of his funk and waved them over. For the rest of the evening, they sat and drank. Different people would drift over, sit and have a beer; but for the most part, the four sat by themselves. By unspoken agreement, they didn't speak about the upcoming operation. They talked about cars and girls and what they would do when they got back to the world. Most of the stories were lies and most of their plans were fantasy, but these excesses were excused and overlooked.

At ten o'clock, First Sergeant Johnson announced the club was closed. Reveille was at 0530. Amid much grumbling and cursing, the club slowly emptied. The men stumbled to their barracks and collapsed onto their cots.

Holt found it difficult to sleep. He quietly left the barracks to sit on the wooden bench by the door. He sat in the cool night air, smoking and staring into the night sky. Behind him, the screen door squeaked, and he turned to see Alfie nosing his way through the door. Don patted his thigh, and Alfie stepped onto the wooded bench. He lay down next to him, and Don idly scratched his ears and stroked his head.

"So tell me, pal. Are you going to miss me when I'm gone?"

Alfie grunted and squirmed about, settling himself a little more comfortably. Don flipped his cigarette into the dark, watching for the small explosion of sparks as it landed. He leaned back against the sandbags and closed his eyes. He slept without dreaming.

Camp shook Don's shoulder. "Did you sleep out here all night?"

17

"I guess so. It was too hot inside."

"Well, get yourself together. We have to go up to the CP. The new guys are in, but we got to see the Lieutenant first."

The sun was up as they walked to the CP. A dusty, mud-caked deuce and a half sat in front of the CP loaded with new guys. They stared intently at everything.

The Lieutenant was standing outside the CP and waved Camp and Holt over. He confirmed that Camp was accepted to advanced NCO school for the next two weeks and would be leaving tomorrow afternoon. He told Holt that he was assuming command of the fourth squad as an Acting Jack, the term used for Acting Sergeant. If he did well, the promotion would be final upon Camp's return.

Holt thanked the Lieutenant, promised he would do his best; and they shook hands. He joined the other squad leaders who had arrived to greet the new guys. They watched as they jumped from the truck and assembled before a pale skinny clerk in pressed fatigues checking their names against a list.

The clerk pointed to the row of twelve men. "You each get three. Just let me know which squad they're going to." He handed the list to them and walked into the CP.

Sergeant Pell, who led the second squad, said, "That's right, you rat-faced bastard, scurry back to your hole."

The four squad leaders debated how they would choose, finally settling on a count-off.

"Count off, 1, 2, 3, 4. First guy goes to the first squad, and so on."

Holt marked the names on the clipboard and told one of them to run it into the CP. They assembled into squads. "Gather up your duffels and follow me. Try and remember the layout. All these shit buildings look alike."

They walked down the boardwalk toward the fourth-platoon barracks, followed in line by the other squads. Holt pointed out the Supply Room and the Mess Hall and the sandbagged bunkers to be used in mortar and rocket attacks.

Someone asked what the foul smell was.

"Piss tubes," Holt said without further explanation.

In the barracks, Holt pointed to where the squad bunked, and specifically to three empty cots. "Those are yours. You get one footlocker and one metal locker against the wall. Stow your duffel bags and get over to the Mess Hall for breakfast. Be back here in one hour."

"Why are there empty bunks?"

"Dead or wounded."

The new guys sat by themselves, nervously looking around the room. Breakfast consisted of scrambled eggs, greasy strips of bacon, and toast. There was two kinds of juice and endless pots of coffee.

You had to feel sorry for the new guys; for seven days, they had been abused at the replacement depot. Their days consisted of filling endless quantities of sandbags. For one full day, they labored under the sweltering, relentless sun, digging a trench only to be told the next day to fill it in. They were cursed at and bullied by the REMFs. They were told horrifying stories of neverending jungle warfare by clerks and typists who never left the safety of the enormous Base Camp. Their taste buds were assaulted by bland, unidentifiable Mess Hall food. Their stomachs ached, and their intestines rumbled and churned with continual spasms of diarrhea. They spent every free minute in the latrines, tormented by runny, green stools which burned and scalded their ass like shitting out shards of glass. Finally, they were unceremoniously loaded on trucks covered in red dust and driven to a place unknown to them. No one had spoken to them like soldiers. They were things to be processed and disposed of in the most efficient manner. Now, they sat silent and frightened, staring at their uneaten food.

"Finish up here, grab a smoke or whatever, and get to the barracks in fifteen minutes. We'll get you all squared away with your gear."

Before going to the barracks, Holt stopped by the supply room. Inside, he saw the Supply Sergeant at his desk against the far wall. "Hey, Sarge. What's up?"

Sergeant Grimes came over to Holt and stood before him, separated by a long wooden counter. "And what can I do for you, young buck? Heard you got your stripes back."

"News travels fast. It happened only 20 minutes ago."

"Good news, bad news, I hear it all," Grimes replied. His black skin glistened like oiled walnuts. "I got some FNGs coming over for supply. Need them outfitted right with a little extra. Extra canteens, magazines, shit like that. In return, I'll look out for you. Anything special you want?"

"I could always use a Tokarev." That's the Russian automatic pistol the NVA officers carried.

"That's a big order, Sarge. Everyone wants a Tokarev. I can't guarantee that, but I can try for an NVA flag or an SKS, some belt buckles or a pith helmet."

"I know you'll do your best, and I always appreciate what you bring me." Holt started to leave, but stopped. "I need two extra M60 barrels and a few extra radio batteries, maybe four? Think you can do that?"

Grimes touched the side of his nose. "Don't worry, son. I'll take care of you."

In the barracks, the new guys were sitting on their cots in sullen silence. They had been ignored by the platoon. They were being inspected by Alfie, who paced before them and growled menacingly.

"Alf, back off and leave them alone."

Holt looked over the barracks and spotted the Wilsons and Elderidge. He called them over. "These are the new guys. You're each responsible for one of them. Choose who you want. Get them over to supply, and get them outfitted with all their gear. Bring them back here and show them how to pack their rucksacks. Lay out all the shared squad equipment and I'll divide that up. Include all the crap you're carrying now. Grimes is waiting for you, so get a move on."

When they returned from supply, Sergeant Grimes had fulfilled his promise. They all had five canteens and extra magazines.

Don sat with Alfie on a cot loaded with the squad's shared equipment. He decided that he would show the new guys how to assemble their gear himself. The first thing he did was discard the bulky flannel lined sleeping bag. Next was the ineffective mosquito net, along with the leaky rubber air mattress. "Put this shit in your locker. The sleeping bag, you can use here. It makes the cot a little softer."

He instructed them how to attach their suspenders to the web belt, and how to adjust it so the belt rode just above their hips. He added two ammo pouches to ether side of the web gear belt buckle; and to one side, he added a pouch containing medical field dressing. To the outside of these, he added two canteens, attaching the covers to the belt.

He showed them how to place their rucksack onto the aluminum frame. There were two positions possible: a high position and a low position. "We all use the high position. Only Mercado, the RTO, uses the low. He needs the space for the radio. You want all your weight high up so that it rests on your shoulders."

He put a rucksack on his shoulders and adjusted the straps and the quick-disconnect pull.

"You reach up here and pull this strap on your right shoulder. It releases the shoulder strap and you can shrug off the pack. You can release the pack when you're lying down or from any other position. It comes in handy if you got to move quickly."

He removed three canteens from their canvas pouches and put them in the three large pockets on the back of the rucksack. He took the poncho liner, an 82" x 62" nylon blanket, and folded and rolled it into a barrel shape. "You're going to use your poncho as a ground cover, and your poncho liner as a blanket. Once you have you poncho liner rolled, wrap it with your poncho into a nice, tight little bundle like this. This keeps the liner dry. Then take this bundle, and using these straps, tie it onto the bottom of your rucksack frame. These loops between the canteen pockets? You each are going to carry two smoke grenades there."

He stood the rucksack frame upright and opened the top flap, revealing a large interior pocket. "In here go your C-rations. We each carry a minimum of three meals, sometimes more. You'll carry two star clusters shoved in along the sides. Any other personal gear goes in here as well, like cigarettes, or toilet paper."

He lifted the top flap and showed them a pocket sewed into the flap. "In here go your writing paper, envelopes and pens. This pocket is almost waterproof so you put your paper into a plastic bag. You will write home at least once a week, if not more. I'm not going to catch shit from the Lieutenant about some worried mother wanting to know what's happened to her son. Tonight, before chow, write a letter home giving your return address and telling them you are fine and having a wonderful adventure and not to worry. Am I clear on this? Don't fill their heads with imaginary horror stories. Give it a few days, and you won't have to make anything up. For now, you tell them how wonderful and exotic Vietnam is and how well you have been treated."

Don saw Little Wilson going toward the door. "Gene, where you going?

"To the PX, Sarge."

"Take these guys with you. Make sure they get writing paper and envelopes and anything else they need. Bring your MPCs."

He was met with blank stares.

"The shit they gave you when you turned in your real money: Military Payment Certificates. You'll need it at the PX. If I were you, I would get a good compass and maybe a survival knife. Do not, I repeat, do not come back here with a big-ass Bowie knife. Only the REMFs carry those. Wilson knows what to get. Don't forget a boonie hat. Make sure you have toothpaste, soap and a razor. There is no Post Exchange out in the field. Inspection at 1600 hours. Pass the word."

As Holt walked off, one of the new guys said, "You know, he never asked for our names."

The inspection started promptly at 4 o'clock. The squad members were all present and sitting on or by their cots. Holt concentrated on the new guys. He had them put on their web gear and rucksacks. He checked the shoulder straps for proper fit and tightness. He made sure their helmets fit correctly. He checked the poncho bedrolls to ensure they were neat and secured properly. Finally, he inspected their rifles.

He gave each a empty Claymore mine bag. "This bag is for extra magazines; you should be able to fit ten mags in each one. Three mags in each ammo pouch and ten in the Claymore bag, and one in your rifle. Twenty-three in total. Eighteen rounds in each mag, for a total of 414 rounds. We all carry the same except for Mercado, Kelly and Big Wilson. Understood?

They nodded nervously.

"The bandoleer that your ammo comes in has seven pockets. We carry seven rounds of high-explosive rounds for Wilson's M79. In addition, we carry a belt of M60 ammunition for Kelly.

"Fisk, you're the biggest, so you're the assistant gunner for Kelly. You carry 4 belts of ammo instead of one, and you also carry an extra M60 barrel."

He turned to Kelly. "Make sure he is squared away before chow. I got some more shit to hand out before we're done."

He handed each a 2-pound block of C-4 plastic explosive. "We use this for cooking our C-rations."

He then asked the two remaining new guys, "Who are you?"

"Kimball, Sergeant. John Kimball. PFC."

"And you?

"Locke, Sergeant. Meyer Locke."

Holt stared at him, "Meyer, huh? Well, you each get a entrenching tool. You can either clip it on the side of your rucksack, or shove it through the top. Fisk, you carry a machete. Attach it the same way."

Holt looked behind him, studying what was left. He handed each three medical pressure bandages. "We carry extra for Doc. They weigh next to nothing, so don't bitch about them. Wherever you put them, make sure they're easily accessible. Let's hope we don't need them. You two, Locke and, what the fuck is your name, don't tell me. Kimball! Take an extra radio battery for the RTO. When you get your ammo, make sure to get six hand grenades apiece. Put one each onto the outside of your ammo pouches, and two up on your ruck straps.

"I see you each bought a compass and knife; that's good. Put your compass in your upper-left jacket pocket, and the knife goes on your web belt or taped to your ruck strap. I prefer it up on the strap; it's easier to get to if you need it. Believe it or not, that's it. Aw, shit! Forgot one thing: your gas mask. Either loop it around your waist, or tie it to your pack; I don't care. We hardly ever use them, but the Officers insist we carry them. Most guys use it as a pillow.

"Gene, take them out back and have them draw their ammo and grenades. Make sure to fill your canteens and get your C-rations, and don't forget your iodine pills. Watch how they pack their ammo. Don't fuck around; do everything right. One final thing: you guys wearing underwear?"

They all looked blankly at him.

"We don't wear underwear in the field. The elastic in the waistband combined with sweating will tear up your skin. You'll get a rash across your whole waist."

Holt looked to Nick Mercado, the RTO. "Nick, divvy up the rations. We got 3 cases, so make sure everyone gets 4 meals. And don't fuck with the new guys and give them all the shit stuff.

Everyone gets a crap meal, including me. Leave mine on my cot. I got to find Camp."

"He's kidding about the underwear, right? You guys are just fucking with us?"

"No one wears underwear in the boonies. You'll sweat so much, your drawers will get soaked and will never dry out under your pants. Your wet drawers will end up chafing your thighs and balls. And like Sarge said, the elastic will give you a painful rash."

"But what about... when we go to the bathroom?"

"You delicate little fucks! You worried about skid marks or pee stains? That's going to be the least of your worries. After two or three days out, we all will be stinking like hobos."

Mercado was exasperated. "Do want you want. But you should do what your told."

As Mercado walked away from them, he dropped his pants and mooned the startled new guys. He looked over his shoulder. "See? No underwear."

Don found Camp drinking coffee. He drew himself a cup from the large silver urn and sat next to Camp. "You excited, Wendy?"

"Yeah, actually, I am. How you doing?"

"I got the new guys squared away. They all look like they want to shit their pants, but I guess that's normal."

"When we were new, we were scared, so lighten up a little. It won't be long before they're blooded and you'll see what they're made of. I almost forgot; go to supply and exchange your M16. Squad leaders now carry a CAR-15."

"Cool! That's a sexy little gun."

"Yeah, it's new perk. Up to now, only the officers got them."

"I'll do it now. Thanks for the info, pal. See you later at chow?"

Holt was cleaning his newly issued Colt Commando AR. With its collapsable stock pushed in, it was 28 inches long, 11 inches shorter than the M16. Oddly enough, it weighed more; at 6.55 pounds, it was a few ounces heavier than the M16, but it just looked mean. The whole center receiver section of the rifle was identical to the M16's. Just the barrel and the stock were different.

He was smiling as he wiped the rifle with a clean cloth lightly coated with gun oil. He didn't move his gear into the Sergeant's room. He'd wait until Camp got his official promotion. His cot was the last in line on the left side; and from his cot, he could observe the entire length of the barracks.

Most of the men were finishing up their packing and were getting ready for chow. He placed his rifle into his locker and selected a clean blouse. The blouse, or jungle jacket, was made from ripstop cotton fabric. It had concealed buttons on the angled pockets and jacket closure. It had shoulder epaulets, adjustable cuffs, and drainage eyelets on the pockets. The jacket was lightweight and comfortable, and dried quickly when wet.

His jacket had his last name and a tab designating 'U.S. Army' sewn over each pocket in subdued lettering. On one shoulder was a subdued version of the 25th Infantry Division patch, and sewn over his left pocket was a subdued Combat Infantryman's Badge. He didn't wear any indication of rank, opting instead for the black Sergeant's stripes pinned on his collar. No one displayed their rank in the field, just the black pins or a black sewn-on patch. He slipped on a pair of Ho Chi Minh sandals he had bought in Cu Chi village, and headed off to chow.

He entered the Mess Hall for the traditional steak dinner served from steaming trays piled high with meat. There were no orders of rare or medium-rare; everything was well-done. He got his baked potato topped with a large dollop of butter and some green beans. He sat with Camp and the squad leaders. The discussion ranged from bitching about the FNGs and the incompetence of the officers.

There was some talk of the upcoming mission, but it was generally viewed as bad luck to dwell on the topic. Instead, they talked about their upcoming R&R, and the merits of Bangkok over Singapore over Hong Kong.

Camp whispered, "You know, now that you're married, you might get to go to Hawaii."

"I doubt if a week in Hawaii would be any better than our so-called honeymoon. Plus she's got to be getting big by now. It's just another excuse not to do anything. Also, my being alive doesn't figure into her father's plans. I should be dead by then. His calculations would have to be done over. Couldn't have that. He spent too much time on them."

"You still did the right thing? Or do you think you were being played for an asshole?"

"My friend, I have asked myself that same question many times, and have come to the conclusion that I am the number-one asshole in all of Vietnam. The absolute top of the asshole tree. That's where I sit, right at the top."

"Fuck it and ruck up."

"I think I'll skip the club tonight and head back and go over my gear again."

"I think we're all heading back. I got a full cooler of ice-cold beer. We'll sit around, tell some war stories, maybe torment the new guys."

"Sounds good, Wendy. I don't think the new guys can stand too much tormenting, though." He pointed to a table. "Poor fucks, all huddled together. Scared shitless on rumors and bullshit."

The barracks slowly filled up with the platoon. Everyone was double-checking their gear. Rucksacks were put on and adjusted. With full loads, everyone was carrying between 70 and 80 pounds each.

Rodney, from the first squad, shouted a shrill, squeaking

"ATTENTION" as the new Lieutenant came through the door, followed by Platoon Sergeant Reynolds. With the exception of Rodney, no one got to their feet. A few looked up, but most continued what they were doing.

"At ease, men. As you were," the Lieutenant said to the men. "Listen up. This is the new platoon leader, Lieutenant Wilkes. He's going to give you the briefing on tomorrow's operation, so pay attention. Lieutenant, the floor's all yours," said Sergeant Reynolds, stepping behind the Lieutenant.

It was hard to take Wilkes seriously. He was overweight and sweating profusely while standing still. It was obvious to everyone that he was nervous. He kept tugging at his pants as if they were too tight. To top it off, he had no combat experience. He was a 90-day wonder, a shake-and-bake instant Second Lieutenant. He'd been in country for five months, begging anyone who would listen for a combat assignment. In almost-total despair, he finally received his posting to the 27th Infantry Regiment.

He started his briefing by referring to the Iron Triangle as the Iron Tit, a name no one could ever recall being used. He threw in some inspiring crap about destroying the Communist stronghold once and for all. All these, to men who had fought there three times before and dreaded the thought of returning. For all the dead and wounded and the misery and pain they endured, they didn't see any appreciable change.

He finished his briefing by giving the wrong map coordinates and the wrong radio call sign; which caused Pollack, his RTO, to storm out of the barracks in disgust. Sergeant Reynolds bowed his head the whole time Wilkes was talking, praying this idiot would not get him killed before he could turn over the platoon to Camp.

"I want everyone to get a good night's sleep, don't drink too much beer, and make sure to write home. Let your folks know you're okay." With that last inspiring message, he turned crisply, but paused as Alfie pushed past him and walked regally into the barracks.

Holt looked over at Camp. "I stand corrected, Wendy. That man right there, he is the number-one perfect asshole."

Alfie walked past the new guys, stopped and bared his teeth, then continued down the aisle separating the rows of cots. He walked to Camp and lay down on his foot.

Camp shoved him with his boot. "Get your flea-infested dog away from me."

"I keep telling you, he's not my dog. He's a free spirit. No one owns him; no one can tame this beast. The way you disrespect him, you're lucky he doesn't just rip your throat out. I've seen him do it. He was a scout dog down in the Delta with the Navy Seals."

"Him," Doc Jaxon said, who just joined the group. He pointed at Alfie, who lay like a lump at Camp's feet.

"Yeah, him. He's trained to kill. He's magnificent. He's fierce and kills without mercy. He's retired now. In the Delta, he was called ACE because he killed five gooks with his bare paws. He just ripped them to fucking pieces. He did it silently, at night."

"'Scout dog' my ass," Camp said. "He couldn't find the door unless you pointed to it."

Don reached down and placed a restraining hand on Alfie's neck. "He's trembling with rage. Actually, fucking trembling. One word from me, and you're a dead man. He'll probably start with your eyes and your soft, squishy cheeks."

"The only way he'd attack me is if I'd tried to take away his beer."

"Perhaps, Wendy, perhaps. Hopefully, you'll never find out. I'm going to turn in. See you morons tomorrow."

He rose from the footlocker and went into the barracks. He packed his final items in his rucksack. A carton of Marlboro cigarettes wrapped in plastic and four squeeze bottles of insect repellent were placed in the center compartment, on top of the four boxes of C-rations Mercado had picked for him. He didn't bother to check the meals, but hoped he got beef and potatoes. He wrapped a washcloth around a tube of toothpaste, toothbrush, razor and a bar of soap in a plastic soap dish; and stuffed the bundle into his rucksack. Finally, in went two bottles of hot sauce, paperback novels, and a small transistor radio.

Janet had sent him some canned goods to supplement the C-rations. He shoved the cans into two socks, forming two elongated tubes. He tied the socks together and draped them over his rucksack, securing them to each side rail with rawhide shoelaces.

Mad Dog came out of the back room and sat on his own cot across from Don's.

"You all set?" he asked.

Don shrugged.

Mad Dog stood and hefted his own pack onto his shoulders. "Jesus Christ, this thing weighs a fucking ton." His pack was probably in excess of 75 pounds. The outside was festooned with extra canteens required to treat heat exhaustion. Inside, the pack bulged with extra bandages of all sizes, medical supplies, and pills of every kind, along with his personal gear. He didn't carry a rifle. He carried a Colt 1911, 45-caliber automatic pistol with six extra magazines.

With packs weighing seventy pounds or more, this was definitely a young man's war. Only the young could endure the endless jungle treks under a blazing sun burdened by such weight. But youth was no protection against heatstroke, fevers and diarrhea that sapped your strength, leaving you weak, shivering and dehydrated.

Mad Dog dropped his pack on his footlocker. He stepped back and stroked his mustache in contemplation. He was a ruggedly handsome young man with a deeply tanned face set off by sparkling blue eyes and light, sandy hair. He was about five-foot-eight, with a solid, well-muscled body hardened by summers working in the sawmills of northern Washington. He was twenty years old and had completed two years of college in Bellingham before dropping out.

Within weeks, without his protective deferment, he was scooped up in the monthly draft. He felt fortunate to have avoided the infantry, only to end up as a medic in a line company. This strange twist of fate didn't bother him too much. Like he did most times, he merely shrugged his shoulders and went about doing the best he could. A medic under fire had a short life expectancy. Unlike in previous conflicts, medics didn't wear or display the large white cross on their helmets or any other form of identification. Gooks always liked to shoot the medic as they aided the wounded. Why give them a better target?

Mad Dog lay back on his cot. "You nervous about tomorrow? Your big day, debuting as squad leader."

"I've been squad leader before. Chances are I'll do something stupid and get busted again, and everything can start over again." Don slid his sandals off and lay back.

Mad Dog extended his arm into the space between the cots and clenched his fist. Holt did the same, and they bumped fists.

"No one dies; we all go home."

"Amen, brother. No one dies; we all go home."

Chapter 3

Departure

Camp found Holt sleeping, slumped against the sandbags that surrounded the barracks. Alfie was curled up on the bench, snoring softly. Camp reached down and touched Holt's shoulder, and he came awake instantly. He pushed Alfie off the bench, landing him on his back. Alfie bristled his hair and growled menacingly. He swiped at him with his boot. Alfie, taking the hint, loped off on some unknown canine errand.

"Is this where you sleep now?"

"They're all farting and snoring. I like it better outside."

Holt ran his hands over his face and scratched at the short, sparse stubble of his beard. He stretched his legs, which were stiff and uncomfortable. He ached all over from sleeping upright in the damp night air. His head throbbed from last night's beers, and his mouth tasted cottony and stale.

Camp lit a cigarette and passed the pack to Holt, holding out his tarnished Zippo lighter. Don drew deeply on the smoke and stared through reddened eyes into the darkness. "What time is it?"

"A little after five. The Mess Hall's open. Let's wake the others and get some breakfast. The trucks will be here at six to load everyone up."

They went through the barracks, waking the squad. The entire barracks slowly came to life as the men rose and pulled on their fatigues. Camp and Holt stumbled along the uneven boardwalk leading to the Mess Hall. Don stopped at a piss tube, holding his breath against the rising stench of urine. When he was done, he fumbled with the buttons on his pants as they continued walking.

They swung through the screen door into the bright glare of the Mess Hall. At the back of the serving line, Sergeant First Class Yokes stood wreathed in steam, berating his Vietnamese KPs.

"Hey, Cookie, what's shaking?" Camp called out to Yokes over the clatter of trays, pans and cutlery.

Yokes turned, wiping his hands on his clean white apron. "Camp. Nice to see you boys up early. You'll be wanting some fresh eggs. Grab some coffee and I'll be with you in a minute."

He turned back towards his KPs and shouted some gook gibberish at them before picking up a spatula and heading toward the flat grill. Without asking, he cracked four eggs onto the grill and proceeded to cook them over easy. Camp and Holt stood in front of the grill holding their thick plastic trays. Several other soldiers started to drift in, and more followed.

"Are you going to join us out there tonight?"

"Not for a few days. The CO wants to let you guys settle in before we bring anything out. Plus I'm not exactly certain anyone knows where you'll be."

"That's good. After a week of C-rats, even your slop will taste good."

Yokes smoothly scooped up the eggs and slid them onto the trays. He dipped into the steam table with a pair of tongs and came up with a generous portion of bacon for each. He pointed with his spatula. "Toast is over there, and the coffee is fresh. And by all means, please, go fuck yourself. Now move out, you're holding up my line."

They ate in silence at first.

"I wish I were going out, just to get you guys settled and everything."

"Stop your worrying. I'll be fine."

"Well, will you look at that."

The squad entered, got their food, and sat together at a large wooden table.

"That's a good sign."

The room was crowded as everyone lined up for eggs and bacon. Some passed on the food, the victims of queasy nervous stomachs. Other stayed behind to enjoy the quiet of the empty barracks and write a quick letter home. It was the same before any large operation. Nowhere was death closer linked with life than for the infantry grunt in Vietnam. It was inevitable that on an operation this size, many would be killed or wounded. No one had to tell the men this. They knew it and accepted it with a stoic indifference of those powerless to change their fate.

At eighteen and nineteen, they were close friends with their own mortality, and had no illusions of the heroic grandness of death on the battlefield. It was March 1968. The past holidays were lost and absorbed in the brutal fighting of the Tet Offensive. There were no special celebrations for Christmas and New Year's. They spent the holidays in the jungle, and the only importance any day had was when it was over and you had one less day to spend in Vietnam.

There was a feeble attempt to link the boys with home. The battalion chaplain flew out for a Christmas service, which few attended. Hot meals were prepared instead of C-rations. Some Red Cross "Doughnut Dollies" arrived to hand out small, gaily wrapped packages of toothpaste, razors and books. But the arrival of the round-eyed girls, the first most had seen in months, only deepened the sense of isolation and depression they felt. So they returned to their foxholes and cursed the young girls who, with their bright eyes and open smiles, promised much but delivered nothing.

The holidays were not easy for those at home, either. Death took no holiday, and any day could be the day a telegram could arrive, announcing the latest battlefield tragedy. Around the dinner tables, the empty chairs marking the place of sons, husbands and boyfriends strangled the joy of the day and muted any attempt at celebration. Packages were mailed, stuffed with canned goods, socks and Kool-Aid; the sort of things you would send a boy at summer Camp. Pictures were mailed and letters were written; and with each act of communication, the sense of sadness deepened because no number of letters could bridge the awful physical separation or lessen the risk of death.

More than anything, what troubled the people at home was their inability to alter or in any way affect the events taking place ten thousand miles away. Those in combat fought for their lives, and there was nothing anyone at home could do to help them. Mothers, wives and girlfriends were reduced to impotent witnesses to events beyond their control. The rage and helplessness they felt overwhelmed them with grief and sadness.

There was little joy at Christmas for those directly affected by Vietnam. What little celebration there was could be peeled back like a thin veneer to reveal a churning morass of fear and pain. All were glad when the holidays passed. They no longer had to pretend to be happy.

As the men finished breakfast, they passed Sergeant Yokes, who shook their hands and patted their backs. He nodded at everyone regardless of rank. "Good luck. Be safe. Don't do anything stupid."

They all headed back to the barracks and waited silently, each lost in his own thoughts. At 6:10 AM, the word came over the loudspeakers to assemble by the orderly room. Wordlessly, the men shouldered their packs and made their way through the company area. In the half-light of dawn, they shuffled down the wooden boardwalks like so many silent, ghostly apparitions.

They formed quickly into squad and platoon order and dropped their packs at their feet. During this formation, before boarding the trucks, there were no clerks or other support personnel present. Those lucky enough to stay behind didn't press their luck by observing the head count. Even the drivers of the trucks stayed in the cabs, looking everywhere but at the lines of quiet grunts.

Finally, the men boarded the trucks, throwing their gear onto the rusty metal floors covered in red dust. The trucks were packed tight, and the men were forced up against each other. Over the noise of the idling diesels came the sounds of mooing cows and baaing sheep, as some gave voice to how they felt. Like animals herded through a stockyard, they allowed themselves to be pushed, prodded and packed onto the trucks.

Mercifully, the ride to the airstrip was short. Once again, they formed into their squads and were given their ship assignments. They moved down the line of waiting helicopters and found their assigned number. They dropped their packs and carefully laid their weapons across them, and settled in for the next period of waiting.

Sergeant Yokes had followed the trucks, bringing with him several large silver urns of coffee and containers of fresh, fried doughnuts. The men stood around, holding steaming styrofoam cups and smoking cigarettes. They drifted back to their squads and sat by the helicopters, talking softly.

The sun was almost up now, moving through the early morning transition from shadow to light. Beyond the helicopters and out past the perimeter of the Base Camp, you could look down onto the flat plain of land shrouded in mists of fog. Soon, the fog would burn off, exposing the neat geometric patterns of the rice paddies. The farmers would be out, trudging through the mud, wading thigh-deep in muck, working their fields. If you were so inclined, you could marvel at the contrast of cultures placed side by side: the villagers and oxen in the muddy fields in sight of the terrible weapons of modern war.

Few of the men gave the farmers any notice. Most didn't even know there was a village beyond the perimeter. The village, to them, was the collection of tin shacks housing the barbershops, tailors, massage parlors and bars just outside the main gate.

There was something unsettling about the scene. Perhaps it was the stillness that shrouded the men and machines, or maybe the feeling of tension that lay just beneath the surface. There was an awful excitement that rippled through the air, bringing with it a warning of danger. It was like watching an animal at the zoo: a tiger or gorilla or any animal with enormous power, sitting placidly behind the bars, waiting for someone to turn it loose. It was as if a force was about to be released; and once free, it would be impossible to control.

It was easy to forget that these were teenagers just out of high school. They handled themselves and their weapons with such deceptive indifference. The helicopters' door gunners were busy with their machine guns, restacking long lengths of belted ammunition. Sitting next to the helicopter was a pimply-faced RTO with the pieces of his 45-caliber pistol spread out on a towel. He was busy assembling it as he talked with another boy who ran a oily rag through the barrel of his grenade launcher. A few feet away, another boy read a comic book as he lay propped up against his M60 machine gun. Everywhere you looked, the pieces didn't match the puzzle. Everything was just a little off.

The fourth squad was gathered near the line of helicopters. Holt leaned against his pack with a cup of coffee and a cigarette dangling from his mouth. Next to him was Nicholas Mercado, the RTO. Nick was Puerto Rican, drafted right out of high school. He lived in Manhattan on the Upper East Side, in Spanish Harlem. The three new guys, Fisk, Kimball and Locke, sat around him.

Mercado was explaining how easy it was to fall out of the helicopters; how, when the chopper banked in a turn, you would just slide down the seat and out the door. "So just grip the seat frame tight and whatever you do, don't let go."

Locke asked him, "Why don't they just have seat belts?"

"Because, asshole, you need to un-ass the chopper as quick as you can. The gooks are gonna be shooting at us. Do you want to be

37

fucking around trying to undo a seat belt?"

"Nicky, c'mon, leave them alone. He's just fucking with you guys. We got sixteen ships and eight guys on each. How many is that? Over a hundred. So maybe three or four guys fall out. It's no big deal. I wouldn't worry about it."

"Four guys falling out of helicopters is no big deal?"

"You guys can sit in the middle this time. That way, you can't fall out."

Holt's assurance did little to calm the three, who continued to debate the merits of even getting on the helicopter.

Little Wilson sat with Robert "Machine Gun" Kelly, the M60 gunner. Kelly was a stocky, muscular Irish kid from Boston. He carried the 26-pound M60 effortlessly. Finally, there was Big Wilson and Edward Elderidge. Elderidge was also from New York City and lived in Harlem. He just turned 21, and carried an M16. Elderidge only had eight weeks in country, but was no longer considered an FNG.

The nine men composed the fourth squad.

Way up front, the lead helicopter was starting. The company commander, First Lieutenant Gary Smith, waved his arm in a circle over his head. This was the signal for the first flight to load up. The crew chief came over to Holt and said they could only take seven guys at a time. Little Wilson and Elderidge were directed to the next chopper in line.

One by one, they boarded the helicopter. Four sat across the webbed canvas seat; Big Wilson and Mercado bordered Fisk and Kimball. Holt sat on the right side of the floor, his feet dangling out the open door. Kelly was on the opposite side with Locke. The door gunner was getting into his body armor, and finally waddled onto his seat behind his mounted machine gun.

The helicopter began to rock rhythmically side to side as the blades began to build speed.

Locke leaned into Holt. "How come the door gunners get to wear body armor and we don't?"

"They cost more to train. They're more valuable than you."

Slowly, the ships rose from the ground and turned north over the rice paddies. There were eight helicopters in the flight; the second flight would soon follow. At the sides of the flight were two sleek Cobra Gunships; and in front of them were two small egg-shaped Loaches, or Light Observation Helicopters, which darted back and forth, dropping low to skim the trees. Together with the Cobras, the Loaches provided security for the airborne convoy. Circling at the top of the formation, at a much higher altitude, was the C and C ship, the command and control ship of the battalion commander, Major Grayson. Major Grayson, from his vantage point, would monitor the full formation and direct the arrivals of the remaining flights. The command ship was crammed with all manner of communication gear spanning the frequencies of all the various units, enabling communication from the squad to the battalion level.

They were in the air about forty minutes when the helicopters slowed down and started to bank to the left. Holt twisted his head and saw a large clearing about four or five klicks up ahead. The Cobras and the observation choppers were working the clearing, trying to draw enemy fire. The door gunner tapped Mercado's helmet and gave him a thumbs-up. Mercado shouted to Holt that the Landing Zone was clear, a cold LZ.

The ships slowly descended. As they approached the ground, Holt and Kelly stood on the helicopter skids and gripped the side posts. The chopper met the earth with a thump; the men jumped from the ships and ran about ten meters before throwing themselves down in a loose defensive perimeter. The LZ resembled a choreographed riot. Leaves and small sticks swirled through the air from the helicopters' downdraft in a stinging, blinding cloud of jungle debris.

As soon as the choppers unloaded and were airborne, the second flight approached. Sergeants and Lieutenants ran about in a near-frenzy in a effort to group their men and get them off the LZ, clearing the way for the second flight.

Holt had the fourth squad up and off the LZ in a matter of minutes. He waited just inside the wood line for the platoon. Lieutenant Wilkes appeared to be aimlessly wandering around the LZ, randomly shooting compass azimuths. His RTO, Pollack, stood several feet behind him with a look of total disgust on his face. He finally went over to Wilkes and, a little harder than necessary, tapped him on his shoulder, pointing to where Holt stood. Wilkes nodded and said something, his words lost in the noise of landing helicopters. He gestured with his arm, and with wide, dramatic sweeping motions, pointed toward Holt. Pollack cursed him and all his family under his breath.

Wilkes walked to Holt. "Goddamn, that was exciting. Nothing like it was in training."

Pollack handed the Lieutenant the radio handset. The Lieutenant listened intently and frowned. "Well, that's not good. Not good at all." He looked at Holt and the surrounding men. "Sergeant Reynolds broke his ankle on landing. They're loading him up now and sending him back. He stepped in a hole as he was getting out. We'll just have to make do for a while. I'm sure they'll get someone out ASAP."

He turned to Pollack. "They won't leave us without a platoon sergeant. Right?"

"I imagine you know better than us what the brass would do?

While the Lieutenant was studying his map, Mad Dog walked over to Holt. "I was on the ship with Reynolds; I saw him fall." He leaned in close to Holt. "I don't think he broke his ankle. I started wrapping it, and it didn't seem broken. What do you think?"

"I think he was short and didn't want to come out this time. Maybe he thinks they can catch Camp before he leaves for training and get him out here."

"That's not going to happen. Camp left right after us. He's gone."

"Then he screwed us. No way they'll wait two weeks before

sending in some shithead to replace him."

At that moment, the LT gave the order to move out. The men settled into a loose formation and proceeded into the jungle. It didn't take long before the jungle was beaten down by the passage of the platoon. They were strung out along the length of the newly formed trail in five-meter intervals. The fourth squad led, followed by the platoon. The battalion was proceeding in a rough diamond-shaped formation.

Holt walked point, then Locke. Mercado was next with the machine-gun crew and the remainder of the squad.

Mercado pushed past Locke. "Hey, Don. Sorry, I meant Sarge. The LT said the Major is bitching about how long it's taking us to un-ass his LZ. He said to pick up the pace."

He held the handset out to Holt, who brushed it away. "Please tell the Lieutenant to tell the CO to tell the major to please go fuck himself. We've only been out, what now, twenty minutes, and he's already bitching about progress? Tell him we're doing the best we can."

Mercado was speaking into the handset and said to Holt, "The LT said okay, but please do your best to accommodate the Major's request. That's what he said; 'Please try to accommodate the Major.'"

"How the fuck can the Major even see us? He's three thousand feet up and we're under the trees. Fucking morons, all of them."

The tall trees blocked out most of the sunlight, and the vegetation didn't seem so thick. The ground was matted and spongy and covered by dark-green moss. Walking became easier; and they did, in fact, make better time. They would occasionally stop and listen. Holt would stare off into the trees before starting again. There was no discernible path or trail to follow, nothing to indicate anyone passed through before them. The fact that the officers wanted to cover a lot of ground was their problem. As far as Holt was concerned, he'd walk just as fast as he wanted. If they didn't like it, let them put someone else on point.

Behind the fourth platoon was the rest of the company in an arrowhead formation. The first platoon was at the point of the arrowhead, with the second and third platoons spaced on their flanks, left and right. In the center of the arrowhead was the Company Commander, Lieutenant Smith and his headquarters element, including Doc White. Following Delta company were the other three companies of the battalion: Alpha, Bravo and Charlie.

Presumably, the first battalion would now be on the ground and off toward their own objective. The plan was that the two battalions would cover their own separate and distinct objectives, but remain in striking distance of each other. The reality was quite different. As they proceeded deeper into the Iron Triangle, the jungle would become so thick and dense that in most places, it was almost impenetrable. It would take hours, if not days, for one battalion to come to the aid of the other if they had to travel over ground. Few clearings existed. Large helicopter insertions were impractical. In spite of the theory of mutual reinforcement, each of the battalions were on their own.

There were other means of assistance available. There were jets and other fixed-wing aircraft. There were the Cobras and helicopter gunships and artillery. But each of these elements carried with it their own problems.

The jets were powerful, accurate weapons whose force could be devastating. You had to go through so many channels to request air support that by the time you got them assigned, it was usually too late.

There was a shortage of gunships, and those available were escorting the lightly armed Hueys. That left the artillery. If you were in range of a firebase and you knew your position, you could call in artillery onto the proper map coordinates. It was seldom you knew where you were with any degree of certainty. It wasn't uncommon to call for artillery support, only to have the shells impact several kilometers away. Also, the probability of a shell exploding in the trees and creating an airburst was a real danger.

In spite of all the support available, each battalion and each company functioned independently. The way the companies were spread out within an area, it was possible for the lead element to be engaged in a bitter fire fight while those in the rear of the formation sat and awaited the outcome. Fire fights in Vietnam were brief and savage. Mostly, the fight was over before other units could maneuver into support. Vietnam was an infantryman's war. It was a lonely, isolated war fought at the squad and platoon level.

As far as the squad was concerned, they could be the only grunts in Vietnam. They had unknowingly extended their lead by two hundred meters. After walking steadily for an hour, they stopped to take a break. Everyone took out their canteens for a long drink of warm water.

Mercado moved past Locke to Holt. He held out his cigarettes and looked toward Don. "A cigarette can't hurt anything. This place smells like shit; how anyone could smell a cigarette?"

"It smells like rotting garbage."

They sat back-to-back, trying to cover as much ground as possible even while taking a break. Behind them, the squad looked exhausted. Their uniforms were drenched in sweat. Don dug deep into his side pants-leg pocket and pulled out his map. He smoothed out the plastic covering and oriented his compass. He looked up from the map while Nick looked over his shoulder.

"Where are we?"

"By my calculations, we are somewhere in Vietnam, north of Cu Chi."

"I was kind of thinking on a smaller scale. You know, a more local level."

"I think we're here and trying to go there. Then again, we could be here, in which case we'd be lost."

"Yeah, whatever." Nick wiped his head with his sleeve. "Jesus Christ, it's hot." He slapped ineffectively at several mosquitoes that had settled on his arm.

Don was still studying the map. "According to this, there should be a small river or stream up ahead."

"What's that say down in the corner? Chevron! Where did you get this fucking map from, a fucking gas station? No wonder we're lost all the time."

"Nicky, you are a laugh riot. Before we get started, give the asshole a call. Let him know what's going on."

Nick brought the handset to his mouth and keyed the squelch button. "Delta Four-Six, this is Delta Four-Four X-Ray. Sit rep negative. Proceeding toward blue line."

A moment later, the radio buzzed. "Delta Four-Four, roger that. Advise when blue line in sight. Four-Six, out."

Lieutenant Wilkes had monitored Nick's transmission and looked at his map. His eyes were all squinted as he held the map close to his face. "What blue line are they talking about? I don't see any river anywhere on here."

Pollack looked at the map and ripped it out of Wilkes' hands. He refolded it with the speed and agility of a circus balloon magician. "If you don't have your map folded right, how do you expect to know where we are?" He jabbed a finger at the map. "See, there's the river. Right there! The way you had it folded, we'd end up in Cambodia. LT, please, you have to pay more attention. Okay, sir?"

Pollack whispered to Mad Dog, "I'm going to kill that motherfucker. He's so stupid, he doesn't deserve to live."

Mad Dog was standing behind the Lieutenant. In the past hour, he heard this same conversation ten different ways. Pollack must be getting tired. He usually extended murderous impulses to include all of Wilkes' living relatives and generations unborn.

They had been out only a few hours, and already Mad Dog was tired. His shoulders ached with the weight of his pack; and no matter how he shifted, he just couldn't get comfortable. His shirt was soaked and plastered to his body with sweat, and it was only 10 AM. A full day of hiking lay ahead.

This would be his last operation. He'd been offered a job, a safe job, back at Base Camp; and he decided he was going to take it. He wasn't going to end up like White, who just kept extending his time in the field. Thirty days or less; that's all this mission would last, and then back to the battalion aid station for good. He'd have cold beers and a soft bed every night. No more of this humping crap, sleeping on rocks and drinking shit-tasting water. Thirty days, and he'd be history.

The funny thing was he knew Holt, Camp and White would be happy for him. And if they weren't? Fuck them. He was doing the right thing and needed to look out for himself. Thirty days, and that's it.

John Kimball was frightened, and not of the gooks. Right now, he'd welcome getting shot. He was so exhausted, he felt like he couldn't take another step. He had five canteens, and he had already emptied two of them. Sergeant Holt had already yelled at him for drinking too much water, but what was he supposed to do?

He was certain he was carrying more than anyone else. That was the only explanation for why he was so tired. He knew he was fit. He ran track in high school, played tennis and swam. He got through basic training and AIT without any major physical challenge. But nothing could have prepared him for the jungle. He couldn't go on much further. He knew he carried too much weight. How could a scarecrow like Little Wilson do it? It was impossible. He'd speak to Sergeant Holt about it the next time they took a break. But for now, he needed more water.

Up front, on point, Holt was lost in his own thoughts. He thought of Janet and the ridiculous situation he'd gotten himself into. He wondered what she was doing right at this moment. He always got the time zones mixed up. If it was daytime here, it should be night back in the world. He thought that was right. But was it today or yesterday, or was it tomorrow? He could never get it right. Her letters were becoming infrequent. When she did write, there was nothing of importance in them. It was a mistake coming back. He did miss her. This time, things would be different. He would be discharged, and there would be no more Vietnam. It would be over for him.

The sudden coolness of the air stopped him. The river was no more than twenty meters ahead. Christ, he could have walked right up to it, fell in and drowned. He realized he had better start paying attention to what he was doing, or there wouldn't be a next time with Janet. He looked back to see if anyone caught him daydreaming.

He could just make out the river through the trees. It wasn't much of a river; it was more like a big stream, maybe ten meters wide and about four feet deep. Just big enough to get everybody wet and miserable. A typical Vietnam stream, muddy and shit-brown. The banks were steeply eroded, and the bottom was soft mud. You could step into a hole and end up over your head before you know it.

He heard Mercado coming up behind him and turned. As he did, he saw a small geyser of mud erupt about six feet to his side. Then another one, much closer, followed by the pop of rifle shots. "Hit it," he hollered, but Mercado was already on the ground.

He threw himself behind a small mound of dirt. Two flashes came from across the river. He thumbed his safety to full auto and fired a long burst. Nick took advantage of the covering fire to crawl up to him.

Two, three, four more shots split the air. Then all at once, four or five AKs opened up on full automatic. It sounded like a whole bunch of corn popping. Bullets whizzed overhead, splitting branches and chopping off leaves. Dirt kicked up all around them. Bark flew off the tree next to them. They were covered with dirt, leaves and splinters.

Holt looked up and fired his rifle into a thick clump of bushes in one long continuous burst, emptying his clip. He reached for a fresh magazine as Mercado fired several short bursts.

Mercado yelled, "What are we shooting at?"

"That bush over there. The big one."

"Why there?"

"Because it's shooting at us."

Once again, the whole other side of the river opened up. AKs from all over fired at them. Tracers filled the air. Rounds were hitting everywhere they looked. Mercado tried burrowing his body deeper into the ground.

"Nicky, stop that! You keep wriggling your ass. You're getting them all excited. That's why they're shooting at us."

Mercado was laughing insanely as he buried his head in the mud.

Don squirmed to the left, and four rounds chopped through the trees just above him. Two hit right in front, spewing dirt into his face, stinging his eyes. He dragged his sweat-slicked hand across his face and heard Nick screaming into his radio.

He stuck his rifle over the dirt mound, put his head up, sighted and squeezed off a long, rattling burst of bullets. No answer. He looked again and fired another clip. All quiet. "I think we won. Shout over to them, see if they want to surrender."

"Fuck you. I'm calling in bombers. Nuke the bastards."

Back in the column, the platoon had dropped to the ground.

Further back, the Lieutenant was shouting orders and calling for his radio.

Pollack cocked his head and listened. Shit, he thought, nothing but AKs. Then he heard an M16, then two. All right! Bring smoke on those fuckers.

Holt looked back at the squad and waved his hand to settle the men. He saw the LT running up toward him. The Lieutenant lay down by his side. Don briefed him. "We'll bring up the platoon slowly, one squad at a time, and spread them along the riverbank."

Holt directed Kelly and Fisk to set up behind a fallen tree. "Spray the trees, keep it low."

The M60 fired as Big Wilson crawled to their side and started firing high-explosive grenades into the bushes.

Holt turned again to the LT. "It doesn't look like much, a few gooks putting out rounds just to fuck with us. They might leave a sniper to hold us up. That's about it."

The Lieutenant nodded and spoke into the radio handset. Off to the side, Kelly was sweeping the bank with M60 fire, and Big Wilson was thumping off grenades. No one was shooting back.

"Take your squad off to the right and find a place to cross. Once there, sweep your way down and come up from their side."

"Sure thing. But they're probably gone by now."

"Understood, but we need security on the other side before we cross."

Holt led the squad upstream about one hundred meters until they found a shallow rocky bottom. The new guys, largely forgotten, followed in glum silence.

Mercado and Holt knelt side by side. Don looked at Mercado and asked, "What do you think?"

Mercado shrugged.

Holt placed Kelly and his M60 behind some rocks that had a clear view of the far side. Fisk crawled to his side, uncoiling a belt of ammunition.

"I'll leave my pack here. Cover me from here. You see anything move over there, you light them up and don't stop until I'm across, okay?" Holt pulled the quick-release strap and shrugged off his rucksack, and got to one knee. He waited just a moment, then darted across the stream. He ran fast, slipped and fell face-down into the water, splashing loudly. He rolled onto his stomach, got up and ran. He threw himself into the soft mud of the bank and stared into the bushes. He moved up the bank and found a dry spot behind a fallen log. Satisfied it was clear, he waved the squad across.

The men crossed the stream one by one. Locke staggered with

the extra weight of Holt's pack. When they all were across, they spread out and proceeded down the opposite bank. They found nothing. Not a thing. No blood trails, no shell casings, nothing. The ground was picked clean.

It took the battalion three hours to cross the stream. It was 2:30 before everyone was on the move again.

Chapter 4

Howdy Doody

Six days had gone by, and they were barely ten miles from the landing zone. It was Wednesday, March 13th, the morning of their seventh day; and the battalion was on stand-down. It was a day of rest and recuperation.

Five days back, Lieutenant Wilkes had requested an immediate replacement for the injured platoon sergeant. Against the recommendation of the company commander, the request was granted in the form of Sergeant First Class Randall Calhoun. Sergeant Calhoun was a transferee from a posting in Germany, eager for Vietnam combat experience. A Germany jungle expert, he completed training in the snowy mountains of Bavaria. Like so many other senior NCOs and Second Lieutenants, they roamed the halls of division headquarters, begging for combat command and a chance to get their Combat Infantryman's Badge, a requirement for advancement. Upon his arrival, he made the rounds of the four squads to introduce himself. He seemed nice enough, but his inexperience was obvious. He left little impression on the men.

Sergeant Camp returned to the squad two days after the arrival of Calhoun. His advanced NCO training class was canceled without explanation. Camp seemed to accept the situation as a normal occurrence of military life; and without question, he assumed his old job as squad leader. Former Sergeant, and former squad leader, Holt went back to being Specialist 4th Class Holt. He could care less about being squad leader, and was relieved Camp had returned. He had long ago given up trying to make sense of how or why the Army did things.

He sat with his back against a tree, stripped to the waist with his boots and socks off. He was reading In Cold Blood and smoking a cigarette. Sitting about ten feet away was the fourth squad minus Camp, who was up at the CP talking to Wilkes. Some were sleeping; others were reading paperbacks or comics, or writing letters. Kelly sat hunched over his poncho, the pieces of his M60 machine gun scattered about him. He carefully wiped each piece with an oily rag.

Since the brief fire fight on the first day, everything had been quiet. They had walked for three days and had seen no signs of the enemy. On the fourth day, Holt, on point, crossed a well-worn trail which bore fresh signs of a fairly large troop movement. They were diverted; and for two days, they followed a trail of footprints and broken branches which eventually lead nowhere. Holt spent half a day criss-crossing the jungle, trying to regain the trail, but it was as if the enemy had been lifted off the ground and had never existed in the first place. For the remainder of the day, they returned to their original heading and continued their monotonous plodding. And now, on the seventh day, they rested.

For the last few days, Holt had been cranky and short-tempered. He wouldn't admit it to anyone; he was more tired than he ever remembered. He usually felt alert and full of energy in the jungle. But now, he was groggy; his movements were slow and clumsy. He felt washed out and drained. It was probably the diarrhea. He was drinking more water than usual. This bothered him the most. He prided himself on his water discipline and the ability to go without water, regardless of how hot it was. He now found himself gulping great mouthfuls like some green FNG. He needed this day to recharge and get his groove back.

He heard some noise and turned his head to see Camp. He was waving something at him. He sat down heavily and brushed Don with his shoulder. Holt grunted with annoyance and slid over. "Here, Smiley, I brought you a present." Camp held out a curved metal box. "It's a banana clip, a brand-new thirty-round magazine for your CAR-15. It's about two inches longer than the standard-issue magazine and holds ten extra rounds."

"Where did you get it?" He turned the magazine over and examined it from all angles.

"Yokes brought a box of them out with him. All the officers and platoon sergeants got one. He saved a couple for you and me. It should be good when you're up on point. This way, you got an extra ten rounds to play with." Camp reached across Holt for his pack of cigarettes. He pulled one out and lit it, and handed the pack back to Don.

"You ever smoke your own?" He looked inside to see how many were left.

"Christ, Don. You get them for free, just like we all do. What are you bitching about?"

"Nothing, all right? Not a fucking thing." Don gathered up his things and walked into the bushes.

Camp looked around at the others and shrugged. He got up and sat by Kelly. "What's wrong with him?" He nodded to where Holt had walked off.

Kelly didn't look up; he studied the bolt of his machine gun. "Don't know, and I don't fucking care. He's been quiet all day, so I figured he wanted to be left alone." He looked at Camp. "So guess what I did? I left him the fuck alone." He continued to oil the gun parts.

Camp walked over to a large tree with plenty of shade. He nestled himself into the tangle of exposed roots. Everybody was acting a little strange. Maybe they could use a few more days of rest. He would mention it to the Lieutenant.

A little after noon, Holt heard someone walking toward him. He sat just inside the wood line. Mosquitoes had forced him to put his shirt on. It was hot, close to a hundred degrees, but he was well into the shade.

It was Little Wilson. He was carrying two C-ration meals. "It's lunch time. You didn't bring any food. I thought you would be hungry." He handed Don a brown cardboard box.

"It's beef and potatoes. You like them, right?" He started to walk away.

"Gene, where are you going? Sit down and eat with me."

"Are you sure? I mean, you didn't look like you wanted any company." Wilson took a hesitant step back before sitting next to Holt.

"The worst part of being in the Army is you're never alone. Try sitting alone; you can't. You end up with guys walking all around you, asking you what's wrong. You can't even take a shit by yourself. You need someone to watch your back. This place can get on a person's nerves." While he was talking, Don was working on a can, cutting the lid off with his P38 can opener.

Wilson was setting up his field stove made out of a can with no lid and holes cut around the base. He didn't answer because he felt Holt wasn't looking for an answer. Don was one of the veterans of the platoon, and Wilson was content just to hang around him.

There were many stories circulating about Holt's first tour in Vietnam. Some said he was highly decorated, having received more than a dozen medals. Other stories were about his heavily scarred legs. He was a mysterious and glamorous figure who contributed to his own myth by rarely discussing his first tour.

Wilson wasn't sure he could call Holt a friend. He had talked to him on many occasions, but usually it was him doing all the talking. He liked Holt and knew he was good in the field. He figured he could learn a lot from him. Since he desperately wanted to leave Vietnam alive, he was willing to take any help he could get.

Don finished cutting his can open and looked up. Wilson began molding a piece of C-4 explosive into a small ball. He looked like such a goofy young kid, yet he was two years older than him. His large, drooping mustache and short spiky hair didn't do anything to make him look older. And he was so skinny. They all looked underweight, but Wilson looked positively anemic. He was all ribs and shoulder blades. It didn't matter, though. He carried as much weight as anyone else and never complained. It fact, he never complained about anything, and Holt knew he had a pretty rough life. "How's your aunt doing?" Wilson's aunt had helped raised him after his parents were killed in an automobile accident when he was fourteen.

"She's doing okay. She got some money from my parents' insurance, and I send her something every month. She'll never be rich, but who will?" Wilson lit a match to the C-4, and it flared up in a blue-white smokeless flame. "She worries about me, though. I guess there's no way to stop that, but it bothers me."

Holt set his can atop the stove and stirred the stew with a plastic spoon. Wilson opened his own meal, a can of beans and franks that everyone called "beans and baby dicks."

"What do you say you're doing over here?"

"I tell her the truth. I promised her I wouldn't lie to her. I don't tell her any bullshit war stories, but I don't leave anything out, either." Wilson bent the cut top of his can over, forming a handle. He took a spoon from his shirt pocket, licked it, and wiped it against his pant leg.

"What's there to tell? We walk through the jungle. Somebody shoots at us and we shoot back. We hardly ever see anybody. We end up shooting a lot of trees and bushes."

Wilson stared down at Holt's bubbling stew. He was tugging at his mustache.

In less than a minute, the stew was boiling. Holt used the end of his shirt and lifted the can off the flame. He opened a second smaller can, and removed a white doughy ball of bread-like substance. He pierced the dough ball with a stick and held it over the flame, toasting it. Surprisingly, the smell of baked bread filled the air.

Wilson waited until Holt was done before setting his own can onto the fire. He concentrated on stirring his meal. "You mind if I ask you something?"

"Depends. What is it?"

"The other day. You and Mercado. What was it like, getting shot at?"

Don laughed. "You've been shot at plenty. You know exactly what it's like."

"I've been shot at like everybody else: in a big group, with bullets flying all over the place. I never had anyone shooting at just me. Those guys were trying to kill you. Just you, and nobody else. They were shooting at you specifically. I can't imagine what that's like."

Holt leaned back. "If the bullet hits you, it's gonna kill you, no matter who it's aimed at."

"Were you scared?"

"At the time, I wasn't. I was too pumped up, too excited. When it's over and I have time to think about it, yeah, then I get scared. Plenty scared. Did you hear Nicky laughing? He wasn't laughing when it was all over."

"I'm always scared. I don't want to die over here. I thought it would get easier, but it hasn't. I can't picture coming back here like you did, not after I was home and all safe. Why did you come back?"

"That's a good question. I've been asking myself that for awhile."

They finished their meal, crushed the cans, and buried their garbage. Holt was full and sleepy, and wanted to take a nap. He saw that the squad was gathered around the battalion chaplain, Major Carltin, and another younger chaplain he didn't recognize.

"Don, Eugene, come over here and meet the new chaplain." Major Carltin pressed his hand on the back of the younger chaplain.

"Boys, I'd like to introduce Father Doody, pronounced Dooday. He joined us just a few days ago."

Camp was praying, "Please, just let it go and don't say anything."

"Dooday? Is that your last name, Padre?" Don asked. "I'm confused. Your name tag says Doody."

"It's pronounced Dooday."

"You must be Canadian or something."

"No! I'm not Canadian. Why would you ask that?"

"That's how Canadians would pronounce it."

Both chaplains clearly looked uncomfortable.

"You know, there was a famous puppet in the '50s called Doody. He had his own show and everything. I thought maybe there was some relation, that's all."

"You thought I was related to a puppet?"

Don shrugged. "He was very well-known."

Major Carltin clenched his jaw, and his face reddened. "Well, Father, I'll leave you to get acquainted with the boys."

Father Doody smiled warmly, looking around from face to face.

Holt sat with his arms extended over his knees. He lit a cigarette and studied the chaplain through the curling rise of smoke. He didn't look any older than the rest of the squad. His skin was soft and smooth, and not darkened by the sun. He couldn't have been in country for that long. He was probably just out of chaplain school or wherever the fuck chaplains came from. His fatigues and boots looked new.

Both Camp and Father Doody looked nervous. The men looked uncomfortable at having the chaplain around so long.

The chaplain was talking about the comfort God could provide young men so far from home who found themselves in such desperate circumstances. He prattled on about how there were no atheists in the foxholes. He sounded like a fifty-year-old lifer spouting the same inane World War Two bullshit.

Maybe he should tell us what a comfort God could be when

you're home on leave and some long-haired punk spits at us or calls us baby-killers, Holt thought. He snorted his disgust and turned to look into the trees.

Camp could sense the men getting more restless by the minute. He'd give the chaplain a couple of minutes, then steer him to another squad. He'd take him down to first squad and give Rodney a thrill. That little Bible-thumping rodent would eat this guy up. The two of them could sit around and debate the scriptures. All he had to do was wait for an opening.

"It's been said that men who are close to death or have been wounded feel the presence God. If that's true, then you boys should be thankful for this experience, thankful for anything that brings you close to God."

The chaplain smiled warmly and looked to each man for encouragement. He couldn't wait to leave. These boys smelled terrible and were absolutely filthy. It looked like they haven't bathed in weeks. He would speak to Major Carltin about this. Perhaps he could introduce a series of lectures about personal hygiene.

"You ever been wounded, Padre?" Holt asked.

"I'm a Catholic chaplain. You can call me Father."

"Sure thing. So, have you been wounded?"

"No, I haven't," the chaplain replied stiffly.

"Then how you gonna tell me or anyone else what it's like to be wounded?"

"You have a point. I'm merely relating experiences that have been passed on to me. I take it you've been wounded... uh, I didn't catch your name, son."

Holt didn't bother to give his name. "I've been wounded twice."

"How you were wounded?" The chaplain sensed he was on dangerous ground, but didn't know what to do. He had no idea of what he was doing wrong. These boys appeared openly hostile to him. At best, they seemed indifferent.

"No. I don't mind." Holt paused and lit another cigarette off the stub of the first.

Little Wilson perked up. He knew Don was wounded, but knew nothing of the details.

Holt continued. "I was shot once. The bullet went through my arm and into my leg. The second time, I tripped a booby trap. I stepped on a hand grenade."

The chaplain's eyes opened wide. "My God! Why would anyone step on a grenade?"

"I didn't do it on purpose. I didn't see it."

"Did it explode?"

"Of course it did. How do you think I was wounded?"

"No. No. It's just that... How close were you? To the explosion, I mean?" The chaplain appeared genuinely interested. He moved closer to Don.

"Two feet, maybe three."

The chaplain shook his head in disbelief. "That's incredible. It really is. Two feet! You were lucky. That only proves my point. God must have been with you."

"Well, I'll tell you something, Padre. If God were with me, I wish he would have stepped on the grenade and not me."

Camp started to laugh, choked it off and turned away from the chaplain. The chaplain, with an embarrassed, self-conscious smile, looked to see if anyone else was laughing. Everyone had their eyes turned down except for Holt, who looked back at him with the same blank, flat stare.

Camp steered the chaplain away. "How about I bring you down to the first squad so you can meet some of the other guys? How about that?"

"Yes, that will be fine."

"You know, Padre," Holt called to him, "if God were there, the least he could have done was point out the grenade. I mean, He can see everything. Right? Why did God want to blow me up?"

Chapter 5

The Listening Post

Holt sat with Mad Dog when Camp returned. It had been over an hour since he left to escort Chaplain Doody to the first squad. He walked over to them, shaking his head slowly. In his hand, he held a small stack of envelopes.

"I stopped by the CP and mail was in. Guess why I was at the CP? Let me tell you. No, I don't have to; you already know. Did this asshole tell you what he did?"

"He didn't have to. I was there when Carltin came by."

Mad Dog started to laugh as he remembered the scene: the Major berating Lieutenant Smith, who endured the outburst in sullen silence. "Serves Carltin right. Him and his little faggot coming out here once a month, telling us what a great job we're doing. How everybody at home appreciates us keeping them free from Communism. Kill a gook for God and all that shit." Mad Dog spat this out in one long, breathless tirade.

"Yeah! Kill a Commie for mommy," said Kelly.

Camp turned to Don. "I've got good news and bad news for you. The good news is Lieutenant Smith didn't think it was fair you didn't get your stripes back because my class was canceled. He put the order in. The bad news is he canceled the order about twenty minutes ago. You can't go around insulting chaplains, even shitheads like Carltin and Doody."

"Whoa, whoa, whoa. His name is pronounced Dooday,

remember?"

"I thought Carltin would piss his pants. I had to stand there and listen to them tell me what a complete, disrespectful fuck-up you are. Wilkes was there, too. I guess he felt he had to pile on. You got the listening post tonight."

"Jesus, Camp. Quite frankly, I don't see good news in any of this."

"Fuck 'em if they can't take a joke."

"So, you're not mad at me?" Holt stretched out his arms. "Come on, let's make up. Give me a kiss, but no tongue."

"Well, you're taking this better than I thought. You seem to be in a better mood."

"Just needed some time. Hey, Wendy. Sorry I'm snapped at you before. Still friends?"

"With friends like you, I should join the fucking Air Force. I got no chance of making rank with you around. I got something that'll make everyone feel better." Camp waved the envelopes and hollered, "Mail call."

Don held out his hand.

"Just cool your jets. It's my duty to distribute the mail in strict alphabetical order. No favorites."

"It's your duty to die on the spot when I put a bullet in your head. Give me my fucking letter."

"Alright, alright. Calm yourself down." Camp handed a letter to Holt.

The squad gathered around as Camp distributed the mail. As Camp walked away to read his mail, he said to Holt, "On the LP tonight, take Little Wilson and one of the new guys."

"Great. I'm sure they'll be thrilled. Hey, Camp, next time you're brown-nosing with the officers, please express my gratitude."

Camp gave him the finger as he walked away.

Don fingered the envelope, feeling its thickness. He examined the postmark before putting it into his pocket. "Gonna save it for later."

"That's cool," said Mad Dog. He stood and extended a hand to help Holt up. "Let's get some chow. Yokes came out again. I think he brought some cold sodas with him."

"Bless his greasy little heart. Yeah. Let's go."

The meal consisted of real comfort food: meat loaf, mashed potatoes and corn, all covered in a thick brown gravy served on droopy, soggy paper plates. There was also fruit salad and two cold sodas per man.

Holt was back at the squad's position, mopping up the last of the gravy with a piece of white bread. He set the plate aside and got out his cigarettes. As he sat there smoking, he took out Janet's letter. He popped the cap on his second soda and settled himself comfortably. Carefully, he tore open the envelope.

He only got three letters from her since he returned to Vietnam, three harmless little bits of fluff that he devoured several times over. They didn't say much. She talked about the weather and her job, which she would be leaving soon. She mentioned her pregnancy and the baby only briefly to say everything was proceeding normally. This letter was no different. She said how she might go back to school and how it was getting warmer. She did ask about him and hoped all was well. The nightly news was horrible, and she couldn't watch it for fear of hearing his name or unit mentioned. She was sorry about how things had worked out. Her last line read, "I hope", and then the words were scratched out. It continued: "when you get home, we can work things out and live like a family." It ended with, "Love Ya, Janet."

Don reread it again. Love Ya, not I Love You or Love You; just Love Ya.

There was no way to explain how important letters were. They were a connection to home, a lifeline to sanity and proof that normalcy still existed. Letters were read and reread. Every line and

61

phrase was dissected in an attempt to reveal the unwritten meaning. Guys hung on to every expression of affection. Letters showed them the real world with a promise of a job or school, a world that held the reasonable expectation of being alive from one day to the next. They could help you endure one more day. Mail was as important as the air they breathed. Mail was water and food for their souls. Without it, they could die. Literally.

He'd seen it happen. Guys who got "Dear John" letters sometimes would just give up. There was a guy from second platoon whose wife stopped writing. After months of no letters, he just stood up during a fire fight. He didn't commit suicide. He let the gooks do it for him.

He promised himself regardless of what happened, that wouldn't be him. Janet might not write enough, but she always sent packages. Then again, he paid her by sending her a marriage allotment from his salary. He knew by the items she sent that she did care for him. She knew the food he liked, the books he read, and the other items of comfort she included without being asked. He vowed he would write her more. He would win her back and prove her father's morbid predictions to be wrong. He would survive this shithole and go home.

Don carefully folded the pages and placed them back into the envelope. He placed the envelope in a plastic bag, and then into his pack with the rest of her letters. He saved them all and reread them constantly.

He leaned back and lit another cigarette. Her letter troubled him. She was making plans for the future. By contrast, he never gave much thought to what he would do once out of the Army. They were drafting so many guys from New York, it was almost impossible to get a job if you were classified 1A. No one would hire you. That's why he had enlisted. At least, that's what he told everybody. What would he do? Eventually, he would have to make some decisions about his future.

He field-stripped his cigarette and pushed the filter into the ground. He needed to prepare for tonight. Before chow, he told Little Wilson and Locke they would be going with him. Wilson took it in stride, but Locke looked like he was going to throw up.

He gathered his gear: rifle, ammo, grenades, poncho liner, and two canteens and two flares. He would leave his helmet with his rucksack and wear his boonie hat. Wilson would carry Mercado's radio, and they all would carry one Claymore mine apiece.

He found them sitting with their gear on, all set to go. Locke looked pale and shaken.

Holt checked their gear to make sure everything was secured and tied tight, and there would be no noise. He told Wilson to get the call signs and make a final radio check. He faced Locke. "This is your first LP, the first time you're going out at night. Right?"

Locke nodded, his throat too dry to speak.

He spoke to him slowly, trying to calm him. "Pay attention and learn something from this. Don't just follow me with your head up your ass. Okay? We'll go out about two hundred meters, wait until it's real dark, and then move to our final position. I'll go first, then you and Wilson bring up the rear. Nothing fancy. We go due north. You got your compass? Good. In case we get separated, you do an about-face and come back due south. You getting all this?"

Locke nodded.

"Okay, keep your mouth shut. No noise. No cigarettes and no canned food. Bring some John Wayne bars to help you stay awake."

"What are they?" Locke asked.

"They're the tropical chocolate bars in your C-rations. They're hard and taste like shit, but loaded with sugar and won't melt. I swear, you could hold them over an open flame and they still won't melt. God knows what they're made out of."

Don pulled out a tube of black camouflage face paint. He squeezed out a small lump and passed it to Locke. "Here, smear some of this on your face; and for Christ's sake, try and relax. You look like you're ready to jump out of your skin. This ain't my first rodeo, cowboy. I know what I'm doing. We have to do this shit all the time."

Locke's hands were visibly shaking.

"Put some on the back of your hands too, and roll down your sleeves. Give it to Wilson when you're done. One more thing, and this is important. Under no circumstance do you fire your weapon. You fire if and when I fire. We're out there by ourselves. All we're doing is providing an early warning for the company. We're gonna hide ourselves and listen and observe. We're not there to fight. Got it? Tell me you understand everything I'm telling you."

"I understand."

"Good. We got time for one more cigarette."

As he lit his cigarette, Camp walked over, carrying three more canvas Claymore bags.

"Well, well. What do we have here? Amos, Andy and Buckwheat?"

"Don't let the brothers hear you. How about just calling us the Black Panthers?"

"You guys all set? Here, take these extra mines with you. They don't weigh much, but they pack a punch."

Don showed Camp where they were going, and Camp objected. "That's too far. Don't go more than two hundred meters. No further. Go easy on Locke; he's scared shitless."

Holt handed Locke a Claymore bag and decided he would carry the extra two.

Camp extended his arm and they shook hands. "Be safe, brother."

"Nobody dies. We all come home." He gave Camp his cigarette, turned toward Wilson and Locke. "Let's go."

As they left the safety of the perimeter, he heard Wilson calling in, letting them know they were leaving. Right outside the perimeter was a large clearing, and they walked quickly across it to get into the wood line. Six days of humping had brought them ten kilometers closer to the Cambodian border. The jungle thinned, and it became cooler and made walking easier.

Holt withdrew his compass and took his first bearing. The forest was much darker; it was easy to lose visual contact. The sun's last rays were absorbed by the thick foliage. Soon, all light would vanish, absorbed into the trees.

They traveled through a world of muted shadows where objects were distinguished in varying shades of gray and black. For Holt, the night held no particular fear. Somewhere during his first tour, he stopped being afraid of the dark. In a way, he missed the tingling sense of apprehension he got when he set out into the night.

Everyone said the gooks owned the night. It was this belief that enabled the NVA to move virtually unchallenged. In fact, all it took was another learned skill to travel in the dark. It was no more difficult moving at night than during the day. The gooks weren't supermen. You had to use all your senses, not just sight. You felt an insect as it flew by you without it ever touching you. You felt the disturbance in the air. A snapping twig echoed in their ears. Progress was slower; but it also felt smoother and quieter, as if all your movements were made through thick liquid. The softness of the ground beneath your boots felt like you were walking barefoot.

If you could let yourself go and suppress your fear, traveling at night could be exhilarating.

For Holt, night movements was commonplace. They routinely had to do listening posts and ambush patrols. He had not conquered his fear; he simply lost it. Locke, on the other hand, was scared to the point of abject terror. He felt that each footfall would send him tumbling helplessly into some dark, unknown void. It was as if he were moving down a long, darkened staircase, searching out the next step. He found himself probing the ground with his toe before committing all his weight to each step. He could barely hear Holt to his front or Wilson to his rear. He was terrified that somehow, he would lose what little sense of direction he had and stumble off between them and the relative safety they provided.

Wilson walked behind Locke and cringed every time Locke would stumble or trip. Wilson suspended his fear with the belief that Don would get them safely to where he wanted to go. This is how he's survived so far: by entrusting his life to the abilities of others. All he wanted was to get out of Vietnam in one piece. He was a follower, not a leader; and he was not ashamed to admit it.

Holt moved slowly, checking his compass often. After every few steps, he would stop and listen. The constant hum and buzz of insects was comforting. The ground bugs would stop buzzing at the slightest disturbance. He walked with his arm stretched out, feeling the air before him, sensitive to the slightest touch.

Holt stopped and looked down at the luminescent dial of his watch. They had made good time; this would be the spot where they would initially set up. In an hour or so, they would move to the final position, the one where they would spend the night.

He turned to look for Locke, and saw him standing about fifteen feet away. Locke was barely visible in the shadows. He was frantically turning his head side to side. Holt decided to let him stew a bit. It would be good for him. It would scare him good. Maybe he won't make the same mistake. He had told to him to stay close.

Locke was close to panic. He had become separated from Holt and was lost. Tears filled his eyes. One minute, Holt was there; and the next, he was gone. Wilson was standing behind him and probably didn't know anything was wrong. What should he tell him?

He never heard Holt come up on him. He was just there, knocking on his forehead with his knuckles. "Anybody home? You just gonna stand here jerking off all night, or do you want to join me?"

Locke was so relieved, so overwhelmingly grateful that he thought he'd cry. Instead, he tugged on Wilson's sleeve and stumbled after Holt, looking through wet, foggy eyes. "Thank you, God," he kept repeating, over and over.

The three of them stepped into a small cluster of bushes and knelt down.

"You two to stay here. I'm going to scout ahead."

"How long will you be?" Wilson whispered, but Holt was already gone.

Locke leaned close to Wilson's ear, a note of concern creeping into his voice. "How will he find us again?"

Within minutes, Holt found the spot he was looking for: a low, grassy ridge set in the woods overlooking a small gully, fifty or sixty meters wide. The gully floor was covered in thick grass. To his left, the forest continued in an unbroken wall. To his right, it thinned considerably, ending in a large open plain. He looked up into the clear night sky, and stared at the moon and stars.

He stood and started back.

Locke was searching for Holt. He heard a soft rustle of branches, and Holt was in front of him. "We'll wait a few minutes, and then we'll go," Holt spoke in a low voice, just above a whisper. "Relax until then."

Relax! He must be out of his mind. He had started shaking at four o'clock when told about the LP, and he hadn't stopped since.

Chapter 6

Graduation

At nine-thirty, they moved to their final position. They settled in a small depression overlooking a dried riverbed.

"What do you see?"

"It looks like a gully or something like that," Locke said.

"Good. How far from are we down to the bottom in meters? A meter is a little over three feet. So, how far?"

"It's about seventy-five feet, so that's twenty-five meters, right?

"You're doing good. How far across to the other side?"

"About one-hundred-fifty feet."

"In meters?"

"Fifty meters?"

"That's right. Get used to speaking this way. A 'klick' is a kilometer, and that's about sixty percent of a mile. So if we walk ten klicks, how many miles is that?"

Locke closed his eyes a moment. "About six."

"You need to speak in meters and klicks to call in artillery."

Holt gathered the six Claymore bags. "I'm going to set four mines about twenty meters down this slope. The remaining two will be five meters behind them." He pulled a mine from its green canvas bag. "See, look here. The mine is about eight inches long and five inches high. See how it's curved? It's made of C-4 plastic explosive, two pounds of it, covered in some sort of epoxy shit. Embedded in the C-4 are seven hundred ball bearings. You fold down these little metal legs and jam it into the ground, curved side out. You can't make a fucking mistake on how you set it. Look."

Locke examined the mine. The curved face was stamped 'Front Toward Enemy'.

"I guess the Army knows they're dealing with morons and aren't taking any chances."

In each bag was a long coil of wire, with a detonator on the end.

"You take this silver pencil-looking thing and put it in one of the two holes on either side. Then you run the wire up to where we are. Cover me while I place them."

They covered Holt as he walked down the embankment. He set the first four mines in a sweeping arc covering their front. He tried to place the mines behind some concealment. He place the second row of two inside the arc of the first row. He came back to their position carrying six strands of thick wire. Attached to each wire was a large clothespin-looking object. This was the firing device known as the clacker. He laid the clackers along the edge of their hole.

He showed Locke the arrangement. "When you're ready to fire the mine, you squeeze the clacker. It creates a electrical charge and blows the detonator, which in turn blows the mine. It's good for about fifty meters. If we have to, we blow the mines and run. You got it?"

"Blow the mines and run," Locke repeated.

"Final thing. We stand a two-hour watch. I'll take the first, ten 'til midnight. Wilson will take midnight 'til two. You take two to four, and then you wake me. We leave here at first light, somewhere around six. Alright? Sack out and try and get some sleep."

Regardless of whether they were on an LP or ambush patrol or just back at the perimeter, they would stand watch. They never got a full night's sleep.

Holt sat cross-legged. His head was barely above their foxhole. His rifle lay across his lap. His web gear containing his ammo, grenades and water was within easy reach. The clackers were laid out in a row. To either side of him lay Wilson and Locke. They had their poncho liners pulled over their heads as protection from the mosquitoes.

At the start of his watch, he called in a radio check. Every hour on the hour, they would call in their situation report, as would the other LPs at their designated times.

Holt settled himself comfortably and peered into the gully beneath them. The moonlight illuminated the ravine. With the exception of the soft, continuous hum of insects, everything was quiet and still.

His thoughts drifted to home and to Janet. It was during the night that he missed her most. He reread her letter in his mind, and it bothered him all over again. In six months, he would be discharged and reluctantly return to civilian life. He caught himself; why did he say reluctantly? He was looking forward to getting out the Army, and especially out of Vietnam. The problem was he had no idea what he was going to do once he was out. Maybe he shouldn't worry about it. According to Janet's father, the grim reaper, the odds were stacked against him. What a fucking asshole, making his money predicting when people would die.

Maybe he would use the GI Bill and go to school. He couldn't picture himself among all those college war protesters. If not school, then what? Janet made it sound so easy. Come home and forget Vietnam. Start a new life and forget the war. It wasn't that easy. He wished she were here so he could talk to her. He often had long, imaginary conversations with her in which he played both parts. He would think out things and rehearse what he would say and how she would respond. At night, he would torture himself with her memory, never letting her out of his mind. The more depressed he got, the more he missed her.

During all the wedding planning, they managed to get a day to themselves. They made a truce of sorts: no talk of Vietnam, and no talk of the wedding. He had borrowed a friend's car and they drove out to Jones Beach on Long Island. It was well after the season, and the beach was deserted. It was a cool, overcast day. Together, they walked along the water's edge, holding hands. They talked quietly as if by not making any noise, they could preserve the peace and serenity of the moment. They walked to the small outdoor snack bar that was open year-round.

He could remember everything as if it were a movie playing in his head. Her blonde hair was pulled back into a loose ponytail. Her green eyes, and her skin reddened to a delicious peach color by the ocean breeze. He remembered how she smelled, and how clean and fresh she tasted when they stopped and kissed.

They sat at a table outside the snack bar and drank cold beer in large paper cups. This was first time since he had been home that he felt relaxed and at ease. The silences in their conversation were just as meaningful as anything they could say. They left the bar and walked across the sand while holding hands. A fog was rolling in, insulating them in a wispy, gauze cocoon.

They sat on the sand, and neither of them spoke. Don was hugging his knees. Janet sat at an angle, looking at him. She thought his mood was subject to change: first bright and cheery, then darkening.

Janet pulled herself close. She nestled into his shoulder, hugging herself to him. She ducked her head under his chin and gently kissed his throat. She placed her hands behind her and leaned back on her arms. Her thin T-shirt stretched tight across her small breasts. She felt her nipples stiffen under his gaze. He felt himself become erect and turned away. His face reddened.

"I'm sorry Don, I wasn't teasing you." She turned to him, and a wave of sadness swept over her. "I'm afraid to say anything. I don't know what to say or do. I'm sorry about everything."

"Don't be sorry. Everything works out the way it is supposed to. I'm supposed to be here with you, doing exactly what I'm doing."

"Tell me something. You had decided to go back before you even saw me. You never thought to ask me what I wanted. Going back is going to hurt you. It may not kill you, but it is going to destroy you. I see how you are now. You're closed off and won't talk to me. Don't you trust me?"

"I know I can trust you. There's nothing to say. I'm afraid of what I'll be without the war, and I'm afraid of what I'll become when I return to Vietnam."

"What do you mean, what you'll be without the war?"

"Without Vietnam, what am I? Out of high school, I pumped gas and made sixty dollars a week. I lived in a roach-infested basement apartment. The jungle was cleaner than that building."

"And in Vietnam?"

"In Vietnam, I was all the things a man should be. I was a squad leader. I had eight guys depending on me for their lives. I had respect that was earned. That's something I'll never have here, pumping gas."

He lit a cigarette and blew out the smoke. He turned his face toward the sky and continued. "There are things about Vietnam that make me sick. It's such a horrible, savage place. Death is all around you. You're treated like an animal, so you behave like an animal."

"What things?" she asked.

"I'm not going to talk about it, not with you or anybody. I'm not some whiny fucking REMF who wails about the things I've seen and the horrible things I've done. I've done horrible things, but I've never done anything I'm ashamed of. It's a war; and in a war, you are supposed to do horrible things. You're trained to do horrible things, and they reward you for doing them. Believe me, you don't want to hear about them. I'll be different to you afterward. So let's just change the subject."

They were quiet on the ride home.

He looked at his watch and picked up the radio handset. He spoke quietly into the mouthpiece. "Delta Four-Six, this is Delta

Four-LP. Sit rep negative."

"Delta Four-LP, this is Delta Four-Six X-Ray. Copy sit rep negative. Out," came the reply.

Shadows moved ominously, creating the impression of movement where there was none. It was a trick of the darkness. Everything seemed to move. The real trick was distinguishing what was real and what was your imagination.

He wondered how Locke would do on guard duty. So far, he was okay. A little noisy and big-time nervous, but that was to be expected. He would get better over time.

Holt wiped his hands across his eyes. He longed for a cigarette, but reached for a John Wayne bar instead. He unwrapped the small, flat bar and bit into it, savoring the crumbly hard chocolate.

This is a good spot; good concealment with an unobstructed view. He concentrated on the jungle sounds. He was tired of thinking and tired of remembering.

The rest of his watch passed quietly. After waking Wilson, he lay on the ground and fell asleep. He slept lightly, aware of the sounds around him. This is why he was awake before Locke touched him.

Locke leaned over him and whispered nervously. "Sarge, wake up. I hear something."

"What do you hear?"

"I hear voices in the woods." The fear was evident in his voice.

Holt sat up and looked into the moonlit ravine. His eyes traveled into the sparse woods. Through the trees, he saw the dark night sky. Nothing on the horizon, he thought. "Are you sure?"

"I don't know. Maybe. I'm not sure now." There was doubt in his voice. He was beginning to feel foolish for waking Holt.

Holt rubbed his eyes. "I'll sit with you for awhile," he said.

It was then he heard something: an unnatural rustling of leaves and branches, followed by some loud whispering. He saw them just as they approached the wood line. There were three of them clearly silhouetted against the dark gray sky.

He reached to wake Wilson. He brought his rifle closer to him and checked the placement of the detonators.

"What is it?" Wilson said.

"Gooks. Three of them, straight across from us."

The figures had started down the slope.

Don leaned close to Wilson. "Get on the horn. Tell them we got visitors. Three NVA in sight, maybe more."

He stared at the soldiers as they moved. They were out of range of the Claymores. Alright, fuckheads. Come closer, and I will blow your shit apart.

His eyes were drawn to the top of the ridge by more movement. Two more soldiers left the trees and quickly joined the others. It looked like they were arguing. There were a lot of hand gestures. One of them emphatically pointed down the length of the gully while the other pointed up the slope toward their position.

"What the fuck is going on? This doesn't look good."

More soldiers came and were standing around, waiting for orders. Don felt his bowels begin to loosen and tightened his sphincter. They didn't seem concerned about noise discipline as they laughed and joked amongst themselves.

Locke, even in the dark, looked as white as a sheet. His eyes were bugged out in fear; and he was breathing in short, shallow gasps.

"Pretty exciting for your first time out, huh? Do you remember where we first set up? Fifty feet straight back, remember?"

He nodded yes.

"If we get separated, that's where we meet up. Stay close to me and do what I do. Everything will be alright. Now gather up your gear."

The enemy was on the move. They started up, straight toward them.

Holt wasn't afraid of the men moving toward them. Those who would survive the initial explosion would be so disoriented, they wouldn't be a problem. It was the men behind the first rank who worried him. It would be better for everyone if they moved down the gully.

"Fuck. Go east, or west. Please, just don't come up here."

Locke was beside himself with fear. He felt tears in his eyes and prayed he wouldn't wet his pants. He couldn't remember ever being so scared. Nothing Holt could say would calm him. He wanted to grab Don's shirt and hold on to him. He didn't want to be left behind.

Wilson seemed oblivious to the danger surrounding them. He calmly worked the radio. If Holt got scared, then he would get scared.

More men joined those at the bottom of the ravine. More than thirty were milling about, all of them well spread out. Add those still coming from the woods, and there might be fifty men approaching their position.

Holt knew two things for sure. The mines would not get them all; now that they were spreading out, fewer and fewer were in the kill zone. Second, they could not win a fight against the survivors. There were just too many of them.

Turn, you bastards, turn, Holt thought. Just turn and get the fuck out of here. Goddamn it, turn, he willed them.

Still, they came. The lead men were fifty feet from the mines. If they got closer, they might spot them. The Claymores were their only chance. If he blew them too soon, they were in for some nasty shit.

Jesus Christ. Turn, you motherfuckers, turn. Please turn, he prayed. Please turn. Walk away; just go.

A few more feet, and their point man would be into the mines. He'd either spot them or trip over the wires.

Holt turned first to Wilson, and then to Locke. Wilson just stared at him, and Locke looked like he was crying. He had his head buried in the dirt, and his shoulders shook with silent sobs. Holt nudged him and pointed toward the approaching men. With great effort,

Locke composed himself and gripped his rifle.

"Shit! I can't remember if I put the detonators in. I put them in, right? Well, I guess we'll find out soon enough."

"You're kidding, right?"

"Yeah, I'm kidding. Lighten up. We'll be okay."

His hands tightened on the clackers taking up the slack in the triggers. He sighted his landmarks, and thought the point man must be even with the mines. It's now or never. They'll be too close soon.

Wilson leaned toward Don. "The Lieutenant wants us to stay and direct artillery."

He leaned past Wilson and shut off the radio. "When the Claymores blow, you and Locke beat feet. I'll stay and cover you. Don't worry, I won't be far behind. Ready?"

Holt squeezed the detonators with both hands. Explosions ripped through the men nearest the mines. He grabbed the next set of detonators and squeezed. Two more explosions shattered the night. He looked, but couldn't see through the clouds of dirt and smoke. He set off the last two mines, sending fourteen hundred steel balls tearing into anyone still standing. The smoke was misted with blood and flesh.

He ripped the wires from the detonators, and stuffed the clackers into his pockets together with his loose grenades. He picked up his rifle and web gear and ran. He ran, and he never looked back. His ears were ringing with the explosions, and he never heard the screams of the dying men.

Chapter 7

Body Count

"It was my call. You weren't there, and now you're gonna second-guess me and tell me what I should have done."

"What I'm saying is that you disobeyed a direct order. I told you to maintain your position and direct artillery fire, and you didn't," Wilkes said.

"The radio wasn't working. I never heard the order," Holt stated flatly.

"I want to see this broken radio. Bring me the fucking radio, right now."

"It's fixed now. Wilson or Mercado fixed it. Probably a loose wire or something like that. It happens."

"Bullshit!"

"I had forty or fifty NVA within fifty yards. You think I was gonna sit there and fuck around against those odds? By the time the arty was up and ready, I would have had gooks all over me."

The Lieutenant struggled to compose himself. "What I wanted you to do was stay in place and direct the artillery fire. How many times do we get the enemy out in the open like that? Here was a chance for a big body count, and you blew it. You missed the chance to make everybody look good."

"How long have you been here? Three, four weeks? You should pray to God you never see forty gooks coming at you. This ain't Iwo Jima, and I'm no John Wayne. Unless I'm one desperate motherfucker, I ain't calling in artillery on top of myself. A lot of us are going to get zapped over here, and I might be one of them. But you can be damn sure I ain't doing anything to increase the odds against myself."

Holt jabbed a finger at Wilkes and took a step closer to him. "You want a body count, then you go out there and kill all the gooks you want. I sure as shit am not putting my life in jeopardy just to make you look good." Holt took a long breath and let it out slowly. He was trembling with rage. He tried to calm himself before continuing. "Lieutenant, do what you want. Write me up on charges. You want to bust me to private? Do that, too. You want to send me in to burn shit? I'll burn shit for the next six months. I'm no lifer and I don't need your fucking stripes. Do whatever makes you happy."

He started to walk away, but stopped and turned. "You know why you're pissed? We did get a body count. But I, Wilson and Locke got the body count. Not you. You know it's not enough we get shot at by the gooks; now we got to worry about getting fucked by our own officers."

Lieutenant Wilkes' fists were balled tight, but he couldn't think of anything to say. Instead, he turned to Sergeant Camp, who was standing a little ways outside the little clearing. "Well?"

Camp walked toward the Lieutenant and lit up a cigarette. He offered the pack to Wilkes, who declined.

"What about this?"

Camp ran a hand across his chin.

"Well?" Wilkes demanded.

"I didn't hear everything that was said, but I heard enough. I think you're wrong on this. Just hear me out. You can't second-guess the patrol leader. You don't know what happened. You have to trust his judgment."

The Lieutenant snapped at Camp. "That's just the point, Sergeant. I don't trust his judgment. And while we're on the subject,

I'm beginning to wonder about your judgment. You plan on making the military a career, isn't that right?"

Camp nodded.

"Well, you'd better decide where your loyalties lie. If you're going to be a career soldier, then start acting like one. A good combat evaluation can carry you through the Army. A bad one can haunt you forever."

The Lieutenant lit his own cigarette before continuing. "Wendell, I like you. This war isn't going to last forever. We've got to make the most of it. There are officers back at Division dying to get assigned to an infantry unit. You need a combat command in your 201 file, or you're finished. Sergeant, you are on your third tour and you are still a squad leader. That doesn't look good."

"Lieutenant, what has this got to do with Holt or the LP?"

"What the Lieutenant is trying to say is you can't make an omelette without breaking a few eggs," Sergeant Calhoun said from behind the Lieutenant.

"Exactly."

"I'm not sure I understand," Camp said, but feared he did.

"To get promotions, we need body count. That goes not only for my promotion, but for Sergeant Calhoun here and for yourself. Now, do you understand?" Wilkes asked.

Camp shook his head sadly because he did understand.

"These boys don't want to risk their lives. So we have to make them do it. We can reason with them. If that doesn't work, then we order them."

"And if some get killed doing it?"

"I read an interview with a World War Two General in charge of logistics. He said his job was to put so many American soldiers on the beach that the Germans couldn't kill them all. Eventually, the Americans would overrun the German positions. This is war, and some of these kids will die. Simple as that. A certain number are considered expendable and the Army plans for this. That's why the replacement depot is loaded with fresh troops. Stop making friends with your squad and learn to command them. You understand?"

"Yes, Sir, I understand."

"I hope you do, Sergeant. For your own sake, and the sake of your career. Get back to your men and tell your little buddy to get his ass in gear. He's going to lead us back to the LP and we'd better find some dead gooks."

"Okay," Camp said quietly.

When Holt returned to the squad, Wilson was holding court, with the men gathered around him. "We fucked them up last night! Fucked! Them! Up! Those motherfuckers were walking around liked they owned the night, then BAM! We blew their shit away. Boom. Boom. Boom. Boom. Four Claymores, one after the other. We tore them a new asshole. And just when they thought the worst was over, boom, boom! Two more Claymores blew their little gook heads off. They never knew what hit them. No fucking clue. Holt let those fuckers walk right up to us. We rocked those assholes. We shredded them! Tell them, Sarge, tell 'em how we fucked those gooks."

"You're doing a good job, bro. I got nothing to add."

Holt saw Locke sitting off to the side. He walked over and sat next to him. "What's up? How come you're not chiming in? Something bothering you about last night?"

"I was so scared, I pissed my pants. I couldn't even open my eyes to see what happened. I cried."

"That's no big deal. I almost shit myself. I didn't see you cry, though."

"You were scared?"

"Fucking A1 terrified." Don fished his cigarettes out of his pocket and took his time lighting it. "We were all scared. I was scared, Wilson was scared, and you were scared. No big deal. When you had to, you came through. We all did what we had to do, and we all made it back. You did alright last night. You are now an ass-kicking jungle fighter. Enjoy your new status with the squad."

"Thanks, Sarge."

"Quit calling me that. I didn't get my stripes back, and I doubt if I will. Now go."

Two guys from the third squad came by to hear the stories. When they saw Holt, they stopped.

"Hey, Killer. Heard you smoked them last night. What's the count? How many?"

"Yeah, how many of those little fuckers you dust?"

"Didn't stop to count. We hauled ass."

"Well, good on you. The more of these little nips we zap, the sooner we go home."

Holt looked at him quizzically. "Nips? Think you got the wrong war."

"Hey, man. Nips. Gooks. Slopes. Who cares, right? Kill 'em all and let God sort them out."

"Yeah, sounds good." Don walked away.

"He going soft on us?"

"Maybe. Or maybe he thinks we're too stupid. He'll be hanging with the college boys next."

The platoon got the news that they would be going to what was being called "the Midnight Massacre". They ate their breakfast and brushed their teeth. They shit in holes they dug and got their gear on. Holt walked point. He didn't like looking for bodies. Vietnam was a war where you shot into the jungle; and if somebody got killed, nobody knew for sure who did it. He had killed before. You got used to it; you had to. He made himself to go emotionally numb. So what was different about this time?

In daylight, the forest was more open than he remembered. He stopped, and held up his hand. He dropped to one knee and rested a moment. He stared into the trees. His thumb caressed the safety of his rifle. He studied the ground to his front and to all sides. He signalled the platoon to maintain its position while he moved on by himself.

Camp silently prayed that they would find some bodies and the Lieutenant would get his fucking body count. This whole incident seemed to be getting out of control, and he just wanted it over. It seemed that Wilkes was the only one who cared about body count. Lieutenant Smith, the company's commanding officer, could care less. His main concern was that Wilkes had the correct map coordinates and would be able to link up with the company later that day. As the fourth platoon was scouting this little valley, Delta Company had moved off with the battalion toward some new objective.

Behind Camp, Little Wilson was whispering to Big Wilson. He was retelling the story of the patrol for the third or fourth time. Each time he told the story, there were more NVA. "The gooks were so close, you could almost reach out and touch them. Don said there were fifty. But I say there were close to a hundred."

Big Wilson rolled his eyes. "Since when you become such a big jungle fighter, bro?"

Camp turned to them. "Shut the fuck up," he hissed.

"See, now you got Camp pissed."

Mercado squatted next to Camp with the radio handset pressed to his ear. "The Lieutenant wants to know what the holdup is."

"What's his hurry? If there are dead bodies up there, they ain't gonna get up and walk away."

"Should I tell him that?"

"Tell him anything that will shut his fucking mouth."

Up ahead, the men started to slowly snake forward. Holt had crested the ridge where their defensive position was. The ground and surrounding bushes were ripped and scorched by the explosive force of the mines. He went down the slope onto the valley floor. He knelt next to a rock, sniffing the air like a dog. The heavy, humid air carried the smell of death. As the platoon came over the ridge and descended into the valley, he moved to the opposing ridge. He would scout the opposite side and the woods beyond.

The men were bunched up and milling around aimlessly. They clustered in small groups for security.

The Lieutenant, seeing the men bunched up, shouted orders at his sergeants. "Get these men in a search pattern. Find the bodies, count them and let's get the hell out of here." He turned to his RTO. "This place gives me the creeps. It's like walking in a graveyard."

It seemed darker and hotter, as if the trees were closing in from the opposing ridges. The air was heavy with a rotting, humid stink. The sweet, coppery smell of blood hung in the air.

They separated and moved cautiously through the undergrowth, searching for the source of the smell.

"Hey! Over here. I found something." It was Parker, from the first squad. He was squatting down, poking at something with a stick.

His squad leader came over. "What have you got?"

"It's a finger, a human finger."

"What the fuck kind of finger do you suppose it would be? Quit playing with it and find the rest."

Parker moved off with a hurt look on his face. The squad leader called in one body found.

Machine Gun Kelly and his ammo bearer, Fisk, had set up security at one end of the valley. "Parker should have kept that finger. He could have given it to the Lieutenant. Didn't you ever want to give the Lieutenant the finger? Shit, he had the perfect chance."

Elderidge came over to Kelly and Fisk. He began playing around with some belted M60 ammo. He hoped he looked busy and could avoid the body search. "Hey, you know, Green Berets do that shit all the time. I heard them dudes go around cutting off ears of dead gooks and stringing them up like necklaces."

"Who told you that shit?" Kelly snapped.

"Your mama. I hear she's down at Cu Chi village, working the steam baths. Number one short time."

"Fuck you and your mother, too. Goddamn it, I hope they find something so we can get the fuck out of here. It smells like shit."

Holt had finished his reconnaissance and had joined the squad.

"Look," Little Wilson said, pointing to a hand sticking up from a shallow grave.

Surprisingly, the smell wasn't so bad. A few more men gathered around, and someone called for the Lieutenant.

"That was fucking brilliant. He's gonna want us to dig this shit up," Holt said to no one in particular.

Wilkes came over with a wet towel across his face to ward off the smell. He looked briefly at the grave. "Dig them up and be quick about it. Let's not waste any more time than necessary here."

Big Wilson started to remove his entrenching tool.

"What the fuck are you doing?" Holt snapped.

"The Lieutenant said…"

"If Wilkes wants them dug up, he can do it himself."

Holt turned to Mercado. "What do you say, Nick?"

"Ten. Twelve maybe," Nick said, shrugging his shoulders.

"You know how many they got already?"

"The asshole is counting each body part as one body. I think they got ten so far."

"Alright, then. Let's not be greedy. Tell him nine bodies, as best we figure. No, no. Make it seven. Yeah, seven is better. Seven bodies, stripped clean, no weapons."

"Can we do that?" Locke asked.

No one answered him.

Someone from the second squad found some blood trails, along with indications that a large body of men had passed through the area heading northwest. This information was radioed to Major Grayson together with the final body count, now inflated to twenty-two confirmed killed.

It was decided that they would follow the trail. The remainder of Delta Company, along with all of Charlie Company, would peel off from the battalion on a heading that would intercept them. If all went well, the two elements would join up sometime around 2 PM. When the link-up was complete, the two full companies would spread out to pick up the trail of the enemy. It was apparent from the signs that they were tracking a large unit, and they were making no attempt at concealment.

This was disturbing. It was unusual for the North Vietnamese Army to mass in large elements. Yet a pattern was developing. It was generally agreed that the Tet offensive was a devastating loss for the enemy. The Viet Cong were effectively eliminated as a fighting force. Tens of thousands were killed. The NVA poured entire divisions into the South. At the Marine combat base, Khe Sanh, it was estimated that forty thousand NVA troops were massed in the hills, completely surrounding the base. Although beaten back, thousands of NVA troops remained in South Vietnam, and in their Cambodian and Laotian sanctuaries. Across Vietnam, sightings of large enemy concentrations were being reported with alarming regularity. The generals predicted a second large enemy offensive.

But for the men of Delta and Charlie Companies, such debate had little meaning. They had far more immediate concerns. Their battles were now fought against the NVA, who were well-armed and battle-hardened soldiers. Instead of the hit-and-run tactics of the VC, they were confronted with well-planned, coordinated attacks. And the NVA stayed and fought from camouflaged bunkers and trenches dug in the jungle. They seemed to possess endless supplies of ammunition, mortars and heavy machine guns. They were willing to take large numbers of casualties in order to kill Americans. The war of attrition was suddenly reversed. Buoyed by the rising influence of the anti-war movement, they determined the American people would have no stomach for a war in which hundreds of soldiers were killed each week. They were correct. Support for the war diminished daily.

The two companies were spread out, almost on line, sweeping through the tangled jungle in a effort to track the enemy. Each individual squad operated in its own isolated orbit, oblivious to the presence of the others.

Both companies left the jungle and entered a sea of undulating elephant grass six to ten feet high. Holt was on the extreme left side with Little Wilson, Elderidge, Locke, and the other new guy, John Kimball. Ten meters to his right, barely visible, were Camp and the rest of the squad. "Roll down your sleeves and stay close. Don't get separated," Holt said.

The elephant grass was so tall and so thick that soon, each man found himself stumbling along almost blindly. Against all rules, it became necessary for them to bunch up to keep in sight of each other.

Circling in the Command and Control helicopter, the terrain didn't seem at all threatening. Major Grayson constantly berated them to maintain decent intervals.

Mercado was staring up at the sky. He squinted into the sun, trying to find the Major's helicopter. "I wish that scumbag was down here. Then I'd like to hear him tell us to spread out. I lost sight of Holt and his guys," he said to Camp.

"They should be to our right."

"This sucks an enormous fucking dick. I can't see three feet in front of me," Holt said.

"Does anyone know where we are?" Locke asked.

"Shut up. You hear that?"

"INCOMING!"

You could clearly hear the thump, thump, thump of the mortars, followed by several loud explosions.

"Jesus Christ! Hit it," Holt hollered as the men threw themselves to the ground.

All around them, they heard explosions, but they couldn't place the distance. There were explosions behind them and to their right.

"They're mortars, right?" asked Locke.

"Yeah. They sound like small ones. Sixty millimeters."

There was another volley of mortars. One of the rounds hit close by, the tremors passing through the earth.

Just as suddenly as it started, the bombardment stopped. The men raised their heads tentatively and listened. There were screams and calls for medics.

Locke raised his head and smiled. "Hey, Sarge. Guess what? I wasn't scared this time."

"Then you're a bigger asshole than I thought," Holt said.

"What are we supposed to do?" asked Wilson.

"You got your compass? Go straight to your right and see if you can find Camp. Ask him what to do. Should we stay put, or what?"

Without complaint, Wilson took off and was soon lost from view.

Suddenly, there were more mortar bombs: a dozen, two dozen, exploding much closer.

"This is fucked," Holt said.

After twenty minutes, Wilson returned. He face was ashen. "Charlie Company got pounded. Six dead. More wounded." He paused. "First squad is gone. All of them, killed or wounded."

"What?"

"All killed or wounded. Mad Dog is down there now. He says they're wrapping up the pieces in ponchos."

"How did it happen?"

"They were all close, and a mortar landed dead center on them. Parker, Rodney and those three black guys that looked alike. All dead."

"Anything else? What did Camp say to do?"

"They're calling in choppers for the wounded. Camp said to stay put."

For two hours, there was a constant stream of choppers. There were billows of colored smoke to guide the choppers to hastily prepared landing zones. First, the wounded were evacuated; and then the dead. The remains of the first squad were tied into neat, bloody packages and removed.

Flying high above, the Major speculated they were getting close to the enemy, and the mortar barrage was a delaying tactic. He ordered them to proceed on their original course. The ground commanders pleaded for more time to allow the men to regroup, but they were denied.

The command was given to saddle up and move out.

Chapter 8

The End of the Beginning

The grass seemed never-ending. It closed in all around them, limiting their sight and hearing. Commands were unintelligible; all they could hear were just muffled sounds.

Holt and his men were on the extreme left of the formation. They had no idea where Camp was. They had started off on line, but immediately lost any semblance of formation.

"I can't see anything. I don't have a clue where we are. We could be ahead of Camp or behind him. Can anybody hear them?"

"I don't hear anything. The wind blowing the grass sounds like static."

"We should have stayed together. Fucking Lieutenant, telling us to spread out."

"You want I should try and find them again?" asked Wilson.

"No. The chances of you finding them now are slim to none. If you're in front and they hear you, they'll shoot you. If you're behind them, you'll wander right past them and get yourself lost. Just stay close. Everybody stay tight. Don't lose sight of each other."

"That's how the first squad got blasted."

Holt looked left and right. He saw Locke rubbing his arms. "Goddamn it, I told you to roll down your sleeves before we started. Your fucking arms are all cut up now. This grass is sharp as razors. From now on, do as you're told."

"Fucking moron!" he hissed under his breath. He checked his

compass and pointed straight ahead. "We'll just keep going north, and we should run into them."

Fifteen minutes of walking produced nothing but clouds of moth-like insects swirling with the disturbed grass. Their gauzy, shimmering wings made them look like silver dust in the sunlight.

The Major, flying high above, was almost apoplectic. He saw the men as moving black dots. There was no organization to their formation. They stumbled forward in a crooked, wavy line.

He shouted orders to the Company Commanders to gain some control of the movement.

"Those stupid pricks are going to end up shooting each other."

Lieutenant Wilkes held his map uselessly in front of him. "The Major says we only got one klick more of grass, and we reach a wood line."

The thump of mortar tubes could be heard clearly.

"Incoming!" screamed Pollack, and pulled the Lieutenant to the ground.

There were six distinct explosions several hundred feet behind them. A second volley of six landed closer.

"They must have a spotter," the Major said. He went on the command net and calmly issued his orders. "Get off your ass and into the woods now. The gooks are walking the rounds toward you. Get your men moving!"

The Captains and Lieutenants shouted commands, but their voices were absorbed in the sea of grass.

"Are they saying move forward?"

"Yeah, forward. I think that's what they're saying."

There were more explosions, closer now.

"This is totally fucked."

"Camp. Camp!" Holt screamed, "Can you hear me?"

Everyone leaned to their right, hoping to hear a voice.

"I heard him. He said go forward now."

"Are you sure, Nick?"

"Go forward. Yeah, maybe. No, I'm sure."

"On your feet. Let's get out of here. Straight ahead. Keep in sight."

They pushed through the grass with arms held ahead, trying to protect their faces and hands. The tangled grass caught at their feet. More close explosions showered them with dirt, leaves and rocks.

"Up ahead, I see the trees."

"That's it. Get into the trees and find cover."

Holt directed them to some logs, remnants of fallen trees. "Take cover here. We got to find Camp."

Mercado had the radio handset pressed to his ear. "It's the Lieutenant. He says go twenty meters, stop and regroup."

"Finally. Where has he been?"

"Eugene, go find Camp. Find out what the fuck is going on. Make sure he knows you're coming, and don't get shot."

"The mortars stopped," Mercado said.

"This is bullshit. There's no control of this movement. We're all spread out with no coordination."

"Can the gooks see us?"

"How? We can't even see each other. I swear to God, they drove us into these woods. They were walking the mortars right in on us."

"Why would they force us here? This was where we were going."

"Here comes Wilson."

"I found him. He's about two hundred meters to the right. Camp is pissed. He says you wandered off, and now Wilkes is pissed at him."

"He's always pissed at somebody. Wilson, lead the way."

Lieutenant Wilkes was with Camp. Even from a distance, you

could sense the conversation wasn't pleasant. Pollack, his RTO, stood off to the side.

"Where the fuck were you? I said stay in sight."

"He did, Lieutenant. I fucked up. I couldn't see shit in the grass. We kind of went off at an angle."

"Did you use your compass? Do you even know how to use a compass?"

"I do, Lieutenant. It must have been polar distortion, or it could have been solar winds. The compass indicated true north, but we drifted west."

"Polar distortion? What are you talking about? And what's this bullshit about solar winds?"

"Solar winds seem highly unlikely. I think you mean solar flares."

"You clearly said solar winds."

"I don't think solar activity played any part in this. I wouldn't put that in your report. Polar distortion, on the other hand, is a distinct possibility."

"Sergeant Camp, do you know what this idiot is talking about?"

"Lieutenant, if I can continue. Polar distortion occurs the closer we get to the poles. Here in South Vietnam, below the equator, it's a fairly common occurrence. The magnetism of the Earth's poles throw compass readings off. Again, my fault. I should have compensated for the distortion."

"You expect me to believe this shit?"

"Ask Sergeant Calhoun. He transferred in from Germany. He'll know what I'm talking about."

"What does Germany have to do with anything?"

"Closer to the North Pole."

"Damn it, Camp. Keep your squad under control. When the order comes, proceed forward. Keep your men close and spread out. Keep them in sight. I don't want this happening again."

Wilkes turned to Holt. "Do you understand?"

"Yes, sir, I do. Keep close, but spread out. Might be difficult keeping close and spreading out, but we'll make it work."

"See that you do."

"Did you ever hear about any of this bullshit? Polar distortion, I mean," Wilkes asked Pollack.

"We get static on the radio all the time. I guess it could be distortion."

"But is it polar distortion?"

"Could be. Sounds reasonable."

"There's Sergeant Calhoun, we'll ask him."

"Sergeant Calhoun, were your radios in Germany subject to polar distortion?"

"Sir?"

"Did your radios and compasses malfunction due to polar distortion? You're said to be knowledgeable on this subject."

"I know about the poles. That's how magnets work. And of course, there is the North Pole, which is very powerful. So... yes, I believe the poles can distort things."

"And this happened in Germany?"

Calhoun looked to Pollack for guidance, who just shrugged. "Well, sir, we adjusted things to not make it happen. Our equipment was calibrated differently. European calibration."

"How so?"

Pollack interrupted, "Sir, the Major. He doesn't sound happy."

"Shit. Tell him I'm not here."

"He wants to know, and these are his words, why your men were spread out all over the fucking country. Should I mentioned the polar distortion?"

The Lieutenant held up his hands.

"Six, we drifted off course due to equipment malfunction possibly caused by polar distortion. Or maybe solar flares. No wait, I'm told to withdraw that last remark regarding solar activity." There was a long pause. "Yes sir, I'll ask."

"The Major asks if you were dropped on your head when you were a baby. Again, his words."

"Not that I know of. How could I possibly know?"

Pollack held up a finger and spoke into the handset. "Possibly, sir. The Lieutenant is unsure."

"Let me speak to him."

"He's gone sir. Hung up, I guess."

The Lieutenant turned his back. "I'm surrounded by fucking morons."

"I heard that, sir. You know, I have feelings. I'm doing the best I can."

"Please tell me all that crap about polar distortion was real," said Camp.

"I wish I could. I made it all up."

"You do know Wilkes will repeat that shit."

"Did it sound real to you?"

"I gotta admit it sounded believable."

"Because some of it was true. There is such a thing as polar distortion. At least, I think there is. So when he repeats it, no one will admit they don't know nothing about it. They'll agree so as not to look stupid. The next thing you know, the Army will issue a pamphlet about compass synchronization to compensate for polar distortion and solar flares."

"Just got the word from Six. We're to break for lunch and be ready to move out at thirteen hundred. Big Six will scout ahead in his helicopter," Mercado said.

At 1 PM, two things happened. First, they were told of a sizable clearing seven klicks due north, suitable for landing one or two choppers. Second, they had to make the clearing in four hours to receive resupply that night. The Major advised there would be hot chow on board.

The forest was thick with tall trees blocking out the sunlight. The sun appeared in golden shafts breaking through the treetops. The forest floor was spongy with rotting vegetation. The air was heavy and thick with humidity. The hum of flies and mosquitoes filled their ears.

Holt walked point. He stopped briefly to smear his face with oily insect repellent and check his compass. They were to proceed on a heading of three-hundred-forty degrees north by west. Each day's march took them nearer to the Cambodian border and the heavily fortified sanctuaries of the NVA.

They had been walking for an hour when they stopped and took a break.

"You fixed for water?" Camp asked Holt.

"I'm good, got plenty left."

"Me too. We might have to share. Some of the guys are pretty low."

"If we have to. These fucking new guys need to learn to conserve their water."

"The new guys are doing okay. It's Kelly and Big Wilson. Both look beat. Kelly is all pale and sweaty."

"As long as he's sweating, that's a good sign. What's ahead?"

"On the map, nothing. Just trees."

"There are so many fallen trees. Great place for a bunker or two. Soft ground, good for trenches. Good fields of fire. The gooks should love this place."

"Let's hope not. Stay alert. Let's not walk into anything."

Holt moved off again. To his right, he could just see the third squad. The Lieutenant and his group were behind them, with the second squad bringing up the rear. At three-twenty, they took another break. Everyone was soaked with sweat and breathing hard.

"Not even four o'clock, and it's dark in here. We should be near the clearing, maybe another hour."

Holt took one of his canteens and threw it to Big Wilson. "You and Kelly share that. If you need more, let me know. You owe me one, brother."

Camp lit a cigarette and passed it to Don and lit one for himself. "This is a fucking spooky place. No sounds, just mosquitoes."

"At least it's not raining."

"Give it a month or so. Monsoon season starts in May."

"You think the Major can see us from his chopper?" Holt asked.

"They fired a flare awhile back so he could mark our position."

"This is like walking through an aquarium. It's so wet and muggy. Smells like rotting garbage and shit."

"Have you seen anything? Any trails? Any signs of life?"

"Not a thing. This is pure prehistoric bullshit. We might be the first people walking this forest."

Camp placed a hand on Holt's shoulder. "Hold on a minute. I swear I saw something. A shadow or something." He pointed to the left.

"Over there, past those trees? I know. I saw the same thing fifteen minutes ago. A shadow passing through the trees. I thought I was just seeing things. I think we're being followed on our left flank. Think we should call it in?"

"No. Our eyes might be playing tricks on us. This place is so creepy; we're all jumpy. Just move out. We can't be far now."

Thirty minutes later, Mercado handed Camp the handset. "Charlie Company has reached the clearing. They're going to skirt the clearing and set up on the north side. We get the southern half."

"Just in time. I hear choppers," Holt said.

The two companies ringed the clearing. The fourth squad settled in a small clearing and went about preparing their night position. They pulled in several logs and dug a shallow fighting position behind the logs. Holt and Elderidge set out trips, flares and Claymores twenty meters out. The Wilsons went and secured water and C-rations. Kelly and Fisk set their gun position and laid out the belted ammo. Kimball and Locke maintained security.

The call went out; hot chow was ready.

Chapter 9

Darlene Honey

Holt pushed the remains of his dinner around his paper plate. It had been days since their last hot meal. The origin of the meat was unknown, but it was still better than C-rations. He flipped a grizzled hunk of meat into the bushes and rolled his plate into a tube. He threw his garbage in a shallow depression where it would later be burned. He settled back against a dirt mound and lit a cigarette, coughing violently with the first drag.

Around him sat a dozen men from the various squads. Camp had come to him, saying they were going to re-establish the decimated first squad. Camp would lead the first squad. Holt would, once again, become leader of the fourth squad. There was no mention of promotion this time. Each squad had to give up two men. After much debate, it was determined Elderidge and Kimball would go with Camp. All the squads were now at seven men each.

"Rumor is we're going in the end of the week," said Kelly.

"No way," said Ox. "That'll be less than a month. We stay out thirty days, no exception."

Ox and Easterwood, the third-squad gun crew, sat next to Kelly. Ox was enormous and well-suited to carry the M60.

When different squads congregated, they tended to group together by specialties. The gunners would sit in one group, the grenadiers in another. This way, they could talk shop and bitch about things in common.

"Is that right? A month, you say? I suppose you discussed this with the Major and he agreed?" Kelly said sarcastically.

"All I'm saying is we usually stay out a month." Ox wouldn't be bullied. He knew what he said and stuck by it. He had the quiet self-confidence that many big men possessed.

For the last ten days, they had wandered the jungle in an aimless search pattern. Each day, they were sniped at or mortared. Four days before, there was a brief fire fight involving the first and second platoons. There were three men wounded, but not seriously. The fourth platoon sat out the fight safely in a small stand of trees.

Camp had gone to the CP to get the mail. The men were reluctant to return to their foxholes until he returned.

"Here he comes," Little Wilson hollered.

Camp was back, his rifle slung over his shoulder, bundles of mail cradled in his arms.

"Listen up. I ain't doing this more than once." He proceeded to call out names and hand out the envelopes and packages. "Kelly, Parker, Easterwood," he said while peeling off envelopes from the stack he held. "Parker, where the fuck are you?"

"Sarge, Parker's dead. Remember?" said Little Wilson.

"Shit. Yeah, right. Sorry guys." He stuffed the envelope into his side pocket. "Wilson, Big Wilson, not you. Sit down and wait your turn." He distributed the rest of the mail. Neither Holt or Camp got any letters.

"Alright! She did it!" said Hansel. He was waving a thick envelope. Hansel was from the third squad and was called "Red". No one could remember how he got the nickname since his hair was brown and nothing else about him suggested red.

"Did what?" Wilson asked.

"My girl, she sent me a pair of her panties. It's about time. I've only been asking her for months."

Wilson was cautious. "What do you want her underwear for?"

"Pussy smell! Man, where you from?" Red said, holding the

panties to his face and breathing deeply. "Pussy smell; it's the next best thing to being there." He said this with less conviction. With the panties held close, he sniffed again. "There's something wrong. Goddamn. They're fucking clean. They're brand-fucking-new. Look here, the price tag is still on them." He held them, stretching them by the waistband for everyone to see.

Mercado was the first to speak. "Man, your girl must think you're one fucking sick dude, asking her to buy girls' underwear. She probably thinks you're wearing them."

"I can't believe it. What does she think I want with new underwear?"

"I don't even know what you want with her old underwear." Wilson declared.

"Wilson, you stupid or something? I already told you, pussy smell. I bet you never got close enough to a pussy to know what it smells like."

Wilson's face flushed.

Holt leaned over and took the envelope from Hansel, examining it closely. "Amazing. How did you teach your sheep to write?"

"What the fuck you talking about?"

"You're from Alabama, right? I always thought you southern boys preferred your girls with wool on them."

"Yeah. Red's idea of a big night out is a six-pack for himself and a bottle of Woolite for his date," said Mercado.

"Fuck you both. I ain't never done no incest," Red declared indignantly.

"Incest?" Holt asked.

"Yeah, incest. You know, fucking animals."

"Red, you are such a dope. That's bestiality. Incest is when you fuck your sister."

Mercado looked at Holt. "You ever see a picture of his sister? It would be like fucking an animal."

"Fuck you," Red said, turning back to examine the panties once again.

Pollack entered the clearing. His fine, white hair was matted in dirty, greasy tendrils. "Anyone got a smoke?"

Holt tossed him his pack and lighter.

Mercado asked him where his radio was.

"At the CP. I had to get out of there for a while. Tell me, who's worse, Calhoun or Wilkes? Lately, every other word out of Calhoun's mouth is nigger this and nigger that. Wilkes doesn't say a thing to him. He shouldn't let him talk that way."

"Who's he calling a nigger?"

"Who knows? He's so stupid, he don't know what he's saying half the time."

"That man is a fucking racist."

"A racist and an asshole," Mercado added.

Garrett, from the second squad, put down the book he was reading and shook his head sadly. "Calhoun is just an ignorant redneck, a product of the old Army. Never learned to change."

"Wait just one fucking minute," Red said.

"No, let me finish. He thinks a nigger is just a black man, but he don't see what's happening here. We're all niggers. Look around, you see anybody living better than anybody else? Shit! We all live like fucking animals. To the officers and the politicians, we're just niggers, every last one of us."

Easterwood sneered at him. "Is that what they teach you in college?"

"It don't take a college education to see we're being fucked over."

"How's that?" Kelly said.

"You see any rich boys over here? Any Senator's kids? Any Congressman's kids? Don't think so. All you see is assholes like us. I may have gone to college, but I'm no different than any of you. Just looking at you, I could guess at your life story and not be too far off. You know why? Because we're all the same. We're somewhere between eighteen and twenty. Some older. We're from lower middle-class families. Our fathers are all farmers, factory workers or some blue-collar job like that. No one here has a father who is a doctor or a lawyer. Most of our dads were in World War Two. They support the war and the president. They worry about you being here, but they're proud you're serving your country."

Garrett paused, warming to the subject. "Most of us graduated high school and got drafted right out of school. All we talk about is girls and cars."

"What's the point? You ain't in college now, and I don't like being lectured at," said Ox.

"You don't like it because you know it's true. It hits too close to home. My point is, we are the backbone of this country: solid, hardworking middle-class kids, and they're killing us every fucking day. They kill us and then shove us in rubber bags like garbage and nobody gives a damn. Thirty days in the jungle, then three days off and back for another thirty days. Nobody can even tell us what we're fighting and dying for."

"We're supposed to be helping the gooks get democracy," Wilson said.

"You fighting for democracy? For God and the American way of life? Bullshit! You're fighting like a desperate fucking savage to stay alive, to keep yourself and your friends alive. You're fighting for the guy next to you regardless of whether he's black, brown or white. War is big business. While we're here, there are guys at home getting rich from making all the rifles and bombs and all the other shit we use."

Holt looked up. "When I was home between tours, I was surprised at how little things changed. New York drafted over thirty thousand guys, yet I don't know anybody else who's in the Army. Some guys enlisted in the Air Force or Navy to avoid the draft. I went to the local bar and nothing's changed. Everybody is still there, just hanging out. It makes you feel a little stupid to be here."

"What's it like for you, Wendy? You've been over here longer than anybody." Little Wilson asked.

Camp didn't answer at first. He lit a cigarette and looked at the ground.

Holt looked at Camp and back to the group.

"I'll tell you what it's like. Outside of your family, your girlfriend and maybe a couple of buddies, no one cares what you're doing over here. Nobody wants to hear about 'Nam. Don't say a fucking word about it cause you'll be talking to yourself. If it does come up, you have to listen to everyone's fucking opinion. If somebody does ask you a question, it's usually 'How many gooks did you kill?', or 'What's it like to shoot somebody?' Bullshit like that. They don't ask you anything about what's real to you. Bunch of fucking ghouls is all they are."

"Not everybody is like that," Locke said. "My girl writes asking about things. How I feel and what I'm doing. She's no ghoul."

"Fuck you, Locke. You're so sensitive and fucking whiny, it makes me want to puke," said Pollack.

"Your girl is probably stepping out with Jody every night, letting him do to her what Uncle Sam is doing to us," Easterwood taunted, making an obscene gesture with his arm.

"Jody?"

"Jody, you idiot. The ultimate fucking REMF."

"Jody is every guy back home who's living the good life while you're over here."

"My girl isn't like that. She's a good, decent girl. Here, look." Locke dug a picture from his wallet and passed it to Camp, who brushed it aside.

"What makes you think she's different from anybody else? You really believe she's sitting at home waiting for you? If you do, you're stupid. She's probably out right now, spreading her legs while you sit here telling us how pure she is."

"Hey, Wendy. Lighten up," Don cautioned.

"I don't have time for this shit. Break this up. Everybody, back to your own position. It'll be dark soon, and that's what you should be worrying about."

As Camp stormed off, Doc White said, "So much for that. You can't talk about your girl being faithful, not around Camp."

"He had no right to say those things. He doesn't know anything about my girlfriend."

Locke looked around the clearing. "None of you do," he said defiantly.

As the men started to leave, he muttered to himself, "You guys think you're so smart just cause you been here longer. You don't know everything. You guys don't know shit." His voice lacked conviction. Finding himself alone, he quickly gathered up his rifle and helmet, and hurried to join the squad.

Holt sat with the squad. Their defensive position was behind some scraggly thorn bushes. He cupped his cigarette in his hand. His legs dangled into the pitiful little foxhole they scraped in the dry, rocky soil. The light was fading fast, with a gloom settling over the men to match the mood of the evening's conversation.

"It's not really like that at home, is it?" said Wilson.

"If you think you're going home and everybody's gonna congratulate you, forget it." Holt took a final drag from his cigarette, savoring the smoke, knowing that it was the last of the night. He crushed the butt between his thumb and forefinger, barely feeling the glowing ember as it scorched the thick pads of callus on his fingers.

"There were times on leave when I couldn't wait to get back. I felt so out of place. I felt like I didn't belong there anymore. All the guys talk about are their cars and how drunk they got on the weekend, who got laid and who didn't. You don't hear Vietnam mentioned. If you wear your uniform, everybody gets pissed off. It reminds them how fucking scared they are about being drafted. Guys you've known your whole life start calling you 'baby killer' and shit like that. Fucking cocksuckers is what they are. We're the same as they are. The difference is we're here and those pricks are home. Do they really think that because we're here, we turn into some psycho murdering killers? I just don't understand why they treat us that way."

He looked at Wilson and put a hand on his shoulder. "It'll be different for you. You come from a small town. People care about each other in small towns."

"Don, do you believe in God?"

"Jesus Christ. No more, not tonight. I'm too tired to think. Grab some sleep. You'll have watch soon."

Camp came out of the gloom. "Just checking on everybody. Hey look, I'm sorry about before."

"Fuck it. You weren't bothering me. I'm used to you being a shithead."

"You think I owe Locke an apology? I don't. He should grow up. He's an asshole if he thinks everything's going to be the same when he gets back. Everything changes."

"Shh, keep your voice down."

"You know as well as I do what it's like at home. If you didn't, you wouldn't be here again. It seems the only guys you're comfortable with are guys who've been to 'Nam. Even then, they gotta be grunts."

"True enough."

"You want to stay up and talk for awhile?"

"Sure. What's on your mind?"

They both were quiet for a long time before Camp spoke. "When I got home after my tour, I thought everything would be great. I was a Staff Sergeant with combat experience. Had some medals. No more Vietnam. During my leave, I met this girl and fell hopelessly in love. Well, more like in lust. She was an animal in bed. Liked sex like a guy likes sex. Couldn't get enough. We fucked three or four times a day. She wore me out. Me and Darlene Honey. Can you imagine anyone actually named Darlene Honey? That alone should have told me something."

"What was she, a stripper?"

"Worse, a hairdresser. Dumb as a sack full of rocks, but goddamn she loved to fuck. Not make love, mind you, but fuck. Anyway, I was coming back here, so I set her up with a nice little house right outside of Fort Gordon. She was a true southern girl. Grew up all her life around Army bases, so I thought there would be no problem."

Camp took out a cigarette, realized he couldn't light it and put it back. "At the end of my tour, I'm gonna surprise her, so I don't tell her I'm coming home. I get off the plane and I'm met by Master Sergeant Soujac. I told you about him. He was my Sergeant when I was stationed at Gordon, and we really hit it off. He kind of took me under his wing. Slow Jack, that's what everyone calls him, says 'Let's go have a drink and catch up.' One drink turns into two, and two into four; and before I know it, it's nine o'clock and we're both shitfaced. I tell Slow Jack I got to go home and see Darlene. He says we need to talk. He gets all serious and says, 'Wendy, your wife's been stepping out on you. What I'm telling you is your wife has been fucking anything that has a dick and can move it. When she isn't fucking, she's blowing guys in the parking lot for free drinks.'"

At this point, Camp stopped and looked past the bushes. It was hot and humid. It was so quiet, you can hear the mosquitoes hum. Camp scratched at his beard, stalling before continuing. "'I don't believe you,' I say. He goes, 'Would I lie to you about something like this?' After a while I finally accept it, so he goes on to tell me everything. She's moved and picked the house clean; there's not a stick of furniture left. Nothing left, no sheets, towels or dishes. She's moved in with some Sergeant from the Signal Corps. Some fucking POG, and to him she's faithful, or so Slow Jack says."

"POG?"

"You never heard that? Person Other than Grunt. Just like an

REMF. A fucking Jody POG. Anyway, we drink more and I go back to Slow Jack's apartment. I can't sleep. Around midnight, I get up, look in the phone book and find out where she's staying. Now keep in mind, I'm so drunk I can hardly stand. I get to their place and decide I'm going to burn their fucking house to the ground. I sneak up to the house, just like in 'Nam. I pile all this dry grass and shit and light it up under their front porch. I make sure it's going good and run like hell. Long story short, I don't get far. Next thing I know, I'm under arrest and trying to sober up in the stockade. Seems that I got about three houses away before I passed out. That's where the MPs found me."

"What happened to the house and your wife?"

"I set fire to the wrong house. I was nowhere near her house. The house I burned belonged to some motor-pool Sergeant. The fire was more smoke than anything. He put it out by himself. There wasn't much damage, just some scorched wood.

"I call Slow Jack from jail. Everybody knows Slow Jack, so he's able to speak to the officers and cut me a deal. I get busted one stripe and pay for damages. The topper is I have to volunteer back to 'Nam. They just wanted me gone. That's the deal he made. So, in less than five days, my leave is canceled, and I'm back on a plane to Vietnam."

"What about Darlene?"

"Never saw her. I'm here about three months and get divorce papers in the mail and that's that. Slow Jack sells the house for me. She gets half, and I get half. I just about break even after the lawyer's fees and everything."

He paused again. "That dumb shit Wilkes wonders why I'm still a Staff Sergeant after two tours. Believe me, Don, it took that long just to get my stripe back. The only consolation is she never fucked an Officer. She did have some standards. Something to be thankful for, I guess. Some story, huh?"

Holt is thoughtful, thinking about the story. "Darlene Honey. No shit, that really was her name?"

Chapter 10

Breakfast with the Dead

The noise was distinct and unmistakable: the snapping of twigs and the rustling of dry grass.

Locke, the sixth man on guard duty, groaned. "Oh God, not again." He peered into the inky darkness and strained to hear the sound. "Nothing. Maybe I'm just imagining it," he said.

No. There it was again: a dry scraping sound.

Little Wilson touched Holt lightly on the shoulder and whispered into his ear.

"Don, wake up. Locke says he hears something out front."

"He's always hearing things. What time is it?"

"I think he may be right. I think there's someone out there."

"Terrific," Holt grumbled as he pushed back his poncho liner and slipped into his combat harness. Cradling his rifle, he crawled to Locke, took the radio handset from him, and handed it to Wilson. "Find out if any LPs are out by us."

Wilson spoke softly into the mouthpiece. "Nobody close to us."

"Shh. There it is again," Locke hissed, barely able to conceal the tremor in his voice.

Holt slipped his knife from its sheath and held up the gleaming blade. "It sounds like one gook is probing our lines. Take this and go kill him. Be quiet about it. Cut his throat."

"Are you out of your mind?"

"Don, cut it out," Wilson said. Turning to Locke, he added, "He's just fucking with you. Don't be such a idiot."

Holt unsnapped his canteen cover and dug out an M26 fragmentation grenade, which he held up to Wilson. Wilson nodded his agreement and scrunched lower into the shallow hole. Placing a hand on Locke's back, he forced him down. Holt straightened the cotter pin on the grenade, and gently tugged the retaining pin free. He opened his fingers and let the safety spoon pop off the grenade.

He counted, "One, two," and threw the grenade thirty feet away. It exploded with a dull thud, showering them with bits of rock and dirt.

The squad jumped awake with shouts and curses. They stumbled over and into the foxhole, tangled in their blankets and ponchos.

"Get the fuck off me," Holt cursed, pushing the men back as they tumbled in on top of him. "Kelly, get your gun going and don't stop. The rest of you, spread out, goddamn it!"

It was if the grenade had set off a chain reaction. The perimeter erupted in explosions. There were shouts of 'INCOMING!' from all sides. The hollow ring of the projectiles as they left the mortar tubes were heard above the continuous explosions. The gooks were walking the mortars across the width of their encampment, filling the air with stinging chunks of metal and rocks. Above the roar of the mortar barrage were the screams of the wounded as they pleaded and begged for medics.

The explosions were concentrated in the northern sector of the perimeter, with only an occasional round straying close to them. This changed suddenly with a large, glowing fireball trailing a shower of sparks across the night sky. The noise was deafening, like a freight train passing overhead. The explosion was enormous, much louder that any mortar. The ground shook and heaved with the detonation; and immediately, a hot, rolling cloud of cordite smoke and dust engulfed them.

"Jesus Christ, what the hell was that?" Kelly screamed.

Their ears were ringing. Holt shook his head and rubbed at his eyes, which stung and teared up from the smoke and dirt. There was another explosion, closer and louder than the first. The concussion sent them reeling. They were covered in swirling black clouds of smoke. Big Wilson, his eyes dazed and unfocused, weakly pulled himself under a small bush. The others clawed and wormed their way closer to the ground, seeking any cover they could find.

"Those are big Chinese rockets," said Holt.

From the north side, they heard the sounds of automatic weapons. AKs and RPGs opened up from concealment in the woods. It took several minutes for the American soldiers to return fire, adding the stuttering chatter of M16s and M60s to the overwhelming din of battle.

A lone AK-47 fired a long, sustained burst over their heads. Before Holt could raise his own rifle, a dozen M16s erupted, firing hundreds of rounds at the enemy position. The rifles were joined by grenades and M79 grenade launchers as the terrified men finding a target to aim at vented their anger and fear.

Holt gazed in stunned wonder as the night exploded into a thousand bursts of white-hot light, all directed at the single, unfortunate, enemy soldier. He rocked back on his heels, his mouth hanging open and his eyes bulging wide. "Un-fucking-believable," was all he could say.

Mercado reached up from his curled position and tugged on Holt's sleeve. "I'm hit. I'm bleeding. Don, look, I'm hit."

Holt pushed his hand away, unable to take his eyes off the fireworks display happening right in front of them.

Little Wilson peeked out from under his helmet. He had the handset pressed to his ear.

"They called Spooky."

"He'll bring smoke on those motherfuckers," Mercado said, his wound forgotten, jubilant at the prospect of the gunship's arrival. "He'll light up those motherfuckers."

The ground attack continued. There was little firing at the fourth squad, just occasional bursts of AK fire. Charlie Company continued to come under heavy attack. As the NVA left the wood line and advanced toward the ring of foxholes, they shifted their mortar barrage toward the center of the encampment. There were no more larger explosions, just the smaller, muffled blasts and flaring light of the sixty-millimeter mortars.

They watched as the battle progressed.

"Charlie Company looks like they're catching maximum shit," Kelly said.

Small arms fire and grenade explosions flashed throughout the company's position. They could clearly see green and orange tracers criss-crossing through the air, forming a deadly spider web of light and steel. Shadows of the enemy soldiers were highlighted by the harsh white light of ground flares. The whole scene looked so surreal.

"Wilson, what are they saying? Are the gooks inside the perimeter?" Holt asked.

"They broke through in one place. It's hand-to-hand fighting."

Mercado was first to hear it, the distinct drone of an airplane drawing closer. "It's Spooky," he yelled.

As the noise grew louder, all firing stopped, as if everyone heard it at once. In that instant, the aircraft could be heard plainly. It was quickly drowned out as the firing began with increased intensity.

The enemy were now firing to cover their withdrawal. The GIs, sensing the turn in battle, fired with renewed fervor, driving the NVA back into the trees. Night turned into day as the battlefield was illuminated under the suspended glow of large parachute flares, dropped by Spooky as it circled above.

Spooky was a large cargo plane, a Douglas AC-47 converted into a flying weapons platform. This particular plane flew out of Bien Hoa, the huge sprawling Air Force base southeast of Cu Chi. The plane was equipped with its own flares and three General

Electric 7.62-mm Mini Guns. The guns were actuated by a control on the pilot's yoke. Each gun had six electronically controlled, synchronized, rotating barrels capable of firing sustained bursts of six thousand rounds per minute. Spooky could cover a football field in less than a minute, placing a bullet every six square inches. Its slow speed and economical fuel consumption made it ideal for ground support, allowing it to stay on station indefinitely over the beleaguered Americans.

"They want us to mark our position. Throw a flare out in front as far as you can," shouted Little Wilson.

The pilot saw a crude circle marked by dozens of pinpoints of flickering light. Flying in a lazy circle, the pilot dropped his left wing and squinted into the electronic sight over his left shoulder. Using the ground flares as markers, he concentrated his fire in a sweeping arc at the edge of the Americans' perimeter. On the ground, a cheer rose from the men, which was drowned out by the machine guns.

Every fifth bullet Spooky fired was a tracer round, but the guns fired so rapidly, it appeared as if a solid stream of liquid fire poured from the plane. The pilot alternated guns so the firing was continuous. Looking into the scrub bushes and trees that ringed the perimeter, it seemed as if large molten raindrops were sweeping the ground in an unrelenting torrent.

Wilson said to Holt, "I pity the men who are under that."

The plane circled once, dropped more flares, and made another pass, expanding its coverage. Finally, with an unseen waggle of its wings, the pilot turned east. It would return to Bien Hoa to refuel and rearm and continue its constant night patrol over the airbase.

"Ain't nothing gonna be alive after that," Mercado said. He brightened even as he remembered his wound. "Hey man, I'm wounded. Get Doc over here. I need a medic."

Holt turned to him and ripped open his sleeve. "Shit, Nicky. It's just a scratch."

"No man, it's a heart. A beautiful Purple Heart, my first. I get one more and I'm out of here, and you dudes can kiss my ass goodbye." Mercado smiled down on his arm, pulling and picking at the long, deep scratch, getting it to bleed again. "Got to make it look good."

"You ain't going in with that."

"Don't matter, just as long as I get my Heart."

Mercado's small, pitiful wound was last to be treated. Mad Dog cleaned the wound and applied an olive drab field dressing after he himself pulled it apart, making it bleed steadily. Mad Dog's eyes were red-rimmed and puffy from lack of sleep. His shirt and hands were speckled and splattered with the blood. With a short, stubby pencil, he filled out Mercado's evacuation card.

"Hey Doc, you can't send him in. Not for that."

Mad Dog suddenly turned and glared menacingly ay Holt. "Don't ever tell me what to do with the wounded. You got that? If I say he goes back, then he fucking goes back."

"It's just that..." sputtered Holt.

"You know how many we're sending back? Seventeen! Seventeen guys, all shot to shit. Nick makes eighteen. They haven't even counted the dead yet. If I can send someone back, even if it's only for a few days, I'm doing it, and not you or anyone else is gonna fucking stop me."

He turned to Mercado. "Get your ass up to the CP; they'll be sending in Medi-vacs soon. If you know what's good for you, you'll kiss ass and get yourself a job in the rear and stay the fuck out of this slaughterhouse." He gathered up his medical pack and stormed off without another word.

The men sat silently, envious of Mercado's good fortune: a good, clean, light wound; and a chance to get off the line. Mercado, for his part, was sheepish, almost embarrassed at this unique turn of events. With a shrug of his shoulders, he hoisted his gear and started toward the CP, cradling his wounded arm.

"Take it easy Nick, and good luck," Holt called after him.

Mercado gave a short wave and trotted off.

"Who's gonna carry the radio now?" Wilson asked.

"You're holding it. You carry it until he gets back."

"What if he doesn't come back?"

"Then you got yourself a new job."

In the morning, the men left their positions and searched the area for dead or wounded enemy soldiers. Four LPs were sent out the night before; three had made it back safely. The fourth LP was found. The three men were dead, their bodies mutilated.

As they searched in front of their position, Little Wilson speculated on the LP's demise.

"Somebody must have fallen asleep. That's the only way the gooks could have gotten so close," said Holt.

"Over here," someone cried.

Holt and Wilson joined a circle of men standing over the dead soldier who had shot at them during the night.

"Not much left of him," Fisk mumbled.

The body was so slashed and torn by bullets and shrapnel, it looked more like a slab of red, bloody meat encased in a khaki cloth bag. Only the hands and feet were clearly distinguishable.

Holt looked at his watch and sighed: 7 AM, time for breakfast. As the men turned away, they left Locke standing alone, staring at his first close-up view of a dead soldier. Like someone unable to turn away from a traffic accident, he gaped in horrid fascination at the mangled remains. When he finally turned away, he was sweating heavily, even though the morning was cool.

The search of the entire perimeter turned up forty-five more dead soldiers, bringing the final count to forty-six. An analysis of blood trails and body parts inflated the enemy body count to one hundred ten killed. The Americans had twenty-three wounded and seven dead.

Chapter 11

Tarzan's Autopsy

Holt left the perimeter and walked a short distance, looking for a place to shit. He carried his rifle and a roll of toilet paper. Finding a spot, he dug a hole with his boot heel. He squatted and gritted his teeth against the painful spasms that rumbled and churned through his stomach. He was drained from the effect of the prolonged diarrhea. It was as if his body was betraying him. On some days, he found it difficult to put one foot in front of the other. After sixteen months, he felt the jungle was finally winning.

He stood, buttoning the fly on his trousers and kicked dirt and leaves into the hole, covering his runny green stool. Once deployed, they don't send you back if you got the runs. Back home, some things seemed so important, like getting a new carburetor, wishing you had the guts to ask your boss for a raise, or asking the new girl at school for a date. Now, if he had one wish, he'd ask to have a solid bowel movement.

As he walked away, he remembered his mother telling him to always wash his hands after using the bathroom. It had been over three weeks since he last washed his hands. No wonder everyone was sick. When he arrived, he weighed one hundred fifty eight pounds. The last time he weighed himself, he was down to one hundred thirty nine. His waistband was cinched as tight as it would go, and his pants still sagged. I'll need a smaller size or have the gook tailors take them in, he thought.

Inside the perimeter, he sat with the squad and made himself some coffee. Little Wilson came over with some coffee of his own.

"I can't believe how torn up that guy was."

"Not much left of him, that's for sure. These sixteens will do a job on you. Small bullet, big power."

Before coming to Vietnam, the only dead people most saw were neatly packaged for viewing inside a funeral home. Now, he could sit and, over a can of coffee, casually discuss the shredded, mutilated remains of a man who just a few hours ago had tried to kill him.

Holt smoked a cigarette, savoring the smoke and coffee in the morning air. He thought about his conversation with Camp the previous night, and felt sad. "You know, Gene, after Vietnam, things ain't ever going to be the same. After this crap, we're different, changed, burnt out. We look the same, but inside our heads, we're sour and gone bad. Fuck it, no one gives a shit. Hey, I meant to ask, how's your aunt?"

"She hears the news and worries."

"She's got good reason to, don't you think?"

They drank their coffee in silence.

"Has anybody seen Wendy this morning?"

"I think he's up at the CP. What are we doing today?"

"Going after the gooks from last night. We'll probably split up again and see if we can track them down, get more body count. That's what's important, body count. Gotta make the officers look good."

"If you feel that way, why did you come back?"

"It's this place. It will haunt you for the rest of your fucking life. It'll kill you inside, even if you make it home. It will stay with you and kill you just as sure as we're gonna hunt down those gooks and kill them."

"Sometimes you scare me, Don."

"Sometimes I scare myself. I'll tell you a story. Me and Janet were at a local bar one night. It was crowded and the music was loud. She was a little drunk and having a good time. She knew more people there than I did. Anyway, she was off in the bathroom and I'm sitting there, looking in the mirror behind the bar. I didn't even recognize myself. I felt so out of place, like I was just visiting. The bartender goes, 'You back for good now?' I tell him, 'I still got time to do.' I'm wearing my uniform. He looks at my ribbons and says, 'Looks like you seen some shit over there. You must be glad to be home and back with Janet. She's a good-looking girl. It's good you're back.' I ask him, 'What do you mean?' He's busy under the bar, washing glasses. 'She comes in here with some of her girlfriends, and guys are always hitting on her.'

"I'm looking at him real steady now, thinking of all the ways I could kill this motherfucker. I ask, 'That go for you, too? You know how it is. No harm in trying. Am I right?' He sets a beer down. 'On the house. Good luck, and welcome back.'

"Janet's back by now, and I say, 'I gotta pee.' I say, 'Let's go someplace else, someplace quieter.' She won't hear it. She says she wants to show me off. She says how great I look in my uniform and how she wants all her friends to see me.

"I come back from the john and see her talking to some guy, some long-haired asshole with bell bottoms and a tie-dyed shirt. 'Real nice,' I say, 'you're in my seat.' He looks me over and goes, 'Christmas ain't for a while, but you're already decorated, all you need is some tinsel and blinking lights.' He turns back to Janet and tells her how pretty she looks and they should go somewhere."

"Now I say to him, 'Get off my fucking seat; I'm not asking again.' He gets up and pushes me and that's it. A white rage came over me and I tore into him. It took just seconds, and this cocksucker was on the floor, whimpering like a baby. I remember throwing some cash on the bar and grabbing Janet. I wanted out of there in case someone called the cops. In the taxi going home, she doesn't say a word. We get to her house and she asks, 'How could you do that? He was just talking to me. You could have killed him.'"

Holt lit another cigarette before continuing. "I tell her, 'If I wanted him dead, he'd be dead.' She goes, 'And I should be grateful for that? You were like an animal. No, you were worse. You had no emotion. You were a mechanic, a machine just doing a job.' I say, 'He put his hands on me.' She shoves me hard and says, 'And that's all it takes to set you off,' and shoves me again. She asks me where I learned such things. I ask her, 'What is it you think I do over there?' She says she doesn't want to know. I tell her I do what I have to do to survive and come back to her, my loving girlfriend. She looks at me and says, 'I could so hate you right now.' She's done and walks into the house. That was just one of the magical nights we had together."

Holt turns and looks at Wilson. "This place won't let go. When you're home, it's in your head. It will grab you by the balls and squeeze. It will make you hurt."

The squad leaders had their maps laid out side by side.

"There's a village five klicks away. No word if the village is occupied or deserted, but Intelligence reports plenty of enemy activity," Camp said.

"Gooks a plenty. Should be a new Vietnam candy," said Holt.

"Considering Charlie got the shit kicked out of them, we'll lead."

"Are we ever linking up with Alpha and Bravo?"

"Not for a while. They're somewhere near Tay Ninh for the next couple of weeks."

"It looks pretty open."

"Yeah, all hardwood forest leading up to the village. Once we get close, it's all cut fields, rice paddies and shit like that. One more thing: be on your best behavior. Major Grayson and both chaplains are going with us."

"Out here? With us?" Holt asked. He folded his map and placed it into a plastic battery bag, and stuffed that in his cargo pocket.

"You look tired."

"Got the squirts. That, and Janet hasn't been writing."

"Probably busy with the baby. When is she due?"

"Who the fuck knows? She doesn't tell me anything. I tried figuring it out; can't make any sense out of what she says. Two or three more months, if you believe her."

"You'll be home soon enough, don't worry about it."

"That's another thing. From day to day, you don't know if you'll live or die. Bet those guys from Charlie Company didn't think they'd be killed last night. How many guys back in the world wake up in the morning and wonder if they'll be killed that night?"

"Don't think like that. It'll only make you crazy."

"Too late. I'm already crazy. Ask anybody."

The sound of an approaching helicopter drew their attention toward the center of the perimeter.

"That gotta be Grayson."

"Look at that fucking thing, all shined and polished. Imagine it, here in Vietnam they got guys shining and waxing helicopters. 'So, what did you do in the war, Daddy?' 'Well, son, I polished helicopters.'"

Camp laughed. "We all have a job to do, even the REMFs. We all serve."

"Some more than others."

"Everybody, back to your squads. It won't be long now."

The two companies broke camp by 9 AM and formed up, Delta in front with the fourth platoon leading. The weakened and depleted Charlie Company was on their right.

Holt walked point for the fourth squad. Wilson followed, burdened by the additional weight of Mercado's radio. The morning remained cool; the grass glistened with dew. Holt set a brisk pace. He walked by instinct, seldom checking his compass. He studied the ground and trees ahead. He heard a noise ahead of him and dropped to one knee, throwing up his hand to stop the company. He crawled forward. Finding nothing, he signalled the men forward.

Walking point was a power trip. You held everyone's life your hands. He was tempted to play with them: Simon says stop, Simon says hide your ass, Simon says go. Everyone followed the point. If he raised his hand, everyone would stop, or go, or fall to the earth. Sixty men, all hoping that the point man knew his shit. He loved walking point and loved the freedom he felt up front, on his own.

The walking became easier. Tall, thick trees were spaced far apart with the usual stunted bushes and coarse grass. The ground was soft and covered in a thick layer of jungle debris, which muffled their footsteps. The air was moist and heavy. In the distance lay a thin layer of fog. Sunlight filtered to the ground in long, golden shafts. The fog would burn off and the air would warm. It would be nearly one hundred degrees by noon.

Holt slowed his pace, comfortable in this part of the forest. He took his compass and shot several azimuths and transferred them to his map. Adjusting his course, he set off again. Rolling his shoulders, he settled his pack. He stopped to see the progress of the squad. He had a cigarette while waiting for them to catch up.

Well back from Holt and the fourth squad, Major Grayson walked, surrounded by his retinue of aides and radio operators. He believed his presence boosted the morale of his junior officers. He had given up any hope of influencing the actions of the enlisted men through example. He fully understood their only goal was to endure Vietnam and return home safely. There didn't appear to be any long-term goals in Vietnam, at least none that were communicated to him. Vietnam was just a series of daily, unrelated skirmishes; deadly little battles which sapped the strength and commitment of the young men who fought here.

The Major heard a loud thud, a curse, and some muffled laughter. He turned to see his aide floundering, his feet hopelessly entangled in several thick vines. The aide struggled to right himself and maintain some semblance of dignity. He made it to his feet and smiled weakly at the Major. He pushed his glasses back on his nose and retrieved his scattered maps and code books. The Major turned away in disgust.

His RTO interrupted his thoughts. "Sir, Charlie Six says they're into some heavy bush and falling behind. He suggests we take a break and let them draw even with us again."

"That'll be fine. Pass the word, Sergeant." Major Grayson found a dry, fallen log and sat down, back erect and feet spaced wide apart. He straightened the crease of his fatigue pants. He debated the merits of spending the night in the field. He took a handkerchief and carefully wiped the dust from his gleaming boots. His aide stood before him; he was not invited to sit.

"Captain, Vietnam is going to change everything. After fifteen years of backwater postings in little shitty nowhere towns, I finally got a combat command. A battalion commander. Not easy to get. I pulled every string and called in every favor owed to me and got what I wanted, and it's going to pay off. I'll see to that. Maybe a posting to the War College, or a staff job at the Pentagon. Maybe Military Liaison in some fashionable European capital. My wife would like that. By God, the Army owes me, and Vietnam ensures they'll pay. A silver oak leaf and a decent job, that's all I want. I deserve it."

"That you do, sir. You'll be needing an aide, I assume?"

"I will. Think you're up for the job? You need to prove yourself here, though. Lose some weight, look crisp. I could do worse. We'll see what happens, Captain."

He dismissed the Captain with a wave and returned to his thoughts of promotion only to be interrupted again.

"It's a pleasant morning, isn't it, sir?" Chaplain Doody said.

"As much as any morning over here can be. Care for some chocolate, Lieutenant?"

"No, thank you, sir. Stomach's still a bit queasy."

The Major shrugged and went about unwrapping his John Wayne

bar.

The Lieutenant dusted the log with his hand before sitting next to the Major. "This is a frightful place, so primitive and primordial. It's no place for white men. Uh… civilized men is what I meant, not just white men. Black civilized men, too."

"What about Oriental civilized men?"

"Yes, I suppose them, too. Have you ever read Joseph Conrad's *Heart of Darkness*? Conrad said the jungle destroys man's soul, brings out primal urges and suppresses everything that's good and decent in man. Do you think about it? The jungle and the war, I mean."

"I obey my orders and do what I'm told."

"But surely you must have an opinion about what's happening here?"

"I'm not in the habit of discussing my opinions with Second Lieutenants."

Chaplain Doody cleared his throat. "Yes, well, I see. Perhaps I should check on the men, see how they're getting along. If you'll excuse me, sir."

"Adios, Padre."

First Lieutenant Smith, Delta Company commanding officer, sat with Doc White. He was clearing mud from his boot with a knife. Smith and Doc White had developed a friendship based initially on the fact that they are both from Chicago. This later expanded to take in other common interests: college, ambitions, and their views on Vietnam and the Army in general. Although two years older, the Lieutenant felt no superiority due to age or rank; and when alone, they addressed each other informally. In the presence of others, White always gave the Lieutenant his rank, treating him with courtesy and respect.

"Hey, Doc. Look who's coming."

"It's Howdy Doody time."

Chaplain Doody approached with his head down, kicking at dirt clumps. Seeing the Lieutenant, he wanted to flee before being noticed. But it was too late; he waved a weak gesture of greeting and advanced slowly, wary of any interaction outside his expressed duties, which he found were almost non-existent. Church services were so poorly attended, they seemed more like individual counselling sessions. Perhaps five or six men would show up regularly; and these men, he disliked almost immediately. The steady churchgoers viewed themselves as members of an exclusive club; they seemed so pompous and superior.

Major Carltin, the battalion chaplain, was of little help. Whenever Lieutenant Doody was granted an audience, it always appeared the Major had been drinking. It was rumored the Major was involved in a physical relationship with his hooch maid, a young girl barely in her teens. He felt his entire presence in Vietnam could go unnoticed, his arrival and departure scheduled by some faceless automaton buried deep within the bowels of the Pentagon. He felt himself sinking deeper into a bottomless morass of self pity.

"Chaplain, how's it going? Save any souls today?"

"What? I'm sorry, I didn't hear you. I was thinking about…"

"I said, have you saved any souls today?"

"No, I haven't. I haven't had the opportunity to…"

"Well then, you best be going. They're not going to save themselves. It's always nice to talk to you. Stop by again when you have the time."

"I don't have anything to do at the moment. Would you mind if I joined you for a bit?"

"I guess that would be alright," Smith said with little conviction.

"Sure, have a seat," said Doc White.

The chaplain sat and began mopping his face with a clean white handkerchief. It was smeared with streaks of reddish, brown dirt. "Is it always so hot over here?"

Smith laughed. "You ain't seen nothing yet. In a month or two, it'll be so hot, you're going to sweat your balls off. Oh, sorry about that."

"That's alright. Chaplains have balls, too. Although some people think they should be removed when you leave the seminary."

"How'd you get into your line of work... uh... do you have a first name, chaplain?"

"Yes. It's Theodore, Ted. Although I understand most call me Howdy."

"Ted, don't try and tell me it's the first time anyone called you 'Howdy'. Not with your last name."

"It's pronounced 'Dooday'."

"That's right, I heard you favor the Canadian pronunciation."

"Canadian? Why do people keep saying that?"

"For argument's sake, we'll assume the American pronunciation."

"I know they're just having some fun. I enlisted after Seminary College. I had to. The Army paid for my degree."

"So, you made a deal with the devil. How are you getting along with the men?"

"These boys seem so angry. I don't understand their anger."

"Look around you. We live like pigs and wallow in our own filth. Give yourself a few weeks out here, and you'll be angry, too."

"Sleep on the ground for a month. Don't shower. Eat shit out of a can. See your friends killed. Then tell me you won't be angry," said Doc White.

"We push these boys to their very limit every day, both physically and mentally, every day for a year. Of course they're angry. You're an officer, so they vent their anger at you. Within accepted limits, of course."

"I'm beginning to see what you mean," the chaplain said meekly.

For a few minutes, they were quiet.

"How did you get here, Lieutenant?"

"Call me Gary. ROTC made me an officer. I was killing time until I could get into the National Guard, but the fucking draft got me first."

"Then you're not a career officer?"

"No way! Three months to DEROS and I'm gone. I'm a double-digit midget. Eighty-eight days and a wake-up."

"He's so short, if he pissed off the edge of a dime, he'd splash his boots."

"If I were a lifer, I'd be a Captain by now. The company commander is a Captain's slot. They won't waste the promotion on me and that's okay. I've made my thoughts known on this fucking war. It doesn't make any sense. We fight over the same territory three or four times. We go in, kill a bunch of gooks, and leave. That very night, the NVA is back, rebuilding their bunkers and waiting for the next time we come back. This is a war of attrition. We kill more gooks than they kill us. The Generals think they'll give up eventually, but they're wrong. Uncle Ho has said they are willing to expend a generation to unite Vietnam. I don't think we're willing to waste a generation defending it. The American people don't have the stomach for a protracted war with no clear, understandable goals. We'll pull out long before they're willing to quit. When we do, all the lives and money spent will have been for nothing. That's why I'm just counting days until I'm out."

"What about you, Doc?"

"One hundred and seven days. My name is Mike."

"What a strange place where you count your life in terms of days."

"It's the only way to keep track of things. If you know how many days a guy's got left, you know a lot about him. There are different stages over here. In your first three months, you get used to the weather and the humping. You're scared all the time, day and night, every minute and every hour of every day. Then things get better. You're still scared, but able to function. Then the old-timers start to rotate home and you become an old-timer. You're the veteran and the FNGs look to you for guidance."

"FNGs?"

"Fucking New Guys. Where was I? So now, there's all these new guys, scared shitless, looking to you to save them. So you start acting like John Wayne: strutting around with grenades hanging off you, knives and all kinds of shit, making like a real bad ass. You do some dumb shit, get a little reckless. Nothing is gonna kill you. Then you start getting short, under a hundred days. Now you get scared all over again. You start to slack off. You avoid walking point if you can, maybe try and go on sick call. Go on R&R. You try anything to get off the line. The goal is to last long enough to get on that Freedom Bird back to the world and forget about this place."

"And you guys are...?"

"Too fucking short to be playing war games. As soon as they find a Captain to take my place, I'm history. In the rear, with a cold beer. Maybe they'll make me Executive Officer and I'll lay around with the REMFs."

"Rear Echelon Mother Fuckers," White said without being asked.

"You feel the same way, Doc?"

"Medics ain't the same as grunts. We don't think we're John Wayne. We think we're God. After we patch up wounded guys while under fire, we can do anything. But the wounded never end. And some of them die, too many die. Just can't let it get to you. My advice is don't get close to anybody; it don't pay to be friends."

"Medics burn out quick. They do six months in combat, and then get assigned to the rear."

The chaplain studied the two men for a moment, uncertain how to phrase the next question. "The men who return for multiple tours, why is that? How can they do that? They're no longer scared?"

"I guess you'll have to ask them that question. Different reasons for everyone. If you want my opinion, anybody who comes back to 'Nam is fighting something inside himself. Something has to be going on in their head to return to this shit pile."

"Amen, brother."

During the break, Holt sat by himself. A premonition of doom hung over him. He wasn't scared, just uneasy. He was waiting for something to happen. He removed his pack and dug out a meal, and cut slowly into the can to discover it was meatballs and beans. Skimming the orange congealed fat from the surface, he ate the food cold with little enthusiasm, chewing methodically on the rubbery meat.

Twenty meters behind were Little Wilson and the squad. There had to be two hundred men scattered behind him. Yet, for all practical purposes, he was by himself. Max, his dog back home, loved walking through the woods of upstate New York. They would spend the day by themselves, Max chasing squirrels and rabbits and just acting crazy. He thought of Alfie and wondered how he made out with the Company gone. Probably hung out by the Mess Hall, begging for scraps.

Holt spooned the last of the beans into his mouth and threw the can in the bushes, then thought better of it. The gooks could use the empty can to make booby traps. He was digging through the bushes for the can when he saw them. At first, he didn't trust his eyes, but knew he couldn't risk another look. He was too far from his rifle. They didn't know he saw them. He found the can and walked back to his rifle.

He stood, looking away from the men he had just seen. There were three of them, crouched down in a shallow trench, their heads just visible. Holt tried to figure a way out. They know I'm on point and let me through. Let the point go and open up on the squad, then bolt into the woods. Shit, how could I have missed them? God, not again. This can't be happening. What the fuck was I thinking? They were there the whole time I was eating.

His mind raced. His eyes darted about. He didn't know what to do. He thought he was going to throw up, and felt the bile rise into his throat. *Run, asshole, run. Get the fuck out of here.* He knew he wouldn't run. Slowly, he reached down for his rifle. Straightening up, he lit a cigarette, needing time to think.

The three men were well-camouflaged, dug in so just their heads were visible above the ground. They were behind him, about fifteen feet. Turn to your left and shoot right to left. Shoot low and sweep the ground. Don't overshoot them. Keep it low.

He remembered a movie, The Magnificent Seven, and one character in particular. He couldn't think of his name, but he was the guy who starred in The Man From UNCLE. He could see his face clearly, but couldn't remember his name. It didn't matter; the story was the important thing. This actor played a gunfighter who had lost his nerve. In the final scene, the big shootout, he was alone. He could run and no one would know, or he could confront his fear and face down the bandits. He shot it out with bad guys. He did the right thing; and Holt would, too.

He dropped his cigarette and let both arms drop straight down. He held his CAR-15 by the pistol grip and thumbed the selector switch to full auto. He drew a deep breath and held it. Fuck you gooks, I ain't dying today. He tensed his muscles. Behind him, the squad was oblivious to the drama about to unfold.

Holt let the breath out and whirled to his left. He fired a long, sustained burst that emptied his magazine, the brass shell casings ejected in a long, sweeping arc from the gun. The bullets chopped through the dirt and two men spasmed and fell backwards, red splotches spreading across their tunics.

His index finger released the empty magazine and he palmed a fresh one into the well. Without hesitation, he stepped forward to search for the third man. The faces of the dead men looked more surprised than dead. The third gook burst from the bushes as if sprung from a catapult, and hit Holt with enough force to send them both sprawling. The man pounded Holt's face, shouting in Vietnamese. Holt chopped hard at the man's neck, and kicked and clawed his way from beneath him. He stood up and swung his leg, catching the soldier in the ribs. He heard bones crack. He kicked again, catching him beneath his chin, sending him backward clutching a mouthful of shattered teeth.

Holt staggered, his chest heaving, struggling to catch his breath. He reached for his knife while the soldier staggered upright. Holt screamed and threw himself on the man.

Locke and Wilson stood slack-jawed, gaping in shock and frozen in fear. From the back of the column, Camp shouldered his way through the men at the sounds of the first shots. Like Wilson and Locke, he froze, immobile at the savagery of the bloody fight less than sixty feet away.

Holt fell upon the man, slashing with his knife. He chopped the blade across the throat, severing muscles and arteries. Blood spurted from the gaping wound in a ghastly red fountain, splattering his face and shirt. The man clawed at Holt and flailed his legs and arms in a desperate effort to break free.

Holt pinned him with his knees and reared back, gripping the knife in both hands. With a loud grunt, he swung the eighteen-ounce blade down with all his strength, tearing a large bloody hole below his throat; and ripped down the chest, through bone and cartilage, revelling in the gore that spewed from the open cavity. Again and again, he slashed at the now-lifeless body. "Fuck you, fuck you," he screamed with each stroke of the knife. His final blow was to the forehead, splitting the skull in two.

It was Camp who pulled Holt from the body. Holt turned on him, snarling through bared teeth, his lips pulled back in a gruesome, hideous grin. He was covered in blood. At first, Camp thought it was Holt who was wounded, but the strength that Holt used to push him away told otherwise.

Holt turned to the body and kicked at the lifeless flesh. He breathed in heaving gasps through flared nostrils; eyes bulged out; the muscles of his neck in thick, rippling cords. After a moment that seemed a lifetime, he threw back his head and gave a blood-curdling roar that echoed through the trees. Camp recoiled from the sound and fell back. The hair on his arms stood out and goose flesh covered his body.

The platoon, hidden in the trees, would later claim they heard an animal howl.

Chapter 12

A Coward's Confession

At the same time Don stood covered in blood, screaming his victory into the trees, Janet, ten thousand miles away, was preparing to go out. She stood before her mirror, combing her hair. She finished and took a step back and examined herself. She stood sideways and thought the weight she had gained was barely noticeable under her loose-fitting blouse. She turned back to the mirror and undid another button on her blouse. She thought she might place a drop of perfume between her breasts, and began searching her cluttered bureau for the bottle. She caught sight of a black-and-white photograph tucked into the corner of her mirror.

It was a photo of Don after he came in from a month in the jungle. He was unaware someone was taking his picture. He was filthy and looked exhausted. His eyes were sunken and ringed with dark circles. She stared at the picture and felt herself begin to tremble. She ran into her bathroom, just in time to be sick.

She sat in the living room wrapped in a old terrycloth robe, trying to ignore her father.

"I thought you were going out?"

"I didn't feel good, so I canceled."

"Your mother and I think you should get out more, enjoy yourself while you can."

She glared at her father, not answering him.

"You're thinking you shouldn't be having a good time while

Don's away. It wouldn't be a bad idea to meet different people, maybe someone better suited for you. We only want what's best for you. Don's changed; he's different now. He's... well, he's done things. You know I'm right. Janet, look at me. Don has no plans, no ambition. Does he want to go to college? He can't tell you because he doesn't know himself. He'd be just as happy working in a gas station as having a real job."

"Grandpa worked in a gas station."

"Your grandfather owned the gas station."

"Not at first. Grandpa turned out okay. He did well enough to put you through college."

"We're not talking about your grandfather; we're talking about Don. If Don likes you so much, why did he go back to Vietnam?"

"Don just doesn't just like me; he loves me."

"Does he? He left you to go back there? He left when he was safe. Does that sound like love? Answer me, if you can." He lowered his voice and continued. "I know what war does to men. After Korea, some of the boys came back and you could tell they were different. Don's in love, I agree. In love with war. He loves the violence and the destruction. It makes him feel important, but he can't stay in Vietnam forever. What will he do when he returns to you and the baby? How is he going to adjust?"

"What matters is he loves me. I know you were prepared to offer him money to marry me. Did he take it?"

"The subject never came up."

"He married me because he loves me, not for your money. You weren't concerned about my reputation. You were concerned about your reputation, about the disgrace of my having a baby out of wedlock."

"It doesn't change the fact that Don will be different."

"What do you know about it?" she screamed. "You weren't in the Army. You stayed safe in school while others fought. You don't know anything," she said, running from the room.

She lay on her bed with the lights out. Her feet were curled under her and her robe pulled tight around her neck. She began to tremble again and couldn't stop herself from crying.

Much later, with the room still dark, she went to the bureau and took the photograph and placed it in a drawer.

They never did reach the village that day. Don and his lonely little battle had sucked the energy from the Company. Charlie Company, stalled earlier in the day, now found themselves mired helplessly in an impenetrable forest of vines and thorns. It wasn't until well past three that they made any progress and found themselves on open ground. The men took to calling them 'Hard-Luck Charlie'. It was decided to bivouac early and proceed toward the village at dawn.

The site where the three dead men lay became an attraction of sorts. The men of Delta Company gathered around the bodies, talking in hushed whispers. It became important to establish where you were when the incident took place, what you heard and what, if anything, you saw. Locke and Little Wilson became instant celebrities by virtue of their closeness to the fight. They retold their stories many times as the day wore on.

Lieutenant Wilkes was talking with Sergeants Camp and Calhoun. He seemed tired and listless, and spoke in a strangely subdued voice. "The Major has directed me to put Holt in for a Bronze Star. He thinks Holt was extraordinarily brave."

"And you? What are you thinking?"

"I guess he was, but I also think he's crazy. What he did to that man... it was... well, at best, it was excessive. I've never seen anything like it."

"He went into a blood frenzy; he couldn't stop himself," Calhoun said.

"Maybe. In any event, he's done in the field. He's changed from being a soldier to a cold-blooded killer. He enjoys killing. He's been in combat too long. When we go back in, he stays in."

The Lieutenant ran a hand across his face as he spoke to Camp. "You think I'm doing this because I don't like him. That's not true. It's for his own good. Most of the men would jump at the chance to get off the line. With his record and his decorations, he'll get a good job. I'll see to it. I mean that, Sergeant. I'll do my best."

Lieutenant Smith and Doc White joined the group.

"I'm putting Holt in for a Bronze Star and recommending that he be removed from combat."

"Why is that?

Wilkes touched the Lieutenant's arm and led him away from the group. "Gary, are you going to fight me on this?"

"We're short-handed now; we can't spare any men, let alone veterans like Holt. Who will be his replacement?"

"It's my platoon. You never interfered before."

"I don't understand your reasoning."

"You saw it. He chopped that man to pieces, cut him open and gutted him like a fish."

"What I saw was a soldier detected an enemy ambush that would have resulted in numerous casualties. I saw that same soldier attack the enemy, killing all the combatants, one of them in lethal hand-to-hand combat. What did I miss? It's your platoon and I won't interfere in how you run it, but I won't have you jeopardizing the platoon just to satisfy some sense of vengeance you developed against this soldier. You can send him back when you get a suitable replacement to my liking. Understood?"

"Yes, sir."

"And word your report so that there's no cloud following that boy. I'm not going to see you fuck up his future because you dislike him. One other thing: he gets his stripes back immediately."

Lieutenant Smith started to walk away, but he stopped and turned back. "You know, most of these boys don't want to be here. But while they're here, they do their job. They live under conditions that civilians can't imagine, even in their worst nightmares. They get wounded and some die. For what? I don't know why they even obey our orders. We order them to attack a hill and they do it, over and over, until we win that hill. A useless piece of dirt, and they attack it until we tell them to stop. Why is that? Do they believe they're defending America? I doubt that. They obey us because they are good boys, brave, patriotic young men taught to respect the flag and authority. We are that authority. You, me and the Major. And when their year is up, we send them home to a country that hates them. They're the best we have, and our country despises them. These boys deserve better."

He walked away and left Wilkes staring at his back.

"Are you alright, Padre?" Major Grayson asked.

The chaplain had emerged from the trees, pale-faced and sweating. He was wiping his mouth with a handkerchief, having just vomited after viewing the man Holt killed. It was like seeing an autopsy done by a maniac. "It's hard to imagine a human being is capable of doing that to another person."

"What should he have done? Convert him to Christianity?"

"I don't deserve that, Major. I don't deserve any of this. None of us do."

"We have a job to do over here; and whether you like or not, we're going to do it. We command these boys because they respect us. You show them that we're weak, and we lose that respect. The last thing I need, the Army needs, is some weak-kneed holy roller who is going to puke every time he sees a dead gook. You pull yourself together, Father, and be damned quick about it. Go find that boy and talk to him."

"What should I say?"

"You hear his confession if that's what he wants. You do whatever the fuck is necessary to make him understand what he did was not wrong. You got that?"

"And you believe that?"

"What I believe is none of your fucking business. Do your job, or I'll get someone out here who will."

"You don't see anything wrong with this? My God, what have we created over here? How are we supposed to send someone like him home? Do you honestly believe he'll ever be the same as he was, that any of them will? We should include a warning with their discharge papers: Contents volatile, could explode under pressure."

"Don't you worry about it, Padre. These boys will be fine. Men have returned from war for as long as there have been men. It'll go on like that long after we're gone."

"You said men. These are just boys, most still in their teens right out of high school. For most, this is their first time away from home."

"You think I should apologize to them for what they endure? Does the carpenter apologize to the hammer? These boys are tools we use to accomplish our mission. Some may break; most don't. You'll be surprised how quickly they'll forget Vietnam once they're home. Your job is to make their time here easier. Interpret their beliefs in such a way so that they don't feel guilty about the things they do."

"'Thou shalt not kill.'"

"Give it a rest. That might work back stateside; but here, you damn sure better kill and kill quickly and efficiently. I wish I had a battalion of men like him, savages who kill without remorse, beasts on a chain that we let loose on the enemy. I hope the gooks who find those bodies are scared shitless and realize this is what we do. We don't just kill you; we destroy you. That's the way you win wars. Kill them until they can't fight. You understand what you have to do?"

"Yes, I do." Play Judas to these boys' souls, he thought to himself.

Holt sat by himself, far from the squad and his friends.

It was Kelly who said to him, "A few days ago, twelve gooks. Today, three more. Back in the States, you'd be a fucking mass murderer. Your picture would be in all the newspapers, cops chasing you across state lines. All-points bulletin: Be on the lookout for Killer Holt. Dig it, man; we should start calling you 'killer' from now on."

"I didn't kill twelve gooks; the Claymores did. I just pressed the button. How about you go clean your fucking gun?"

Holt didn't feel like a mass murderer. He didn't feel like much of anything. There were two Holts sitting under the tree. One felt light and free, released from a heavy burden. The second was disgusted with his actions and realized that, like the Lieutenant said, he had crossed a line from which he couldn't cross back. Released from one memory, he had created another that he must carry with him. He willed himself to go numb.

He might have crawled off into the jungle if he hadn't seen Camp walking toward him.

"You pulling your own LP. Come back with everyone else."

"I feel like being alone."

"You want a beer? I've been saving two."

"Where did you get these?"

"I saved them from the other night."

They drank the warm beer in silence.

Camp was first to speak. "Wilkes said maybe you'll get a job back at Cu Chi. You're getting your stripes back and he's putting you in for a Bronze Star."

"I don't care what he does. I don't want any more medals. I don't need nothing from that prick."

"Maybe so, but think about it. Will you do that?"

"Sure."

"How about MEDCAP? You could hook up with Doc White."

"Yeah, maybe."

"You want to talk about it?"

"Nothing to say."

"You sure?"

"Not really." He stared into space until his eyes misted over and he had to blink back the tears. "Today was a repeat. It all happened before. Only the first time, it turned out differently. My first tour, I thought I was a real hotshot, a real badass. I was wounded about six months in. Nothing life-threatening, but enough for a few weeks' hospital time. That only made things worse: got a Purple Heart and thought nothing could kill me.

"We were somewhere around the Black Virgin Mountain. Real rough country. Big hills, thick jungle and NVA everywhere. You know what happens; you start thinking and believing you're some kind of John Wayne instead of what you are: a kid carrying a rifle. Maybe that's how you survive. You trick yourself into thinking you're something you ain't. I was almost done with my ninth month when they made me squad leader. I kept walking point; I liked walking point. So one day, we're humping through really thick shit and I pass a bunker. An old rotten, falling-down, piece of shit bunker. There are shadows all over the place playing tricks with my eyes. At first I saw some movement, but I convinced myself I didn't. I should have checked it out; but I was scared, simple as that. I was fucking scared. I didn't have the balls to check it out. I tell myself there is no use wasting time checking on phantom gooks."

He stops and takes a long pull from the can. "So, I... just walked by. Nothing to see. I kept on walking. The rest of the squad, my squad, follows. Those phantom gooks, well, they had real guns and they lit up the squad. Once the shooting started, I acted okay. I fired back, charged the bunker, threw grenades. When the smoke cleared, two guys were dead, three wounded. All because I was too fucking scared to do my job."

"And you been carrying this around with you all this time?"

"Oh, that ain't all. They gave me a Bronze Star for busting up the ambush and killing the gooks."

"Did you?"

"That was the easy part. They never saw me coming."

"But you did go back. You could have stayed hidden."

"That ain't the point, and you know it!"

Camp shrugged and waited for Don to continue.

"Not long after, I'm wounded again. Real bad. I was in for good. Didn't happen too soon. I'd lost my nerve. Couldn't handle it anymore. When I got out of the hospital, I got a job as night CQ, just marking time until I go home. One night, the camp gets shelled and I'm so scared, I puke my guts out."

"You were short. Everybody is scared when they're short."

"At home, the only time I could sleep is when I was drunk. I relived the ambush every night along with vivid, detailed nightmares. So I stayed drunk. I'd drop Janet off and spend the night in a bar. The drinking didn't help. I knew what I had to do. So here I am, back in the fucking jungle where I belong."

"To prove something?"

"Exactly."

"To prove what? That you're not a coward?"

"Yeah."

"Everyone thinks you're so gung ho, that you're nuts. Wilkes thinks you are a stone-cold killer."

"It's what I think that matters."

"Your first tour, how old were you, nineteen? You had every right to be scared; it's normal. You can't keep blaming yourself."

"I don't blame myself for being scared; I blame myself for getting other guys killed."

"Would it have been better if you got yourself killed instead?"

"Who knows?"

"So how do you feel now? You feeling better about yourself?"

"I guess so. I did the right thing today, I know that. But that poor fucking gook, I did get carried away."

"You had to kill him. Does it matter how you did it?"

"I kept chopping at him. Hacked that motherfucker to pieces."

"The new guys don't think you're crazy. I guarantee they'll run down to the PX and get a knife just like yours. I don't think you're crazy, and I damn sure know you're no coward."

"Thanks, Wendy. I appreciate you talking to me."

"You ever talk about this with anybody?"

"I started to tell Janet, but I knew she wouldn't understand."

"You coming back to the squad now?"

"In a little bit. One thing still bothers me. The gook, he didn't shoot me. He could have. He charged at me with his bayonet."

"Maybe he thought he was the gook John Wayne. Who knows?"

Camp left him sitting alone. Holt felt tired. He felt as old as he ever would be. He lost his guilt; but with it, he also lost a part of himself, the part that cared whether he lived or died. He felt empty, as if something essential had been taken from him. He felt alone.

He wished he could go home, and wondered if he ever could.

He smiled. "Robert Vaughn! That's the guy. The guy in the movie. I knew I'd remember his name."

Chapter 13

Fire from the Sky

Delta was on the left; and Charlie, on the right. It was 10 AM, only three hours behind schedule.

The men woke up at dawn and rushed through breakfast. They were told to assemble in Company formation. The headquarters element, Major Grayson and his entourage, brought up the rear. For three hours, the men held in place. No explanation was given. Finally, at 10 AM, the orders were given to saddle up and move out. It took time before the men found a comfortable pace. At first, the platoons would bunch up and then overcompensate and spread out in a straggling loose formation.

Holt was the left flanker, as good as being on point. He just wanted to be left alone and think. Throughout the night, he weighed the possibilities of his new situation. Off the line, out of combat... it was difficult to comprehend. Toward dawn, he accepted it as fact; and with acceptance, a peace he had not known since coming back to Vietnam.

It was over. He'd get a job in the rear and pass his remaining months in safety. Camp was right; this was the best thing for him. It would give him time to decompress. It would let him get back to normal. "Damn straight I'll lie around, work on my tan and gain weight. Cover up these ribs and stop looking like a skeleton. I'll write Janet tonight and tell her."

The thoughts came so quickly, they were a jumble in his mind. I'll buy a stereo at the PX. I'll go on R&R to Singapore or Bangkok. Better yet, I'll see if I can get Hawaii and send Janet the money for her ticket. No, her father would never let her go. I'll fix Alfie up with some shots and send him home. That little fucker would terrorize the neighborhood. Stateside dogs wouldn't stand a chance against Alfie.

He was happy and excited and afraid all at once. He wanted to scream out loud. Nothing would happen to him at Base Camp. Five months, and he would be home, gone from this shit hole for good. He wouldn't touch another gun for as long as he lived. He'd sleep dry; shower ten times a day in water so hot, you could boil lobsters in it. Home! The fucking end, and he made it.

I got to find Camp, he thought. I'm not waiting 'til the end of this operation. I'll go in tonight. If Camp can't swing it, I'll get Doc to send me in. Either Doc White or Mad Dog, one of them will do it. I ain't taking any more chances.

He never would have asked to be sent in, but he was alright with it if someone else made the decision.

"That stupid fuck Wilkes thinks he's screwing me. That dumb shit don't know it, but he's saving me. I'll hang out with Nick. He ain't coming back. The three of us, me, Nick and Alfie. We'll sit around and drink beer all day long. Stay fucked up and Di Di this fucking place.

He kicked his feet, raising little clouds of dust. "Alright, be cool. You got one more day to get through. Just pray there are no gooks in that ville. A few more hours, and I'm history."

The jungle was quiet, the sounds muted by the mist of ground fog. Everything looked new. Blades of grass poked through the ground, shiny and fresh, not trampled and crushed under the lug soles of heavy boots.

To the left, he heard the rapid flutter of wings. Birds or bats? He wondered why they never see animals, and he knew why. In this jungle, we're the animals; and we don't leave room for anything else. He lifted his head and tried to see the sun, but the leaves are too thick. There's a heavy, sweet smell of rotting vegetation and green mold. Moss covered the rocksin a soft, green blanket of fuzz.

His next step breaks a branch, and the sharp snap echoes like a rifle shot.

"Shit. Watch where you're going, asshole, or you'll go home in a box."

A spasm of pain rumbled through his stomach, and he ran into the bushes. From where he squatted, he sees Camp coming toward him.

"Wendy, over here," he called while searching for his toilet paper. "What's up?"

"You look like shit. You're all pale and sweaty. You feeling okay?

"I got cramps and fever. I want to go back tonight, or as soon as the chopper comes in."

Camp raised his eyebrows.

"You see any reason why I should stay? If Wilkes wants me gone, he'll be happy I'm going in."

"I guess. Oh, what the hell. Go for it. No use to have you fucking around out here. You'll be missed."

"Damn straight."

"Don't worry about it. I'm sure the war will continue without you. We got to move now. Wilkes wants us to swing left, and circle the village." Camp pointed at his map with dirty, ragged fingernails.

"These maps ain't worth a damn. How old are they?"

"Michelin maps, from the days of the French."

"The village isn't marked on mine."

"I got it drawn in. See, right here."

"If it ain't on the map, how do they know where it is?"

Camp pointed a finger at the sky.

"God?

"Grayson. He's up in his chopper. That's why we were so late jumping off; his chopper wasn't ready. He's somewhere up there and got everything pinpointed. He says we're about a klick away from it, maybe two."

"Did he say what it looks like?"

Camp pushed his helmet back and scratched at his forehead.

"He says it looks deserted. No people, no dogs, nothing."

"Should there be people there?"

Camp scratched vigorously at his ass. "Who knows? Anyway, we got the easy job. We'll swing wide on the flank and do a quick recon. We hang out while Charlie sweeps the village. Goddamn it, I feel like I'm crawling with bugs."

"You probably are. Then what?"

"Then it'll be lunch time. Why you asking me all these questions? They don't tell me anything."

"I'm a short-timer. I'm concerned for my well-being."

Camp laughed. "You got five months, short-timer, and then you start worrying."

"Five in 'Nam, but only one day in the field."

"Take point short-timer. Get us to the village, and don't fuck up. Then maybe we'll let you go in. Okay? I'm coming with you guys. First squad will tag along behind us."

"Yes, Sergeant!" Raising his arm, he gave Camp the finger as he walked away.

"Short-timer, my ass," Camp mumbled. "Saddle up, girls. Break's over."

As they approached the village, the forest thinned. The farmers had tried to clear the land, but gave up against the enormity of the task, succumbing to the inevitable encroachment of trees and vines. The vines were everywhere: thick ones covered with short, prickly thorns; thin ones entangling your feet with the strength of wire. The vines snaked and coiled up the tree trunks, lacing themselves up through the branches. They moved as the trees swayed.

It was through these vines that Holt first saw the village. It lay beyond an open field. In the monsoon, the field probably flooded and rice was planted; but not recently. The dikes which defined the rice fields were crumbling and in disrepair, and didn't look like they could hold water. Short, stubby weed clumps dotted the fields.

Everything about the village looked old and worn out. It was separated from the fields by a ring of hedges and palm trees. Just over the hedges, the walls and thatched roofs of the first house could be seen. The mud walls of the houses looked dry and cracked, and large patches of thatch were missing from the roofs. There was a total absence of activity; there were no fires or wood smoke. It looked, as promised, deserted and abandoned.

"Nobody home?"

"That's the way it looks."

Holt took his floppy bush hat and mopped at his face. "So what now?"

"We'll stay inside these trees and swing over there. There should be a stream that runs through the village, with enough cover along the bank to work our way closer. Keep out of sight."

"Why? Ain't nobody here?"

"You never know. It does appear quiet."

"Too quiet," Holt said eerily, drawing out the words.

As they circled the village, Camp gave a site report to Wilkes, informing him of their progress. They were to call in when they reached the stream.

Charlie Company left the cover of the trees and started across the field. It was after eleven, and the cool of the morning was replaced by the smoldering heat of the afternoon.

The first shots sounded like firecrackers: first one, then two, then a whole string. Holt, who had stopped to light a cigarette, turned with a quick, startled look.

Camp listened to the radio, but he didn't need it to know what was happening. The sounds were unmistakable. AK-47s sprang the ambush, and it was sometime before M16s were heard returning fire. They were soon silenced by the thunderous booming of Russian-made 51-caliber heavy machine guns. There was more than one; maybe two or three.

Charlie Company was caught in the open and pinned down as the guns swept the field at ground level, like a scythe through wheat. For several awful moments, only the machine guns could be heard. The Sergeants saved the moment, kicking, cursing and threatening the men to return fire. The earthen dikes offered little protection from the 51-caliber bullets which pummeled the ground. Clumps of dirt and grass disintegrated into powder, forcing the trapped men to crawl helplessly toward whatever cover was available.

Delta Company was stunned; they lay immobile, watching the slaughter. Finally, they moved on Charlie's left flank to relieve the pressure of the ambush, confident the NVA would flee, leaving only a harassing sniper or two.

The fourth squad was ahead of both Delta and Charlie Companies and had not been detected by the entrenched enemy. They had an unobstructed view of the carnage taking place.

Holt turned to Camp. "What should we do?"

Camp pressed the handset to his ear and shushed Holt. "The gooks are dug in all along the hedgerow. There are heavy casualties: two KIA and a bunch wounded."

As Delta moved into the field, another machine gun opened fire. The gun fired diagonally, trapping the men in a withering crossfire. They struggled to within a hundred meters of the hedgerow before being pinned down. An RPG fired into a group of men huddled behind a large tree stump. The rocket-propelled grenade exploded in a blinding, fiery flash, shredding bodies into a red cloud of bone and blood. Holt watched a severed leg tumble through the air as if in slow motion. Holt swore he heard it hit the ground over the noise of battle.

Mad Dog was there, kneeling over the wounded man, frantically working on the remains of the leg. He was tying a field dressing on the stump. A thick geyser of blood spurted onto his face and shirt. He looked up and shouted something. He followed his gaze and saw Doc White running toward him. He was hunched over, burdened by the weight of his field packs. Bullets kicked up dirt all around him.

"Jesus Christ. He must be crazy. Get down, Doc," Holt hollered.

"Take it easy, he can't hear you."

White lumbered along, oblivious to the bullets and explosions. Dirt flew up at Doc's feet, and he went down hard.

"Oh, God, no!" Holt started up, but Camp grabbed his sleeve and pulled him down.

"He's alright."

White got to his feet, looking dazed and dopey. He reached down, picked up his glasses, and carefully fitted them to his nose. He gathered his packs and continued his slow, clumsy running.

"That fucking idiot. What does he think he's doing?"

"His job. He's fine; he's with Mad Dog."

"They're not even paying attention to what's going on. Those assholes don't even know they're being shot at. Shit, Wendy. We gotta do something. We can't just sit here."

"You're right. Wilson, get your ass over here with the radio."

Wilson raised his head slightly.

"Now, shithead! If we can take that gun, it'll break the crossfire. We can sneak up on them. What do you think?"

Holt picked up a stick and quickly sketched in the dirt. "The wood line runs right into the village. We can use the stream bed for cover. We should be able to get right up on the gun before they see us."

"Let's hope so. That fucking fifty will tear us apart if they spot us."

He relayed the plan to Wilkes. He listened and nodded. "Okay, let's go."

Crouching low, they started moving. To their right, the battle raged on. Both companies were raked by murderous machine-gun fire. Grenades and rockets exploded among the men, clouding the air with dirt and smoke. The stench of cordite and blood hung in the air.

High above the battle, Major Grayson calmly coordinated the frantic calls for Medivacs, artillery and air support. He easily handled several radios at once, pressing the handsets to his ears as he hunched over his map table.

"Delta Six, Charlie Six, stand by, fast movers inbound. Group your men and prepare to pop smoke."

In another handset, he coordinated with the jet pilots who had just left Ben Hoa. He pulled out a chocolate bar and turned to his aide. "In about fifteen minutes, we'll see some show."

He looked out the open door. "Hang on, boys. We'll get you out."

The stream was more like a big ditch, with a few inches of green, scummy water lying in stagnant pools. The machine gun was much closer now. They crowded together, shoulders touching.

Holt held his up hand. The stream curved to the right, toward the field. In front was a ten-foot sloping embankment. He carefully removed his pack and moved toward the embankment. It was slick with mud, but there were enough exposed roots and vines to allow him to climb the ten feet to the top.

Twenty feet away, in an old bomb crater, was the gun emplacement. The gun was manned by three ragged, young soldiers. He was so close, he could hear the metallic chink of the spent shell casings hitting the ground. He slid down the mud wall and crab-walked back to the squad. He placed a finger to his lips. Turning to Camp, he whispered, "They're right there. You can see them from the top: three gooks and the gun. They couldn't have picked a worse spot. They have a great view of the field, but they're blind on their right side. Bunch of assholes. We climb up and take them with grenades."

"You sure about this?"

"If you can throw a grenade, we can fuck them up. Come on."

Holt was at the top of the embankment, and looked back with annoyance at Camp and the rest of the squad. They were moving slowly. Holt gestured irritably to hurry.

Reluctantly, the men climbed up besides Holt. He withdrew a grenade and counted off, one, two, three; letting them know to throw their grenades on three.

Locke whispered to Big Wilson, "Why is he telling us what to do? What's wrong with Camp?

They waited for Kelly to lay out several belts of machine-gun ammo. It was hard to do quietly. Finally, Kelly nodded. Everyone was ready. Holt held up his grenade and worked the pin loose; everyone did the same. He silently counted 'one' and let the spoon fly off the grenade body. He mouthed two and three, and lobbed the grenades. They landed and exploded as one. Before the dust settled, Kelly was on his knees, firing long bursts from his M-60. Big Wilson pumped round after round of 40-millimeter grenades into the smoking pit.

"More grenades," Holt shouted.

The deadly little spheres landed with muffled blasts of earth and stone.

Holt peeped his head over the edge and saw the barrel of the big gun tipped up, pointing toward the sky.

"Shit, we did it," Camp said, poking at Holt's ribs. "You fucker, you were right."

"Let's get out of here."

From the field, the sounds of firing changed. Without the crossfire, Delta was free to move forward.

From the crater came several low moans. Through the smoke

rose a silent, swaying figure. Blood ran from his nose and ears, and his clothes were torn and shredded. He staggered slightly and tried to lift his arms.

Kelly was first to fire, stitching the soldier across his chest with a burst from his gun that sent the man reeling backward. Everyone fired into the bodies. The moaning stopped.

"What are you doing?" Locke shrieked. "They were trying to surrender."

Holt looked at the bullet-riddled bodies and shrugged. "They should have tried harder."

"Locke, quit wetting your diapers over a bunch of dinks. Do you think they'd treat you any different if it were you doing the surrendering?"

"It's not right, that's all I'm saying."

"Learn to keep you stupid mouth shut and just do as you're told."

Locke started to say something.

"Did you just hear what I said? Shut the fuck up. Keep your whining mouth shut. You're driving everyone nuts. Our guys got killed today. You want to feel sorry for someone? Feel sorry for them."

In the time it had taken to knock the gun out, the tide of battle had shifted. Delta had advanced fifty yards and had gone into a defensive perimeter with Charlie Company. The wounded were being treated and assigned priorities for the incoming Medi-vacs. The two companies would consolidate their position and sit out the strafing and bombing, now only minutes away.

The jets had an ETA of two minutes when Camp was informed of their arrival. There was no time to run.

"Jesus Christ! Everybody in the bomb crater. Jets are coming to bomb the village."

"There're dead gooks in there."

"Throw them out. There's no other place to go. Hurry!"

Kelly and Little Wilson were struggling with a body when

150

Wilson dropped his end.

"Oh shit! I'm getting blood all over me."

"Clear this fucking hole. Do it now! Locke, pop smoke. Let them know where we are."

Locke took a yellow smoke grenade, pulled the pin, and tossed it a few yards. It sent out a rich, billowing cloud of bright yellow smoke which drifted through the trees.

Camp ran to the sputtering canister, picked it up and threw it deep into the woods.

"You moron, you want them to drop the bombs on top of us?"

Before getting into the crater, he counted to make sure no one was missing.

Little Wilson gagged, "I got guts on me."

"Better his guts than yours."

Circling above the village, Major Grayson was speaking with the Forward Air Controller.

"Be advised, we have men within the village, fifty yards west of the yellow smoke."

"I see the smoke. Will relay to Blue Bird."

Everyone was hunkered down, awaiting the jets. The FAC came first in his spindly, single-engine Piper Cub. He chugged over the village at treetop level, firing a pair of white phosphorous marking rockets defining the area to be bombed. The rockets nearest the gun pit were barely thirty yards away.

"Jesus Christ, that's too close."

"If those assholes sneeze, we'll be dead meat."

"Look, there they are."

"Get your fucking head down."

The jets made a false pass to line up their bombing run. They roared overhead in a thunderous, explosive whine of turbines, trailing a hot wind reeking of jet fuel. Their second pass was the real thing; and if anyone was watching, you could see the bombs release and fall to the ground.

The ground jolted and heaved under the men. The shockwaves lifted them off the ground and snapped their mouths shut so hard, their teeth clicked. The actual explosions were lost in the high-pitched scream of the jets as they passed overhead. Dirt, rocks and jungle debris filtered down upon them as they crouched, doubled over, awaiting the next pass.

"Two-hundred-fifty pounders," Camp said with authority. His ears were ringing so badly, he couldn't hear his own voice.

The next run was even closer, and the explosions seemed to tear at their skin and push against their eyes: a sharp, jolting pain, followed by a long-drawn-out, vibrating ring.

"Those fuckers are trying to kill us." Kelly started to raise his machine, but was restrained by Holt.

"Easy, bro. They're ours, remember? Be cool."

"Napalm next," Little Wilson wailed in despair.

The jets came low and flared upward, releasing two long metal cylinders which tumbled end over end into the trees.

"Whump. Whump," the tree line erupted in a rolling wave of liquid fire. Bright balls of orange flame blossomed with a rushing whoosh, only to be consumed in oily, black clouds of thick, pungent smoke.

Crouched at the bottom, they felt as if the air was being sucked from their lungs. When they tried to breathe, they choked, caught in a cloud of superheated air. A hot dry wind rushed over them, ruffling their hair, and pulling and tugging at their clothes. The roar of the fire was deafening.

"Is it over?" someone screamed.

Camp slapped at his ears. It felt like an enormous pressure trapping him inside a buzzing jar.

Big Wilson rolled to the bottom of the crater, his arms and legs hanging at awkward angles. Locke was curled in a ball, shuddering in silent sobs. Kelly got up on wobbly, uncertain legs. He dragged Little Wilson and Kimball by their shirts, shaking them like rag dolls. His machine gun lay unattended at his feet.

Holt couldn't focus his eyes. He kept rubbing them, trying to see through the drifting pall of smoke. He realized he had bit his lip, and blood was dripping from his mouth. His fuzzy vision cleared and he looked upon a real-life nightmare. Small, crackling fires burned what little vegetation remained. Long, greasy tendrils of congealing napalm hung from the bare, blackened branches of scorched trees. Everything smelled like burnt flesh and gasoline. Through shimmering waves of heat, he could just discern the ruined eastern edge of the village. There appeared to be little remaining.

"Aw, shit," moaned Little Wilson. "I pissed my pants."

"Be thankful. It probably kept your legs from burning."

Camp crawled to where Holt stood and asked him, "You ever come that close to bombs before?"

"Un-fucking-believable." Holt struggled to light his cigarette, his hands shaking too hard to control them.

Camp held out his lighter for Holt and then lit his own cigarette. It tasted like gasoline. "No more firing."

"I can't believe anyone is left in there, not after that napalm. That stuff is horrible."

"Can you imagine what it must be like?"

Holt sat down heavily and shook his head. He brought his wrist up to his eyes and brushed the caked dirt from his watch. The crystal was cracked and glazed with trapped condensation. He squinted. Twelve thirty-five. Lunch time.

Chapter 14

The Village

The fourth squad rested in the shade on the western edge of the open field. Where earlier the jets had strafed and bombed, they now sat and watched the cleanup of the residue of war.

The men had regrouped and consolidated their defensive position. Medivac helicopters were called to ferry the casualties and the dead back to Cu Chi.

Another chopper was landing, emblazoned with a large red cross. It settled clumsily amid swirling clouds of dust and was immediately surrounded by men carrying collapsible stretchers bearing the wounded. Camp had the radio handset pressed to his ear, listening to the details of the evacuation.

"Any word who got it?"

"No names. Charlie Company got hit hard. Seven KIAs, double that in wounded. Delta got three dead, but they ain't saying who."

"Any wounded?"

"Here comes Mad Dog. He'll know what's going on."

Everybody gathered around and watched Mad Dog's slow, exhausted progress across the field.

"He really looks beat," said Kelly.

"He's dragging ass, that's for sure," added Little Wilson.

As the tired medic came under the trees, they could see how bad he looked. His shirt front and sleeves were covered in dried blood. His cheek was tinged a dull, coppery color where blood had splashed him. Dried blood and dirt encrusted his hands and fingers.

"The Lieutenant's dead," he said without preamble.

"Which Lieutenant?" Holt said quickly.

"Smith, not Wilkes," Mad Dog said, a trace of annoyance in his voice.

"Oh," Holt said and shrugged.

"That's not all," Mad Dog said, pausing to accept a cigarette offered by Camp. "White flipped out. Just went nuts when he heard the news. They put him on a Medivac and sent him back with the Lieutenant's body." Mad Dog dragged deeply on the cigarette and began to cough violently. He spat out some phlegm. He wiped his mouth with a blood-encrusted sleeve before continuing. "He really freaked out. Was screaming it was his fault and that if he were there, he could have saved him. Shit like that. No one was gonna save him. Caught a fifty-round right here, just below his left eye. Splattered his head like a dropped watermelon. There wasn't anything left to save, just a bunch of red stringy junk hanging off his neck. He was all fucked up."

"'Remains unfit for viewing'," Camp said, referring to the tag that would be placed on the coffin and accompanying the body when it was shipped home.

"Hope if I get it, they don't have to scrape me up with a spoon," Big Wilson said.

Holt grimaced and made a face. "How's Doc gonna be?"

"He'll be okay. They'll shoot him up with dope and let him rest. He probably won't be out anymore. They'll get him something in the rear. Maybe as battalion aide."

"Wish I could have said goodbye," Holt said wistfully.

"You'll see him soon enough. We're going in tomorrow, day after at the latest. I heard them talking at the CP, what with the Lieutenant getting killed and Charlie Company beat to shit. Man, those guys are so fucked up, you can't believe it. They're down to half-strength. Got maybe thirty-five guys left."

"You think they'll make Wilkes CO?" asked Camp.

Mad Dog scratched at the stubble covering his chin. "Probably, he's Senior Lieutenant. They got nobody else. All the Lieutenants are brand-new."

"They make that 'weasel dick' CO and we're all fucked."

"Maybe. Maybe not," Camp said. "If he's CO, then he'll be fucking around with Grayson all the time. Won't have any time for us."

"His replacement won't be any better," Holt said. "He'll either be a 'ninety-day wonder' or worse, a 'ring-knocker.' Either way, it'll be bad news."

"All officers suck," Little Wilson said. "They want to get promoted regardless of how many of us they gotta kill to do it."

"Fucking A," mumbled Kelly.

"Anyway, they do it, it don't mean nothing. At least we're going in."

"Big fucking deal! So they let us in a few days early," said Holt.

"Yeah, big deal," echoed Little Wilson.

"Not to change the subject, but did you hear anything about the village? We going in?" asked Camp.

"Waiting for an interpreter. They're gonna fly one in. They think there are people in the village."

"Not anymore. Not after the jets got through with them."

"But we are going in?"

"Definitely. They already sent two platoons around back to cordon it off."

"Don't want them Chucks getting away," said Little Wilson.

"Only Chucks left in there are dead crispy critters."

"Napalm sure does a job on them."

"'Better living through chemistry'. DuPont should put a few pictures of napalm in their annual report to impress the stockholders."

Mad Dog lit another cigarette and looked over at Locke. "Why's he so quiet?"

"He sulking 'cause we killed some gooks?" taunted Kelly.

"But they had their hands up," mimicked Little Wilson in a high, whiny voice.

"Locke's gonna hang around and wait for the chaplain. The two of them will say a few prayers, maybe bury the fuckers. Ain't that right, altar boy?"

"Make sure you call in the body count first."

Locke turned with a look of sheer disgust on his face. He started to say something, but thought better of it.

Little Wilson teased him. "Maybe you'd better change that face. Didn't your mother ever tell you an angel could fly over and freeze your face like that?"

"Any angels flying over this place would die of a fucking heart attack," said Mad Dog.

"You said it all, brother. You said it all."

Major Grayson was brushing the dust from his uniform, squinting into the sun as he watched the second helicopter approach. His own command ship stood several feet away, rocking gently on its skids as the blades slowly turned, coasting to a stop. As the second ship landed, he shielded his eyes and turned from the swirling downdraft.

Two figures emerged from the helicopter: one barely five feet tall, and the second, well over six feet. Lieutenant Wilkes stood by the Major's side. When he saw the two men step from the ship, he turned his head away and groaned. The Major stood with his mouth open, staring in disbelief at the apparition that approached him.

"Lieutenant, who the hell are they?"

"They would be the prisoner interrogation team, sir," Wilkes said. "The little one is the Vietnamese interpreter, Sergeant Zion; and the big one is his American counterpart, Sergeant John John."

"John John?"

"Yes, sir. John is his first name, and also his last. They call him Little John for short."

"What's he made up for, Halloween?"

"He's a bit eccentric, sir. I'm told he was formerly with this unit and was... uh... transferred out after some problem developed."

"He looks like a real nutcase."

Sergeant John was dressed in tailored, tiger-striped camouflage fatigues. His face was completely covered in three different shades of camouflage grease paint. His head was shaved except for a short, spiky ridge of hair down the center. His bald pate was also camouflaged, no doubt in order to prevent detection from above. The diminutive Vietnamese Sergeant was dressed in identical tiger-striped fatigues, but they were tailored to such an extent they appeared to be skin tight. On his head, tilted at a jaunty angle, was a maroon beret. Perched on a small delicate nose were dark-tinted aviator sunglasses.

"They look like a psychotic version of Mutt and Jeff," the Major said.

"It's more than looks, sir; they are."

Before the Major could question him further, the two men head approached and were standing before him.

"Sir!" said the Vietnamese, snapping to attention. "Sergeant Zion, reporting as ordered."

But the Major was staring past the Vietnamese at Sergeant John, who stood in an insolent slouch, a Remington 12-gauge shotgun balanced on one cocked hip.

"Soldier, you look like a horse's ass. Look around you. These are real fighting men. You see any of them dressed up like you?"

"Yes, sir. Thank you, sir," Sergeant John said, smiling broadly and exposing a mouth full of discolored teeth.

The Major stared at the Sergeant without saying anything. The Sergeant continued to smile at the Major, unconcerned at the criticism directed at him.

"Get this clown away from me, Lieutenant. Keep him out of my sight."

"Sir, you had asked to see me about...?"

"Yes, about Lieutenant Smith. We'll discuss that later. For the time being, I'll direct the activities of Delta Company. Get back to your platoon. Now that our interrogation team has arrived, we'll search the village."

A cordon was formed around the village. On cue, the men slowly advanced from all sides, closing the noose around the hedgerows and trees which define the outer perimeter. The fourth squad entered the village from the southeast corner. Inside the hedgerow was a wide dirt track which defined the hamlet's outer limits. Branching off the track at right angles were narrow footpaths.

The damage done by the bombs and napalm was evident. The whole southern half lay in ruins. The thatch roofs had burned from the huts, leaving crumbing mud walls pockmarked by shrapnel and bullets.

Even in the best of times, this would have been a mean, dirty village, surviving on what little could be scratched and clawed from the surrounding fields. Now shattered and burning, there appeared little reason for its continued existence. Enormous craters lay in a haphazard pattern of aimless destruction. As they passed by the hedgerow, they could see the remains of bunkers and foxholes dug by the defenders.

"Where are all the gooks? And what is that smell?"

"That's burned human flesh. Smells just like roast pork."

The village appeared uninhabited. Despite the apparent destruction, there were no bodies.

"Search inside the hedges there," directed Camp. "Be careful, and watch out for booby traps."

"I'll go on ahead," said Holt.

"Yeah, okay. Be careful."

Holt followed a footpath into the village. He passed a shattered hooch and stopped to examine the interior. Nothing, he thought, stripped bare. He moved further and passed more ruined huts. He came to a large open area bordered by small, thatched buildings. It was the town square, empty and deserted.

The northern half appeared to have escaped damage. The houses remained intact, walls and roofs untouched. Across the square, he saw soldiers from Charlie Company moving from house to house. He waved, making sure they saw him.

To his right, he detected some movement from a hooch. He watched as several Vietnamese civilians stumbled into the open, hands held high above their heads. As if a bell had been rung, other villagers appeared, all with their hands up, eyes darting nervously from side to side.

A Charlie Company lieutenant shouted at his men to search all the huts and get everyone out. Behind him, Holt heard someone shout they had found some bodies.

About twenty men were crowded around a covered well, peering over the edge into the dark interior. The bodies of the North Vietnamese soldiers had been thrown into the well. No one could figure out how to get them out without actually climbing in on top of them.

"Over here! There's more, over here."

As Holt approached, he saw and smelled the hastily dug grave barely covering a grisly collection of badly mutilated bodies. Soldiers from the first and second platoons were already busy dragging the bodies from beneath the thin dirt cover and laying them out for inspection.

The bodies were arranged in neat rows, affording them a measure of dignity otherwise lacking considering the circumstances. Holt had seen it all before; mutilated bodies had long ago lost the ability to shock or disgust him. The newer guys would crowd around, horrified and fascinated all at once, nauseated, but unable to turn and look away.

Holt remembered the first dead man he saw in Vietnam. He was a Viet Cong guerilla who had been split in two after being hit in the chest by a forty-millimeter grenade. Spilling from the open cavity were a variety of shiny, wet things: heart, lungs, kidneys, liver; it was all such a mess. He remembered the intestines clearly. They were an iridescent, purplish color; and fat and squirmy, like raw sausage. They looked all swollen and puffed up, and he remembered wondering how they could fit inside the body.

That was last year. Now, nothing bothered him. Not even the sight of some guy called Moon Dog, some spaced-out California surfer freak, carrying a severed head by the hair and rolling the head into a group of soldiers busy watching the body count. Seeing the head roll toward their legs, they shouted and jumped back; then started laughing at their own squeamish, nervous reaction. They looked like they might kick the head around, soccer-style, but a first-platoon lieutenant came by and told then to stop playing with it. That didn't stop a man from lifting the head and getting his friend to take a picture of him. When he was done, he dropped the head like discarding a candy wrapper.

For some reason, Holt thought of Janet and what she would think if she could see him right now, right this minute. What would she think of all this? He closed his eyes to wipe the thought from his mind. When he looked back, he saw that somebody had put the head on a shattered tree stump and placed a lit cigarette in its mouth, the smoke drifting up past the lifeless, open eyes. A couple of guys were taking pictures of it.

Somebody was calling him. "Hey, Don. Over here." It was Pollack, standing with Camp and Sergeant Calhoun. "C'mere. You gotta see this old geezer."

Don walked to where they were standing and looked at the body.

"You ever seen such an old gook soldier before? He must be near fifty. What do you think? At least fifty, maybe older?"

"Wilkes thinks he must have been an officer, that he was in

charge."

"Yeah. He had a pistol and everything. The lieutenant snatched it," Calhoun said nervously.

"Look at this shit," Pollack said, bending down to pull the man's shirt apart, revealing a large, discolored scar. "This dude's been fucked up before."

"You think he was an officer?"

Holt examined the man's face, then his body. He couldn't see what had killed him. Maybe he was just tired and gave up. "I think he came a long way just to die here."

"Yeah, but is he an officer?"

Holt shrugged.

"Look here, pictures of his 'mama san' and 'baby san'."

The pictures were passed around before being returned to Pollack. "I'm keeping these."

"You're supposed to turn all documents in to G-2."

"These ain't documents. They're pictures and I'm keeping them," Pollack said defiantly. "And don't you go telling the Lieutenant. Okay, Sarge?"

"Go ahead, keep them if you want. What the hell. Pictures of 'dink' kids don't matter none."

Calhoun was scratching his crotch when they heard some rifle shots.

"Snipers," somebody yelled from inside the village.

"C'mon, Pollack, let's go," Calhoun said, trotting off down a worn dirt path.

They watched them go, with neither saying anything. Camp lit a cigarette and passed the pack to Holt. Holt yawned before lighting his cigarette. The two of them stood there, smoking, trying to ignore the stench of blood, feces and burnt flesh that hung in the air. The smell was so heavy, it was almost solid so that when you move around, you could feel it clinging to you.

Breathing through an open mouth to avoid the smell, Camp said,

"Let's go see what's happening with the snipers."

Holt agreed, more for something to do than for any interest in snipers. To get to the snipers, they passed through the village center. They walked down a red dirt path, polished to a glossy smoothness by years of bare, padding feet. The path was bordered by trees and bushes that crowd in from both sides. It led them to the center square, where Holt had been before. There were about two dozen Vietnamese civilians squatting in the dirt, eyes downcast. There were no young men among them, just old men and women and some young women cradling babies. No one made a sound. An old Papa San who could be anywhere from fifty to eighty stood with a bowed head before the Vietnamese interpreter, who is shouting at the man. The old man glanced nervously from Sergeant Zion to the bizarre spectacle of Sergeant John.

"Hey, fuckhead, don't eyeball me," Sergeant John screamed, cuffing him on the side of his head.

The man staggered a little, but remained standing. The other villagers didn't look up.

Sergeant Zion screamed something else, and spittle landed on the man's nose.

They watched as Sergeant John punched the man in the stomach. He fell, and Zion started kicking him. The man curled up into a ball and lay very still.

"This makes me sick," Holt said.

"There's nothing you can do. Just stay out of it."

"How can they turn a lunatic like Little John loose? That guy is certified. Just look at him, made up like a fucking insane clown." Holt took a long drag on his cigarette and threw it to the ground in frustration. "Asshole couldn't hack it in the field, so now he flies in when all the shooting's over and beats up old men. Shit, he's a foot taller and a hundred pounds heavier than that old guy."

"Calm down. I don't like this, but there's nothing we can do. This is none of our business."

Sergeant Zion grabbed an old woman by her hair and roughly pulled her to her feet. Little John took his shotgun and started poking the woman's crotch. "You short-time, bitch?" he shouted at the same time Zion was screaming.

Soldiers have gathered, drawn by the shouts and curses. Holt looked at their faces and tried to gauge their reaction to the interrogation. Some, like the villagers, stare at the ground, as if they're embarrassed to be part of it. Others stared in wide-eyed fascination, openly excited by the brutality.

"You dink motherfucker," Little John screamed, backhanding the woman across the face.

"You lying VC cunt," he shouted as he punched her in the chest.

The woman fell to her knees. She bowed her head but didn't make a sound. A younger girl, maybe seventeen or eighteen and holding a baby, glared with pure, open hatred at Little John. It was the first sign of emotion any of the villagers displayed.

Little John was ready to punch the old lady when he saw the girl glaring at him. "What are you looking at, bitch? You little slope whore, get over here!"

When she didn't move, he took two large steps and stood in front of her. "Get on your feet," he screamed.

He grabbed her blouse and pulled her roughly to her feet. The fabric tore. At first, the girl didn't know what to do first, grab her baby or keep her blouse shut. Somehow, she managed to do both. Little John leered at her.

"She VC whore," Sergeant Zion said in pigeon English.

"You think so? Then she won't mind putting out for us." Little John turned to the soldiers gathered around. "Any of you guys want a piece of this?"

The baby was crying now, and this enraged Little John. "Shut that brat up."

When she was unable to quiet the baby, he leaned his face close to hers. "Either you shut it up, or I'll do it for you."

"I don't believe she understands you, Sergeant."

Little John whirled around, startled by the voice behind him. Major Grayson was standing there, hands on his hips, his face as cold as stone. At his side stood his aide and Chaplain Doody. "Sergeant, I've been watching this little spectacle for several minutes, and I haven't heard you ask one question that even remotely could be considered a legitimate source of inquiry."

"Hey, Major, we're just having a little fun. We don't mean no harm. Uh... you know, we find that by disorienting the interrogation subject... uh... prior to actual questioning... we get... uh... sometimes, we obtain better results." He stammered out his little speech, desperately trying to remember the phrases he learned at the training center. "Uh... Sergeant Zion here has a lot of experience... "

"Shut up, Sergeant," Major Grayson said quietly.

He turned his head and saw Chaplain Doody kneel next to the young girl, trying to comfort her. The girl scowled and pushed the chaplain away. She turned and said something to the old lady, who remained bent over, head bowed. He looked at the rest of the villagers and they stared back with blank, lifeless eyes. No one moved or made a sound; just the baby cries.

"You were just having a little fun. Is that right, Sergeant? Then you won't object if I have some fun with you. Is that all right?" Before Little John could answer, the Major continued. "Consider yourself under arrest. There'll be a supply ship along soon. The Captain will accompany you back to Cu Chi, where he will place you in the custody of the MPs. My aide, on my behalf, will file formal charges based on your actions which I have observed. The Captain will relieve you of your weapon and escort you to the landing zone. So tell me, Sergeant, are you still having fun?"

As the Captain led Little John away, the Major turned to Sergeant Zion, who had backed away several feet, trying to make himself as inconspicuous as possible. "You sadistic little midget, I am personally going to see that you are assigned to a regular South

Vietnamese infantry unit. We'll see if you're as brave against your North Vietnamese brothers as you are against women and children."

"Please, Major," Zion stammered, "these people are VC peoples. They are bad. Do not be fooled. They old, but they VC. They VC for sure. They number ten people."

The Major ignored him. "Instruct the villagers to gather their belongings. They're being relocated to a government-protected hamlet closer to Saigon. Do not lay a hand on anyone. Do you understand?"

"Yes, Major. But I tell you, these VC people. They no good."

"Do as you're told."

"Good for him. The Major did alright," Holt said.

"Coming from you, that's high praise for an officer," Camp said.

"That Little John is a sick creep. I hope they throw his ass in LBJ," he said, referring to the stockade at Long Binh, informally called Long Binh Jail or LBJ.

In the commotion caused by Little John, the snipers, who were still active, were all but forgotten. Holt and Camp crossed the square and entered the trees on the northern edge. Pollack, Mad Dog, and several others were standing in a grove of palms. In front of them was a dirt path deeply rutted by wagon wheels. Across the path fifty feet away were several thin-walled mud hooches with dry thatch roofs.

"What's going on?"

"Shh. Calhoun's over there," Pollack said, pointing to where the fat sergeant was stealthily advancing toward one of the huts.

"What's he doing?"

"He's going to attack the hooch. He thinks that's where the snipers are."

"Are they?"

"Nah. They beat feet as soon as we got here."

They watched as Calhoun creeped along the wall. He stopped and withdrew two hand grenades from the pouch on his belt.

166

"Uh-oh," Holt said.

"Maybe somebody should say something."

"Let's wait and see how this plays out... It'll be a good lesson for him. How else is he going to learn?"

"I shouldn't be here," Camp said. "I'll see you guys later. You can tell me what happens. Or better yet, don't."

Calhoun flattened himself against the wall. He was sweating profusely. He looked over to Pollack, who gives him a thumbs up and smiles.

"He's not such a bad guy once you get used to him."

Calhoun edged closer to the door.

"They probably taught him how to do this in Germany," Mad Dog said.

"Just like in the movies."

"Is he gonna pull the pin with his teeth?"

"Not even Calhoun is that stupid."

"Only John Wayne can do that."

"I think we need the Duke here in 'Nam. Have him kick some gook ass," Mad Dog said as he searched his pockets for a cigarette. Without being asked, Holt handed him his pack.

"Hey, here he goes."

They all watched as Calhoun pulled the pin on one grenade, then the second. He had a grim, determined look, his jaw set firmly. He edged to the door. He leaned into the doorway and tossed the grenades inside. After a second or two, the hooch exploded outward, consumed in a muffled roar and a cloud of smoke. Calhoun was sent reeling, flying several feet, half-stumbling on churning legs. He landed on his stomach in a heap, fluttering his arms weakly.

Mad Dog was the first to reach him. "You're gonna be okay, Sarge. Let me get a look at you." He cut away the shirt with surgical scissors. "Not too bad, you'll be fine."

Calhoun's chalky white back was peppered with dozens of small shrapnel punctures. The wounds appeared to continue down onto his buttocks and the tops of his thighs.

"How is he?" Pollack asked.

"All superficial." Mad Dog scraped a fingernail across Calhoun's back. "See?" he said, holding up a tiny piece of metal. "The wall absorbed most of the impact."

Calhoun moaned weakly. "Did I get them?"

"You sure did, Sarge. You're a hero. You'll get a Purple Heart for sure, maybe even a Bronze Star."

"What happened?"

Pollack shrugged, not wanting to tell him the mud walls couldn't possibly have contained the grenade explosions.

"You did okay," he said instead.

This seemed to satisfy Calhoun. He let his body sag and turned his face toward the dirt. Pollack was on the radio, calling in the dust-off as Mad Dog put the finishing touches on the field dressing.

"Let's get him up to the LZ. The dust-off is inbound."

Together, Pollack, Holt, Mad Dog and Sugar Bear, a big black guy from the third platoon who just happened to pass by, struggled with Calhoun's bulk slung between them on a collapsible stretcher. They stumbled through the village unnoticed as activity swirled about them. The villagers had been instructed to gather their possessions; they were to be relocated to a secure, "pacified" hamlet northwest of Saigon.

"You would think foreign soldiers coming into your home and forcibly evicting you would create an uproar of protest."

In Vietnam, relocations were commonplace. Indeed, more than half the villagers had abandoned their homes some months before rather than become slave labor to a Viet Cong battalion.

"Who is this dude, anyway?" Sugar Bear asked.

"Our Platoon Sergeant."

"You mean your former Platoon Sergeant," Sugar Bear said to the barely conscious Calhoun.

"He don't hear what you say, he's all doped up."

"Bullshit! The man hears fine. He don't want to say anything gonna fuck up his chance to get off the line. Sergeant or not, he knows he's got it dicked. Old Sarge here is gonna get a soft job, maybe run the EM Club. Hey, Sarge, you need an assistant, you call the Bear and I'll come running. I don't need no more of this shit, that's for damn sure."

"Who you shitting? You black guys eat this shit up. You get free meals, clothes, and a good-paying job. You never had it so good."

"You get to travel and live right next to white people. Vietnam is a black man's dream come true."

"Shit, living with you 'white people' is like living with farm animals. The pigs on my daddy's farm live better than you 'white people'."

"Yeah, but eventually they go to slaughter," Mad Dog said.

"So do we or ain't you looked around you lately? Fuck the 'Nam. You ever been to Alabama? There ain't no way I'd fight for Alabama. Can't expect me to travel halfway round the world and fight for Vietnam. No fucking way. I know some people back in Alabama don't live much better than these gooks. I ain't got no quarrel with these folks."

They walked in silence toward the LZ.

"Let me tell you something. You sure this dude is out?" he asked Mad Dog, who nodded. "I sent me home an M16. Before I leave, I'll send home some grenades and maybe an M79 if I can swing it."

"What are you going to do with that hardware back in the world?"

"Next time some white redneck motherfucker calls me 'boy' or 'nigger', I'll just stand there, all smiles, and say, 'Yes, sir boss.' Then I'll wait 'til it gets dark just like here, and blow his cracker head clean off. That's what I'm going to do with all that shit."

"You are going to be one dangerous fucking nigger!" Pollack said.

"You got that right! Hey, man, how much further we got to lug this fat boy?"

"This should be about right," Jaxon said.

"Then I'm off."

"Hey, Bear, thanks for the hand," Holt said.

"No sweat. Hey, I hear this dumb fuck tried to blow himself up."

"He tried, but couldn't quite manage it."

"Somebody should've told him not to play with these bad-boy toys."

Around the landing zone were groups of men standing guard over a wounded friend. Off to one side lay figures covered by ponchos: the dead, awaiting their final ride. No one stood by the dead.

"You think this was worth it?" Holt asked.

"If you're an officer, I guess it is."

Pollack looked at the dead bodies. "Somebody should ask them what they think."

Chapter 15

The Mystery of the Missing Arm

A small, rough wooden table and chair had been brought from one of the hooches for Major Grayson to use. He sat, strategically placed, where he could observe the evacuation and relocation. He stared at his map spread across the tabletop. From time to time, he would smooth the wrinkled surface of the map and then go back to just staring.

Behind him sprawled his radio operators: one was reading a comic book, while the two others tortured a huge, hard-shell beetle. They took turns slicing at it with a knife, seeing how close they could get without cutting it.

"Shit, man! Look what you did now. You chopped off a leg."

"Big fucking deal. He's got like twenty others."

The Major turned and stared at the two boys. "Would you morons kindly hold it down and quit fucking with that bug?"

As the Major turned back to the table, the smaller of the RTOs mimicked him, mouthing his words. The other raised his leg and brought his boot heel down onto the beetle with a sickening crunch. He then pushed the small carcass away with his foot.

The Major sighed as he heard them snickering behind him. He seldom used profanity in front of the troops, but he was so tired and disgusted with the day's events, he couldn't help himself.

"Ten dead," he said, staring at the map as his hands smoothed back the curled edges.

"Ten dead, and not a damn thing to show for it."

The bodies of the dead and the wounded were brought back to Cu Chi less than an hour ago, and already he had received orders to abandon the village and proceed 'with all due haste' toward another objective: a pacified, secured village approximately ten miles away.

The Major pinched the bridge of his nose and rubbed his eyes. The men were in no condition to march ten miles, or more than sixteen klicks. It would take two days to cover that distance. He checked his watch: two-thirty. If they left within the hour, maybe they could cover five klicks. He traced his finger over the map. Five klicks would leave them in the jungle searching for a clearing. Too late for resupply, too late for hot food, too late to dig in and prepare a proper defensive perimeter.

The Major leaned back and heard the chair crack ominously under him. He leaned his head back and rolled his shoulders. "What the hell were they thinking back at headquarters? We should stay here for the night and send out patrols to see what lies ahead." For no reason at all, he thought of those signs you see in shopping malls with a bright arrow pointing to a spot: 'You are here.' "We're in the middle of nothing and going nowhere fast."

A noise made him look up. The villagers were being herded across the square toward the waiting Chinooks, the big, monstrous double-rotor cargo helicopters capable of carrying fifty men or more. These people had probably never been in a car, and now they were being flown to God knows where to start life all over. "Welcome to the modern world."

The Major saw Chaplain Doody wander into the square and stop, seemingly bewildered by all the activity swirling about him. He saw the Major and started toward him. The Major rested his chin in his hand and watched him. "Howdy, Doody," he said to himself. But to the chaplain, he merely nodded his head.

The chaplain stood beside the Major and looked back into the village. "It's a real mess." He took off his helmet and rubbed the red indentation the sweatband had left across his forehead. "A real mess," he repeated. "I gave everybody last rites. You think it means anything?"

"What's that? Last rites?"

"No. No, not that. I mean this village. You think what happened here will mean anything?"

"That's hard to say. We kicked their ass, that's for sure. But if it means anything, that's not up to us. It's difficult without knowing the big picture."

"The big picture?"

A small smile creased the Major's face. "That's right, the big picture. We're just a small part of this operation. It's just hard to know what's going on. If I were back at Division, it would be a different story. But out here..." he said, leaving the thought hang. "I believe I understand what it's like, being a ground soldier with somebody flying overhead, telling you 'Go here, go there' but not telling you why."

"A different perspective on the ground?"

"Yes, it sure is, Lieutenant."

"I wonder how Major Carltinwould react if he spent more time out there. Out here with the men instead of..."

"Instead of back at Base Camp doing other things? We've all heard the rumors about Major Carltin. Just remember, they are just rumors."

"Oh, I don't care about those stories. It's just that sometimes, he's so critical of the men, of their behavior. It doesn't seem fair after spending time out here."

"You've been out here all of three weeks. That doesn't make you a veteran."

"I gave last rites to ten brave young men today. Am I still an FNG?"

"You got a point there, chaplain. You're no FNG, not anymore."

The chaplain reached into a pocket and brought out a small box of raisins. He took some and passed the box to the Major. "What will happen now?"

"We'll be out of here when they wrap things up with the villagers. We're going to another village, Ben Tre, about ten miles from here."

"Another village? Not like here, I hope?"

"No, nothing like here. It's secure. It even has ARVNs stationed there, so you know its safe. We should be able to relax, get resupplied and get some replacements."

The Major was interrupted by his RTO, who handed him the radio handset. The Major listened, and his face turned red. "Roger. Out," He slammed the handset onto the table. "Shit!"

"What's wrong?"

"Jesus Christ! One of the wounded men got his arm shot off, his left arm. Before we sent him back, we found his arm, wrapped it up, and sent it back with him." The Major ground his teeth before continuing. "It was the wrong fucking arm. Can you believe that! The wrong fucking arm!"

"How could they tell?"

"For one thing, it was a right arm, not a left."

"Does it matter? I mean, they can't sew it back on, can they?"

"No. they can't. The problem is the boy is married and wore a wedding band. Apparently, the ring is still on the hand, wherever it is. He's back there now, crying to some Colonel about the ring, how it's a family heirloom and how he's got to have it back. It has an inscription or something on the inside from his grandfather to his grandmother, some bullshit like that. So now, we got to hunt down the missing arm and find the fucking ring."

"It shouldn't be hard. If we know where the boy was wounded, the arm shouldn't be far away."

"Maybe you're right. It's not like the arm could get up and walk off." The Major pushed himself away from the chair. He turned to his RTOs and snapped his fingers. "Let's go. You come with me, chaplain."

They walked until they came upon a row of North Vietnamese bodies laid out in a small clearing. A short, plump lieutenant was pacing in front of the dead men. He stopped as the Major approached. "Oh, Major, good thing you're here. We got a problem."

"What is your problem, Lieutenant..." he trailed off, unable to recall his name.

"Jesup, sir. Lieutenant Jesup. The body count, sir," he said, as if stating the obvious.

"What's wrong with the body count?"

"It's all fucked up, sir." Seeing the chaplain for the first time, he stammered an apology.

"Exactly, what is the problem?"

"Well, we got these gooks here, sir. Seventeen. With these, there's no problem. But over here, we got these parts and we don't know how to count them."

"Parts? What parts?" the Major said wearily.

"These parts." He held up his hand and ticked them off. "We got three arms, a foot, and two legs. Right over here."

The Major brightened up. "Arms! You have loose arms. Where? Let me see those arms."

"The arms? Yes, sir, right over here. We have several for you." He showed the Major the pile of severed limbs. "Oh, shit, sorry, chaplain. I almost forgot; we have a head, too. Thompson, get that head, will you? Bring it here and add it to the pile."

"The arms, Lieutenant. I want to see the arms."

The Lieutenant held each of the limbs for the Major's inspection as if it were a normal thing to do.

"Hot damn! We got it, chaplain. Here it is. Look, here's the ring. This must be our lucky day. You, soldier, wrap this up and get it up to the LZ. You tell the chopper pilot to make sure it gets back safely and in one piece. If anything happens to this ring, it's his ass. You make sure he understands that. You got all that?"

"No sweat, sir," the soldier said, proud to be entrusted with the

175

arm.

The Major slapped his hands and rubbed his palms together. "So much for the missing arm, eh, Padre?"

If Lieutenant Jesup was confused, he didn't show it. "Would you care to examine the legs now, sir?"

"No, Lieutenant, I would not care to examine the legs. I was just interested in arms. You said you had a problem?"

"About the parts, sir. How do we count the parts?"

The Major pointed to the bodies. "Are any of those over there missing any of these?"

"No, sir. All them gooks are complete."

"Given the state of medical care available to the North Vietnamese, do you think it's possible for their soldiers to live after losing a limb, let alone a head?"

"No, sir! If a gook loses a leg or arm, he's as good as dead."

"If that's the case, Lieutenant, add each of those individual parts to the body count."

"Right, sir! Let's see, we got seventeen whole bodies, more or less; and to those, we add two legs, the foot, and the head. Now we only got two arms left, so that makes twenty-three."

"Major, if we previously sent an arm back, that means they got one of our arms in Cu Chi. Shouldn't we add that one to our count?"

"Good thinking, chaplain. Add one more to your count, Lieutenant."

"Twenty-four, sir!"

The Major did a quick calculation and groaned. A kill ratio of less than three to one. Headquarters wouldn't like that.

"Are there any more parts, Lieutenant?"

"No, sir, but we do have some bodies in a well, and we can't get them out."

"How many bodies?"

"Maybe three, sir. It's hard to tell. Nobody wants to climb in and hand them out."

"Only three, Lieutenant?"

"Uh... maybe more?"

"How many more?"

"Maybe three more?"

The Major waited.

"Maybe five more?"

"Five will do."

The Lieutenant did some quick calculations. "That's thirty-three in all, sir."

"I believe it's thirty-two."

"Thirty-two it is, sir. Shall I call the body count in, sir?"

"Please do, Lieutenant. Please do. Good work, son." Major Grayson turned to Chaplain Doody. "Well, everybody's happy. Cu Chi got their arm. We got our body count. A good kill ratio will make the General happy. Everyone is satisfied. It's good you remembered the arm. Quick thinking, Padre."

In another clearing, Lieutenant Wilkes sat with Sergeant Camp. "What's bothering you, Sergeant? It seems to me you should be happy. You're the Platoon Sergeant now. You'll get your promotion soon."

"Under different circumstances, maybe. It's kind of ghoulish, getting a promotion because somebody got wounded."

Lieutenant Wilkes patted Camp on the shoulder. "You'll make a fine Platoon Sergeant under any circumstances. You've nothing to feel guilty about. From what I've heard, Calhoun's wounds were his own fault. I wonder what got into him? Platoon Sergeants are not supposed to lead attacks. You keep that in mind. That's what enlisted men are for."

"Yes, sir."

"We do have a slight problem, though. We need a replacement for you as squad leader. Any suggestions?"

"Elderidge. He's the only one with any experience, and I trust him."

"Yes, you're right. He's black, isn't he? That's a good choice. We need more black NCOs."

"What about Sergeant Holt? You were going to send him in. Remember, sir?"

"Still plan to. Not just yet, though. The Major says no replacements for NCOs while we're still out in the field. He stays out another week or two. No big deal. Hell, he should thank us. This way, he goes back a Sergeant instead of Specialist 4."

"Gets him out of KP and the other bullshit assignments."

"All assignments have value. Please remember that. In any event, he'll only remain a Sergeant until he gets busted again."

"He'll do alright. He's the best point man we got."

"No argument there, Sergeant. Everyone agrees about that. There's more to being a good soldier than being good in combat. What good is walking point going to do him in Cu Chi? Promotions count, and this promotion will do wonders for your career. Do a good job for me, and I'll see that it happens. Sergeant First Class. How does that sound?"

"That sounds good, sir."

"Keep this under your hat, but things look good for me, too. I'm Senior Lieutenant and next in line for Company Commander. That is, unless they come up with a Captain in the next week or so."

Camp looked at Wilkes and nodded.

"And to answer your unasked question: No, I don't feel bad about getting promoted because Smith got killed. It's the breaks. Sometimes, they're with you; sometimes, they're not. It's a foolish man who doesn't take advantage of a situation that's presented to him."

"I guess you're right."

"I know I am. Now go break the news to your buddy. Tell him not to fuck up, and everybody will get what they want."

Camp found Holt sitting by himself under a tree. He was writing a letter. "Been brown-nosing with the officers again?"

"Yeah. Got a smoke?"

Holt handed Camp a rumpled pack after first taking one for himself. He held out his Zippo for Camp. They smoked in silence for a few moments.

"I'm gonna be Platoon Sergeant," Camp said abruptly.

"That's no surprise. They got nobody else."

"Who are you writing to? Janet?"

"Yeah, I was just telling her about how I'm going in. You remember, off the line. No more combat."

"It'll happen. You just gotta be patient. As soon as they get replacements, you'll go in."

"In a week or two?"

"That's all. A few more days."

"I guess I can hang on. It shouldn't kill me. At least, I hope not."

"We got it dicked for the next two weeks. The Lieutenant told me we're pulling out of here this afternoon. Going to some safe village named Ben Tre to relieve some ARVNs."

"Ben Tre? I've been there. My first tour, we went through there. Big place. Nice and clean. It's some sort of government showcase. Good farmland producing a shitload of rice. But I heard a rumor we were going in."

"You know better than to listen to rumors. We go in when they tell us to go in. Is this place safe?"

"Last time I was there, it was. It's closer to Saigon." Holt suddenly brightened up. "It's out of the fucking Triangle. Well, not technically, but it's right on the edge. Shit, where's my map? Here, look here, Ben Tre. See?"

"You're right. Looks like the bad part is over. Let's hope the gooks cooperate and leave us alone."

"As we get closer to Ben Tre, we'll pass through this rubber plantation. If I remember right, it's a working plantation."

"That's good news."

"Definitely! The NVA 'tax' the plantation owners, protection money. The owner pays and they leave him alone."

"Which means they'll leave us alone. They don't want to do anything to disrupt their cash flow."

"Money makes the world go around. Anyway, once in the rubber plantation, it should be smooth sailing. Maybe a sniper or two just to slow us down, let us know they're still with us, but nothing heavy."

"You know, I remember once when I was with the 1st Division, we got hit inside a rubber plantation. We shot the shit out of the place. The fight lasted the better part of the day. When it was all over, this French dude who owned the place sent the Army a bill for the trees we damaged. Can you believe it? He actually sent us a bill! And the worst part is we paid the asshole and promised to be more careful in the future," said Camp.

"This is a different kind of war. It's like we're not really trying to win."

"Tell me about it. Can you imagine the Army paying for the houses it damaged on D-Day? This whole place is fucked up!"

"It's like Alice in Wonderland: 'Curiouser and Curiouser'."

"People may call Vietnam a lot of things, but Wonderland it ain't."

Past the village, in the cleared fields, another Chinook took off in a clatter of rotor blades and swirling clouds of dust. Camp saw the huge helicopter rise over the tops of the trees and slowly lumber off. "We're gonna finish here soon, then it's off to Ben Tre. If I tell the Lieutenant you've been there before, he's gonna want you to lead the way. You mind me telling him?"

"No problem. It's an easy walk. We can do six klicks easy, and be halfway there by nightfall. Make sure you give him my best."

With the evacuation nearly completed, it was decided that the village was to be burnt to the ground. Anything that wouldn't burn was to be blown apart. Up and down the pathways, small fires burned, consuming the thatch roofs of the standing hooches.

The engineers were busy laying charges of C-4 and detonation cord in the enemy bunkers and tunnels, which had been uncovered earlier. Seeing an opportunity to lighten their loads, they'd doubled up on the explosives, laying massive charges to destroy flimsy mud structures.

Throughout the village, cries of "fire in the hole" preceded muffled explosions as soldiers ran from hut to hut, tossing grenades inside. One soldier, the California surfer Moon Dog, waved a huge flaming bundle of dried palms. "I am the God of Hellfire!" he shouted while igniting the dry thatch roofs.

The officers stood around, helpless to control the mayhem they unleashed.

At the farthest end of the village, as yet untouched by the orgy of fire, stood a small knot of Vietnamese awaiting helicopter transport. They stood and watched the destruction of their homes with totally blank, impassive faces, as if they were watching a newsreel of events in a faraway land. Not even the children cried. Standing among them was Chaplain Doody, towering over the stooped figures. His face was creased with fatigue and sorrow as if he were absorbing their misery and fear.

A cloud of sooty, black smoke hung over the village. Small bits of ash fell from the sky like a snowstorm in hell. Somewhere close, an enormous explosion blew the sides of a hut outward in a rush of bright orange flame. Everyone flinched and ducked at the sound.

"Fire in the hole," someone called a warning too late.

"Dickhead," someone shouted back, and there was laughter in the jungle.

Major Grayson stood among his Lieutenants. "Charlie Company is assembled and ready to go. Have a squad escort those villagers up to the LZ. The last chopper is inbound."

Major Grayson surveyed the destruction of the village. He pulled his sweat-soaked shirt away from his body and looked with distaste at his ruined fatigues. Nothing remained of the sharp-creased, pressed perfection of the morning. Large patches of sweat discolored his underarms, chest and back. Not wanting to look, he knew his crotch and waistband would be wet, too. He felt the beginnings of a painful rash forming at the elastic of his underwear. He imagined he could smell himself. Could the others?

"Get out there and control those men. We need to be under way in thirty minutes. Lieutenant..." He turned his head, searching for Wilkes, spotting him at the edge of the group. He waved him over. "Get your man... The one who knows Ben Tre..."

"Holt, sir."

"Whoever. Get him started. I want him to have a good lead on the rest of us. Make sure he takes a radio and that he stays in touch."

"Yes, sir."

"Lieutenant, tell him to pick an easy route, the easiest he can find. We need to cover as much distance as we can, and the men are in no shape to be busting jungle."

"Right, sir."

"And Lieutenant, no gooks. No more firefights today."

"Can't promise that, sir. The gooks have a habit of finding us. Usually, we don't have to go looking for them."

"Just tell him to do his best and be careful."

Chapter 16

The Grassy Dome

When he learned that he was to take along an RTO, Holt asked for Pollack. Little Wilson needed a break. Pollack was more experienced, both in the jungle and with the radio. He considered having Locke carry the radio, but he felt he couldn't predict how he would react under pressure and he no longer trusted him. A two-man point with a half-mile between them and the rest of the company was no place to evaluate someone's strengths and weaknesses. It was at times like these when Holt missed Mercado. With Nicky, there was never a problem with trust.

Any uneasiness Holt felt about moving from the village was unwarranted. The march to the new NDP was anticlimactic after the chaos of earlier events. The jungle thinned considerably once they left the village. It opened up, exposing wide spaces between the trees. Long, yellow grass and round, puffy bushes with brilliant red and yellow flowers flourished in the shafts of sunlight which spread through the treetops, bathing the earth in a milky yellow warmth. The ground was shaded, spongy and damp.

As the afternoon passed and evening approached, the darkness brought with it a stillness and absence of sound, which always amazed him. It was as if someone had turned the volume off in anticipation of night. Even the insects, caught in the lengthening shadows between dark and light, were hushed. Holt, unaffected by night, was at home in the darkness. He didn't need to study his map to know where he was or where he wanted to go. He was headed toward a grassy knoll overlooking a wide, shallow valley. It was marked as six kilometers on the map; and by setting a brisk pace, he planned to arrive an hour before dark.

When they first started out, he was brooding about having to spend more time in the field. He'd been overcome by a feeling of dread as the uneasiness he felt at the mission's outset had returned to haunt him. He had allowed himself to believe he was going to survive Vietnam and return home.

But he was determined not to die in this shithole. He would beat the odds against his second tour, and he would vanquish the ghosts of his past that threatened to destroy him. He had made a mistake, and others paid for it. He suffered for it with countless nights of screaming nightmares and a shroud of guilt which covered him and distorted his every thought and action. That was his past, not his future. He was through with guilt. He had proven himself back on that narrow, jungle trail and cleansed himself in the blood of the enemy. To hell with his ghosts. They were gone for good. He'd make it through his last five months, regardless of where he had to spend them. In the jungle, walking point, or in the rear with a safe job; it didn't matter. He was going home.

He heard Pollack whisper his name and turned. Pollack held up the radio handset.

"They want to know how much further."

"They got about another forty minutes. Tell them to stay on the same compass heading. It's easy walking. They'll be here before dark."

Pollack relayed the news in a harsh whisper. He didn't share Holt's enthusiasm for walking point. He felt his white hair, even covered by his helmet, made him an easy target. He squinted nervously into the gathering gloom, turning his head from side to side with sharp, rapid movements. "This place better be good. The Lieutenant's awful antsy."

"So what else is new? We got about fifteen minutes or less. I figure they're about a half-hour behind. You okay? Why are you being so pissy?"

"Because I shouldn't be here. Wilson's your RTO, not me."

"I wanted to give Gene a break and you were available."

"I worked hard to be the Platoon Sergeant's RTO, not to be out here walking point with you. Those days are over for me, or at least I thought so."

"Fine. I'll find somebody else next time I need someone reliable whom I can trust."

Pollack shrugged, not knowing what else to do.

The site Holt chose for a night defensive perimeter was everything he said it would be. It was a small clearing ringed by large, thick trees which gave way on one side and overlooked a wide, flat valley. There was little depth to the valley; it was more like a concave, grassy plain. The clearing in which they would spend the night was centered on a dome of earth. It was dry and afforded a good field of vision in all directions.

The company arrived without incident, but later than Holt predicted. It was too late for resupply, which would wait until morning. There would be no fires; they would eat their C-rations cold. It was too late and too dark for everything but patrols. It was never too dark for patrols. Major Grayson decided on the LPs, placing them at the compass points with two extra LPs deep in the trees. He dispensed with the usual ambush patrols; the men were too tired to be effective. They would have probably just faked them, anyway.

Major Grayson realized it was up to him to call and adjust the artillery fire which would ring their perimeter, and with that realization came a sudden loss of confidence. He couldn't remember the last time he adjusted artillery fire. Had he ever? In training at Fort Benning, maybe, but never in a real combat situation, and never while on the ground. He always flew above the perimeter, and always had a forward observer with him. He thought of asking one of his Lieutenants to do it, but decided it wouldn't look right. He held his map and tried to read the coordinates in the weak disk of red light filtering thought his flashlight lens cover. He heard his RTO relaying map coordinates without realizing he had spoken.

"Two smoke fired for effect," said his RTO.

In the distance, a soft thud could barely be heard, and he had to strain his eyes to make out the twin puffs of white smoke a half-mile away.

"Good shooting, sir. Might want to walk it in a bit, though," he said, all the while wondering if this shithead knew where they were. Any farther out, and the shells would have landed in another time zone.

The Major glared at the boy and told him to drop 500 yards. The RTO relayed the order to the artillery battery.

"Five hundred yards? Are you sure? Please confirm, over."

"Repeat: five hundred yards," the RTO said softly, not wanting the Major to hear his orders were questioned.

"What's the problem?" the Major snapped.

"Nothing, sir. They just wanted to confirm the distance, that's all."

"Give me that! This is Big Six. When I give an order, I don't expect to have that order questioned by you or anyone else. Is that clear? Over."

"Affirmative, sir," came the reply.

"Your job is to adjust artillery fire, not to second-guess field officers. If we were under attack, do you think I'd have time to debate my orders with you? Just do as you're told and keep your opinions to yourself." The Major took a deep breath and let it out slowly. "Now, if it's agreeable with you, I would like to finish plotting our coordinates. Over."

"Yes, sir. Please continue. Over."

"Fire the goddamn marking rounds. Over."

"Two smoke, out," came the immediate reply.

The rounds landed less than a quarter mile from their perimeter. "Mark that as Dog One. Over," the Major barked, then went on to provide three other map points, each calculated using Dog One as the reference. In this way, Dog Two, Three and Four were identified.

The artillery Lieutenant marked each of the coordinates on his map using a soft black grease pencil. His map was thumb-tacked to a piece of thick cardboard and covered in acetate, which could be wiped clean with a damp cloth and used again. Delta Company now had four predetermined reference points plotted by the artillery fire support base. In case of an enemy attack, Major Grayson could simply call in the code words with the proper adjustments. In the heat of battle, "Dog One, left fifty" was a lot simpler to say than trying to establish the proper coordinates.

With artillery plotted, he was more relaxed. He instructed his RTO to contact the platoon leaders and arrange for the evening staff meeting and briefing. While he waited, he ate a can of beef stew provided by a young specialist. All in all, he had done a good day's work. Not perfect, but he was confident that if he stayed on the ground for any length of time, he'd get better.

The fourth squad had prepared a hastily dug position overlooking the valley, and had settled down to eat. They ate their rations cold, without talking, adhering to the strict requirements of noise and light discipline. Holt finished a can of greasy meatballs and beans, and dug through his pack to find the plastic bag containing his writing paper and envelopes. He wanted to write to Janet; but realizing it was too dark, he decided to clean his rifle instead.

How it could be too dark to write, but he could still take apart and clean a rifle? It should be the other way around. After all, he'd been writing all his life.

He lay his CAR-15 across his legs, and reached into his rucksack and drew out the canvas pouch containing his cleaning kit. There was a soft, clean piece of towel wrapped around the pouch, held by a thick rubber band. He assembled the various parts of the cleaning kit and began the process of taking the rifle apart.

The CAR-15 was identical to the standard M16, only shorter. It consisted of two main parts and upper section containing the receiver group: bolt, firing pin, ejector mechanism, the barrel and plastic hand guards. The upper section was topped by the metal carrying handle, which gave the rifle its distinctive profile. The lower section consisted of the trigger mechanism, pistol grip, magazine well, and the stock. The CAR-15 had a collapsible tubular stock, unlike the solid plastic stock of the M16. The two sections were held in place by metal pins. By removing the pins, the sections could be separated, allowing access to the smaller parts.

Holt had separated the rifle and was disassembling the bolt. In the dwindling light, he allowed his fingers to feel out the cotter pins and grooves which held the bolt together, not concentrating on what he was doing. It was a task he had performed hundreds of times, and it had long lost any ability to occupy his mind. He lay the small parts of the bolt on the flat of his thigh, wiping each with a section of towel dampened with gun oil. He let his mind wander and, as he often did at night, he began to compose the letter he would write to Janet.

So much had happened since his last letter. Did he tell her about the knife fight? He decided he wouldn't tell her about that.

What would he tell her? Did the incident change anything? Did he feel he had redeemed himself, as he had told Camp, or had it only temporarily pushed the guilt aside? Maybe he was just fooling himself. If he felt he was responsible for his friends getting killed, then nothing he could do would change things. They were dead and would stay that way. That wouldn't change.

Janet could put his feelings into perspective. If he could just talk to her, she'd see through his words to what was troubling him. She had done it before. He remembered when he had only a few days left on his leave. It was a warm day, weeks away from the oppressive summer heat. They were alone in her house. Her parents and brother had gone off somewhere and were not expected to return until late that evening.

He had brought her some albums that he had bought when he first came home. When he gave them to her, she looked at him strangely.

"Why are you giving me these?" Her voice was hard and accusing, not at all what he expected.

"You said you liked them and I won't be needing them. There's no ulterior motive."

"Are you sure?"

"Did I do something wrong? Something I should know about?"

"You're giving away your things now?"

"I'm giving you some albums that I have no use for."

"I sometimes think you don't expect to come back. Is that it? Am I right?"

"Ask your father, he has it all worked out. Your future and mine."

"Why are you going back?"

"You tell me. You seem to have all the answers."

"You want a beer?" She went and got him one without waiting for his answer. She poured the beer carefully down the side of the glass so it wouldn't foam. She watched the glass fill up. "You're going back to kill yourself." It was a statement without emotion.

"That's stupid!"

"It's not something you're doing consciously."

"Are you nuts? What makes you say something like that?"

"Because you feel guilty that your friends died. You feel responsible. I read an article about it; it's called 'survivor's guilt'. Tell me I'm wrong."

"You're wrong."

She moved to sit close to him on the couch. "You're full of guilt over something that can't be changed, about something that

189

probably wasn't your fault. Do you want to feel guilty? Because if you do, then feel guilty about what you're doing to me. You'll be in Vietnam doing whatever it is you feel you have to do, but what about me? I'll be back here with the baby, waiting. What am I waiting for? Am I waiting for you to come home, or am I waiting to hear that you're dead?"

She reached out and gently turned his head so he was facing her. "I want you to understand what it's like for me, what this is doing to me. Do you think it's easy being left behind?"

"According to your father, it might be better for you if I were killed. You would have a better life."

"Don't listen to my father."

"I know it's not easy for you. We've talked about this before, and I know how you feel."

"I don't think you do. Do you know how I found out you were wounded the first year?"

"I wrote and told you."

"That's right, and if you didn't write, how would I have known anything was wrong? What will happen if, God forbid, something serious happens?" She couldn't even bring herself to say what she meant. "If you can't write, how will I know? How will I find out?"

"We're married; the Army will tell you. Can we please change the topic? I don't want to talk about this anymore."

"Well then, you'd better go home because this is what I'm gong to talk about. You complain no one wants to hear about Vietnam; but the minute I bring it up, you refuse to talk. Is that fair? You accuse me of not listening, but you never talk. When should we talk about this? You have three days left; that's not a lot of time."

"Three days? You keeping count?"

"Yes, as a matter of fact, I am. I have since you got home. The same as I will when you leave. I mark the days off the same as you. We have to talk now; there's no time left. You torture yourself with your memories. You've made Vietnam the best part of you and the worst part. You've got to let it go. Nothing you can do will change the past. Getting killed will not bring your friends back. Please, just let it go."

"It's not that easy. I wish it were. Tell me what to do."

She moved close to him and wrapped him in her arms. Her face was against his chest.

"You can come back to me. Promise you'll come back. Promise you'll come home."

"I promise. You'll see, everything will be alright."

It was easy to tell her what she wanted to hear and to make a promise while sitting in Brooklyn. It was not so easy to keep that promise in Vietnam, not after the carnage of the last few days.

He had cleaned and assembled his rifle without any conscious effort, his fingers working with a mind of their own. He took the cloth and absently rubbed down the black plastic hand guards. He noticed, as he did so, that they were stained a chalky gray color from the sweat of his hands.

He thought of Janet and wondered what to tell her. Would she want to hear he had faced his private demons and won? He'd tell her the outcome without the details. No need to tell her all the blood-and-guts stuff. She could live without that. He would tell the truth of what he had done and how it made him feel. Most of all, he would tell her he intended to keep his promise. He would come home to her.

Chapter 17

The Major's Big Plan

The next morning, the Major was ecstatic. "Hot damn! That is great news. Wonderful news! The men will be excited to be part of this. I really appreciate your confidence in the plan, and in me. Once we reach Ben Tre, I'll return to Cu Chi and we can finalize the details. Perhaps we can have dinner tonight. Wonderful, I'm looking forward to it. Once again, thanks for your approval."

"Who's the old man talking to?"

"Battalion Commander."

"Why is he so happy?"

"He's been working on some asshole plan. I guess the Colonel just gave the go-ahead."

"Anything he's developed is going to be bad news for us."

"Get the Company Commanders up here, on the double," the Major said to his RTOs.

"What about Delta Company, sir?"

"Have Lieutenant Wilkes join us for the time being."

While waiting for the officers to assemble, the Major spread out his map and traced a route to Ben Tre. His RTO handed him a second cup of coffee.

"Good news, sir?"

"You'll hear soon enough."

"Sir, they're all here."

The Major stood before the assembled group. "Gentlemen, at

ease. I have some good news. Since Tet, we have been chasing the NVA as they make their way back to their Cambodian sanctuaries. During this period, we have fought on their terms: hit-and-run skirmishes at the time and place of their choosing. That ends today. I have developed a plan to trap and eliminate the remaining elements of several depleted NVA battalions before they reach Cambodia. I have presented the plan to our Regiment Commander; and today, just now, I have received his full support to initiate the plan. We will proceed to Ben Tre and rest for three days while we resupply and receive replacements. We will then make a helicopter insertion about fourteen miles northwest into a valley used as a staging area by the 274th NVA battalion. We will engage this battalion and all others and destroy them.

"This will be an old-school infantry operation. We will use artillery and air support sparingly. I want to show the American public and the politicians that the North Vietnamese are no match for the American fighting man. We will provide the folks back home a clear and decisive victory. There will be no dispute as to who is capable of winning this war. The coverage of Tet has been shameful and cast doubt on the outcome of our involvement in Vietnam. At this moment, the media is all about Khe Sanh and the surrounded Marines. They are waiting for another failure. Our Marines will deny them that failure, of that I'm sure. We, in turn, will produce a victory so decisive as to eliminate all doubt of who will be victorious if provided the material and emotional support we require. We will reverse the perceived failure of Tet and invigorate the support of the public. The people back home are not tired of this war; they are tired of failure. Questions?"

"This all sounds good, sir. But the men are exhausted, both physically and mentally. Will three days' rest be enough?"

"You underestimate these boys. They're ready for a fight, and we'll give them one. They're exhausted from marginal victories. They see daily casualties with no clear purpose. They need this as much as we do. This will be 'mano a mano' and we will prevail. The country will be made aware of their victory. I have secured reporters and photographers who are anxious to accompany us on this operation. We'll have full coverage of every aspect of the mission from start to finish."

"When will 1ˢᵗ Battalion join us?"

"We will secure the valley as a base of operations. The 1ˢᵗ Battalion will arrive a day or two later. At that time, the major portion of the operation will commence. We will sweep through the valley south to north, engaging and eliminating all opposition. It's a straightforward objective: clear the valley and completely destroy the enemy down to the last man."

The Major surveyed the officers. "If there are no more questions, return to your companies and brief your lieutenants. They, in turn, will brief the squad leaders. You can brief them now or when we arrive at Ben Tre, your choice. Have your men saddle up and be ready to leave in one hour. I want to arrive at Ben Tre no later than 2 PM. I want everyone on board with this. Lieutenant Wilkes, if I may have a minute."

"Sir?"

"I don't know if I can make you Company CO. It depends on who is back at regiment. If there is a Captain available, then you'll have to wait. I have confidence in you, but we do have to follow protocol. I want you to brief the platoon leaders in the interim. Do I have your full support?"

"Always, sir."

"Good. Be on your way, then."

Holt returned to the fourth squad after the briefing by Lieutenant Wilkes.

"Start getting your shit together; we move out in thirty minutes. The Major has some new fucking plan and we're not going in. We'll rest up and resupply at Ben Tre; and after that, we get to chase down some NVA regiment before they get to Cambodia. Don't even think about bitching to me. It's orders, and we follow orders. Now pack up and get ready to move."

"We're not going back to Cu Chi?"

"Eugene, what part of 'pack up your shit' don't you understand?"

"We were supposed to get some rest, get our three days off."

"And we will, at Ben Tre. Then we go out and kill gooks, just like we always do."

"This is bullshit!" said Kelly. "The Major comes up with some wild-ass plan and that's it. No discussion?"

"I didn't realize you and the Major discussed military objectives. I have to be honest with you: I doubt if the Major gives a flying rat's ass about your opinion."

"It's just that..."

"Where the fuck is Fisk? I never see that guy. Is he still part of the squad?"

"He's off taking a shit."

"Well, I'm changing things around. Locke, you're now assistant gunner, and tell Fisk he's a rifleman now. I want him available for LPs and walking point."

"Sarge, I just got used to Fisk. I don't want Locke anywhere near me."

"Well, once again, Kelly, you're welcome to discuss your grievances with the Major. But until he tells me otherwise, just do as your told. Locke is your assistant. Have him switch gear with Fisk."

Locke started to say something, but Holt cut him short.

"Think carefully before you speak. I'm in no mood to listen to your whining. All of you, get your shit together. Kelly, go find Fisk, wipe his ass and get him back here."

"Yes sir, Sergeant."

"Kelly, you got anything to say to me, say it now."

"No. I got nothing."

Little Wilson was strapping smoke grenades to his radio. "Sarge, you seem a little pissed."

"I don't understand why everyone is bitching. We get three days rest and then another mission. It's what we always do. So we don't go back to Base Camp. What's the big fucking deal? Cu Chi is a cesspool, anyway. It stinks like piss and shit."

"I know, but it is the routine we always follow. No one likes to break routine. It's bad luck."

"Think of it this way. This is a interesting break in routine. We get to visit the exotic local people and sample their way of life. Then we get to go on a new adventure and meet more interesting people and kill them. What could be better?"

"When you put it that way, it sounds delightful."

"Gene, you are a ray of sunshine. You always have a positive attitude. Try and pass that off to these other morons."

They left for Ben Tre on time. Holt walked point and led the men on an uneventful march through the forest. Far to the north, storm clouds gathered over the mountains, an indication of the coming rainy season. But for now, the morning was cool and the forest shaded. There were several well-defined trails that led toward Ben Tre, an indication of its importance as a trading and supply hub. They tried to avoid the trails. As they neared the village, they passed over wide expanses of well-tended rice paddies, with farmers working the fields. The farmers appeared indifferent to the Americans. Only a small child atop a water buffalo welcomed them with a wave of his arm.

"A nice easy walk, and here we are."

They stood about four hundred meters outside the village. There was a large berm, about three feet wide, rising from the rice paddies which led to Ben Tre. Between two cement bunkers was a tall, elaborately carved teak gate welcoming you inside. Lounging on ether side of the gate were several ARVN soldiers. Holt caught their attention and waved one over.

"Let's see where this gook walks. I want to make sure the berm is clear."

"Here he comes, and he don't look concerned," said Little Wilson.

"He's a well-dressed little fuck. Tiger-striped fatigues and a big-assed forty-five hanging off his hip."

"I love his beret and the sunglasses."

"They all look like stick figures with rifles. They make us look fat."

As the soldier approached, his wide large smile revealed a row of gold teeth. "Welcome, welcome. No VC here, you relax. Have good time." Pointing to the path, he said, "No VC, no booby traps, all good here."

"You speak good English. Please, would you lead the way?"

"We all friends here, no VC," he said over his shoulder as he made his way toward the open gate.

"Oh, fuck me. This is too good to be true. Wait until the Lieutenant sees this. Get him on the phone."

"Lieutenant, you got to see this for yourself. They have a big banner stretched across the entrance. It says, 'Welcome, Wolfhounds'. I guess they knew we were coming."

As they waited for Wilkes, they admired the thick-walled cement bunkers.

"The whole place has a stone wall around it, running right up to the bunkers. Can you imagine the work it took to build that wall?"

"And the ground is smoothed out fifty feet in front and ringed with barbed wire. I bet there is a bunch of trip flares and Claymores placed out there."

"Here comes Wilkes. You know, he needs a beret like the gooks."

"How the hell did they know we were coming? We just found out this morning."

"Anytime we want to know something, we ask the Vietnamese.

Their sources are better than ours."

"Get your squad inside, take a left and follow the wall. Find a good place to stop and hang out until I find the Major. We need to get both companies inside and find out where to set up."

As they passed through the gates, they were immediately swarmed with children of all sizes and ages offering cold, bottled Cokes and fruit.

Holt called the ARVN who greeted them. "Tell these kids to back off until we're settled. Then they can sell all the shit they want. You have any idea how long we're staying?"

"Three days you be our guests. You sleep and rest. No VC here."

"You keep saying that. Hope you're right."

"You have good time. Many things to buy. You take showers and women clean clothes."

He leaned in and whispered, "Now you smell, you get clean and feel better. I be your friend and interpreter. Get you and your friends good deal on everything. No one will cheat you here. You the Sergeant, very good. What's your name, Sergeant?"

"I'm Holt, this is Gene."

"I'm Chinh. I also Sergeant. You call me for anything you want."

"How do you say Sergeant in Vietnamese?"

"Trung Si."

"You Trung Si, I'm Trung Si."

"Yes."

"Chinh, you can greet the others. We need to wait for our Major."

"Major is Thieu Ta in Vietnamese."

"That's good to know. See you later, Trung Si."

If the Major was concerned, he didn't show it. "I imagine the Colonel had to clear our arrival with the province chief. They had to pass on the information. I wish they had been more discreet, but you have to admit, the banner is a nice touch."

"You think the NVA know we're here?" asked Lieutenant Wilkes.

"I would imagine so, but I doubt they know where we're going."

"And this place is safe?"

"Safe as anywhere in Vietnam can be. Ben Tre is part of the rubber plantation. The French owners ensure the safety of the town and the plantation by paying the NVA to stay away. Half the people here work on the plantation. Can't have them getting shot or hauled off to some labor battalion. The NVA gets paid and they stay away."

"Maybe we should do that?"

"Well, we wouldn't have a war if we did that. Settle your men on the west and north side of the village. Charlie Company will take the south and east. Resupply and replacements are scheduled for this afternoon. I don't want the village overwhelmed with our guys. Work with the platoon leaders to set up a schedule so that all the men get equal time inside. I want half the men to maintain guard positions at all times. I'll be leaving for Division when the resupply arrives and will return tomorrow. Tell the men to stay alert, but to rest and enjoy themselves as best they can."

"Yes sir, stay alert, but relax."

"When you say it, Lieutenant, it sounds stupid. Get on with it."

Holt and the other squad leaders were briefed by Camp and Lieutenant Wilkes on the orders given by Major Grayson as to their behavior and conduct while at Ben Tre. When he returned to the squad, he saw they had settled in a fighting position prepared in the stone wall. It afforded them good fields of fire and concealment. The next position was a hundred meters to their right. The men were involved in an animated conversation.

"What are we discussing today, world peace or blow jobs?"

"Daredevil, Sergeant."

"What about Daredevil?"

"I say his whole back story is bullshit! This normal goober pushes a blind man out of the way of a truck. The truck is carrying radioactive waste and it splashes in his eyes. Next thing, we're supposed to believe he develops super-senses and goes on to become a superhero. First off, the radioactive shit would burn his face off. Second, where does he get this body from? He's jacked up like a weightlifter. How does that happen? He swings through the city on little ropes guided by his super-senses. That's just fucking nuts. How does he carry hundreds of feet of rope?"

"What about Spiderman? He does the same shit, and you think that could happen?"

"That's way fucking different. He was bitten by a radioactive spider and got all the spider's powers. And he swings on spiderwebs, not rope. That could happen."

"On what fucking planet could that happen? I got bit by a dog once. I didn't get the powers of a dog."

"Was the dog radioactive? No! So, no dog powers."

"What superpowers does a dog have?"

"He can lick his own dick."

"Hey, Sarge, if you could blow yourself, would that make you a fag?"

"Are we still talking about Daredevil, or what? You morons are making my head hurt. Please, just for once, talk about normal shit."

"When can we go into the village?"

"As soon as resupply comes in. Half you assholes go in and the other half stays on alert. You get one hour inside today. Look around the shops and get back here on time. Tomorrow, you'll get longer."

"They got any short-time girls in there?"

"Put it back in your pants, Kelly. I'm sure by tomorrow, they'll arrive by the truckload. Do not, and I repeat, do not fuck with the village girls. They are not whores. You'll get your ass in a world of hurt if you get busted in here. The Major wants us on our best behavior. Do I make myself clear?"

"Kelly, try sucking your own dick and you can save some money," said Big Wilson.

"When I get bit by a radioactive dog, then I'll try."

"One final thing. They had latrines dug for us. Use them. Don't go shitting anyplace you want."

Two of the massive Chinook helicopters circled the village. One landed and disgorged over forty replacements. They were hustled off the LZ to be greeted by a group of Sergeants. The second Chinook landed, and large pallets of supplies were pushed off the back. The pallets were set upon by the various squads and ripped apart in a frenzy reminiscent of Christmas morning. Two Lieutenants arrived and attempted to bring some semblance of order to the chaos. Eventually, the supplies were distributed in accordance of need.

The fourth squad was back at their position, breaking down boxes of ammunition, grenades and C-rations.

Holt returned from the CP, his arms stacked with various items. "I got three cartons of cigarettes, some comics and paperbacks. Here's a full box of John Wayne bars and a shitload of writing paper and envelopes. There's some razors and toothpaste and best of all, four bars of soap."

"What are we going to do with all those cigarettes?" asked Little Wilson.

"The cigarettes and chocolate are good for trade with the gooks. So are all the shit rations we don't like: the ham and lima beans and the scrambled eggs.

"Kelly, you, Locke and Big Wilson can go first. Just bring your forty-fives and some clips. Remember, best behavior. One hour and not a minute more."

"Don, do you think they'll have short-time girls tomorrow?" asked Little Wilson.

"Why you asking?"

"I was just thinking about it, that's all."

Holt looked around before speaking. "Gene, you're still a virgin, right? This ain't going to be the right time for you. Relax and wait until your R&R. Go someplace nice, like Singapore or Bangkok. Nice hotels; beautiful, clean girls who speak English. Good restaurants and bars. It'll be like you're dating them. They'll treat you right."

"But they're still whores?"

"Yeah, but it don't feel like it. They're nice girls who will show you the attractions and act as an interpreter. Guaranteed, you'll fall in love with them. And if you tell them you're a cherry boy, they'll fight to be with you. This place and these girls, this ain't for you. Trust me on this. Okay?"

"Sure, Sarge. I appreciate you looking out for me. This cherry-boy thing, the guys don't have to know."

"Between you and me. You got my word."

"Holy shit! Look who's coming."

"Nicky! What are you doing back?" Holt jumped up and wrapped Mercado in a bear hug.

"Jesus Christ, you guys stink. Get off of me."

"Give it a few days and you'll be back in full bloom. The unforgettable fragrance of the infantry grunt: thirty days without a shower."

"No, really man, you guys really smell bad."

"I revel in my stench. You, on the other hand, smell like a pampered, powdered REMF. Tell me you're not wearing cologne?"

"It's aftershave, asshole."

"New fatigues, new boots and smelling good. You fit right in with the FNGs."

"Most of them are going to Charlie Company. They are absolutely terrified. Charlie really got caught in a shitstorm. It was all over Base Camp."

"You were here. You know what happened. So tell me how was life in the rear, with the queers?"

"FUBAR."

"What's FUBAR?" said Little Wilson.

"Fucked Up Beyond All Recognition. First off, there's nothing to do. It is so fucking boring, and the days drag on. I got put with

Sergeant Grimes in supply, and I thought I had it dicked. All I did was sweep the floors and after lunch, I was on my own. How many times can you go the PX? I actually volunteered to wash the Jeeps for something to do. The EM Club is filled with REMFs, so I had nobody to talk to. I finally told Top I was ready to go back out."

"You were missed, brother. We all missed you."

"You'll be wanting your radio back."

"Who doesn't want to carry an extra twenty-six pounds? Sure, I'll take it back. Base Camp is all excited about the Major's big plan for world conquest."

"So much for being discreet."

"Here comes Kelly, right on time."

"You want to explore the village with us?"

"I'm going to hunt down some of my bros. Get the Latin Mafia back together. Tomorrow, for sure."

"Hey Nick, how's the arm?"

"Nice scar, it'll make for some good stories."

"Where's Fisk?"

"He wandered off to visit some friends."

"He has friends? I can't even tell when he's around. He's like a fucking ghost. Fuck him. Let's go and buy some shit, Gene."

As they entered the village, they were confronted with dozens of stands and kiosks selling everything imaginable.

"Where do we go first?"

"Right here. I want to get some Ho Chi Minh sandals to let my feet dry out, then let's find a cold beer."

They stopped at a bar made from two barrels topped with rough wooden planks and some stools.

"Mama San, what kind of beer you have?"

"Tomorrow, we have GI beer. Today, Ba Mui Ba or Biere Larue."

"What are you having? Beer 33 or Biere Larue, the beer of the streets?"

"Whatever you're having."

"Mama San, two ice-cold Tiger Beers. They call Biere Larue 'Tiger Beer' because it has a tiger's head on the label."

They both drank deeply from the large brown bottles.

"Goddamn, it's fucking ice-cold. It's good, right?"

"Is it safe to drink this stuff?"

"They drink it, so it must be alright. Mama San, is that noodle soup?"

"Best in Ben Tre, number one."

"Two, please."

"This is so good, spicy and hot enough to burn your tongue."

They finished their meal and walked down the main street. There were shops selling leather goods, wallets, watch wristbands and woven leather bracelets. Another had hammered metal work and custom Zippo lighters. One shop had duplicate NVA ammo vests.

"I want one of these," Holt said. "See, it's like a shirt front that ties in the back with pouches for eight magazines. How much?"

"Ten MPC."

Holt held up his hand with spread fingers. "Five, no more."

"No can do. For you, GI, I give you for seven MPC."

"Seven," Holt said, counting off the colored MPCs. He tried on several vests before finding one that fit comfortably. "Most of the real gook ones are too small to fit us."

"Get a pith helmet, and you'll look like an NVA."

"Time to head back. Tomorrow, we'll explore down the street and the other side."

Chapter 18

Showers and Shopping

"Trung Si Chinh, how are you this morning?"

"I am good, Trung Si Holt. Good news, showers are ready. You take shower while Mama San washes your clothes. Only five MPC. You follow me, one at a time. Get clean, smell good. You have soap?"

"Boys, rank has its privileges. I'm going first. Work it out among yourselves, the order you're going in. Lead the way, Trung Si."

The makeshift shower consisted of two wooden pallets pulled together with three plywood sides. A poncho was stretched across the front as a shower curtain.

"You get undressed and give me clothes," said the Mama San.

Holt undressed, and was surprised when she followed him into the shower stall.

"I wash you, while clothes get washed."

Holt handed her the soap and she lathered his back, scrubbing him with a rough cloth. She washed his hair while he cleaned his face. She used a small blue plastic bucket to rinse him. He turned so she could wash his front. She did his chest and sides, and squatted to wash his legs.

She saw his scars and said, "VC do this? VC number ten."

As she approached his crotch, she said, "I jerk you, five MPC."

"That's okay, Mama San, I'm good. You keep the soap."

"Thank you. Girl bring clothes. You send next."

The squad followed in a steady progression. Holt sat and waited for his clothes to dry. They were laid out on the stone wall. They looked surprisingly clean and smelled much better.

Holt saw Little Wilson return from the showers with a ear-to-ear smile on his face. "You enjoy the shower, Gene?"

"I feel so much better now."

"Did you get the complete shower experience?"

"Oh, you mean... Yeah, I did."

"Good for you."

A little girl came running up with Wilson's fatigues. He gave her a bar of chocolate. She grabbed it and ran off.

"Lay them on the wall. In this heat, they dry in about ten minutes."

"Look how weird we look. Our faces and arms are dark brown, and the rest is bone-white."

"An infantry tan."

"Back home, we'd call it a farmer's tan."

When the squad was showered and dressed, they agreed on a schedule to visit the village in two-hour increments. Holt, Little Wilson and Mercado would go in second. Camp and Pollack, now his RTO, came by to visit.

"Good news. While we're here, Charlie Company is doing all the night patrols. They have over thirty replacements and need to break them in. Couldn't find a safer place to train those guys."

"When's the Major coming back?"

"This afternoon. I guess then we'll get our briefing on the big plan."

"Is that what everyone is calling it?"

"I'm sure it will have some snappy name, something to inspire us and sound good in the news reports."

"How you making out as Platoon Sergeant?"

"It's mostly paper work. I have to keep a journal recording all the shit we do: who went on patrol and who did LPs, all the map coordinates and radio frequencies, all the boring shit the Lieutenant doesn't want to do. He also made me in charge of ordering the supplies. All that's left for him to do is hang around the Major, sniffing his butt."

"A task he's well-suited for. Do you know anything about this big plan?"

"The only thing I heard is that we are to be choppered north, into some valley. The valley is supposed to be crawling with NVA left over from Tet. We're supposed to run them down before they get to Cambodia."

"What if they're not running from us, but setting a trap for us?"

"Do you ever look on the bright side? Maybe they're worn out and just want to get away. Fuck, we just gave them a three-day head start. I wish them well, and hope they make it to Cambodia before we ever see them."

"A head start don't mean shit. We can jump ahead of them with one chopper ride."

"Hopefully, we'll go north and they'll go west and make it across the border."

"Maybe that's his big plan: we don't stop at the border and we chase them into Cambodia."

"That will never happen. The people back home will never let these fuckers expand the war. They want us out of Vietnam."

"Look at the map. Northeast is the Fil Hol rubber plantation. We ain't going there. The only place with a sizable valley is northwest. It looks perfect for the gooks to hole up and rest. It's got water and triple-canopy jungle. I bet they got a ton of supplies stashed there."

Camp studied the map. "You might be right. It's over a hundred miles from here. I doubt even the NVA could do that in three days. It would be about an hour's flight, and we could insert somewhere in here and cut them off from any base area they might have."

"It's the only valley large enough to warrant a battalion-sized operation. This has to be it."

"We'll know soon enough; the Major is due in this afternoon. Are you going into the village today?"

"Yeah, Eugene, Nick and me."

"Can you get me a new boonie hat and a Zippo? I lost my hat somewhere and my lighter took a shit. I can't go. Have to inventory the supplies and see what we need."

"Sure thing. See you later, 'gator."

"In a while, crocodile."

The village was even more festive than the day before. It was crowded with GIs buying everything in sight. They stopped for ice-cold beers and noodle soup before continuing down the street. Holt bought two new Zippo lighters emblazoned with the Wolfhound crest on one side and inscribed on the other with their names and dates of service. He got Camp a new camouflaged boonie hat. He bought himself a new plastic box that fit a pack of cigarettes perfectly to replace his old, cracked one. Mercado bought a deck of pornographic playing cards and a woven plastic hammock. On their way back to the squad position, they each bought a freshly baked small loaf of bread.

"Do you think I have time for another shower before chow?" asked Little Wilson.

"Sure, knock yourself out; it'll be your last for a month."

They watched Wilson make his way to the shower.

"Mama San is going to have arms like Popeye from jerking off all these guys."

"At five bucks a pop, she's going to be rich."

"I bet she has to kick half up to the village chief as an employment tax and something to Sergeant Chinh for steering us her way."

"Death and taxes. Everybody's got to pay; no one gets out alive."

"You're a wise man, Nick. Here comes the Major's chopper. We'll find out soon enough where we're going. Fun and games are over."

"I'm going over to the second squad. You okay here by yourself?"

"I enjoy my own company. Please give those assholes my best."

After being briefed by the Major, Camp briefed the squad leaders. He walked with Holt to the fourth squad. "You were right. Good guess."

"Wasn't a guess; it was my superior knowledge of tactics and strategy. I should be running this show."

"I'll mention it to Wilkes. He always values your opinion. What bothers me is if a mope like you could figure this out, won't the gooks know the same shit? What if they're ready for us?"

"That's what I said. Are you telling me I got the same brainpower as these gooks? Considering they are always one step ahead of us, I take that as a compliment. But any plan thought up by that dimwit is sure to end in a bloodbath for us. He's just looking for his next promotion and don't care how many of us get killed to get it."

"You know, he got reporters coming along: two of them and a photographer."

"Has to make himself famous. You wait and see; after the fighting is over, he'll crawl out of his bunker and have his picture taken with a bunch of dead gooks."

"You hold the officers in such high esteem. They're not all bad. I've met some pretty good ones."

"They can all suck my dick. Each and everyone of them."

"I was meaning to tell you, I like your new NVA vest. You sure you can carry extra ammo? Eight more mags means eight extra pounds."

"Seven mags and a pocket for my cigarettes and lighter. Listen up, old man. Don't you worry about how much I can carry. I can walk you into the ground."

As the squad drifted back, Kelly said, "What are you ladies bitching about now?"

"Grandpa here says he can carry more weight than I can. I can out-hump you any day of the week. I'll walk you into your grave. Now that you're Platoon Sergeant, I'm surprised you still carry your own ruck."

"I was fighting gooks when you still had mother's milk on your breath."

"Milk? From my mother? I doubt if my mother had anything but alcohol running through her veins."

"Well, with that rather dark revelation, get yourself cleaned up. Yokes came out and is cooking up some steaks."

"Eugene, you good, or do you need another shower?"

Little Wilson blushed red.

They sat and quietly ate their dinner. At the back of the serving line stood several children and young girls. When all the GIs had been fed, Sergeant Yokes made a point of wrapping the leftovers in foil and handed it to the children.

"Yokes is a decent guy. Most of these scumbags would have thrown the leftovers in the garbage and made the kids fight over them," Holt said.

"That meat he gave them is probably more meat than they eat in a month," Camp said.

Kelly asked, "Who are those guys hanging with the Major?"

"The guy in civilian clothes is some sort of CIA spook. The dude in the tan pants is the Frenchie who owns the plantation. And that little gook with all the medals is the province chief. They're all here to congratulate themselves on what a success our visit was. See them three civilians in the back? Those are the reporters coming out with us to make us famous."

"The Major is calling that one guy over. I knew it. He wants his picture taken. What a fucking whore."

"That guy is a reporter from the New York Daily News. You know him?"

"Camp, you are such an embarrassing hayseed. There are over

eight million people in New York City. But, yeah, I do know him. He came by the hospital when I was wounded and asked for New York guys. We talked and he wrote a story about me, how I was the ultimate jungle-fighting hero. It was actually in the papers. Hey, Nick, round up all your New York spic buddies and I'll make sure I steer him your way. I can see it now: the brave Puerto Rican freedom fighters, here to free the Vietnamese from their cruel Communist masters."

"That would be cool."

"Who's that Puerto Rican-Irish guy in the second squad? He'd be perfect. The fighting Mick Spic or Spic Mick, whatever sounds better. The story writes itself. He needs a better name. Something like Jesus O'Brien."

"I'm sure he'd want to use his real name. But I'll ask."

"Watch this. I'll go burst the Major's bubble."

Holt walked to the group surrounding the Major. "Mr. Freed, is that you?"

"Yes it is, and you are? Don't tell me... Donald Hall."

"Holt, sir. Don Holt. We met in the hospital."

"Yes, I remember. What are you still doing here?"

"I could ask you the same thing."

Major Grayson interrupted, "You know this soldier?"

"I sure do. Wrote an article about him when I visited the hospital at Cu Chi last year. In fact, I did a series of columns about boys from New York fighting in Vietnam. I'd like to do the same this time. Are there many boys from the city here?"

"I'd have to check the roster and get back to you."

"There's a bunch; at least six in Delta Company alone," Holt said.

"Well, I'll be kept busy."

"Sergeant, if you will excuse us, we have to go over the upcoming mission."

"Sure thing, Major. Nice to see you again, Mr. Freed."

The reporter said to the Major, "As I recall, he was wounded twice and was awarded some medals. A good soldier, well-liked. You must be glad to have him."

"I would hope you'll cover the entire scope of this operation."

"The Daily News is a big-circulation local paper. Stories like his, about local boys, sell papers. But, yes, the entire operation will be covered. With emphasis on the local boys," he added quickly.

"Nicky, tell your Latin brothers they'll be famous. He wants to meet them."

"What did you say to the Major? He looked like he wanted to kill you."

"I just let him know there were a lot of city kids here. That's what he likes. He likes to write about regular blue-collar kids, not officers. I guess the Major doesn't like to share."

"If he had a gun, I think he would have shot you."

Chapter 19

Bible Study

Holt saw Mr. Freed approach them. Mercado started to get up to leave. "Stay, Nicky. I want to introduce you to Mr. Freed."

As the reporter got closer, Holt said, "What's kicking, chicken?"

"Not much, just walking around and trying to introduce myself."

"The proper response to that greeting is 'You babe'. Here, I'll show you. Nick, what's kicking chicken?"

"You babe."

"See, it's a universal greeting. Very common in 'Nam. Try it out and you'll fit right in. As a matter of fact, try it on Major Grayson. He's a cool cat, hip to all the jive."

"That doesn't sound believable, even coming out of your mouth. Sounds like something from the forties. I believe I'll pass on using that phrase. I'm curious; what are you doing back here?"

"Long story short: couldn't stand the Stateside Army. Spit-shined boots, pressed fatigues, and saluting second lieutenants too young to shave."

"That's reason enough to come back?"

"Had twelve months to do, This is as good of a place as any. Maybe I can do some good here. Keep some of these rookies alive."

"I'm sure there's more to it than that."

"We'll have plenty of time to talk. I hear you're staying out with us the whole operation, all thirty days? You must be crazy. No offense, but you're not a young guy. This place will kick your ass and then some."

"How old do you think I am?"

"You got to be mid-forties, somewhere around that."

"I'm thirty-seven. I still have some life left in me. I'll keep up."

"Thirty-seven, huh? Anyway, why are you still here?"

"I live here; never left. Been here three years now. This will be the first time I'm going out for a full month. After this op, I'm going to try and start a book. Got a lot of stuff written I've never published."

"So you were here for Tet?"

"Yeah. And you?"

"Yes, I was. That was a real fucking horror show. Am I right?"

"I thought the reporting was pretty biased against the military. I tried to do better, but all my stuff ended up on page six. I swear, I actually believe the North Vietnamese had their own publicist, the way the news was reported. You guys kicked ass everywhere you met them. You decimated the Viet Cong. They're gone as a fighting force. The NVA let them do all their dirty work and they paid in blood. I made my way up to Hue and spent some time at Khe Sanh. The Marines there are really going through some major shit. Surrounded by forty-thousand NVA and getting shelled every day, a thousand rounds a day on some days. You can't even imagine what it's like 'til you have gone through it. Constant, unrelenting explosions. Nowhere is safe. They are some tough SOBs. I was happy to leave."

"What about Hue?"

"It was the most beautiful city I've ever seen, reduced to rubble. Like something out of World War II. The Marines are smart. They have hundreds of reporters working with them. Some extraordinary reporting and photographs coming from them."

Mercado had busied himself making coffee and now handed a cup to each of them.

Mr. Freed held out a dull, worn aluminum flask. "Let's Irish that up."

"I like the way you think." Holt poured a generous measure into his cup and passed the flask to Nick. "Is that a First Cav emblem on that?"

"This is mine from the Korean War. I was a war correspondent with them."

"So you have seen some shit. I've just developed a newfound respect for you, Mr. Freed."

"Please, call me Joe."

"Joe when we're alone and Mr. Freed when the officers are around. Deal?"

"Sounds good."

"Speaking of officers, how did you detach their noses from your ass and break loose?"

"It wasn't easy. All the Lieutenants have their own story of blood and guts, and want to tell me about them. Grayson wants to describe his operation in detail and how it's going to end the war. The operation is called 'Adler Falls', whatever that means."

"Sounds like a town in Vermont. I think they just string two names together. Maybe the Major is from there, or the Colonel. Maybe its just phonetically easy to say. You ever notice how most firebases have girls' names?"

"I think the commanding officer chooses the name. Maybe after his wife or daughter. Although I can't believe naming some shithole in Vietnam after your wife is a fitting tribute. Speaking of which, I heard you're married? When did that happen?"

"Joe, come on, we're just getting reacquainted. For now, you can feel me up a little. But we have to know each other better before you put your hand under my skirt."

"I like your use of metaphor. We got time; we got a whole month."

"What else did the Major say? Any details?"

"I did ask him about projected casualties, and he became a little vague. I had to remind him I was to be given full access to everything I wanted to know and do. He finally said casualties were anticipated to be less than twenty percent."

"We can figure that out. You a got a notebook or something? Write this down. The whole regiment is supposed to be involved. Right now, we're really under strength. A platoon has maybe thirty-four or thirty-six guys in it. Four platoons to a company and a headquarters and weapons element, so that's about...?"

"Rounded off, about one hundred and fifty."

"Four companies to a battalion..."

"Seven hundred and fifty."

"Two battalions to the regiment."

"Fifteen hundred guys, give or take. A casualty rate of twenty percent is three hundred guys."

"Three hundred men killed or wounded, and that's acceptable to him and the higher-ups?"

"Folks back home are going to go apeshit."

"According to Stars and Stripes, we're averaging somewhere around four hundred killed a week. They say 1968 is going to be the worst year ever. He's not saying three hundred killed; he's saying three hundred killed and wounded. I guess according to his calculations, that isn't so bad."

"How do you feel about it?"

"I try and not to think about that shit. I don't think you should be discussing this with the guys. Nothing specific like we just did. Save it for the officers. To them, we're just numbers in their body-count ratio."

"Sure. Who's this coming?"

"That is Chaplain Doody."

"Doody, like the clown?"

"He pronounces it 'Dooday'."

"Fucking Canadians. But he's American?"

"Claims to be."

"What's up, Padre? Did you meet Mr. Freed, the reporter?"

"Yes, briefly at the CP. I was hoping we could talk."

"Perhaps later. I should be on my way."

"Nicky, why don't you take Mr. Freed and introduce him to the other guys from New York? Start with the city guys, and save the upstate assholes for later."

"Mr. Freed, this is our Platoon Sergeant coming up. Camp, come over here and meet Mr. Freed."

"A pleasure, Sergeant. If you have time later, perhaps I can ask you some questions."

"I'll be at the CP later."

"Away from the officers, if you don't mind. You can show me the village. How would that be?"

"Whatever I can do to assist you."

They watched as Mercado led the reporter to the third squad.

"I understand you know him from your first tour?"

"Yeah. He wrote a small story about me. About getting wounded and stuff like that."

"He seems to favor the enlisted men."

"He's a man of the people, in the tradition of Jimmy Breslin, a famous New York reporter. A salt-of-the-earth type of guy. So what brings you to my humble dwelling?"

The chaplain looked uncomfortable.

"Feel free to speak. Me and Camp don't have secrets."

"The Major wanted to make sure you're doing okay after the... incident."

"Right as rain, Padre. Not a care in the world. And you?"

"It's just that you've been through a lot."

"1 Samuel 15:3: 'This is what the Lord says: Utterly destroy all they have, do not spare them, kill both man and women, infant and suckling.' So according to the Bible, I'm doing okay. Maybe I'm slacking off; I just killed the one guy. No women or kids."

"You know the Bible?"

"No, I'm just fucking with you. There was an article in Playboy about all the batshit-crazy stuff that's in the Bible. I ripped it out and saved it. This way, we can have intelligent conversations when you drop by."

"You memorized them?"

"Just the one. I was hoping you'd stop by before I forgot it. I'll pick out another passage for next time. There's some really weird shit in there. I'd like to get your opinion on them."

"I look forward to that."

"There is one thing you can help with me with. You know I'm married."

"Yes, I know."

"Well, here's the problem. My wife's pregnant."

"That, I didn't know. Congratulations."

"Yeah, but the problem is... This is just between you and me and Camp here. Right? You can't tell anyone?"

"I would never disclose our conversation, under any circumstance."

"Good. So me and her, we never did it. We never consum... I can't think of the word."

"Consummated?"

"Yeah, that's it. We never consummated our marriage."

"But she's pregnant?"

"Now you see the problem. So I'm thinking, maybe this could be one of those immaculate-birth things. Like Jesus."

"Are you sure you never had relations?"

"Camp, did I ever fuck my wife?"

"No sir. You did not."

"How would Sergeant Camp know?"

"We discuss everything. I value his opinion. So how about it? An immaculate birth, or do you think my wife is lying to me and is really a raging whore, slut?"

"I really don't know what to say. Is your wife Catholic?"

"No, we're both Episcopalians. It's just like being Catholic, right?"

"There are subtle differences. Perhaps I should discuss this with the Episcopal Chaplain before commenting. I'll see if I can arrange it so that he visits with you to clarify this."

"Let's not waste time; she getting ready to pop. I should know before it happens. Could this be the 'second coming of Christ' thing? That's in the Bible, too."

"I would have to do more research."

"Good talk, Padre. Next time, we can discuss the Bible in more detail. There's a passage in Deuteronomy about eating the flesh of those you kill. I'd like to discuss that. I don't think I'd like that, but I do want to get your thoughts on cannibalism before I decide."

"Why do you fuck with him all the time? He's a nice guy; he just wants to help us if we got problems."

"My problem is there are people out there who want to kill us every day. That, and diarrhea. He doesn't seem to be able to help with either one."

"Do me a favor and leave him alone. Okay?"

"Alright, I promise. You can tell him I was just fucking with him about all that stuff."

"Let's wait a bit. I want to see if he does try and come back with an answer. Is cannibalism really in the Bible?"

"According to Playboy, and I can't see them lying to us."

"As much as I enjoyed this whole conversation, I came by for a reason. We're getting a detailed briefing and they have new maps for us. Get somebody to watch this position and make your way to the CP."

The four squad leaders, Lieutenant Wilkes, Major Grayson, the chaplain and Camp were all crowded in a small clearing designated as the company command post.

"Men, we'll keep this brief," said Wilkes. "Tomorrow, choppers will arrive at 0700. We'll load up and proceed about fifty miles north. There is a clearing large enough for about four choppers to land. Delta Company is going in first. Major Grayson has given fourth platoon the privilege of clearing the LZ. Fourth platoon will insert first, followed in order by the rest of Delta. Tonight, check your gear. Carry as much water, rations and ammo as you can. Cobras will scout the area prior to our insertion. To the left of the LZ are open, rocky fields, not suitable for landing. To the right is a stand of trees. Once on the ground, we go through those trees and turn north and travel up a dry riverbed. The riverbed is the beginning of the valley we are to clear. These are the new maps of our area of operation. Turn in your old maps to Sergeant Camp. Major, do you have anything to add?"

"Delta Company will lead this operation, followed by Charlie. We need to allow their new men time to acclimate to the weather and the terrain. At some point, we'll be joined by Alpha and Bravo companies. There's a full regiment of NVA in this valley. We'll pursue them, engage them and destroy them. Every last man. They will not escape. This operation will be documented by the reporters who will accompany us. We will provide the American people with a clear, decisive victory that will leave no doubt of who is the superior fighting force in Vietnam. Any questions? Good. Get a good night's sleep and be ready to kick ass tomorrow."

In addition to new maps, Camp distributed small bundles of mail to each of the squad leaders.

"That was certainly informative. Get on the choppers, head north, land and kill gooks. How come fourth platoon is leading?"

"Wilkes volunteered the fourth. He wants to lead this operation. He thinks Grayson will make him Company Commander if he does a good job."

"I can only speak for myself, but you can tell the Lieutenant I will happily endanger my life to ensure his promotion."

"Hand out the mail and we'll grab a beer before chow. The village is open until four."

The squad was gathered, sorting their gear and packing their rucks. Holt briefed the men as he handed out mail. There was a letter from Janet, which he sliced open. The letter was brief, barely a page, but there were two recent pictures of her.

"Jesus Christ, she's getting huge," he said.

"Let me see," Camp said.

"Look at the fucking jugs on her; she must be a D-cup. I thought you said she was skinny."

"Camp! Please, that's my wife you're talking about. And I never said she was skinny. I said she was slender. There's a difference."

"She's got some rack."

"Let me see," said Kelly, grabbing the photos from Camp. "Can I borrow these for a minute?" he said.

"Sure. I'm certain she would like knowing I lent her pictures out so you could crawl off into the bushes and jerk off. If you want some nude photos, I got some of your mother."

"Where would you get photos of my mom?"

"She working the strip clubs outside of Fort Benning."

"That's bullshit. My mother doesn't dance, and she's never been outside of Boston."

"It looked just like her."

Kelly handed the pictures back to Holt. "With tits like that, you just know her nipples must be fucking gigantic."

Holt sighed. "Let's end all this conversation regarding my wife's breasts. I'll pass on your compliments; I'm sure she'll be very pleased. For now, get your shit together. Extra water, ammo and Cs. Load yourselves up; I'm afraid we are going to need it. The Major says once we're in that valley, we ain't leaving until every gook is dead."

Chapter 20

The Rock River

On the morning of their departure, Holt was busy frying up two thick slices of Spam in his mess-kit frying pan. He added a can of C-ration scrambled eggs and mashed them into the grease from the Spam. He covered both with Louisiana Hot Sauce and stirred. The final addition to his breakfast was a can of white bread toasted over the C-4 explosive. He settled back to enjoy his meal as Little Wilson approached.

"What's kicking, chicken?"

No response.

"Why so glum, chum?"

"I need to ask a favor."

"Must be important. Ask away."

"You're in a good mood today."

"I got clean clothes. I got my hair cut and showered. I'm prepared to eat a good meal. I'm locked and loaded, and awaiting a new adventure. What's not to like? What's your favor?"

"I got a letter I want you to carry and mail if..."

"Stop right there. I ain't carrying any death letter for you. Put it back in your pocket."

"C'mon Sarge, please."

"Not doing it, so don't ask."

"Why?"

"Don't be a maudlin little prick. You're jinxing yourself, writing some bullshit death letter. I'll tell you what. Tonight, when we stop, you write a proper letter, to your aunt, I assume. You tell her everything you said in this letter while you're still alive. Don't wait until you're dead to tell her what's important to you. You tell her now. Everything you want her to know, tell her now. You love her and want to thank her for taking you in after your parents died, tell her now. Don't make her wait until you're dead. You do that and you still want me to carry your letter, I will, but not before you write her tonight."

"But everyone has a letter to be mailed in case something happens."

"Yeah, I know, and I would tell them the same thing. You guys are being all fucking dramatic assholes. World War Two bullshit. The only person I write to is Janet, and if she doesn't know how I feel about her by now, then no bullshit death letter is going to change things. You do as I tell you. Now, get the fuck away from me and let me eat my breakfast in peace. You need something to do, check and make sure everyone's canteens are full. Get your gear squared away and be ready to move out."

Mercado walked over to Holt and said, "Choppers are thirty minutes out. Wilson looks bummed out. I know he asked you to carry his letter. You didn't have to shut him down; it was important to him."

"Mind your own fucking business, Nick. And Wilson can kiss my ass. Go ruck up, I'll be there in a minute."

"Fucking morons," he said to himself as he shouldered his rucksack and walked to the squad. "Saddle up. The landing zone is out in the field. We need to hustle. And smile. Today, we embark on a glorious mission to defeat the enemy in one decisive battle that will change the course of the war. Those are the words right out of Grayson's mouth. We will do everything we can to ensure the success of this mission, and to ensure the Major gets promoted. His promotion is more important than your life, remember that. Now that I gave that little speech, you forget all that shit. You do exactly what I tell you to do. No one is risking their life for that cheese dick. We do what we have to, and no more. We all go home; no one gets left behind. Head out to the LZ."

As the men filed past, Holt put a hand on Wilson's shoulder. "Give me your fucking letter. I'll return it tonight."

"Thanks, Don."

"Fuck you."

"We're in the first insertion. Same position as when we came out. When we're ready to land, you un-ass that chopper as fast as possible. You run ten feet and hit the ground. You get up when I get up and do what I do. Do not fuck around. Get off the ship and hit the ground. Any questions?"

Locke raised his hand.

"I wasn't serious about questions. What don't you understand? Get off the fucking ship and hit the ground!"

The helicopters landed in the usual downdraft of dirt and debris. Holt sat with his legs out the open door. The door gunner, looking like a giant insect in his helmet, grinned and gave him a thumbs-up. Holt nodded in return. The ship nosed over and slowly began to rise in the air.

The trip to the new landing zone passed quickly. Holt sat mesmerized by the rolling carpet of jungle passing underneath them. It wasn't until the door gunner tapped his helmet that Holt became aware of the passage of time. The gunner pointed forward and down. Holt strained to see the open field coming up beneath them. As the first ships approached the LZ, Holt could clearly see green tracers erupt from the woods.

He leaned toward the gunner and shouted, "Tell the pilot not to land in front of those trees. Land ahead of the trees. Tell him to land short."

The gunner spoke into his microphone, turned to Holt, shook his head and shrugged.

"Fuck!" Holt shouted at the squad. "The LZ is hot. Get out as quickly as you can."

"Can't hear you. What did you say?" asked Mercado.

"Hot LZ! Gooks in the trees. Pass it on."

The green tracers crossed with the orange tracers from the door gunners' M60 machine guns, forming a deadly web of bullets.

Their ship approached the ground much faster than normal and flared hard, throwing the men against each other. Holt jumped from the ship while it was still several feet off the ground, and hit the ground hard. He stumbled forward and fell behind a small mound of dirt. Nick followed and fell on him, and rolled to the side. They both fired their guns into the trees.

They heard bullets strike the helicopter behind them. Holt saw the door gunner slumped over his machine gun, his ceramic armor plate hanging from his chest armor. Bullets raked the chopper from the rear forward, shattering the plexiglass door glass and windscreen surrounding the pilot. The chopper veered violently up and to the left before gaining level flight. Men tumbled from the open door. Bullets filled the air above their heads, forcing them to claw at the earth, seeking cover.

The two Cobra gunships came from behind them in line and tore the trees with their mini-guns, firing a seemingly continuous stream of tracers. They raked the length of the wood line with bullets and, at the end, turned in a tight circle for another approach. The small observation Loach chopper bravely came to ground level and fired several rockets into a concealed bunker, sending logs exploding outward. The Cobras followed with more rockets, killing all that remained.

"We need to mark our position with smoke," yelled Mercado.

Soon, the air was filled with brightly colored yellow smoke. The Cobras made one final pass, expending their remaining munitions.

"Two jets are coming in."

"Everybody, get down. Jets are coming."

Two swept-wing fighter bombers flew in line, dropping two hundred and fifty-pound bombs into the trees. They came around for a second pass, firing their forty-millimeter cannons, filling the air with splintered branches. They were gone, and it was silent.

"The Lieutenant wants us to move forward into the trees."

Holt turned to give the orders and counted only three men. "Who's missing? Sound off."

Kelly shouted from ten feet away. "Fisk and Big Wilson didn't make it off the chopper. They were thrown back inside when it flared up."

"What are we supposed to do with five guys? Kelly, take Locke, set up your gun and cover us. Eugene, come with me. Mercado, stay behind us."

They sprinted to the edge of the trees. There were sporadic firefights as they entered the woods.

"I can't see shit. Nothing but dust and smoke. Up ahead should be that bunker with the machine gun."

"I see it up ahead, about thirty feet," said Wilson.

The bunker was destroyed, logs all askew, with black smoke drifting from the ruins. As they approached, they saw one lone soldier crawling from the ruins. Nick shot him in the head. There were four more bodies in the bunker, and they all fired into them.

"Those Cobras lit these fuckers up. Look at that guy, almost cut in half," said Nick.

"This guy only has his lower jaw left. The rest of his head is gone. Where are his arms?"

"Eugene, what are you, a fucking medic going to patch them up? I think these assholes are beyond repair. I count five."

"We can make it seven if we count parts."

"Nick, call in five. No, go ahead and make it seven and see what's up."

After several minutes, Nick said, "Nobody killed. Can you believe it, no one killed? A bunch with scrapes, cuts and bruises, but no one dead. They're all good to go. Walking wounded. Holy shit, I can't believe it."

"God bless the Cobras and those jet assholes. And that little fucker in the Loach, he must have enormous brass balls. Hovered right at ground level marking the bunkers. They saved our asses."

"Quiet; there's more coming in. Three of the choppers are shot to shit. The gunner in our ship was shot up pretty bad, but he'll live. Our pilot was killed, shot through the throat. Wait, repeat that. Are you sure? You're certain?"

"What is it?"

"Fisk is dead. Took two fifty-caliber rounds through his chest. Blew a hole in him you could see through. Bullets went through him and hit Big Wilson. That's why they never left the ship. Tore up Wilson's arm and shoulder. He might lose the arm."

"I keep forgetting Fisk was even with us."

"Will Rich be okay?"

"Who's Rich?"

"Big Wilson. His name is Richard."

"Sorry, Gene. I know you two are close. I forgot his name is Richard. Think I would have remembered that."

"He's on his way back to Cu Chi, at the 25th Evac. They'll patch him up; I'm sure he'll be fine."

"We've been together for so long. He's Big Wilson and I'm Little Wilson. We're brothers. He's gotta be okay."

"I guess we can just call you Wilson from now on."

"I hope he's alright."

"Nick, what are they saying? What are we to do?"

"The second lift is delayed. We are supposed to search the bodies, gather up their weapons and wait."

"I ain't moving these bodies all around. It's like sorting through a butcher shop. It's nothing but guts and shit."

"Sarge, you got blood on your shirt. Are you bleeding?"

"Where?"

"On your side, above your hip. You're all bloody."

Holt lifted his shirt. "Fuck me. It's a Nicky wound."

"Mine was bigger. But you're still gonna need a couple of stitches. You're not going in, are you?"

"No. Doc won't send me in for this. It's just a deep cut."

"You must have been clipped by an AK round or something."

"Gene, what have you got there?"

"It looks like a diary."

"Good. Run that up to the Lieutenant and while you're there, tell Mad Dog to come see me. And be quiet about it." Holt kicked at the bodies.

"Leave this shit alone. I'm not digging through guts for no reason."

Locke sat on a log with his head between his knees.

"You okay?"

"No, Sarge, I'm not. I can't take this anymore. I'm no good out here. I can't sleep and I got the runs. I'm so nervous, I keep shaking all the time."

"Well, fuck. I haven't had a solid shit in sixty days. Your being nervous is no reason to send you in. We're all nervous."

"It's just that death is so sudden out here. Fisk was alive, and then he's dead. We could all be dead ten minutes from now. We could have been shot up on that helicopter."

"I don't want to speak ill of the dead, but Fisk was a ghost when he was alive. He barely registered as a member of this squad. I'm assuming he had a first name, but I'll be damned if I know it. I really don't know anything about him."

"You keep saying we're just numbers to the Major, but that's exactly how you treat us new guys."

"You may have something there. But I can emphatically say that you are the biggest pain in the ass I've recently encountered. You ain't going in, so suck it up, buttercup. You're here for the duration. Get yourself wounded or killed, and I'll load you on the chopper myself and smile while I'm doing it. But until that time, tighten your shit and soldier on."

"Don, here comes Mad Dog."

Without preamble, Mad Dog said, "Show me your boo-boo."

Don lifted his shirt.

"Three stitches. Take off your shirt and sit down over here."

"Wow! What are you doing? It burns like hell."

"Antiseptic. You need something to bite on; this is going to sting."

"Could you wash your fucking hands first?"

"I never realized you were such a delicate little faggot. Shut up and don't move."

Holt looked down at his side while Doc stitched him up.

"That's gonna leave a big fucking scar. Christ, you're a butcher. It's a fucking shame. I was beautiful when I came over here. I had skin like a baby's."

"And now you're pieced together like Frankenstein's monster. You bitch like this when they did your legs?"

"I was flying high. Morphine! It's a hell of a drug."

"Change this bandage in a day. Sooner, if you get it wet. Try and keep it clean. I'll give you a shot of penicillin."

"I'll change it after my bath tonight."

Mad Dog pulled out a journal and wrote a notation. "This is good for a Purple Heart. We got five other walking, lightly wounded. Get another and they'll take you off the line."

"While you're here, Locke's got the shakes. Can you give him anything?"

"Nothing that will let him function. He's not suited for this shit. He's gonna crack. You should keep an eye on him."

"Next time we're in a firefight, I'll shoot him in the leg."

"You serious?"

"I felt like shooting him every day since I met him."

The second lift of helicopters offloaded more troops, and the order was given to move out.

"Are we still walking point?" asked Mercado.

"Until we're told different. There's about a klick of jungle ahead, and it opens up onto the dry riverbed. We turn north and keep walking. We follow the riverbed until it ends. Couldn't be easier."

"Anybody figure that the gooks know exactly where we're going? They could have ambushes all up and down the river."

"Nicky, we're just the little worm dangling off the hook. We're here to find gooks and kill them. Hopefully, the Major has artillery dialed in and air support on call."

"What if he's serious about all this man-to-man fighting?"

"That's what your bayonet is for." Holt turned to the squad. "Nick, you follow me, then Kelly and Locke. Gene, you pull drag. Let's go, boys. Glory awaits."

"This is pleasant. Like a walk in the park, if the park was filled with violent fucking animals waiting to kill you."

Nick was studying the map. "The river should be just ahead. You should go ahead and scope it out."

"I appreciate your concern for my well-being. How about we all go together? Tell them jerkoffs to spread out and keep a decent interval. It looks like it clears out about fifty yards ahead."

They stood inside the trees, surveying the area that lay ahead. The river was dry, filled with tumbled rocks of all sizes. It was wide, a quarter-mile across with an open expanse to the trees on the other side.

"Call Wilkes and see how we're doing this. Are we crossing to the other side or what?"

"He says to wait. He's coming up here."

Holt lit a cigarette and passed the pack to Mercado. They smoked in silence until the Lieutenant arrived.

"What do we have?" he said.

"The river or former river. It goes pretty much straight north. Look south, it's all open sandy field. The rocks stop right here. It's just pebbles and sand behind us."

Wilkes studied the southern expanse with his binoculars.

"Where's the Major?"

"Back with Charlie Company."

"You think he should see this?"

"He said he flew the whole length of it, from the sandy shit south of here all the way to where the jungle closes in about five or six miles north."

"Don't step out too far, but look north. See ahead of us, there are cliffs on both sides. Back a few thousand years ago, this must have had water in it a hundred feet deep. Once we hit those cliffs, we're going to be boxed in. This ain't a dry riverbed; it's a dry canyon. We'll be committed to going north, no turning around."

"What's your point?"

"I guarantee the gooks know where we're going. Going north is not the problem. They are up there, and that's what we're here for. But what if they fall in behind us? Then we're trapped. Gooks north and south of us, with the cliff walls boxing us in."

"The Major said it was clear south of us."

"Oh, then I guess it's okay."

"Let me get on the horn and let him know what we've found."

Holt gave the Lieutenant some space and walked over to Mercado. They each lit cigarettes. When Nick asked him about the plan, Holt shrugged.

After several moments, Wilkes waved him over. "The Major wants us to proceed north. Take your squad and stay on the edge of the trees. I'll put a squad in the woods to protect our flank. Once we're deployed, he'll bring Charlie up and they will cross over to the other side. Then both companies will continue north. He wants us into the jungle by nightfall."

"That's about eight or nine klicks. Shouldn't be a problem."

"You seem a bit apprehensive, Sergeant."

"I'm always nervous in the service. My guess is they'll let us commit ourselves more than halfway before they hit us."

"If they do, we'll engage and kill them. This whole operation is based on us being aggressive and denying them any sanctuary."

"'A curse on him who keeps his sword from bloodshed.'"

"Sounds like the Bible. The chaplain said you were reading the Bible."

"Jeremiah 48:10. It's from Playboy. I assume they got it from the Bible. They could have made it up."

"Read the real Bible, Sergeant. It will help dispel those nerves. I'll have the chaplain get you a copy. For now, move your men out. I'll tell you when to stop."

"If you speak to the chaplain, ask him if he found anything on the Second Coming."

"What?"

"He'll know what I mean."

They moved north for a half-mile and were told to halt while Charlie Company crossed the river to the eastern side. They skirted the trees as told, all the while keeping an eye on the interior of the wood line.

"You ever feel like you're being watched?" said Mercado.

"Third squad is supposed to be in there, protecting our flank. Maybe it's them you feel."

"It's so quiet. No birds, no animals, nothing."

"I've said it before: in this jungle, we're the animals. The birds and shit know to stay clear of us."

Nick nodded. "There goes Charlie, crossing over. Doesn't seem like a good idea splitting us up."

"Wilkes assured me the Major has thought of everything."

"That's good. I feel better now. With the Major planning this whole thing, what could go wrong?"

"Not a thing."

Nick pressed the radio handset to his ear. "The Lieutenant says let Charlie come even with us and then move out."

"Pass the word back. Keep five-yard intervals. Make sure Kelly is locked and loaded."

After more than an hour, they had barely covered a mile. Walking was extremely difficult. They stumbled over stones and rocks the size of softballs. Care had to be taken not to twist or sprain ankles under the heavy weight of their packs. It was twelve-thirty when the stopped for lunch. They sat in the shade in sweat-soaked fatigues.

"Christ. My thighs are burning. It feels like we're walking on marbles," said Holt.

"This is ankle-breaking country," echoed Mercado.

Wilson drank deeply from his canteen.

"I'm so tired, I don't even feel like eating."

"Eat some fruit. You have any peaches or pears?"

"All I got is fruit cocktail. Anyone want to trade? Don't everyone jump at once."

Holt opened a can of franks and beans with his P38 can opener. He set up his stove and lit a small ball of C-4.

"Beans and baby dicks, good eating," he said as he stirred the beans.

"Why is Charlie walking in the woods and we're walking out in the open?" asked Locke.

"I'm assuming the Major wants us as bait."

"What's that you're eating?"

"A can of tuna my girl sent me."

"That oily shit is no good when you're overheated. Eat some crackers with it."

"Kelly, how you doing?"

"I'm fucking dragging ass. This pig is beating me today. It's got to be a hundred ten degrees today."

"The pig might be bitch-slapping you, but there's no one better on the M60."

Kelly grunted his thanks.

"Roger, out," Mercado said into the handset. "The Lieutenant wants us moving out in ten."

Holt got up and stretched his back. He lit a cigarette and looked across the riverbed.

"Can't see Charlie. They must be tucked into the trees."

"All their new guys must be suffering. Hell of a way to get broken in."

"I gotta take a leak," said Holt, going behind some bushes. "Can't see third squad, either. I hope we didn't get ahead of everybody. Nicky, can you get Charlie Company on your radio?"

"Yeah."

"Ask if they can see us, and if we are online with them."

"They say we're about twenty yards ahead of them. He wants to know why we ain't trying to conceal ourselves."

"Tell him we wouldn't be good bait if we hid."

"Yeah, good luck to you too," Nick said, throwing the handset down. "Fucking wise guy."

"Who were you talking to?"

"Some fucking wise-ass RTO."

"Alright, girls, let's saddle up and dangle our asses out front."

Chapter 21

There's a Man with a Gun

They walked until three o'clock without taking a break. When they finally did stop, they dropped to the ground, exhausted. The towel Holt had wrapped around his neck was soaking wet with sweat. His boonie hat was drenched. He had strapped his helmet to his pack. He took off his hat and wiped his face. "My knees are killing me. These rocks are getting worse."

Mercado was talking on the radio. "That was Camp. The Major is pissed. Said we barely covered a mile in two hours."

"The Major can go fuck himself. The lazy bitch doesn't even carry his own gear. He's got guys carrying all his shit."

"My thighs are twitching," moaned Kelly. "They feel like they're on fire."

"It's like walking on wet, slippery softballs," said Wilson. "Why can't we walk in the woods? This is killing my ankles."

"The Major wants us out in the open. I'm telling you, we're just being used as bait."

"Everyone just calm down," said Holt. "Nothing we can do about it, so quit bitching." He sat against a tree with his head between his knees, drawing deep breaths. His once-clean fatigues were sweat-soaked and beginning to smell. The were large salt circles in his armpits and crotch. He dropped his pack and stood on trembling legs.

"We've got at least four more miles of this shit. We'll never make the jungle by nightfall, regardless of what the Major says."

"Let him come up here and walk point if he thinks he can do better. Shouldn't he be leading by example instead of always ragging on us?"

"Nick, he's an officer. I doubt he ever walked point in his life, and I'm sure as shit he ain't gonna start now."

"Fuck him! Shit, I can't stop sweating."

"That's a good thing. When you can't sweat anymore is the time to worry."

Holt felt his side. "Fuck me! My bandage came off."

"Let me take a look?" Mercado examined Holt's stitches, poking at his side.

"Christ, Nicky, are your hands clean? Quit poking at me with those filthy mitts."

"Stitches are holding; you look okay. Smear some ointment on them, you'll be fine."

"Nick, your radio's talking," said Wilson.

"The prick wants us on our feet in five."

Holt looked at Wilson, and he struggled with his rucksack. "Eugene, how about taking point? It's just you and me, brother. It's time you learned. I'll walk slack. You keep your eyes forward and I'll watch to the sides. You see anything you don't like, you stop."

"Sure. I'm ready. I want to learn."

"Everybody, make sure you're careful with your water. I guarantee you Grayson is going to punish us by canceling our resupply tonight. Let's saddle up and move out."

They walked for several minutes when Holt turned around and looked backward. "Nicky, give me the fucking radio. Look back; those pricks are all going into the woods." Holt spoke into the handset. "Delta Four-Six, are we moving into the trees?"

The Lieutenant answered, "Big Six wants you to maintain your route. He says you have a clearer field of vision. We'll follow in the woods. Be observant and be careful."

"Roger, out. Even the Lieutenant knows he's using us for bait. Told us to be careful. When did he ever tell us that shit?"

"Look ahead. There are giant boulders rolled right up against the trees. It means we got to go around them. We'll be even more exposed," said Wilson.

"Let's just go. This sucks any way you look at it."

They walked in silence, passing huge boulders bigger than cars. They skirted the boulders, bringing them twenty feet into the center of the river. They slowly worked around the rocks.

Suddenly, Wilson held up a clenched fist. Holt came up behind him. "What you got?"

"I'm not sure. I might be delirious, but I swear I saw a man over there."

"Was he telling you to beware?"

"What?"

"Song lyric. Buffalo Springfield."

"I'm serious. Across the riverbed, just behind those giant rocks."

"You sure?"

"Yeah, I'm sure. Right over there."

"I don't see anything. Maybe it's Charlie Company. Maybe they got ahead of us. Nick, call Charlie and confirm their position. Ask if they got anybody up by those rocks."

"Negative."

Holt wiped sweat from his eyes and stared across the open ground. Heat shimmers distorted his vision. He leaned into Wilson. "Look across at that big fucking rock, the one with all the moss all over it. Look to the right and back about ten feet, and tell me what you see."

"Nothing, just shadows."

"Keep looking."

"They're moving. The shadows are moving!"

"Damn straight, they're moving."

"Charlie Six, this is Delta Four-Four. If you ain't in front of us, then you got company. There are some guys to your front."

Holt listened and replied. "There are three large boulders all crashed into each other. Just to the side, there's movement in the trees. If you want, I'll have my gunner fire a burst and mark the position. Kelly, get up here."

"What's up?"

"Fire a short burst to the side of those rocks."

Kelly steadied the machine gun and fired two three-round bursts where directed. Almost instantly, there was return fire directed at them.

"Light them up, Kelly."

"Charlie says they are moving forward to engage and to hold our fire."

Kelly rested the M60 on a smaller boulder and crouched behind it. Holt stood over his shoulder. The squad took cover. It was quiet for several moments, then a burst of AK fire shattered the stillness, followed by M16s and M60s. Red and green tracers bounced off the rocks and flew up into the sky. There were grenade explosions, then the whoosh of an RPG and a larger explosion. They heard another whoosh, and a second RPG was fired at them.

"Get down," screamed Holt.

The RPG hit a boulder ten feet to their left, and shrapnel sliced through the trees.

"Anyone hit?"

"Why are they shooting at us?" whined Locke, who was balled up at Wilson's feet.

The firing continued with intensity, then died down and finally stopped. Silence, then four single shots.

"That's our guys making sure they're dead."

Then the calls for medics began.

"That's not good," Holt said.

"Wilkes says hold our position. They got wounded to be evacuated," Mercado said. "We're gonna be here for a while."

"Maybe we'll hole up here for the night. It's four-thirty. It'll be an hour before the choppers are done."

A Hunter-Killer team of two Cobras and a Loach accompanied the Medivac ship. The Loach flew at ground level, trying to draw fire while the Cobras circled above. The evacuation helicopter had difficulty landing on the rocks; it kept touching down and tilting when trying to land. They finally found a stable place to land and the wounded were brought out and placed aboard the ship. As the hospital ship took off, the Cobras remained behind to prowl the valley. Not wanting to return to Base Camp fully loaded, they strafed the trees ahead of them with rockets and mini-gun fire. There was no return fire.

As predicted, they were told to prepare to spend the night. Delta Company drew into a circular night defensive perimeter, with fourth squad nestled behind some rocks with the trees to their backs. It would be their job to watch for movement through the length of the valley. They set their cook fires against the rocks and prepared their C-rations. Holt cooked and ate ham slices on crackers with cheese. He made a cup of coffee and lit a cigarette.

Nick came over with the radio. "Major wants to compliment us for spotting the ambush."

"Tell him it was Wilson, our newest and best point man."

Wilson looked around, beaming. "You don't have to do that, Don."

"Credit where credit's due. You did good today. Like I said, until we get replacements, it's just me and you."

"You really think I was good?"

"Out-fucking-standing!" Holt addressed the squad. "We'll do one-hour shifts on guard. I'm so wiped out, I can't pull a two-hour shift. We'll start at seven, and each will take two shifts. That'll bring us to dawn. Choose your position; I'll go last. There's gooks about, so don't fuck up and fall asleep. Camp should be around to check our position, so don't shoot him."

Camp came to their position just before seven.

"Looks good here. Good fields of fire. You got the whole valley covered." He knelt besides Holt. "The Major's not happy with our progress, but he is happy you spotted the ambush."

"Not me; Wilson did. Saw a man with a gun."

"I like that song. Good work, Eugene."

"What song do you keep talking about?"

"Wilson's a country-music guy. Not into all this rock-and-roll stuff."

"You guys look beat. You still have to stay alert tonight. Gooks will be crawling around."

"Every fucking bone in my body is hurting. Walking on those rocks was horrible. But you wouldn't know. I saw Wilkes move you pussies into the trees. Nice, soft ground and in the shade. Hoped you enjoyed yourself."

"It was quite pleasant, thank you for asking."

"We getting water tomorrow?"

Camp shrugged.

"Would have been just as easy to bring in a resupply ship along with the Medivac."

"I told you, the Major is pissed."

"Please, prior to inserting your nose up his ass tonight, express our deepest regrets over our performance today, and tell him we hope to do better tomorrow."

"Yeah, I'll do that. I will ask him about water. You guys stay safe tonight."

Kelly woke up Holt during his second shift. It was close to 2 AM. "Wake up. You have to see this shit."

Holt stretched and yawned, and looked where Kelly was pointing. A mile or so up the valley, the woods twinkled with lights. The sound of whistles could be heard.

"Holy shit, where's the radio?"

Kelly fumbled in the dark. "Delta Six, this is Four-Four. Are you seeing this?"

"Big Six is calling in artillery as we speak. Shot out."

They watched as four artillery rounds screamed overhead and impacted short of target.

"Delta Six, relay this, you're good left to right but short. Add two hundred yards."

Four more rounds impacted on target, then another four rounds. The night was lit ahead by the explosions. Big Six, the Major, walked the rounds forward, covering a half-mile of ground with more than thirty rounds in all.

"That should fuck them up."

"Don't these bastards ever sleep?"

The full squad was awake, looking at the drifting clouds of smoke. The smell of cordite hung in the humid air.

"What happened?" asked Wilson.

"Gooks down the valley with lights and whistles. Grayson fucked them up good."

"That asshole will have us looking for body parts tomorrow."

"Not us, Charlie Company. It all happened on their side."

"You think there are gooks on this side, too?"

"Locke, this is their country. There are gooks everywhere."

"Why were they blowing whistles?"

"Could be one of two reasons. One, there's a large force up ahead and they are trying to control their movements. Or two, there are two or three gooks with flashlights and whistles, trying to scare the shit out of us. In your case, Locke, it worked."

"In Korea, they blew trumpets. I don't like gooks with trumpets or whistles," said Wilson.

"You are a peculiar young man, Eugene. Very strange, indeed."

"Gooks with whistles or trumpets means there are a lot of them. A whole regiment, according to the Major."

"Or, as I said, one or two trying to fuck up our sleep, which they succeeded in doing."

"The Major did good with the artillery."

"Even an asshole can accomplish one thing perfectly. Who got guard? I'm going back to sleep."

But Holt couldn't sleep. The North Vietnamese were known to use whistles to control the movement of large units. Maybe they were ahead, lying in ambushes and in bunkers, just waiting for us. He did finally drift off fifteen minutes before being woken up for his turn on guard.

In the morning, everyone was on edge. Exhausting days of difficult humping and lack of sleep were taking its toll on everyone. Tempers were short, and everyone remained silent as they prepared breakfast. Holt studied his map over coffee and cigarettes. They still had a day of ankle-breaking walking ahead until they reached the jungle.

But fourth squad was given a reprieve of sorts. Mercado was smiling. "Just got the word. We are trading with the third squad. They're taking our spot, and we'll walk flank."

"Thank you, God," said Wilson.

"Speak of the devil. Here come our saviors now. Howdy, boys. Welcome to the world of Vietnam fishing, where you are the bait at the end of the Major's pole."

"Good morning, and fuck you too. What should I know?"

"Lace up your boots tight and walk carefully. Those rocks are a motherfucker. And the flank?"

"Like walking in a steam bath. No sunlight, but easy walking. You got the cliff on your left and you were on our right. The woods are only about two hundred feet wide, left to right. Lots of fallen trees, so watch out for bunkers and gun emplacements. Have fun, shitheads."

"Guys, saddle up. Into the woods we go."

Chapter 22

Nightmares Come When It's Dark

The trees on the western side of the river were evenly spaced will tall, leafy canopies. The ground was spongy with moss and plant debris, which made for easy walking.

"Just heard, the Major is still bitching about the time. He's going to have third squad fall in behind us. He wants us at the end of all this rock shit in two hours," said Mercado.

The squad watched as third squad entered the trees and fell in behind them.

"You delicate little fucks couldn't handle the rocks, I see," Holt said to Gibson, the third squad's leader.

"I can't believe you guys walked there all day. My dogs are barking."

"The Major wants us clear of the rocks in two hours. I hope you girls can keep up with us."

"You set the pace and we'll do fine. Hey, did you hear anything about water?"

"I would hope that prick is going to call in resupply before we enter the jungle. I'm down to about two canteens."

In an hour, they stopped to examine the remnants of several bunkers. There were fresh tracks leading ahead of them. They kicked apart the bunkers and moved on.

Holt stopped to light a cigarette. "Well, it's no surprise the gooks know where we're going," he said to Mercado.

"You think we're chasing them, or are they leading us into an ambush?"

"I guess we'll find out soon enough."

Wilson came up to them. "You want me to take point for a while?"

"Not now, Gene. Maybe later. What you can do is walk slack. Stay behind me and watch left and right, and I'll watch straight ahead. You good with that?"

"Sure thing, Sarge."

They walked for another hour, and were told they were nearing the end of the rock river.

They were taking a short break when Wilson jumped up and fired a burst into the trees in front of them. "I saw gooks. Two of them behind those rocks. They got up and ran."

"Did you hit them?"

"Wilkes wants to know what's going on," said Mercado.

"Tell him we spotted two gooks who ran off when we got close."

"He said to move out. Look for blood trails. The Major wants us in the jungle by noon. When we get there, we're supposed to hold up and some resupply choppers are coming in."

As the river ended, the trees thickened. To their right, the river ended at a wall of thick jungle. The cliff to their left sloped down to a jumble of jagged rocks jutting from the ground.

"This is some weird shit. Back in dinosaur times, this must have been a real river. If you look at the cliffs, the water would have been two hundred feet high. This whole area would have been underwater," said Holt.

"I guess the force of the water swept all these rocks down here."

"And when it dried up, the rocks stayed and the jungle just took over."

Wilson knelt and swept the ground. "This is good soil. It's so black and moist. Anything could grow here."

"In a couple of years, the jungle will grow over any evidence we were ever here."

"Choppers are inbound. Wilkes says to send two guys out to get food and water."

"Wilson, you and Locke go get our shit, and we'll cover you," said Holt.

The helicopters landed quickly, and supplies were kicked off by the door gunner. They lifted and were gone before the men arrived. Men swarmed over the supplies and broke them apart. Wilson came back carrying three cases of C-rations, and Locke struggled under the weight of two five-gallon plastic jugs. Wilson distributed the rations while everyone filled their canteens. There was some water left, which Locke brought to the third squad. The baling wire from the cartons was coiled and placed in their packs; and the boxes were ripped apart and shoved under bushes, where they would quickly decompose. The five-gallon jug was cut apart and scattered, leaving nothing of value for the enemy. The whole process took less than twenty minutes.

"Wilkes says to move out, heading due north. We'll break for lunch around one."

They entered a world of darkness. This was true, triple-canopy jungle, where sunlight struggled to enter. Tall trees with broad, leafy canopies shrouded the jungle. Smaller trees grew, competing for sunlight; and beneath them were an assortment of plants and bushes. Vines were everywhere: lying on the ground, wrapped around trees, and lacing through the bushes. The air was heavy and moist, and almost had a weight to it. Everyone was soon drenched with an oily sweat. And it was eerily silent. Their feet made no sound, muffled by a thick mat of moss.

"This is some spooky shit," said Holt.

"I'm soaking wet. My balls feel like they're boiling. Can't hear anybody."

"I'm guessing Charlie Company is off to our right?"

"That's what Wilkes says. About a hundred yards or so. Their left flank should be closer."

"It's past noon, and water is still dripping from the trees. Everything is wet and slimy and black with mold."

Mercado pointed at some large boulders. "The moss on those rocks must be six inches thick. Every tree is covered with moss and mold. It stinks like rotting garbage."

"Breathe through your mouth. It's not as foul."

"Breathe? I can't; I'm panting like a dog. It's like I'm underwater."

"As far as I know, this shit is gonna last for three days or more. After that, we break out into the valley."

"That's when the whole battalion hooks up?"

"That's the plan."

The radio squawked, and Mercado held the handset to his ear. His face was streaked with dirt and sweat. "Wilkes says find a place and break for lunch."

"Up ahead by those rocks looks good."

They settled behind the rocks and started the procedure of setting up their stoves and preparing their food. For the first time, they saw third squad about thirty feet behind them. Off to the left, Charlie Company's left flank was visible. They waved at each other before they sank into the bushes.

Holt opened a can of chicken and noodles, and put it on his stove over a lit ball of C-4. He stirred his meal and watched it bubble and boil. He removed the can by the folded lid and set it aside to cool. He worked his P38 to open a small can of crackers. "Man, I'm wiped."

"People back home pay good money to take a steam bath, and here we get to live in one for free," said Kelly.

"What's that you're eating?

"Turkey loaf."

"Don't eat that shit cold. Use my stove before the C-4 goes out."

"Cold is good."

"You are one hardcore motherfucker."

"You guys are crazy if you like this. We live like pigs and smell like pigs," said Locke.

"Excuse me, but, pigs smell better," said Wilson.

Holt studied Locke. "Dude, you gotta get used to this. It's your life now. Think positive."

"This is a picnic in the park. It's like a day by the Charles River," Kelly added.

"Guys get killed in the blink of an eye. Gone forever. How can you get used to that?"

"I never asked, what kind of name is Meyer?"

"German."

"Are you Jewish?"

"No, I'm Lutheran. Why?"

"I didn't think you were Jewish. Jews aren't stupid. They all got some college smarts and are back working at Division."

"That's a dumb thing to say."

"Never said I was smart, that's why I'm just a grunt. Just a dumb fucking pack mule that fights."

"I'll never get used to this."

"I heard a chaplain ask this guy how he would feel if a baby died. The guy say he'd be sad, and the chaplain asks why. He says, if you believe in God, then you have to believe that the baby is now with God, having lived his full, complete life, the life allotted to him by God. The point is whether you're nine months old or nineteen or ninety, when your number's up, it's time to go. You either believe in God and accept that he has a plan for you, or you don't."

"Since when have you become so religious? I hear you always ragging on the chaplain."

"I'm not a holy roller, but I believe in God. I make sure I'm doing everything possible to stay alive; but if God sends a bullet your way, you ain't gonna dodge it. Stop making all your plans. Stop thinking about the car you're going to buy. Stop worrying about your girlfriend and your job and where you're going to live. Don't think about all that shit and live in the present. You don't hear me whine about Janet and the baby. Sure, I read her letters and what's happening back home. But that's her life, not mine. My life is here, with you assholes. And at this moment, life is good. I got my chicken and noodles with hot sauce, I got water and plenty of ammo. What else do I need? Ten minutes from now, I could be dead; but worrying about it won't change things. You're worried about shit you can't control. Worry about the stuff you can control and forget the rest.

"Look at these guys; you don't hear them bitching. Kelly carries his full pack plus the pig and four belts of ammo. I never heard Eugene bitch about anything. He always has something good to say and a smile on his face. Nicky carries his stuff plus thirty pounds of radio gear. You gotta make this place your home for the next ten months."

"I don't see how."

"You better find a way, or you ain't gonna make it."

Mercado interrupted them. "Wilkes says we move out in ten."

"Ten minutes is plenty of time for me to take a nice, relaxing dump. Police the area and bury the garbage, like we were never here."

They plodded through the jungle for two hours before taking a break. Everything was wet and soggy. There were pools of green stagnant water buzzing with mosquitoes. In a small clearing, they found boot prints in the soft mud. The Lieutenant asked how many, and Holt said about twenty.

"Are you saying twenty pairs of prints, or just twenty prints?" asked Wilkes.

"They're all mashed up, but I would say between ten or twenty guys."

"Which way are they heading?"

"Same way we're going. Also, there are some rocks piled up in a little pyramid to the side of the prints."

"I'm coming up for a look-see."

Holt and Nick lit cigarettes and waited for Wilkes. The Lieutenant came with his RTO and Mr. Freed.

"How goes it, old-timer?"

"I'm hanging in there. This is good exercise; I could stand to lose a few pounds."

"That why we do it. To stay in shape and control our weight."

Wilkes examined the rocks and boot prints. Mr. Freed took some pictures. Kelly posed with the M60 cocked on his hip. Wilson, with his goofy smile, gave the peace sign. Mercado stood with his back to everyone, taking a leak, while Locke stood to the side with a sullen look.

"What do you think the rocks mean?"

"Could be anything. I've never seen anything like it before."

"Maybe it means supplies are up ahead," said Wilson.

"Why?"

"It looks like a little building, maybe a supply depot."

"As good a guess as any," said Holt.

"And the boot prints? They're going our way?"

"The same way, due north."

"I'll let the Major know."

"Is he still with us?"

"He's up above, scouting out a night position for us. He'll rejoin us tomorrow. He left me in charge of the company. Sergeant Camp is running the platoon."

"Good to know."

"Move out on the same heading. Keep me apprised on any new developments. We should be stopping in two or three hours for the night."

Before they left, Holt put a hand on Mr. Freed's shoulder. "Still having fun?"

"I've never experienced anything like this. I want to tell this story. What you guys endure, how you live. But to be honest, I'm exhausted."

"After a few more days, you'll never want to leave."

Chapter 23

The Real God of Hellfire

Major Grayson scouted out a night defensive perimeter for them, one thousand yards from their present location. It had a small clearing suitable for one or two helicopters. He ordered the NDP be set on the western edge of the clearing, and he went about laying in artillery coordinates.

Lieutenant Wilkes came forward to relay the Major's orders. "Look at your map, and you'll see a clearing straight ahead. It's too large for us to encompass it, so we'll be here on the west side. Charlie Company will set up facing the clearing to the south. Delta will take the north and west sides."

Holt looked up. "Is that thunder?"

"The Major is spotting artillery for us and firing some Harassment and Interdiction fire."

"Good. This way, the gooks will know where we'll be."

"According to you, the gooks know exactly where we're going already."

"That's true. I did say that."

"Let's move out. The sooner we get there, the sooner we break."

"Lieutenant, the guys were asking about mail. It's been a couple of days."

"Not tonight, maybe tomorrow. Get your men moving."

The walk to the NDP was uneventful. They arrived just before five. Sergeant Camp came around with Mr. Freed to set the squad's positions.

"This looks good for your squad. Wilkes is setting too big of a perimeter. We're going to be spread thin, so put Kelly here at the end and the rest about five yards down. Second squad will be to your right. Third squad will be to your left, at the corner; and first squad is taking the western edge."

"That leaves a lot of gaps," said Holt.

"I told him to tighten things up, but he won't listen."

"Are we putting out LPs?"

"What do you think?"

"Got you. But what if he checks?"

"Wilkes won't leave the CP at night, guaranteed. If he wants to check, I'll do it. Here, I brought you this." Camp handed Holt an M79 grenade launcher and three bandoleers containing eighteen rounds. "Set your trip flares out about ninety feet and as second row in closer."

Mr. Freed stopped taking pictures. "What do you say to my spending the night with you guys?"

"Not tonight; some other time. Everybody's on edge. There were signs of gooks all over the place. They're sure to fuck with us tonight. Stay at the CP; the Lieutenant will love showing off for you."

"That's what I'm worried about. Every officer wants to tell me his life story. It's not why I'm here."

"There'll be other nights, just not tonight."

"Kelly, drag that big log in front of you, then help Mercado with his over here. Dig in behind the logs. Me and Wilson are going to set trip flares and Claymores."

They walked silently for about thirty yards. Wilson was chewing on his nails. "I don't mind telling you, I'm scared."

"Me too, brother. This place is like an old graveyard you see in the horror movies."

They spaced out a row of three trip flares, and moved ten yards closer and set a second row of three. Behind these, they spaced four Claymore mines. They walked back until they were fifteen feet from their position and set the remaining two Claymores.

They climbed over the log and settled into a three-foot-deep trench Mercado had dug in the soft earth. Holt laid out the detonators in order of fire. "Get your grenades out and a bunch of magazines, and keep your ruck close. I'll check on Kelly and Locke."

Kelly had dampened his towel and was scrubbing his face and torso. He then dropped his pants and cleaned his crotch.

"Tomorrow, you'll use that towel to wipe your face," said Holt.

"It's my dick and I know where it's been all day. Same sweat as my face."

"Kelly, you are a hulk. Did you work out back home? What can you press?"

"On a regular basis, I can do two-twenty; on a good day, two-fifty."

"Vietnam's been good to you. You don't have an ounce of fat on you. Me, I bet I weigh under one-thirty and I still feel flabby."

"No, you look good. You have that whole concentration-camp look going on."

"I see you got your belts laid out. Here's two more," he said, handing Kelly two linked belts of M60 ammunition.

"I got one thousand rounds. I'm ready to rock and roll."

"Just be ready to duck. You draw RPGs like shit draws flies. Where the fuck is Locke?"

"Taking a crap. That dickwad is shaking like a leaf. Can't we trade him to someone?"

"I was thinking of asking Camp to make him an RTO in the CP if a space opens up. We need replacements, though."

"You think we'll get hit tonight?"

Holt dug into his pocket for a cigarette, and offered the pack to

Kelly. He lit both. "I think so. At the very least, they'll probe us, keep us awake all night. I hope they lay off that whistle shit. That stuff just scares the shit out me."

"I know what you mean. My hair was standing on edge, like a cat."

They smoked in silence for a moment.

"The Major's plan, you know, man against man, regiment against regiment. You ever think the gooks want that, too? That they're drawing us into a trap?"

"Yeah, I thought of that. Maybe they want a big, decisive victory. Show the world what they're made of."

Holt field-stripped his cigarette and watched Kelly do the same. "Stay frosty, brother. No one dies; we all go home."

"From your lips to God's ears."

"Nicky, we'll do one-hour shifts. You take first."

"I doubt if I'll sleep. This place makes me nervous. Fucking Major is back at Cu Chi, probably getting laid by some round-eyed pussy."

"I'm sure he's very concerned about our well-being. He even laid in artillery. We're group Bravo. Just call that in and we adjust from there."

"Won't we get air bursts in these trees?"

"The artillery guys can set their fuses differently, or so I've been told. Try and relax. It's just about seven. I'm going to try and get some sleep. Wilson knows he's got second shift."

It was twelve o'clock straight up when Wilson woke him.

Holt grunted and sat up.

"Sarge, I hear voices."

"Where?"

"Out front."

Holt came fully awake and grabbed his rifle. "You sure?"

"Yes."

"Wake Nick up and have him call it in. I'll make sure Kelly and Locke are awake."

Holt crawled to Kelly's position. "Who goes there?" whispered Locke.

"Shut up and wake Kelly up."

"I'm awake; we heard them. Voices, way out there."

"Stay alert. Maybe they're just trying to scare us."

"If that's what they're doing, then they're doing a good job."

Back with Wilson and Mercado, Holt asked, "Anyone else hear noises?"

"First and third squads heard shit and are on full alert."

For the next hour, it was quiet.

"Did you hear that?" Wilson asked.

"Yeah. Sounded like a branch breaking."

"Nick, call in and ask about artillery."

"Wilkes said he was going to fire three rounds at the compass points."

They heard the rounds pass overhead and impact far off.

"I couldn't even see the explosion. Tell him again, but drop one hundred."

At various points around their perimeter, artillery was fired and adjusted until the explosions were visible.

Another hour passed, and it remained quiet.

Out of the corner of his eye, Holt saw the wire for one of the detonators move. Without hesitation, he blew the mine. They heard screams and cursing, and Holt blew another mine. More screams.

"They're fucking with the Claymores."

"How did they get past the trip flares? We hid them!"

"Christ, Gene, it's not like we built the Berlin Wall. We stretched a fishing line between some bushes. Maybe they walked around them and missed the flares completely. We just guessed where to put them."

Then the whistles started. It began from far away and muffled, then moved much closer.

"You know, I was just thinking, the only thing missing were the whistles."

They heard groans, pitiful sounds of pain.

"We must have gotten a few," said Mercado.

Someone screamed from the forest, "Fuck you, GI, fuck you."

The hairs on Holt's arm went up.

"Fuck you mother, GI."

"Now that's uncalled for," whispered Holt.

"Fuck you mother in the ass."

"This is bullshit, Nicky. They're talking to you."

"Or you."

"My mom doesn't do anal. I tried."

"You're fucking nuts. Ain't you scared?"

"I'm about to crap my pants, if you must know. Let me try a few blooper rounds." Holt loaded the M79 and fired off three high-explosive rounds in rapid succession. In the flash of the explosions, they saw the silhouettes of the NVA soldiers. They fired bursts from their M16s and saw several of the figures fall.

Kelly started with the M60, firing short three-round bursts into the advancing figures. From all over the perimeter, firing started. They saw the flash of an RPG and followed the smoke trail as it passed over Kelly's position and exploded behind them.

"Third squad is getting hit," screamed Kelly. "I got rounds coming from the left and the front."

Holt blew the two distant Claymores, and the jungle was backlit with fire. More screams, more whistles, both up close now.

Wilson grabbed the blooper and fired four rounds into the advancing enemy. Artillery rounds flew overhead.

"Nick, tell them to drop one hundred. We need it closer."

Artillery shells ringed the northern and western sides of the perimeter, lighting up the night.

"Closer, Nick. Drop fifty."

Kelly was on his knees, firing directly into the NVA soldiers. The arcs of spent shell casings twinkled in the night.

"Smoke those bastards. Smoke them, Kelly," Holt screamed.

Kelly rose and fired long bursts from the machine gun. It seemed like dozens of NVA fell before him. The barrel of the gun glowed a dull orange as he hollered at Locke for more ammo.

It was then that two bursts of AK-47 fire came from behind them. Holt whirled and fired at two shadows, dropping them both. "Kelly, be careful. We got gooks inside the perimeter."

"We're surrounded!" screamed Locke, who got up and ran past the two bodies.

"You cocksucker, you coward bastard, get back here!" shouted Kelly.

Immediately, Wilson ran to Kelly's side and began feeding the machine gun.

"Did you see that? That fucking prick ran out on me," Kelly said. He fired off another fifty rounds and forced the NVA toward Holt. Mercado and Holt fired nonstop, swapping out magazines in quick, fluid motions.

"Barrel change," yelled Kelly. He hit the release lever and grabbed the glowing barrel with his bare hand, and replaced it with a fresh barrel in seconds, never stopping an unending stream of curses. Kelly was up on his knees. "C'mon assholes, keep coming. I am the fucking devil, and I'm sending all you fucks to hell. Gonna fire your asses up. More! Send me more! I want more!"

"Kelly, get down," shouted Holt. "Wilson, get Kelly down."

As Wilson tugged at Kelly's fatigues, he slapped him away. "Keep feeding me. More ammo, more ammo."

Wilson clipped two belts together and held them ready. "Goddamn it, Kelly, get your ass down!"

Two RPGs fired. The first passed overhead; the second hit the logs in front of Kelly's foxhole, throwing him and Wilson back with the concussion.

Kelly never missed a beat. He scrambled to his gun and resumed firing. Wilson crawled to his side, blood streaming from his nose.

"You can't kill me! I ain't dying tonight, you cocksuckers."

"Look at that guy, he's a fucking war god. He's a fucking beast," Holt said to Mercado.

He blew the two remaining Claymores, filling the air with blood mist and flesh.

Kelly turned to Wilson and calmly said to get ready to change barrels. "Use your towel; I burnt my hand to shit. Ready?"

With the barrel swapped out, Kelly resumed firing. Mercado fired until he emptied a magazine and slapped in a fresh one. Holt was throwing grenades. The air was filled with gun smoke and screams. The trees were filled with tracers: the incoming green tracers from the AKs, and the red tracers from the Americans. It seemed like nothing could survive out in the open. From behind a rock, three NVA soldiers burst out, firing from the hip. Nick cut them down in a long, sustained burst. The momentum of their charge carried the dead soldiers onto the logs. One was still moving. Holt placed the barrel of his gun against his head and fired a single shot, bursting his head like a dropped melon.

"Jesus, that's disgusting. Couldn't you push him away first?"

The firing died down to sporadic shots. The second squad was killing the NVA as they attempted to withdraw. The third squad was quiet.

"You still want to fuck my mother?" Kelly screamed. "My mother's a tough Irish bitch, and we just fucked you."

"Nicky, tell them to add twenty to the artillery and keep adding. We'll blow their asses to hell. They won't get away."

As the artillery rained down shells on the retreating enemy, Kelly and Wilson crawled to Holt and Mercado.

Holt punched Kelly in the chest. "You, my man, are a fucking monster. A god of fucking death. A fucking death-dealing monster. You saved our asses tonight."

"Where's that fucking coward? Locke ran! Did you see him run?"

"I'll deal with him myself. Fucking prick!"

"Where did he go?" asked Wilson.

"Who the fuck knows? You guys get your shit and bring it over here. We'll dig out this hole. We ain't splitting up no more."

"What about these guys?" Nick said, pointing at the three bodies on the logs.

"Leave them until morning. They ain't going anywhere."

Chapter 24

A Coward Reinvented

Holt sat, smoking a cigarette. He stared at the three dead North Vietnamese soldiers draped over the logs.

Mercado came over and handed him a steaming cup of coffee. "Kelly made a shitload of coffee. Thought you'd like some. Light and sweet?"

"Perfect, Nick, thank you."

"Why are you eyeballing those dead gooks?"

"You ever watch war movies at home? John Wayne movies. I remember one called Iwo Jima something."

"Yeah, it was called Sands of Iwo Jima."

"Remember when the Duke was killed? It was a clean, painless, bloodless death. After saying some inspirational shit, he just closed his eyes. Look at those fuckers. That one guy, what's left of him? I see some teeth, part of his nose, and one ear. The rest of his head is gone."

"That's because you shot him in the head from two inches away. What did you think was gonna happen?"

"That's what people should see. See what war really looks like. People blown apart, nothing recognizable left of them. They should see guys screaming with missing arms and legs. Heads blown off. Not some bullshit John Wayne death."

"You want me to move him?"

"Nah, me and him are pals. This guy has more balls than that gutless wonder Locke. You heard anything about him?"

"Wilkes called for a casualty report. Told him Kelly fucked up his hand and we can't find Locke. He said he's coming over. He sounded pissed."

"What am I supposed to say?"

"Tell him straight up what happened. Speaking of the shithead, here he comes with Camp." Mercado looked up at the sound of an approaching helicopter. "And that, I wager, is the Major coming to take credit for last night."

Holt went back to staring at the dead gooks as the Lieutenant, Sergeant Camp and Mr. Freed approached.

"Jesus Christ! It looks like you guys had fun last night."

"Fun?"

"You know what I mean. How many are there?"

"These three, two you passed walking in, and maybe seven or eight out front. In front of Kelly's position, there are a lot more, a least a dozen."

"You searched the bodies yet?"

"No. I was going to have breakfast first."

"The Major will want an accurate count. What's this crap about Locke?"

"You don't have him?"

"No, why would I have him?"

"He ran back toward the CP. I figured he landed there. Can you call around and see if someone else picked him up?"

"Wait here." He walked to his RTO and spoke into the radio, leaving Camp with Holt. Mr. Freed started taking pictures of the carnage.

"What happened?"

"Locke happened. He thought we were surrounded and ran off."

"He ran away? He didn't say anything?"

"Just ran. He did take his rifle."

"He ran because he was scared. He just left you guys?"

"That's the way it looks."

The Lieutenant came back. "Nobody has Locke. No one has seen him."

"He didn't just vanish," said Holt.

"What do I tell Major Grayson?"

"You better think quick; he's here."

"Don't say a word about his fatigues. Not one fucking word," Camp said.

They all turned and watched as Major Grayson and his entourage approached. They were all wearing brand-new, pressed, camouflaged jungle fatigues.

"Am I hearing this right? You have a man missing?"

"Yes, sir," said Wilkes.

"That won't do. We can't have anyone missing. Just what the fuck happened?"

"Kelly. Come over here and tell the Major what happened with Locke."

"That weasel dick ran out on us, simple as that."

"Men just don't run off. What happened before he... left?"

"We had gooks charging our position, and some gooks got behind us. I told that piece of shit to get me more ammo. He hollered we're surrounded. Next I knew, he ran."

"So he could have been leaving to get you more ammunition?"

"We had plenty. I meant for him to get another belt."

"But could he have misunderstood?"

Kelly looked at Holt, who just stared back. "I have no idea what he was thinking. All I know is that he ran."

"Thank you, Specialist. You can return to your position."

They stood in silence for a moment.

"As I see it, the soldier..."

"Locke, sir."

"Locke may have been confused in the heat of battle. He may have thought he was being ordered to go get more ammunition. As

261

he ran, he got turned around and became disoriented. He's probably outside the perimeter right now, scared and alone. Lieutenant, send some men out to search the area. We have to find him."

"At once, sir. What you said sounds reasonable. Wouldn't you agree, Sergeant Holt?"

"I want to put Specialist Kelly in for a Silver Star, and Private Wilson for a Bronze Star. They saved our asses last night. I'd like to see them get it."

Wilkes stared at Holt for a long moment, then nodded. "You write it up, and I'll push it through."

The Major looked confused.

"It probably happened as you said, Major. He got confused."

"Agreed, then. Lieutenant Wilkes, try and find that boy and when you do, send him to me. One final thing. I'm surprised you haven't mentioned our fatigues. We're testing them out. Once we evaluate them, they will become standard issue. What do you think?"

"Very impressive, sir. You wear them well."

As the Major's group walked away, Wilkes turned to Holt, who held out his hand.

"Deal?"

The Lieutenant shook his hand without saying anything.

"Should I have heard all that?" asked Mr. Freed.

"If you heard what I heard, then none of it makes sense."

"What did this Kelly do?"

"See that foxhole over there? Look out there. That was all Kelly. When Locke disappeared, Wilson ran through heavy fire and took over as assistant gunner. Without them, we would have lost this section of the perimeter."

"Let me help you. You tell me what happened, and I'll write it. I know what they want to hear and how they like to hear it."

"Hey, Nicky. Is there any more coffee? Could you whip up a couple of cups?"

"Yes, sir, Sergeant. I'll get right on it."

"Two, cream and sugar, with less sarcasm. So here's what happened."

"That should do it. Sign and date it on the bottom, and I'll bring up to the Lieutenant."

Holt was looking over at Kelly.

"What's going on?"

"That's Kelly. He's with the chaplain."

The two were sitting on the edge of the foxhole. The chaplain had his arm around Kelly's shoulders.

"It's horrible, what we make you do. It's why I need to tell your stories. A few months ago, you were kids just out of high school. Now you're in the jungle, fighting like savages just to stay alive. I fear this will stay with you all your lives."

"'Thou shalt not kill.' I guess we get an exemption during war. There is really some crazy shit in the Bible. One chapter has 'no killing'; the next chapter has 'kill all living things, let nothing be spared.' Whoever wrote it had to have a split personality."

"This Locke kid. You think he ran out of fear?"

"At this point, I don't even care."

"You think Major Grayson is concerned about what the family will hear?"

"I think he's concerned about himself. Can't have cowards in his unit. But yeah, maybe the family, too."

"What happens now?"

"I hope we get moving before these bodies start to stink."

"I can't believe we didn't have anyone killed. I have to admit, I was scared shitless. I can't imagine how you guys deal with it on a daily basis."

"After a while, you just get used to it. It just becomes normal."

"Normal?"

"I mean, it becomes your life and you have to accept it. If you don't, you end up like Locke. When Mad Dog was wrapping up Kelly's hand, he did say we had wounded. He treated seven gunshot and shrapnel wounds. The choppers already came and went."

"Kelly didn't go in?"

"He's a fucking boneheaded Irishman. Says he'll go in when he really gets hurt. He will get a Purple Heart, though."

"I'll go drop these letters off to Wilkes myself. If he knows I've seen them, it might carry some weight. I'll keep after him, make sure he follows through."

Holt walked over to Kelly. "What's up with you and God boy?"

"Nothing. We were just talking. Figured I could use a tune-up. I kind of flipped out last night. Got a little carried away."

"You think? You were a fucking animal. And thank God you were. You saved our asses. They would have overrun us for sure. If they got inside the perimeter, who knows how many would have been killed? You did good, bucko."

"I never would have thought I could take pleasure in killing someone. But last night, I was in the groove."

Holt lit cigarettes for them both and let Kelly talk.

"You remember reading about Richard Speck? He's that pussy who tied up eight nurses and then killed them. Papers called him a mass murderer, a monster. What are they going to call us?"

"They are already calling us baby-killers and murderers."

"You think we'll be able to forget this shit?"

"I pray we will. But I think this is going to stay with us for some time."

"Did anyone take a body count?"

"I told Wilkes there were forty killed. He'll tell the Major sixty. And Grayson will call in eighty."

"We killed forty?"

"How the fuck should I know? I ain't rooting through those bodies. Forty sounded like a good number."

Around noon, the search for Locke was abandoned and he was listed as Missing in Action. Resupply choppers came in with ammo and water, which were quickly distributed. Enemy weapons were gathered and thrown on the choppers. The order was given to move out. No one wanted to stay around the dead, which had begun to smell.

Chapter 25

Into the Valley and Beyond

Three days' hard march brought them through the jungle and into the valley, where the big operation would commence. The Alpha and Bravo Companies arrived on choppers.

"How come those pussies flew in and we had to hump the whole way?" asked Kelly.

"Three days of humping through booby traps and snipers when we could have flown. That's straight-up bullshit," added Mercado.

"I know," said Holt, "four more wounded and two killed for nothing."

"And we never saw a gook the whole three days."

"Gene, are you itching for a fight?"

"I can't stand booby traps. The fuckers should come out and fight if they want to kill us. A booby trap ain't no way to die."

"I got a feeling you'll get your fight soon enough. So, are we excited? This is it! The beginning of the big plan. The Major says this valley contains a whole NVA regiment. Mano a mano. Fix bayonets and on to glory."

"As long as I got bullets, I don't need no bayonet," said Wilson.

"The gooks love using their bayonets, especially on our wounded."

"Must be some bullshit gook samara thing."

"One good thing about being here: we should be getting a proper resupply," said Holt.

"No mail for five days. I'm down to one C-ration and half a canteen."

"I'll find Wilkes and see what's up."

"Tell him we need C-4, too. I ain't eating any more cold rations. They taste like shit when they're cold."

"I'll register your complaint; I'm sure he'll respond accordingly."

When Holt returned, he said, "You boys better sit down. You are not going to believe what I just heard. They found Locke."

"Where? Where did that cocksucker end up?"

"A chopper picked him up about two miles west of our position. It took him this long to make it back to Cu Chi. The Major flew back to greet him. He's telling a whopper of a story. Of course, he didn't run away. After being prompted, he agreed he was going for more ammo. He got lost and ended up heading west, where the chopper found him. Said he had to escape and evade the gooks the whole time. He credits his training with helping him to survive. He's being hailed as a hero. A fucking hero!"

"That miserable little cunt. And they're believing that shit?"

"Kelly, they had the story prepared. All he's doing is stepping right into it."

"That little fuck is going to skate himself right into a job in the rear."

"Ah-hah, here's the wrinkle. The Major promoted him to Specialist Fourth Class and made him one of his RTOs. He's returning as one of Grayson's ass buddies in the Command Post. Probably going to get a medal, too."

"If I see that piece of shit, I swear I'll kill him myself."

"Behave yourself, Eugene. He outranks you."

"He must be pissing his pants at the thought of coming back out."

"If there is a God in heaven, he'll get his just rewards," said Kelly.

"Everyone in Delta Company knows the true story. He won't be making any friends. The guys in Headquarters Company pride themselves as true Wolfhounds. And I guarantee they'll know soon enough. But enough about that asshole. We take a break, chow down, then at one o'clock we have to march to the far end of the valley to make room for the 1ˢᵗ Battalion."

"That has to be three miles or more. I'm guessing those guys are also flying in?"

"Excellent observation, Kelly. It is three miles exactly. And yes, they are flying in."

"What about supplies?"

"I did tell the Lieutenant about your concerns, and he said to divvy up what we have and we'll be supplied tonight. We're all in the same boat. Everybody's running on empty."

After his meal of 'meat chunks with beans and tomato sauce' laced with hot sauce, Holt leaned against his pack, smoking a cigarette. "Eugene, make sure everyone has at least one full canteen to get us to the end. Here, take one of mine; I have two left."

Mercado joined him, leaning against his radio.

"You know Nicky, this is the rock river all over again, with grass instead of rocks."

"The same type of growth on either side for cover, but not as slimy. It should be easy walking."

"Maybe this is all part of the same river system, but up here it scoured away all the rocks and just left dirt. I feel like I'm inside a bowl, though."

"I know what you mean. High grassy hills on each side instead of the cliffs. I thought it was always important to take the high ground?"

"Yet here we sit at the bottom. You know, there are gooks up in them hills right now. They're up there, eyeballing us and counting how many of us there are."

"Did you hear what we're supposed to be doing?"

"When this grassy shit ends, the jungle begins again. A mile or so in, the valley splits in two. The 1st Battalion takes the left split and we take the right. I think for a few days, we'll run patrols, maybe get some rest before the big push. It's gonna take that long to get everybody in and supplied."

"Are we getting replacements?"

"Wilkes is having each squad give us one man."

"You can be sure it's not their best. We better not get three more like Locke."

"Whoever they are, they all got a month under their belts. They're not FNGs anymore."

At precisely 1300 hours, they moved out. The fourth squad was in the lead, with Delta Company following. Behind them was Charlie Company. The Alpha and Bravo companies crossed the valley and slipped into the trees on the east side.

"At least this shit ain't all wet and moldy like before. I smell like a pile of wet dogs."

"You ever forget your gym clothes and leave them in you locker over the weekend? You smell like that: a damp jock strap."

"Maybe the Major will bring us some of those fancy camo fatigues."

"Your fatigues are already camouflaged. They're all striped with sweat, mud and piss."

They walked in silence for the remaining miles, too tired to talk. When they reached the jungle, they stopped.

Lieutenant Wilkes came up to them. "Move in about one hundred feet, and stop and dig in. Delta will spread out and link up with Alpha Company. Charlie Company will stay behind you on a right angle, forming our left flank. Bravo Company will be our flank on the other side. The 1st Battalion will do the same behind us, forming a big box. The resupply choppers will land inside the box. Any questions?"

"Replacements?"

"I got three for you. I'll send them over. One more thing. I signed off with my recommendation on your commendations. They'll go in tonight."

"Thanks, Lieutenant."

"You okay about Locke?"

"Please, Lieutenant, I don't want to hear any more about that coward."

"He had quite a story to tell."

"And a complete bullshit story it was."

"He's one of the Major's RTOs now, so just leave him alone."

"Understood. I'll pass the word."

"Here comes our replacements. There's a familiar face. It's Kimball back from first squad."

Holt and Kimball shook hands.

"And you two are?"

"Bill Kane, Sergeant."

"Carlos Menendez."

"Welcome to the fourth, or what's left of it."

"You guys had some bad luck," said Kimball.

"Shit happens. After a month out here, you're no longer FNGs, and don't let anyone give you any crap about being new. This whole operation has been a horror show, and you've seen enough to last a lifetime. We all share equally and we look out for one another. Pull your weight and we'll get along fine."

"What's the story with your guy Locke?"

"He's gone and we don't speak of him again. Agreed?"

"Kimball, take your old spot as assistant gunner with Kelly. Menendez, you good with the blooper?"

"Better than most."

"You'll keep your M16, too. We'll all the share the grenades with you. Kane, you'll stay as a rifleman and fill in where needed. Any questions? When the choppers come in with supplies, you three and Kelly will get them. Wilson, Mercado and I will stay and prepare our position."

As the afternoon passed, Holt sent Wilson, Kane and Menendez out to place trip flares and Claymores. Kelly and Kimball laid out the ammo belts for the M60. A long shallow trench had been dug as their fighting position. They would sleep outside the foxhole. As night approached, they lit their last cigarettes and talked quietly, getting to know each other. Guard rotation was set, and the men settled in for the night. Later that night, there was sporadic rifle fire from Bravo Company. Mercado had the handset against his ear.

"Bravo reports they are getting probed. A couple of trip flares went off, then nothing."

"They are just fucking with our sleep. I doubt they'll hit us again after the beating they took. Just stay alert," Holt said.

The next morning, they awoke damp and stiff with morning dew. Wilson set about brewing coffee. "Sarge, where are we crapping?"

"Go to the left about twenty feet. Dig a deep hole and make sure you bury everything, paper included. Mark your spot with a stone or something so the next guy doesn't dig up your shit. Take somebody with you for cover."

Wilson handed Holt his first cup of coffee, and he settled back with a cigarette. Mail had arrived with the supplies, and he got two letters from Janet. The letters were the usual harmless fluff: the weather and her health were the main topics.

"Any pictures?" asked Kelly.

"Behave yourself."

Menendez noticed Kelly's bandaged hand and asked what happened.

"That's what happens from furious masturbation. Tore the skin right off," Holt said.

"Jesus, what does your dick look like?"

"His dick is so calloused, it looks like a German sausage."

"That's right. It's a big, thick, foot-long German blood sausage."

"Dream on, asshole," said Mercado. "Here comes that reporter and Chaplain Doody."

"I heard the chaplain is Canadian. What's he doing with us?" asked Kane.

"He won't say. Keeps it a mystery. Hey, Menendez, where you from?"

"The Bronx."

"Nicky, let Mr. Freed know he's from New York."

"Good morning, gents. You look like you're all settled in."

"Good morning to you, Mr. Freed. Chaplain, how you doing? How come you ain't wearing camo fatigues? I heard all the headquarters guys have got them."

"I'll wear them when they become standard issue. Until then, I think it's premature."

"Good for you. Stay a man of the people."

Mercado introduced Menendez to Mr. Freed, and the three of them sat and talked.

"Chaplain, how about some coffee?"

"That would be nice, thank you."

Holt brewed two cups and handed one to the chaplain, along with an open can of cookies. They sat for a time in silence.

"You had a rough time a few nights back. You okay with everything? Want to talk about it?"

"Nah, it's all done with. We're doing good. Business as usual."

"You're not bothered by all the death?"

"It's what we do, what we're trained to do. It's why we're here."

"But still?"

"It's something you just have to accept. What bothers me is what'll happen when we get home. How are we going to act then? We're going to be different. At home, I felt alone, even when I was with people. I guess that's how it always been for guys coming back from war. Everything stays normal back home; but for us, nothing's the same. I couldn't even sleep in a bed for a week; I slept on the floor. I cursed all the time and drank way too much, got in fights without knowing why. I feel better here. I like the jungle."

"It doesn't have to be. You can always talk to me. That's why I'm here."

"Fucking Army gives you no time to decompress. You are here one day and home the next. How the fuck do they expect you to fit back in? It's FUBAR."

"What's FUBAR?"

"Fucked Up Beyond All Recognition."

He laughed. "That's good. I'll have to remember that. I will tell you that I find it difficult to get used to this. The fighting is so savage. Death is so quick and absolute."

"Lighten up. You're spoiling my cookies and coffee. You want a cigarette?"

"I quit. You should, too."

"I know it's bad for my health." He held up the cigarette. "But out here, this is the last thing that's going to kill me."

"I thank you for the coffee. I'll be on my way. Third squad is toward the right?"

"Yep. Then second and first. Don't wander out in front. The guys are still itchy. They'll shoot first, then ask questions."

They spent the rest of the day lounging bare-chested by their position. They read car magazines and comics, and discussed where they would take their R&R. They talked about girls. They smoked cigarettes and ate lunch. They slept, or tried to. They cleaned their weapons and cleaned them again. They tried not to think about the next few days.

Chapter 26

The Lieutenant's Patrol

At 9 AM, Lieutenant Wilkes held a squad leaders' meeting. "I've just met with Major Grayson, and I want to go over the plan as it has developed so far. The plan is fluid and will adapt to changing circumstances. He wants a platoon-sized patrol to scout the valley ahead. We'll go one mile and set a defensive perimeter, and wait for the battalion to join us. I was able to secure the fourth platoon the honor of the initial reconnaissance. I will be leading the patrol, and Sergeant Camp will accompany us."

"On the map, it seems that there is a road. Are we going to be following that road?"

"That's a good question, Sergeant Holt. A road exists, although its condition is unknown. This region was a central hub for the collection of raw rubber. Three miles from here is a former French town that was quite built up. It has been fought over several times in the past during the French occupation. My understanding is not much is left. It sits at an intersection of two large roads. One road is the one you mentioned that leads into this valley, and the second skirts the valley to the east. The Major is seeing if he can obtain armor participation in this operation from the 25th Division or the 11th Armored Cavalry, both of which have units in the general area."

Holt looked at the other squad leaders, who made a point of studying their maps.

"If this town was so vital to the French, then it should be

important to the gooks. Is this where the gooks are supposed to be?"

"If the town is occupied, then the town will be cleared. If there are buildings intact, then we might resettle it and use it as a base of operations. As I said, the operational plans are fluid. We are trying to get photo reconnaissance as we speak."

"Can choppers land there?"

"As I understand it, there was a contingent of French soldiers stationed there, and there were barracks and an assembly area large enough for choppers to land. There is also a fort there, which we hope to secure for the Major's command post. That's why this town is of such importance. It could provide a fortified position in some very valuable territory. We can deny the North Vietnamese access to this valley, both as a supply area and as an assembly point for offensive operations to the south."

Holt looked at Camp, who shrugged.

"Are there any other questions? Good. Get your men ready, fill your canteens, and draw rations for three days. It may be that long before the Battalion joins us. We're leaving at eleven. Fourth squad will be on point, and we will we proceed in a diamond formation with my headquarters element in the middle. We will move slowly and cautiously. For once, time is on our side."

When Holt returned to the squad position, he found the men relaxing. Mercado was reading a week-old issue of Stars and Stripes, the Army newspaper.

"It says here the 1st Cavalry launched Operation Pegasus to break through the siege at Khe Sanh. I hope those jarheads appreciate the effort. It also says NVA tanks were spotted in the surrounding area."

"Enough of that shit. Listen up. We move out at eleven. Kimball, you, Menendez and Kane go get four cartons of Cs. Kelly, you and Wilson get water; and everyone, top off your canteens. Make sure you have enough ammo. Mercado, are you fixed for batteries?"

"Got a fresh one in the radio and two more for spares."

Holt did some quick calculations and said, "Get four more. And if you see any LAWs lying around, grab some."

"You expecting gook tanks?"

"Bunker-busting, Nick. Plus, you never know."

"What will you be doing?"

"Studying the map. Remember, I'm the brains of this outfit. I got you donkeys for the brawn. Chop chop, let's hustle."

They spent the time until eleven packing their rucksacks until they bulged.

"This sucks! I ended up with three Ham and Egg meals. C'mon, someone trade with me," said Kimball.

"I'll give you my Ham and Motherfuckers for one," said Menendez.

"Keep it; that's no trade."

"Nicky, nice job on scoring the LAWs. Four is just about right. Let's check everyone's packs. I don't want anyone overloaded. We should all be carrying about seventy to seventy-five pounds."

"I got so much shit hanging off my pack, I feel like a mule," said Wilson.

"In this heat, we wouldn't load a mule this badly."

Everyone shouldered their packs, rolled their shoulders and adjusted their straps, settling the weight.

Holt lit a cigarette. "Everyone, gather round. We all remember what happened to Fisk. Pure, bad fucking luck. Wrong place at the wrong time. Nothing to be done about it. But out here in the bush, we control how we act. We look out for each other and we protect each other. We don't take stupid risks, regardless of what some officer tells us to do. Our job is to make it through this shitshow and go home. We do our job, but we do it as safely as we can. We're all brothers out here, and we look after and protect our brothers. No one dies; we all go home."

They left at eleven o'clock. Holt was surprised to see the reporter, Mr. Freed, walking alongside Lieutenant Wilkes.

"What are you doing here?"

"I'm going to accompany you guys on the patrol today."

"You might want to reconsider that."

"Why's that? You don't think I can keep up?"

"It's not that. No one knows this area, and anything can happen. We'll be at least an hour or more from any help if we need it. The Major thinks this is going to be easy: hunt down the NVA and kill them. If we run into a larger force, it could really get hairy. You'd be much safer back with the Headquarters Command."

"I didn't come out here to be safe. I came here to get the story of how you live. You don't get that story hanging around the CP."

"You got a weapon?"

"I'm a journalist; I'm not supposed to carry one."

"So that means someone has to watch over you. In combat, that ain't going to happen. Hey, Kelly, let Mr. Freed borrow your forty-five. Here, put this on."

Mr. Freed held the holstered pistol and belt dumbly.

"Put it on, or you ain't going."

"You are aware that you can't order me around?"

"Put the fucking pistol on. We can't dick around here. We got to be moving out."

Mr. Freed stared Holt in the eyes, but did finally strap the pistol around his waist.

Holt walked past the Lieutenant. "Bad idea, bringing him along," he said as he passed him heading to the front of the column.

The road began two hundred feet from their position. They stayed at the sides, aware of any disturbance on the surface. Traveling at a leisurely pace, it was two hours before they stopped at four.

Lieutenant Wilkes came up to Holt. "You need a break?"

"We should stop here. We've gone more than a mile. That hill over there is a perfect place to dig in for the night."

"That hill, as you call it, is nothing more than a mound of dirt."

"It's high ground. It's gotta be fifty or seventy feet high. It's big enough to hold the whole platoon, and we can see the road in both directions. It's got trees for shade and rocks for cover. I haven't seen a better place. Have you?"

"You may be right. Take your squad and check it out. Give us a wave if it's all you say."

To Holt, it was perfect. The ground was level and grassy, with trees to provide cover and shade. Large rocks rimmed the perimeter, and the earth was moist and soft. Easy digging. The Lieutenant, and the platoon, came to the top. Wilkes began to give orders in a crisp fashion, placing the squads in a tight perimeter.

"Fucking ass-kisser is showing off for the reporter," said Mercado.

"Let him play soldier, as long as he does what I say. Quiet, here he comes."

"I have to admit, this is a good spot." Wilkes looked over the rocks down to the road. "Place some trip flares out from the base, about ten yards. Put half your Claymores down at the base, and the other half midway pointed down."

"Front toward enemy?" asked Kelly.

"What? Why are you asking? Of course, put the front toward the enemy. Are you all right?"

"Kelly's from Boston," Holt said, as if no further explanation was necessary.

"Good call, Lieutenant," said Mercado. "This ground is like digging in sand. We'll have our holes prepared in no time."

Wilkes nodded in agreement. "No fires after dark. Chow down and stay alert."

"Good advice, Lieutenant. We'll get it done."

As the Lieutenant walked away, Kelly said, "What a dimwit! Did he really think we'd light fires at night?"

"Obviously, he thinks we're the dimwits. Kelly, you and Kimball set your gun at the end. Let's set the flares and Claymores."

Later, the men prepared their C-rations.

"How is it I got 'Meat Chunks' again? The least they could do is call them 'Beef Chunks'."

"What makes you think they're beef?"

"Kimball, gimme that shit. I'm going to fix your Ham and Eggs Spanish-style. I guarantee you'll love them," said Mercado.

"Just don't fuck them up. I can barely choke down that crap as it is."

Mercado scooped the contents into a larger pan and mashed the eggs, adding several different spices and hot sauce. He folded the eggs several times, finally adding a dollop of cheese and letting it melt in. He handed the pan to Kimball without saying anything. He watched as Kimball took a tentative taste.

"Jesus Christ! This is delicious. You've got to show me how you made them."

"Anything tastes better with spices."

After dinner, the men settled down to reread mail.

"You didn't say how Janet and the kid are."

"She says everything is fine; no problems. Here, she sent me another picture."

Mercado looked at the picture, then at Holt. "Are those her nipples?"

"Apparently."

"Ask her to unbutton her shirt in the next picture."

"You know, I might just do that."

"Let me see," said Kelly.

"As long as your hand is bandaged, I guess there's no harm."

"God gave me a left hand for just this type of condition. I've practiced. I'm ambidextrous. My God, you could hang your hat on those pups."

"You could hang your steel pot on them, and I doubt they would flex," said Mercado.

Holt sighed. "Once again, we find ourselves debating the merits of my wife's breasts. Believe me, they weren't that big last I saw them. She says they got big and firm with baby milk."

Kelly groaned. "Could you imagine having them nipples in your mouth?"

"Again, please remember, this is my wife you're talking about."

"Here comes Camp. Wendy, you gotta see Janet's tits."

Camp studied the picture. "I feel like I could use a cigarette after looking at this. If she sends more pictures, could you ask her to let down her hair and maybe pull up her blouse a little?"

"Here's what I'll do. I'll tell her to get naked and open her legs so we get a proper beaver shot. How's that?"

"Have her cup her tits at the same time, maybe play with herself a little."

"Does she have blond pussy hair?"

"Enough! Please, dear God, no more. This is the last picture you assholes are ever going to see."

Kelly groaned again.

Camp spread out his map. "We are somewhere around here."

"I think we've gone too far. We were only supposed to go a mile."

"Agreed. Tonight, we are going to stay put; and tomorrow, maybe run a patrol up the road. You want to do it?"

"Sure. I need some time to work with the new guys. I want to see how they handle themselves."

"I made sure they didn't give you any fuckups. They're all good guys. You got your Claymores out? Trip flares?"

"Yes, mother. No need to worry about us."

"Right now, we have no artillery cover, and we won't have any until a day or two. That bothers me."

"This whole thing seems rushed. It's like they're still in the planning stage."

"This isn't bad. We have a nice, tight perimeter. Just stay alert."

The jungle was alive with night noise. The 'fuck you' lizards were active together with crickets and frogs. You could hear bats fluttering in the upper tree branches, hunting insects.

Mercado leaned in and whispered in Holt's ear. "I just heard. The NVA overran a Special Forces camp at Lang Vei outside of Khe Sanh. They used tanks to roll right through the perimeter. Fucking tanks. Can you believe it? The gooks, using tanks."

"Who told you that?"

"Us RTOs share information. Do you think they got tanks this far south?"

"I doubt it. Maybe in Cambodia, but not here. They got trucks and shit in Cambodia. All up and down the Ho Chi Minh trail. I heard they got Russian and Cuban advisers in Cambodia."

"What would Cubans be doing in Vietnam?"

"Well, you're here."

"I ain't no fucking Cuban. I'm Puerto Rican. There's a big difference."

"Sorry, Nick. I didn't realize that there was a hierarchy of spics."

"I'll tell you what. When we get home, you come see me in Spanish Harlem and tell a Puerto Rican he's a Cuban, and see if anyone gets offended."

"I'll do that, brother, as long as you promise to protect me."

Just then, the jungle went silent, as if a switch was thrown, shutting off all noise. The hair on Holt's neck stood up. There was nothing but dead silence. "Nick, wake the others up."

They all huddled in the foxhole.

"Did you hear that? A branch cracked," said Wilson.

"Is that someone whispering? Is it out front?"

"First and second squads got movement in front of them," said Mercado. "Wilkes says stay alert, and don't fire unless you got a target."

They heard another branch crack and a muffled curse.

"Where's that coming from?"

"Kane, be quiet."

"Ask Wilkes if we can we throw out some grenades."

"He said no. He's afraid we'll blow up our Claymores."

Holt swore he could hear his heartbeat.

Silence again.

"I don't hear anything. Maybe they were just fucking around, keeping us awake."

"It could have been an animal."

"Man, when I get home, I ain't never sleeping in the dark again. I don't care who makes fun of me," said Mercado.

"I know what you mean. There are bad things in the dark."

The night passed in silence; no more 'fuck you' lizards, no crickets or frogs. Just silence.

In the morning, they felt exhausted before the day even began.

Chapter 27

Day Two of the Patrol

"Second squad reports two of their Claymores are missing. Gooks cut the wires and took them," said Mercado.

"Why are the gooks crawling all over our shit? Don't they ever sleep?"

"I guess they sleep during the day, Gene."

"It gives me the creeps, knowing they're out there at night."

Holt saw Camp approach. "Good morning, Sunshine. Did you sleep well last night?"

"No, I did not. Same as you, I would imagine. Wilkes was on the radio all night. The Battalion was getting probed all night long. Some trip flares went off, and the LPs reported activity all around the perimeter. They are going to remain in place another day and send out patrols. Wilkes wants you to scout up the road another half-mile and find another location for tonight. He doesn't want to stay here two nights in a row."

"We're putting too much distance between us and the main group. If we run into any shit, it'll be two hours before they can get to us."

"I told him that. He says the Major is okay with extending our patrol."

"You sure this isn't Wilkes just trying to look good?"

"What should I do, ask to speak to Grayson myself? Go slow and be careful."

"We'll leave at nine and go a half-mile. I don't like spending the night here again, but I doubt we'll find anything as good."

Mad Dog came by with Mr. Freed to check on everyone.

"Mind if I join you boys for breakfast? I brought my own," said Mr. Freed.

"You guys get any sleep?" asked Mad Dog.

"Ten, fifteen minutes at a time. The gooks were playing with us all night."

"Everybody reported noises. Some unsettling shit. Seems like they're preparing something."

"Nothing good, I imagine."

"What is that you're eating?"

"Boned chicken with cheese and crackers," said Holt.

"I got 'Beef in Spiced Sauce'; it's not bad. Not good, but not bad. I've tried C-rations before, but never had to eat them on a daily basis. I guess you get used to them."

"Mr. Freed, you never get used to eating this shit. It's dog food for humans. We won't see any hot chow for awhile. So, bon appetit."

"I was reading somewhere that C-rations are made high in calories and engineered to be highly digestible to reduce stool."

"If reducing stool means giving you explosive diarrhea, then you're correct."

"It's the water that gives you the shits, not the Cs. I got some pills that may help," said Mad Dog.

"You got anything to stay awake? I'm dead on my feet."

"I have some Benzedrine. The Long-Range Reconnaissance guys use them."

"I'll pass for now, but keep them handy."

"I heard you are taking out a patrol. Can I come along?"

"Absolutely no fucking way. And where is your forty-five?"

"I left it at the CP."

"What fucking good is it going to do you there? With all the stories you've written, you should know it's not safe anywhere. What the fuck is wrong with you?"

"I should have mentioned, I do have the honorary rank of Lieutenant."

"And that's an excuse for being stupid. I'd say the same thing to Wilkes if he were to walk around without his weapon."

"What would you say to me, Sergeant?"

"Jesus, you're getting like the gooks, Lieutenant. Sneaking up on us. That's good. I was just telling Mr. Freed he can't be walking around unarmed, not out here."

"Carry your pistol, Mr. Freed, and make Sergeant Holt happy. I want to go over the patrol with you. Scout another place for us to stay tonight."

"Sergeant Camp relayed your orders."

"Gather up your Claymores and be on your way. I don't want us sitting here all day."

The fourth squad left their hilltop perimeter and started down the road, keeping to the trees and avoiding the road surface. They stopped after a quarter of a mile.

"Nick, get the Lieutenant on the horn."

"Lieutenant, we got a bunch of converging foot paths down here." He listened, then replied. "Some are well-worn and look fresh. Others, not so much. They're coming in from the west."

He listened and handed the microphone to Mercado. "Fuckhead wants us to keep going. We're in the middle of a gook highway, and he wants to set up camp. Says it might be a good place for an ambush. Fucking moron is going to get us all killed."

Holt rose from his bended knee and lit a cigarette. He turned to his left and saw two NVA soldiers coming down the trail, frozen in midstep.

Before he could react, Kelly fired a stream of tracers into their chests. He was exuberant. "Did you see that? Made those fuckers dance the chicken."

"Wilkes wants to know what happened."

"Tell him, Nicky. Tell him what the fuck happened. Wilson, Kane, check out the bodies."

Wilson came back holding some documents and cloth patches, and handed them to Holt. Holt examined them and gave then back to Wilson. "Stuff them in your pockets and give them to Wilkes."

"What about their AKs?"

"Disassemble them and throw the pieces in the woods. You keeping their belts?"

"Damn straight. I need a belt. They got a red star on them."

"Wilkes said to hold in place. He's bringing up the platoon."

"Cross the road. Get over in those trees and we'll wait."

The remainder of the fourth platoon arrived an hour later. Holt was fuming. "This is why I'm worried we've gone too far. It takes you an hour to get here and you were prepared. How long do you think it'll take the Battalion to put together a reaction force and get to us?"

"Relax, Sergeant. The Battalion is prepared to respond to any request for assistance at a moment's notice."

Holt frowned and went to retrieve his rucksack. "Petulant little prick. They all believe they know better, and they all have an opinion."

"But you're in charge, and it's your opinion that matters."

"Correct, Mr. Freed. I can't have every decision, every order, debated."

"Dwight Eisenhower said, 'Leadership consists of nothing but taking responsibility for everything that goes wrong and giving your subordinates credit for everything that goes well.'"

"General Eisenhower didn't have to lead a group of misfits through the jungle. He fought his war from behind a desk. He was a glorified supply clerk. You quote Patton to me, and I'll listen."

"'Never tell people how to do things. Tell them what to do and they will surprise you with their ingenuity.' General Patton said that."

"Well, let's see how that works out."

Holt found a place another quarter-mile up the road. It was a ditch that ran alongside the road, four feet deep, carved out by water drainage.

"This is adequate. Good views up and down the road. Sparse trees behind us allowing for good fields of fire. Good work, Sergeant."

"A kind word goes a long way," said Mr. Freed.

"Patton again?"

"No, me. I just made it up."

"Sergeant Camp, put two squads behind us in those trees. You take charge of them, and I'll take the remaining squads and set up in this ditch. The ditch will be your fallback if necessary. Have the men try and conceal their Claymores and trip flares. We have several hours 'til dark, so don't have them rush. Sergeant Holt, take your squad to the right. The third squad will be on the left, and I'll be in the middle. I want Claymores out to the left and right, with trip flares beyond them. No fires or cigarettes after dark."

"Again, with the fucking fires after dark. He really believes we're idiots," said Mercado.

"In your case, Nicky, he's not that far off."

"Have I told you today to go fuck yourself?"

"I have no idea. I barely listen to anything you say. Your jumbled spic English is barely decipherable. No wonder you're on the radio; you're like a Navajo code talker in WWII. Only in your case, no one can understand you. Menendez should be on the other end of all your transmissions."

"Carlos doesn't speak Spanish. I'm trying to teach him."

"How can a New York Puerto Rican not speak Spanish?"

"I know; it's sad. He has no sense of the beauty of our language, or of our heritage."

"Yeah, that's sad."

"You know, I was thinking, and I wanted to assure you that if you get killed over here, I'll get with Janet and raise the baby like it were my own. You should let her know."

"That would be something I'd like to see. Her father barely, and I mean barely, tolerates me. A Manhattan spic raising his grandchild would kill him. You're just thinking about her tits again?"

"I can't get those nipples out of my mind."

"How about this. If we survive this shit patrol, I'll ask her to send me a picture of her in a tank top with no bra. It'll be yours."

"I'm getting hard just thinking about it."

"Thank you. That's another image I could do without."

They used their entrenching tools and helmets to clear out the trench and to dig a shallow hole for their cooking stoves. Mr. Freed, with his pistol strapped to his leg, took numerous pictures in the afternoon light. At around four, they began to prepare their evening meal.

"I got Chicken and Noodles in Broth. I'll trade for some Beans and Baby Dicks," said Holt.

"Please don't eat beans tonight. Your farting will give away our position," said Kelly.

"You're probably right. I'll stick with the chicken."

Holt lit his last cigarette of the night and took out Janet's letter. She's probably sitting down to dinner in her house in Brooklyn. There will be a tablecloth, nice dishes and napkins. And here I am, eating canned chicken in a muddy ditch. Her hands will be clean. I haven't washed mine in a week.

"Don't get yourself all moody. We need to stay sharp tonight," said Mercado.

"You ever wonder what they think we're doing? I mean, Janet will go to bed tonight in clean sheets and plan her next day. We go to sleep and pray we don't get killed before dawn."

"Hey brother, you're optimistic. We'll probably get killed tonight; forget about making it to dawn."

"Fuck it! You're right. Wilkes wants fifty-percent watch. I'll take first shift. Try and catch some sleep."

At one o'clock, they heard what they thought was thunder.

"Oh shit, the Battalion's getting hit with heavy mortars and artillery from the hills."

"Nicky, are you sure? Artillery?"

"That's what they're saying. Big guns."

"Listen to that shit. There's no letup."

They all strained their necks and looked to the south. Star clusters and flares exploded in the night sky.

"Here, listen, they're getting pounded."

For more than an hour, they listened as the thunder of mortars and artillery continued.

"Ground attack! Hundreds of gooks everywhere."

They listened as Mercado relayed the information as he heard it.

"The gooks drove a wedge between the Battalions. They're forcing the Battalions apart. Our guys are shooting at each other."

"What do you mean they're shooting at each other?"

"The gooks are in the middle of the two Battalions. If they shoot at them and miss, it's going into the other Battalion." Nick held up his hand for quiet. "NVA broke through First Battalion's lines and are inside the perimeter. There's hand-to-hand fighting."

"The Major finally got his battle."

"Shut up, I can't hear. Second Battalion is falling back into the woods. Fuck! They're getting hit from the west. They're pouring out of the hills. The First Battalion is getting hit from the south, too. They are rolling over their positions."

"How many?"

"Someone is screaming that there are thousands. Over and over again, thousands!"

"That's bullshit! They're just panicking. They better get their shit together and fight back."

"Spooky is on the way, along with air support."

They watched in stunned silence as the gunships worked the ground, pouring thousands of rounds onto the perimeter. As one ship left, jets came in and dropped high-explosives and napalm on the surrounding hills. When the jets expended their ammunition, a second Spooky arrived and continued to devastate the enemy. The sky, two miles away, had a dull orange glow. By three-thirty, the fighting died down. Everyone was on full alert. At four, the word was passed down the trench line: there were gooks on the road. They strained their eyes to see shadowy figures moving toward them.

"They got stretchers. They're evacuating their wounded," Holt whispered in Mercado's ear.

"Not for long."

Third squad let most of the NVA walk past their position into the kill zone before they opened up. Fourth squad leaned over the trench so they could fire down the road. Claymores were blown, filling the air with hundreds of steel pellets and smoke. Four NVA jumped into the trench and charged third squad from their left, firing at close range. The fighting was fierce and bloody. As quickly as it began, it was over. The road was strewn with bodies. The smell of blood and cordite hung in the moist night air. Men from the third squad left the trench and fired single shots into the dying North Vietnamese.

Behind him, he saw Camp crawling toward them. "Is it over? Everyone okay?"

"Sound off, anyone hit?" shouted Lieutenant Wilkes.

"We're all good," hollered Holt.

Someone called for a medic.

"Doc, down here," came another voice.

Holt sagged back against the trench.

"Man, that was brutal. Those fuckers didn't stand a chance. We tore them up."

Wilson crowded in. "What are the battalions saying?"

"Nothing. I hear nothing. No one is on the net."

"That's impossible. Someone has to be talking."

"Here, listen for yourself. There's nobody there."

Holt listened, then handed the handset back to Mercado.

"It's like they're all fucking gone."

"That's not possible. There were over a thousand guys there. Two battalions just don't vanish."

"Can you hear any more firing?"

"Nothing."

"Well, where are they?"

Chapter 28

The French Fort

It wasn't until 9 AM that they could raise the Battalion and the Major.

"Lieutenant, I want you to get your men somewhere that's safe and sit this battle out. As it stands right now, we are surrounded and cut off from the First Battalion. We have several hundred NVA to the north effectively standing between us and you. Estimates range from one thousand NVA to well over that committed to this fight. Second Battalion alone has over two hundred casualties. Hopefully, the mortars and artillery in the hills have been suppressed by the air support. This is the fight we were looking for, and we will prevail. Are my orders clear? Hunker down and wait this out. The 11th Armored Cavalry is running a relief column to us. Once they arrive, we will bust through the enemy and come get you. Am I clear?"

"Yes, sir! Crystal clear."

"Conserve your ammo, food and water. There will be no resupply until the Cavalry arrives."

"I'm glad to hear you're in good spirits, sir. Give them hell!"

The squad leaders gathered around the Lieutenant and Sergeant Camp. Mr. Freed stood at the side, taking pictures.

"Unfortunately, we have orders to sit out this fight. The NVA has a blocking force between us and the Battalion. As much as I would like to tear into that force, the Major has advised it would impede the effective use of air support. We need a safe place to wait for a relief column. I know just the spot: the French Fort. We are less than a mile from it, and it will serve two purposes: the first being a safe, defensive place to wait; and the second, it will become the Major's command post for additional operations in the valley. Any questions?"

"Lieutenant, these gooks we killed last night, where do you think they were going?"

"Enlighten me, Sergeant Holt."

"They were bringing their wounded up the same road we'll be going. There must be something up there, a facility manned by troops. If the gooks are coming in from the hills to the west, we should go east to be safe. We shouldn't be heading to a place where we know there are more gooks."

"That's a valid point. We easily took care of this group, and we can do the same if we encounter additional opposition."

"These fuckers were all involved in carrying their wounded; they weren't expecting us. It was like shooting fish in a barrel."

"Sergeant Camp, do you have an opinion?"

"I kind of agree with the Lieutenant. A fort sounds like it would provide a good defensive position."

"And what if the fort is occupied? Are we going to fight our way in?"

"Your objections are noted, Sergeant Holt; but we're going to the fort. Tell your men we will be on half-rations and to conserve their water. We won't be getting resupplied until relieved. We move out in ten."

"Sarge, I couldn't help but overhear. What is 'shooting fish in a barrel', and why is it easy?"

"Because they are fish, and they're in a fucking barrel. It's an expression. You never heard it before?"

"No, Sarge. Wouldn't they be swimming and underwater?"

"Kimball, what the fuck is wrong with you? Are you some sort of cave-dwelling Amish fuck?"

"I'm Kane, Sarge."

"You two blonde hicks look too much alike. Don't stand next to each other anymore. Get your gear on. Ask someone else about shooting fish."

"Mercado?"

"Yeah, ask Mercado. He's a Puerto Rican from Manhattan, but I'm sure he knows all about fish. Just get out of my sight, you dimwit."

Mercado shrugged on his radio and rucksack and walked over to Holt. "What was that all about?"

"Don't be surprised if Kane asks you about fishing. I told him you were an expert."

"Fishing?"

They hadn't walked more than three hundred feet when Holt stopped the column. A large trail intersected the road from the west.

"Tell Wilkes we got a fresh trail with beaucoup tracks, all converging and heading north."

"Wilkes said he's coming up."

Lieutenant Wilkes, his RTO and Mad Dog came to where Holt was standing. Holt pointed to the trail. As Wilkes went to examine it, Holt lit a cigarette and turned to the medic.

"Who got hit last night?"

"Two guys from first squad. A bullet graze in the leg and some shrapnel wounds. Patched them both up. They'll be fine."

"This is bullshit. Any other time, they would be evacuated and be back at Cu Chi. Instead, we got John Wayne who thinks he's going to be in charge of a fort."

"This plan doesn't appear to be fully thought out."

"You think?"

Wilkes joined them. "How many tracks would you say?"

"There are sandals and boots all overlaid with each other, so it's hard to tell. Maybe a hundred or more. For certain, the tracks are fresh."

"I'd say those tracks are at least a few days old, and no more than thirty men. Let's continue. I want to be at that village by eleven."

They walked on the right side of the road, but were soon forced back onto the road by a wall of rocks and boulders. As they approached the village, there was a gigantic boulder to their right. It was more than fifty feet tall and equally as wide.

Wilkes came up to Holt. "Look at your map. This rock is such a distinctive feature, it is actually on the map."

They signaled the men to stay and walked forward. They knelt behind some rocks.

"There's the village."

"This ain't no village. It's got actual fucking buildings."

"We should map it out. Here, you draw it." Wilkes handed Holt a sheet of paper and a worn pencil. "In front of us, we got a line of single-story buildings and a wide, packed dirt street. On the other side of the street, we have two rows of two-story buildings, back to back. Then another street, and another row of buildings. See down the end of the street? Those are the warehouses where the raw rubber was stored. There's the assembly area for the French troops, and way off to the right are their barracks. On the other side of this boulder is the fort."

"This had to be some place when it was active. Now, it's just a bunch of bombed-out shit."

"My understanding is over two hundred of the French lived here. The rubber plantation is still active in the northwest. Out there, somewhere, was where the Vietnamese workers lived. They had their own village. This was just for the French."

"That big building in the center looks like some sort of government building."

"This will be good for us to stay in, and could make a great staging area for the next phase of the operation. Still nervous, Sergeant?"

"It's too big for a single platoon to secure. We would need a company to search all those buildings."

"Once we're settled, we can run some patrols and see if anybody's home."

"This place could house hundreds of gooks. Remember when Wilson found those stacked boulders? Those warehouses could be the supply depot."

"If it is, Battalion needs to know."

"I've had my fill of house-to-house fighting during Tet. This place could be a nightmare."

"Or it could be empty."

"Let me borrow your binoculars, Lieutenant." Holt studied the street, looking for any movement. Whatever windows contained glass were now shattered, dark, gaping holes. "You see that house in the corner? I'll go over there. I'll be able to see more from there. You guys stay put until I signal you."

"Sounds like a plan."

Holt sprinted to the house and threw himself against the wall. He inched his way to a blown-out window and looked inside. It was a large interior room, with another window at the back and a door facing the street. He high-stepped through the window and was inside. He perceived movement to his rear, and looked as the squads raced around the boulder toward the fort.

"Fucking moron couldn't even wait five minutes," he said to himself.

The room was dark and smelled musty. It was empty except for a broken desk. He made his way to the door. He took the binoculars and stared at the windows and doors across from him. A dozen men ran from the fort across the open area to the large two-story building facing him. They saw him and waved. He waved back and indicated they should stay put. "What the fuck is Wilkes doing?"

Some movement in the upper windows caught his eye. He trained the binoculars on the dark, black holes. A shot was fired from behind and hit him in the back. He spun around and grabbed his rifle. A young soldier was at the window, pointing an AK at him. Holt fired first, hitting him in the shoulder and knocking him down. When he got to the window, he saw the soldier running down an alley behind the house. He fired a burst and hit the soldier in the leg. He got up and continued running. Holt fired again and missed.

"Goddamn it."

He went back to the door. He felt a hot, oozing liquid spread across his back and pain in his side. He took his pack off and felt his side. His hand was covered with blood and peach syrup. He lifted his shirt and saw a gouge in his side oozing blood.

Fuck me. That gook shot me and hit a can of peaches. The bullet must have deflected and skimmed along my side, he thought.

He turned to look back out the door and was greeted by a long stream of green tracers fired at him from an upper window. The bullets chewed up the door frame and sent shards of cement into the room. A piece cut his cheek, beneath his right eye.

At that moment, the Lieutenant and his RTO entered the room through the window.

"What the fuck are you doing here? You were supposed to wait for my signal."

"I thought you were shot and came to see if you needed help."

Suddenly, there was a deafening whoosh as an RPG was fired from the upper window across from them. You could follow the projectile as it hit the Lieutenant square in the chest, blowing him to pieces and filling the room in a mist of blood, bone and smoke. Holt had turned his face away and felt the stinging bite of shrapnel in his right leg. He slid down the wall to the ground. The stench of the explosive was choking him. Another RPG was fired and impacted the building. Holt turned and saw Camp at the window.

"Get inside. Why are you here? What is going on? Who's with the men?"

"Wilkes sent the men to the fort."

Holt looked outside and saw two guys making their way up a staircase to the second floor. The dark interior of the building exploded in light as a short, vicious firefight took place. Someone appeared in the open window and gave a thumbs-up.

"We need to get out of here now!"

"Where's Wilkes?"

"See that pile of meat over there? That's him."

"Where's his RTO?"

Completely forgotten, Holt searched the room for the missing soldier and saw him slumped in the corner. A large piece of shrapnel had decapitated him. "He's in the corner."

Camp gagged and vomited. He appeared dazed and disoriented. "Where's his head?"

"Who knows? Camp, listen to me, we have to go."

"We have to find his head. He's a new guy, and I don't remember his name. We need his head to identify him."

"Are you out of your fucking mind? What's wrong with you! I keep telling you this place ain't safe. We gotta leave."

"Here it is. I found it," he said, holding the head, still wearing its helmet.

"Put that fucking thing down and let's go."

"We have to bring it with us," he said numbly.

"You ain't bringing that fucking head with you. Get rid of it, goddamn it!"

"I'm bringing it with us."

"Please, Camp, leave it. We need to go."

"No!"

"Ah, fuck it. Bring it with you, but let's go, please."

Holt got into his rucksack and went over to the Lieutenant. He gingerly removed his forty-five pistol and dug into his pants-leg pocket for his maps and code book. His rifle was bent in two, and he threw it aside. His ammo pouches were nowhere to be found. He looked at the radio and saw the side was ripped open.

"Okay, Camp, you go first and I'll cover you. Give me the head and I'll bring it."

"Okay, sure. Just don't forget it."

"How can I forget a fucking head? When you get across the street, tell them to cover me, okay?"

Camp handed him the head and ran out the door. Holt tossed the head in a corner and covered Camp. There was no firing. Camp waved him over.

Holt started out the doorway and ran, his legs pumping furiously. Someone was shooting at him from behind. The men across the street fired back. He threw himself on the ground, panting like a dog, and was handed a canteen.

"Where's my squad?" asked Holt.

"Third and fourth squad took the fort. We came over to check out this building. Where's the Lieutenant?"

"Back there. Him and his RTO, both dead."

"Who's in charge?

"Camp is. Where is he?"

"He's over there. But he's acting weird. All fucking dazed and dopey-like."

"He'll be okay. We need to get back to the fort. It's no good out here."

A barrage of RPGs hit the building walls from both sides. One hit the right side, exploding amongst three men, shredding their bodies.

"Check those guys. Gather up anything we can use: ammo, water, grenades, food. Strip the wounded and dead, and let's get moving. We're sitting ducks out here."

"Sarge, we got four killed. We got everything off them. What about the bodies?"

"We gotta leave them for now. We'll come back for them. Get your sixty gunners to cover us. We'll stop halfway and cover them."

"The gooks are pouring out of the buildings like somebody kicked over an ant hill."

"Get your men moving, and don't forget Camp."

The two gun crews put down a heavy volume of fire to cover their withdrawal. They ran across the open ground and stopped to cover the gun teams. Half the men continued without stopping, helping the wounded or too loaded down with extra equipment to be effective.

"Keep going. Don't stop until you get to the fort," Holt yelled as the gunners passed him.

Holt continued to fire for several minutes and started to run. To his left, he saw Camp staggering back. He grabbed his arm and pulled him along.

"You forgot his head."

There was a loud 'ping'. Camp's helmet flew off, and he cartwheeled to the ground. Holt ran to him and saw a deep crease along the side of his head. He tried lifting him, but he was dead weight. Another soldier came and helped. Together, they dragged Camp between them. Seventy feet from the fort, Holt's right leg flew out underneath him; and he landed square on his tailbone, the wind knocked out of him.

"Keep going, get Camp back. I'm okay."

But he wasn't. When he tried to rise, his leg buckled and he fell. He started to crawl. Bullets struck all around him in deadly little puffs of dirt.

Kelly ran out and reached Holt, and began to drag him by his combat harness. Kelly ran, dragging Holt as if he were weightless. When they reached the fort walls, Kelly gently lifted Holt over the edge and climbed in after him.

Holt struggled to sit upright.

"Give me a head count. Is everybody back?"

Mad Dog came over to him. "Jesus, dude, you are fucked up."

"Is everybody back? We didn't leave anybody, did we?"

"No, we're all here. Thirty-one here, and six dead out there."

"Wounded?"

"Not counting you, we got three seriously wounded, and seven with gunshots and shrapnel who can still fight."

"What about Camp?"

"He's unconscious. Got shot through his helmet. It left a gouge a half-inch deep from his ear to his eyebrow. The bullet just followed his skull."

"Will he be okay?"

"At the very least, he got a bad concussion. He might have brain swelling, or worse. His brain could be bleeding. I put him and the other serious wounded inside the bunker. Let me see your leg."

"I'm okay. Check on the others and come back to me."

"Sit tight and try not to move."

"Hey Nicky, come here and help me sit up."

"What happened to Wilkes?"

"Took an RPG to his chest and was blown to pieces. The only thing left of him you could recognize was his legs. His RTO got his head blown off."

"You find his head?"

"What is it with you fucking guys and his head? Yeah, Camp found it and wanted to bring it back. I left it out there."

"I was just thinking maybe his folks might want it."

"His head? What would they do with it? Put it in a jar so they could bring it out at family gatherings?"

"They might want to bury it."

"It's still out there. We'll get it when we retrieve the bodies." For the first time, Holt looked around. "This ain't much of a fort. I have never seen so many pockmarks from bullets and shrapnel."

"The wall you're leaning on, you can stand behind it. It's two feet thick. The ledge you're sitting on is four feet thick and two feet off the ground. It's got separate blast walls that will protect our backs. The bunker can hold twenty guys, and the walls and ceiling are three feet of reinforced concrete. It's got steel fold-down shutters and a two-inch steel door. This area here is the same on the other side. This is a good position. We can hold out here as long as our ammo lasts."

"You wonder why they let us have it?"

"What do you mean?"

"If it's so good, why did they let us take it without a fight? Because now they know where we all are. They don't have to hunt for us. They put us in this box for a reason."

"You think they wanted us here?"

"Damn straight! They forced us here. They have us surrounded. Nicky, we're trapped here!"

Chapter 29

Our Private Khe Sanh

Mad Dog was first to say it. "With the Lieutenant dead and Camp out of commission, you're in charge. You got the most time in grade."

"I don't want to be in charge."

"No choice. Suck it up. We're stuck with you. First, take off your shirt and drop your pants. I want to check you out."

"Faggot. How long have you wanted to say that?"

"Don't flatter yourself. I could do better than you. Way fucking better."

"I need to tell Grayson what's happened. Nick, get him on the horn."

Holt lit a cigarette while he waited.

Mercado gave him the handset. "Big Six on the line."

"Six, this is Delta Four... Ah, fuck, Nick, what's my call sign?"

"This is Six, say it clear."

"This is Sergeant Holt. Sit rep follows. Lieutenant Wilkes is KIA, along with his RTO and four others."

"Goddamm it, how did that happen? I told him to get somewhere safe. Where are you?"

"We have occupied the French fort at coordinates..."

"I know where the fort is. Why are you there?"

"It's where the Lieutenant wanted to go."

"Where's your Platoon Sergeant? Why am I talking to you?"

"The Platoon Sergeant is seriously wounded and unconscious. We also have three other serious wounded and seven, no eight, walking wounded."

"You're the senior NCO?"

"Yes, sir."

"You are to assume command and you're promoted to E-6. Now give me your sit rep."

"Situation is as follows: the fort itself is a good defensive position. I have to count ammo and supplies. I'm guessing we'll be here for awhile."

"It will be at least two days until we get you reinforcements. Can you hold for that long?"

"Do we have a choice?"

"I'll try for artillery support. I'll get a flyover to access your situation. Just hang on and we'll come for you. Can you do that?"

"We'll hold, sir. How are you guys doing?"

"Same as you, hanging on. Six out."

"This sucks a huge dick. I mean, one giant-sized, scabby, monster dick. They can't get to us. We gotta hold for two days. Hey, Mr. Freed, how you doing, old-timer? Bet you wish you stayed with Battalion right about now."

"I could ask you the same question. You look pretty chewed up."

"We'll soon see. C'mon, Doc, I'm ready for you now."

"Let's do your leg first."

The medic wiped his wound with an antiseptic cloth and prodded the area with his fingers. Mr. Freed took pictures of the procedure.

"The bullet has to come out. You want morphine?"

"Yeah, I want morphine, lots of it. But no, I gotta stay clear-headed. I'll do without it. I'm afraid you'll need it later."

"It's going to hurt. Bite down on your towel and stay still."

Mad Dog inserted a long, thin probe to locate the bullet. He spread the hole with some small forceps and inserted a tweezer of sorts. The muscles on Holt's neck stood out in thick cords as Doc dug the bullet out. He held the bloody piece of metal for Holt to examine.

"You want to save this?"

"Sure, I'll make a necklace for Janet."

"I can numb your skin while I stitch you up. You're going to have another scar. I'll try and make it look especially ugly."

Holt bit down hard on his towel as Doc stitched him with some coarse black thread.

"Nick, hold his leg still." Mad Dog stood back and admired his work. "Not my best job, but it'll do. Let's wrap it up. What's next?"

Holt said his side.

"Deep, gaping flesh wound; might need stitches. For now, we'll just bandage it and keep an eye on it. Same goes for your cheek. The shrapnel in your side will wait until you're back at Cu Chi. There are too many tiny pieces. Alright, you're done. I'll send you my bill."

"What are you writing in your book?"

"Day, time and place of wounds. A description of each wound, and how I treated them. I need this as backup for the Purple Heart recommendations. You are finished in the field, brother. Once we get back to Cu Chi, you are staying there. Your time in the bush is over."

"Let's just get back there before you plan my retirement." Holt attempted to stand and sat back down.

"Stay off your feet for awhile."

Holt nodded and lit a cigarette. "Nick, get the other squad leaders over here."

"I'm taking over for Camp until he's back on his feet. First off, we need to ration our food and water. We're going to be here awhile, two days at least. Have everyone keep one full canteen and bring everything else to Doc. The same with your rations. Don't hold back. We're in this together. Doc will inventory our supplies and determine how much we can have each day. Collect all the ammo and grenades and distribute it evenly. Single shots on the sixteens and three-round bursts on all the sixties. We have to make our shit last. Guaranteed, we'll get hit sometime this afternoon or tonight. We're on our own until reinforcements arrive. This is a solid position, and we can survive as long as we conserve our ammo. I want third and fourth squads on this side of the bunker. First and second squads, on the right side. Try and get some sleep. I have a feeling it'll be a busy night. Any questions or comments?"

"Resupply?"

"Your guess is as good as mine. The Major says he'll do a flyover to access our situation."

Holt tried to sleep. The throbbing in his leg had subsided, and the nausea from the stitching had passed. He was just dozing off when Wilson woke him.

"Wake up, Sarge. You have to see this. There's a gook out front hollering at us."

"Give me a hand and help me stand."

"See, over there, by the building where the Lieutenant was killed."

"I can't hear him. What is that skinny little runt saying?"

Another soldier ran out and gave the first one a bull horn.

"Hey, GI, you missing something?" He held up the RTO's severed head.

"You need this? You want it back? Come out and get it, we won't shoot you."

"The fucking head again. What is the fascination with this head?"

"Come on, come out, we give it to you. No lie, you come get it."

Kelly sighted his M60 and fired a short burst. Three bloody spots blossomed on the man's chest; and he fell backward, dropping the head.

"That's okay, you keep it," Kelly shouted.

"Jesus, Kelly. How did you do that?"

"Right? That had to be two or three hundred yards, and I sniped that motherfucker with a machine gun."

A barrage of AK fire came from every window and peppered the fort. A second soldier picked up the head and threw it into the open square. For the next half-hour, the NVA shot at the head, pinballing it across the parade grounds. When they tired of the game, it was barely recognizable as anything human.

"Those pricks don't seem worried about conserving ammo. Wilson, you might be right. Maybe this is their supply depot."

They stood and watched as the NVA moved about the buildings, apparently unconcerned about return fire.

"Sergeant Holt, we got a lot of movement over here by the French barracks."

Holt limped over to the right side. It was extremely generous, calling the burned-out and bombed buildings barracks. NVA soldiers were moving into the shattered buildings.

"They're getting ready to do something. They will probably hit us from both sides. On the left, they'll come down along that giant fucking boulder. Here, they got no choice, they gotta come across the open field. Let them get halfway across. Once they're committed, cut them down. They'll fire some RPGs to keep you down, but ignore them. These walls can take it. Who's in charge here?"

"I am, Sarge."

"Goddamn, Elderidge, I forgot you were here. Long time no see, brother. How are you making out?"

"Good. How's Camp?"

"He's still out; hasn't woke up. Doc's worried. So am I."

"I was thinking, I'm not going to commit our 60s at first. Just M16s. When they get close, we'll open up with the guns and make them dance."

"Sounds good. Don't use your flares unless you have to. I'm going to call about getting some illumination tonight. Let me know if there are any problems. Good luck, boys."

"There's some good news. I just spoke with Grayson. He's getting us a flare ship tonight. We should have some artillery in about three hours. They're setting up a fire base about two miles away on some low hills to the east."

To the south, they heard explosions.

"Sounds like Battalion is getting hit again," said Mercado.

"Those gook fuckers must be dug in good. How could they survive the bombing and napalm?"

"You ever wonder how we would do against jets and napalm?" asked Wilson.

"If the gooks had napalm and all the shit we have, they would have driven us out years ago."

"They are some hardcore, committed motherfuckers, that's for sure," said Kelly.

"Robert Kelly, the only M60 sniper in Vietnam. You are an artist with the pig, my friend. I'm glad you're on our side. How you fixed for ammo?"

"Got about eighteen hundred rounds per gun. They want us, they're gonna pay. They'll pay for every fucking step they take. Gonna send them back to their ancestors tonight."

"Kane, go find Doc and see when he's going to feed us. We should eat early."

They ate their meal at around four-thirty.

"I think we should limit everyone to one box a day. Break it up into three separate meals. Coffee and a biscuit or crackers for breakfast. Eat the entree at lunch and dessert at dinner time. We have a shitload of coffee. More coffee than water," said Mad Dog.

"Calling anything in those cans an entree is very generous of you, Doc. But, yeah, I agree. How's the water situation?"

"No more than one canteen a day, and we should be all right. It's not like we're humping the bush. We'll be able to get by."

"How about you go and tell the men? It'll sound more official coming from you. You're a medic and they believe anything you say."

"Got to be careful with my water. I need my morning coffee, and I like a cup at night. I can live on cigarettes and coffee."

"Let's see. There are thirty-two ounces in a quart. Your coffee can is eight ounces. That's sixteen ounces for coffee and sixteen ounces for water," said Wilson.

"Thank you, Eugene. Every ounce will be precious to me, just like you are, brother."

Wilson stroked his mustache for a while.

"Maybe they won't attack. Maybe they'll just wait and try to starve us out."

"Sure, that could happen. That's what I would do. Get some sleep while you can."

The attack started after dark with a mortar barrage. At first, they could hear the 'thunk' of the mortar bombs being shot from the tubes. But after a minute, the explosions were constant and they couldn't hear anything. They crouched down between the thick outer wall of the fort and the interior blast walls. Their only real fear was a direct hit. The air was filled with lethal shards of shrapnel and chipped cement. They gagged on the combination of dirt, smoke and cement dust. Their eyes teared up. Then came the whistles. That, they heard. They peeked over the wall and saw dozens of khaki-clad men run from the buildings under the cover of the continuing mortar bombardment.

"Hold your fire," Holt shouted. "Let them get closer."

To either side of the advancing men was a large fifty-one caliber machine gun. The bullets hit the wall, tearing large divots from the cement. When the NVA were committed to the attack, Holt gave the order to fire. The soldiers were cut down, some in mid-stride.

They fell, sliding several feet, then lay still in pools of spreading blood. The carnage was awful. Their advancing men were torn to pieces, and the attack ended as quickly as it began. Several more mortar explosions followed; but they seemed almost halfhearted, an afterthought.

"Why would they do that? Why would they run across an open field?" said Wilson.

"I have no fucking idea why. I can't explain it. It makes no sense."

"Fuck them! If they want to die, I'm happy to oblige," Kelly said.

"Nicky, go to the other side. See how they made out."

The men peered into the darkness. Soft moans could be heard coming from the wounded. Mercado returned.

"Second squad took a bad hit. A mortar exploded on top of the wall. Two guys wounded, one killed. All from shrapnel. Doc is over there now."

"Enemy dead?" asked Holt.

"Too dark to count."

"This wasn't combat. This was a slaughter; it was a turkey shoot. I guarantee they won't try that again."

"They had to be testing us," Kimball said.

"Menendez, what's wrong with your arm? Come here, let me look at it."

"I don't know what happened, Sarge. I just felt something hit me."

Holt ripped his sleeve down, exposing three small shrapnel wounds. "You'll be okay. We'll get it bandaged until Doc gets here."

"They're not coming back, right? We beat them bad; they won't be back."

"Not tonight. But tomorrow, they'll attack again. They can't leave us here. They have to kill us or die trying. It's what they do; it's what we do."

Chapter 30

We Got Them Right Where They Want Us

"Nick, get the Major and find out about our artillery and air support," Holt said.

"Good morning, boys. Quite a night."

"Good morning, Mr. Freed. I trust you slept well?"

"Please, call me Joe. I think the time for formality has long gone."

"Where did you spend the night?"

"Doc had me in the main bunker with the wounded. I managed to sneak out and take some pictures. I need a favor. Can I borrow a radio so I can call in my story?"

"Are you allowed to call in your reports direct? Don't you have to go through the censors?"

"Not that I'm aware of."

"Go to the other side and use their radio. Tell them I said it's okay. What are you reporting?"

"The truth."

"The truth in Vietnam is elusive. Give it a try and good luck. Nicky, what did Grayson say?"

"We should have guns up this afternoon and maybe some helicopter support. But that's a big maybe. Everything is committed to the Battalion. I spoke to his RTO. They got hammered again last night. Gooks overran the First Battalion's perimeter, and now an entire company is cut off and surrounded. Jets keep pounding the hills, but it doesn't seem to have any effect on them. They have to be in caves or deep bunkers."

"Casualties?"

"He says the American casualties are in the hundreds. NVA casualties are unknown, but are estimated much higher."

"Of course they are. Hey, Eugene, come here. I just noticed that huge crack in the boulder, all the way in the back corner. Could you check it out?"

"Sure thing, Sarge."

"Hey, Sarge, you got to see this. There's a gook outside with a white flag."

"Nicky, you go; find out what's going on. My leg is throbbing like a bitch."

Mercado stood and hollered over the wall. "He wants to get his wounded."

"You want me to shoot him?"

"Do not shoot that fucking guy, Kelly. Leave him alone. Nick, help me up."

"He's over there, by that building."

Holt studied him through his binoculars. "Go ahead, get your wounded. No weapons. Don't bring any guns, or we will shoot you," he shouted.

They watched as a half-dozen NVA left the building and began to examine the bodies littering the field. They carried several off and returned for more. The soldier with the flag gave it a wave. "Thank you, GI, thank you."

"Go fuck your mother, you fucking gook bastard," yelled Kelly.

"Our very own ambassador of goodwill. He should be at the Paris peace talks."

"That was pure, fucking bullshit, Sarge. You think they wouldn't have just shot our wounded if they had the chance?"

"They probably would have, Kelly, but we're not them. We're Americans, and we're supposed to be better."

Wilson was back. "What did I miss? What was all the shouting about?"

"It's all over now. What about that crack?"

"It's huge, Sarge. About three feet wide, and I can see straight through to the road we came in on."

"Can someone get through it?"

"No. It's all packed with branches, vines and shit. The Frenchies must have known about it because they stuffed it with barbed wire."

"Good. One more thing, find Doc and see if there is anything that could pass as a latrine. We can't dig one in this ground, and we can't just be shitting and pissing everywhere. The French had to have something they used."

"There's one behind the bunker. The seats are all gone, but I'll see if I can rig something up. I'll let everyone know that's what they got to use."

"Nick, get Kane and Menendez to check out that back wall. There are no fighting positions along the back, and I want to know why."

It was mid-morning when the shelling started. Heavy mortars pounded the fort for more than twenty minutes, followed by a flurry of 122-millimeter rockets. The first two rockets flew over the fort and impacted in the jungle. Having adjusted their sights, the next three slammed into the fort's front walls, causing enormous explosions. Two men from the third squad were violently thrown backward. A large gaping hole was left in the wall, and the blast wall behind it was shattered. After the rockets, the mortars began again. After what seemed like an eternity, it was quiet.

Doc raced to the downed soldiers. "They're dead," he shouted. He dragged their bodies behind the wall and covered them with ponchos. He then came over, wiping his hands against his pants.

"What killed them, shrapnel?"

"Not a scratch on them. They were killed from the concussion of the rockets. They looked flattened and squashed. I guess the blast just crushed their insides."

"Anybody else hit?"

"Just a bunch of scratches and cuts from chipped cement."

"Call it in, Doc. That's what, eight killed now? They're just going to blow us to pieces, and knock us off one by one."

The compound was littered with cement chips and shards of metal. Menendez and Kane came from the bunker. It sounded like they were walking on broken glass.

"Glad to see you rode out the shelling. What did you find?"

"There's nothing there. Behind the rear wall, it drops straight off about four hundred feet. If we went more to the east, we would have seen it. Cliffs, straight down."

"So there's nothing to defend since no one can climb up the cliff."

"There is a narrow trail down to the bottom of the valley," said Kane.

"What kind of trail?"

"It's only about a foot wide. It's more like an animal trail than any footpath. It would be scary as shit to try and get down it, but it could be done."

"I'll have Mercado call it in."

"Sarge, I found this for you. It's a bent piece of rebar; it'll make a good crutch for you if you wrap the top."

"That should work. Thanks."

Holt rummaged through his pack and found a compression bandage. He placed it around the rebar and wrapped the straps tightly around the bandage. "This will work. I think I'll test it out and see how the boys on the other side are doing."

Holt shuffled through the debris until he came to the first and second squads. "Gentlemen, how are you getting along?"

"I called in my report. It does have to pass through the censors before they'll release it for publication," said Mr. Freed.

"Good luck with that. This doesn't appear to be the Army's finest hour. Don't know if they want to broadcast it."

"What were those big explosions we heard?"

"Chinese rockets. 122 millimeters of pure shit. They're like eight or nine feet long and weigh about 140 pounds, half of it explosive. Something new to make our life miserable. They actually blew the wall apart."

"That can't be an infantry weapon."

"I doubt it, Joe. Usually, they're mounted on some sort of vehicle. You need a truck to carry the launcher and the spare rounds."

"And it blew the wall apart," asked Elderidge.

"Split it in two and blew out a three-foot-wide section. Killed the two guys behind it from the concussion alone."

"So much for the French's construction abilities."

Holt looked out over the open area toward the barracks. "They won't risk another frontal attack, not without cover fire. They'll use the rockets, mortars or RPGs to keep your heads down, and then they'll rush you. If they use rockets, they'll blow this outer wall to pieces. Get behind the blast walls; and if they don't hold, fall back to those stub walls sticking out from the bunker."

"If we had artillery, we could flatten those barracks. That's got to be where they are staging from."

"The Major claims he's working on it. They're in worse shape than us. The two Battalions are separated into four perimeters and each one is surrounded. Plus, they got artillery firing at them from the hills."

"The Major got his fight; he should be happy."

"Not on the terms he wanted. We should be surrounding them."

"If they have artillery and trucks, then they need gas and some place to store it."

"That's what I think those warehouses in the back are, Joe. They don't appear to be short of ammunition."

"So, this could be the big assembly area the Major was looking for?"

"Could be. Mr. Freed, why don't you come back to my side, where I can keep an eye on you?"

"What do you think, Slim?"

"Tonight, for sure," said Sergeant Pickens, the third squad's leader. "If they come from the front, it'll be a diversion. Their main attack will be on the left."

"Agreed. At the end of the wall, where it meets the boulder. They can snake their way along the face of that fucking rock, and we won't see them until they're right on top of us."

"Once there, they can toss in a satchel charge or grenades and come over the top."

"Won't take many to fuck us up. If they get four or five guys inside, we'll be shooting each other."

"Tonight, we got to get some Claymores out there."

"As soon as it's dark, I'll go myself and set them along the boulder."

"Try and place a couple of trip flares in front of the Claymores. Be careful, Slim, and be quiet."

"Kelly, move away from the corner. I want you to come in about ten feet. Get some guys and fill in the space between the inner and outer walls. Use all this concrete rubble and block it off. I'm thinking they'll try and come from the left and jump the wall. When they do, they'll be trapped in a little concrete room, and we can use our grenades. Tell that nitwit Kane it'll be like shooting fish in a barrel, and see what he says."

Wilson sat with Holt. Holt had made coffee using water from the dead men's canteens. To the west, dark storm clouds had gathered; and there were flashes of lightning over the hills.

"They won't attack if it's raining, will they?"

"I don't think the rain will stop them. If anything, it will provide cover for any noise they make. They'll come tonight, and we'll be ready for them."

"Can I join you men?"

"Please do, Joe. You have a cup? I'll share my coffee."

"Have you heard anything from Battalion?"

"Not a word. It sounds quiet. Maybe the worst is over."

"From your lips to God's ears."

"Wilson, hand me that sixteen and a few magazines. Joe, give me your forty-five and take this rifle."

"We've been through this; I'm not supposed to be armed."

"Take it. I can't spare anyone to watch over you. You said you would never be a burden out here. You need to be able to defend yourself. You do know how to use it?"

"I do, and I'm a good shot."

Holt put on the belt with the holstered forty-five. He took the Lieutenant's pistol and shoved it inside the belt. Mr. Freed examined the M16, worked the action and inserted a magazine.

"We'll be in big trouble if it comes down to me using this."

At dusk, it started to rain, the first rain they had in over a month. It rained steadily. Sergeant Pickens and two men slipped outside the wall and proceeded to the boulder, where they placed four Claymore mines and trip flares. They returned and gave a thumbs-up to Holt.

The mortars started around midnight. The barracks side of the fort was taking RPGs on a repeated basis. Mercado was on the radio, pleading for flares. Machine-gun fire was coming from the buildings directly across from them. The bullets chipped at the walls and forced them down. A trip flare snapped, producing a bright flash of light. Immediately, two Claymore mines were blown. Another flare lit the night, and the remaining two mines were triggered. Several Chinese hand grenades arched over the wall, followed by five NVA soldiers.

The trap worked perfectly: they were in a concrete enclosure without an exit. Kelly threw two hand grenades at the men, and they exploded in a shower of blood and concrete. More North Vietnamese came over the wall, avoiding the smoldering room. One raced toward Kelly, who shot him at close range with his forty-five. The soldier sprawled at his feet. Another passed Kelly and lunged at Kimball with his bayonet. Kimball, in perfect fashion, parried the bayonet and broke the soldier's jaw with an upward butt stroke of his rifle. He pounded the soldier's head to mush with his rifle butt.

The third squad rushed to join the fight. In such close quarters, rifles were useless and functioned only as clubs. The ground was slippery with mud and blood. The men slashed at each other with knives and bayonets. Kelly used a rock to crush a soldier's skull. Kane was pinned to the ground and was being stabbed repeatedly until Menendez pulled the soldier from him and shot him point-blank through his eye. Holt stared helplessly, unable to fire into the tangle of men fighting in a narrow corridor between the inner and outer walls.

Rockets started impacting the right-side positions. The walls began to crumble. NVA poured from the trees and barracks, firing as they ran. The two squads poured gunfire into the advancing men. They fell, but more still came. Grenades were thrown by both sides, and explosions sent shrapnel ripping through flesh. There were screams and curses, tracers and blood. Handheld flares were fired in a feeble attempt to illuminate the night. Murderous shadows ran through the dark, bringing death with them. The NVA tried to breach the walls, but were repulsed and killed just feet from their enemies.

The left side was locked in its own desperate struggle as more men ran from the buildings. Holt and his group fired single shots and ignored the carnage on their right. A bullet hit Wilson on his right shoulder, and he spun backward and lay slumped against the wall. Mr. Freed went to his aid and dragged him to safety. RPGs were fired, showering them with concrete and metal. Mercado cried out in pain, grabbed his head and dropped to his knees.

"Nicky, are you alright?"

"The motherfuckers shot my ear off!"

Holt pulled him upright and pressed against him, shielding him with his body.

Mercado beat against his legs. "Get off me, you fucking homo. Get your dick out of my face. You're smothering me. I can't breathe."

To the left, Kelly roared in rage and threw himself on an attacking soldier. He stabbed the man through his boonie hat and into his skull. Unable to extract his knife, he kicked the body aside and picked up his machine gun. He first shot anyone to the front, then turned his attention to the retreating men on his left. The spent shell casings sparkled like diamonds in the light of the flares. Gradually, the firing died down; and the men sat in stunned silence in the swirling mist of rain and gun smoke.

No one spoke. Only the wounded moaned.

Chapter 31

Conflicting Orders

Dawn came slowly the next morning. The hills to the west were shrouded in swirling mists and clouds. The lingering rain turned the compound into a slurry of concrete dust, mud and human fluids. The bodies were locked in rigor, producing awful, grotesque poses of death. The stench of decomposition was something that clung to their fatigues and could almost be tasted.

"I don't care how used we get to this shit. The smell of dead bodies is something I'll never forget," said Holt.

Mad Dog sat down, exhausted from a night of tending to the wounded. Holt passed him his pack of cigarettes. "Do you have a count, Doc?"

"Three dead and eight wounded. We got eighteen guys who can fight. Of the eighteen, fifteen have been wounded, some more than once."

"Is Kane one of the dead?"

"No, he's alive. It's fucking unbelievable. He got stabbed about six times, all in the same area. Left side, just below his shoulder."

"And he can fight?"

"He's in a lot of pain, but he can hold a rifle if he has to."

"How about Wilson?"

"Wilson is out of the fight. The bullet broke his collarbone. He'll recover and hopefully, there's no permanent damage. I got his arm taped to his body, and he's all doped up."

Mercado was sitting next to Holt, who slapped his shoulder. "You got Nicky fixed up, good as new. You can't even tell his ear has been pieced back together."

"No thanks to you, you fucking jackass. You almost killed me."

"That's the gratitude I get for shielding you with my own body. I was ready to take a bullet for you, you ungrateful little spic."

"I kept thinking: this is how I'm going to die, smothered by your crotch."

"You're welcome."

"I'll call in the casualty report. What should I tell Grayson?"

"You get some sleep. I'll talk to Grayson."

"Major, we're about done here. We're low on everything: ammo, food and water. Doc's out of bandages; he's using ripped-up towels. There's no morphine left. I got my guys policing up the gook weapons. Maybe, and it's a big maybe, we can hold off one more attack."

"You do have a way out, though."

"How's that?"

"Your RTO said there's a trail at the back of the fort that leads down to the valley."

"It's a fucking goat path about ten inches wide. There's no way the wounded would make it down. Don't forget, we also got four or five stretcher cases who can't walk. How do I get them down?"

"You'll leave them. You lock them in the bunker. When the NVA see you've abandoned the fort, they might not even search the place."

"And if they do?"

There was silence on the line.

"Major?"

"I will not lose an entire platoon due to misunderstood orders. You shouldn't even be there."

Holt signaled Mad Dog to come over to him. "Major, my medic

is listening in. Could you repeat those orders?"

"I am giving you a direct order to abandon your position and get those men who can walk to safety. Am I clear?"

"Yes, sir. Let me get back to you in just a minute. Well, Doc, did you hear all that?"

"Fuck him. I'm not leaving the wounded, and that's that. Camp is back there. You just going to leave him?"

"If he hasn't woken up by now, he ain't waking up."

Doc shook his head in disgust.

"I'm staying."

"Is everything all right?" asked Joe Freed.

Holt slowly scratched his head and lit a cigarette. "No, everything is not alright. Doc, gather up the men. Leave a couple on the wall."

When they were assembled, Holt addressed them. "I've been given orders to abandon the fort. Mad Dog is going to stay with the wounded. I'm shot to pieces and can't climb down that trail, so I'm staying with Doc. Get your shit together and get ready to leave. Once you've gone, we'll raise a white flag and see what happens."

"You know what will happen. The fucking gooks will kill you," said Kelly.

"Maybe not. We let them get their wounded; maybe they'll return the favor. Maybe they'll let us stay here and use us for bait."

"And maybe they'll just shoot you outright."

"Enough, Kelly. This ain't open for debate. It's an order."

"Fuck the Major, and fuck you. I'm staying right here."

"Goddamn it, Kelly."

"You think any of us are leaving you guys? So what happens? We go, and then as we're walking down the trail, we hear the gooks put single shots into the back of your heads? I ain't living with that. We came here together, we fight together and if it comes down to it, we die together. So shove your orders up your ass."

322

"They're Grayson's orders, not mine," Holt said defensively.

"Then I'll tell that fucking prick myself. No one tells us to retreat. We're fucking Wolfhounds. We are the death dealers. We don't run from a fight; we run to it. No fear!"

"You're right. No fear, brother."

"How did it go?" asked Mr. Freed.

"That's a conversation I hope I don't have again anytime soon. He got his RTO as a witness and repeated his direct order. I told him I couldn't obey that order. I said get us the helicopters and artillery he's been promising because we ain't going nowhere. I told him I obeyed a lawful order that got us into this shit, against my better judgment. I made it clear I ain't listening to any more officers and their bullshit orders. I also reminded him that you were here with us; and you'll be reporting on what happens, including his order to run and leave our wounded."

"What did he say?"

"Nothing. The line went dead."

"What's going to happen to you?"

"Nothing as bad as what already has happened, and probably will happen tonight."

"If we make it out of here, this will make for a great story."

"I'd go ahead and call it in before he thinks to cut you off. Just lay it all out."

They spent the afternoon inventorying their equipment. They gathered the enemy weapons and ammunition and stacked them along the wall. They laid out their ammo and grenades, and cleaned their weapons. On the bunker's right side, Elderidge and what was left of the two squads made an attempt to repair the outer wall. The interior blast walls were reduced to rubble. They prepared their fallback position behind the bunker's stub wall. Mad Dog passed out canteens and C-rations. Then, they waited.

"We have to do something about these bodies. They're really beginning to stink," said Doc.

"Take the gooks and throw them over the back wall. Take our guys and wrap them in ponchos and stack them over there. That will help with the smell," said Holt.

Mr. Freed returned and sat with the group. "Story's out, for what it's worth." He took an offered cigarette from Holt. "These guys look like ghosts. Their fatigues and faces are all covered in grey dust."

"Nicky looks like a snowman. He's got more bandages than face showing."

"Let me ask you, did Doc do a good job sewing up my ear?"

"It did sort of resemble an ear when he finished. It had the general shape of an ear and it was where an ear should be."

"What does that mean?"

"He did put it back on the side of your head. It did look a little droopy, though. I'm sure people will know it's supposed to be an ear. I wouldn't worry about it."

"Hey, Sarge."

"What is it, Gene?"

"You guys ain't leaving, are you? I can still walk. I don't need any help walking."

Holt ruffled Wilson's hair. "Nobody's leaving; we're staying. Like Kelly said, we came here together and we're staying together. We'll ride this out together, right to the end."

"I can fight."

"I know you can. Rest easy, Gene. We're staying put."

Kelly held up a survival mirror and was covering his face with camouflage paint. From his hairline to the bottom of his nose, he covered his face solid black. From the nose down, he did vertical stripes. He looked like an Indian warrior. Soon, all the men were painting their faces in the most ghoulish manner possible. Holt joined in and painted his face in vertical stripes of black, green and brown. They all laughed and modeled their war faces while Mr. Freed took copious pictures.

"I got some Colonel asking for you," said Mercado.

"What Colonel? Are you sure you heard him right?"

"My left ear is working fine. Here, take this."

Holt identified himself and waited.

"This is Colonel Thomas Lynne. I have assumed command of the regiment. Major Grayson has been reassigned. I'm rescinding his orders to evacuate the fort. You know the road you came in on? It runs all the way north, and at some point parallels the Cambodian border. It separates two rubber plantations. A large number of NVA have been spotted coming south along that road. The only thing that separates them from us is the fort. You are to hold the fort and delay the enemy advance at all costs. We cannot allow those men to reinforce the NVA we are currently engaged with. Do you understand?"

"Uh, yeah, sure. We weren't leaving anyway. How many gooks are we talking about?"

"Approximately one thousand. We have observation planes trying to spot them. If we find them, we'll blow them to bits before they ever reach you."

"Colonel, you are aware I only got eighteen men left. We need water and ammunition."

"You'll be resupplied this afternoon. You'll have artillery and helicopter support, too. You need to delay their advance until a relief column arrives. You hold on, son; we're coming to get you."

"Doc, get Elderidge and Slim over here."

"Sergeant Pickens was KIA last night."

"Fuck me. Get Kelly, then."

When Kelly and Elderidge arrived, Holt described the new

situation. Kelly counted on his fingers. "That's like fifty to one," he said.

"More than that, but they won't use all their men to attack us. They're reinforcements. They're not here to fight us. We're just in their way. They'll use maybe one hundred against us and hold the rest in reserve."

"That's still ten to one."

"Kelly, where the fuck did you go to school? It's not ten to one; it's half that. Do the math, it's like five to one. You mean to tell me you can't kill five gooks?"

"I'll kill as many who come at me. As long as I got ammo, I'm an unstoppable killing machine."

"That's what I want to hear. You take charge of half the men here and I'll take the other half. Elderidge, you got your guys. Let everyone know what's going on. Tell them help is on the way. Nicky, get on the horn with your pal at Battalion and find out what's really going on."

"I got the story, and it's a wild one. The Colonel flies in on his helicopter, lands, and he and this huge Sergeant Major get off. Danny, my friend, says this guy, the Sergeant Major, is as big as a fucking grizzly bear. Just enormous. They march over to Grayson and the Colonel is shouting at him. Then, the Sergeant Major grabs Grayson and half-drags him to the chopper and throws him on board like a rag doll. Throws his fucking ass on the chopper, and it's gone. The Colonel starts barking orders; and him and the Sarge start repositioning the perimeter, pushing out here and pulling in there. Within minutes, he got our guys on the attack and they break through to Alpha Company and consolidate the perimeter. Next, he gets another attack going to combine the two regiments, forcing out the gooks who were between them. This all happens within thirty minutes. The Sergeant Major was working three radios, coordinating artillery, air and ground troops. Boom! It's done. This

Colonel accomplishes more in a few hours than Grayson did in three days."

"Who is this guy?"

"He's the Regimental Commander. They call him 'Ginger' because his hair is red. Some sort of Korean War legend. Both the Colonel and the Sergeant Major got two stars on their CIBs and have been together for thirty years."

"What about us?"

"Danny says the Colonel went absolutely apeshit over Grayson's order to abandon the fort and leave the wounded. He says to expect a relief column from the 11ᵗʰ Cavalry. As soon as they reach the regiment, they'll send them our way."

"That's the best fucking news I've heard all day. And this guy Danny is solid?"

"Never once did he relay shit info. If he says it's true, then it's true."

"We have to tell the guys."

"Also, he said they are loading up a chopper with ammo and a bunch of other shit for us."

Mercado said to Holt, "I got the Colonel on the line."

"I have choppers on the way. A slick loaded with supplies, and four gunships. I can't spare any men at the moment, but I guarantee you they'll be coming. I need everybody I got to clean up this mess and get back on track. Have targets ready for the gunships. They'll also provide cover for the supply slick. Their call sign is Dragon."

"Thank you, Sir."

"Do your job, and I'll be thanking you."

The first helicopter to arrive was the egg-shaped Loach. It buzzed the fort. "This is Dragon One. Pop smoke for supplies."

Over the trees came two Huey gunships and two sleek Cobras. Behind them was a lone Huey slick. Holt popped purple smoke.

"That's for the supply ship. My boys are hungry; give us something to eat."

"Dragon One, the buildings directly across from us and the barracks to the east. They need to be gone. Be prepared for return fire. Have your Cobras rocket the warehouse at the end of the village. We think it's a gook supply dump. The gooks are dug in with heavy machine guns. Have fun and bon appetit."

"I understand you have a reporter with you."

"Affirmative."

"Make sure he gets our call sign right: 25th Aviation Battalion, at your disposal. Time to go to work. Dragon One, out."

As the Huey supply ship came over their position, it was fired upon from the buildings. Dragon One fired two white phosphorus marking rockets at the building. One of the gunships peeled off and fired hundreds of rounds from its mini-gun, collapsing the upper floor. It was followed by the second gunship, which fired a batch of rockets into the building. Almost in slow motion, the building folded in on itself. Several NVA ran from the building and were cut down by murderous machine-gun fire from the Loach.

"Hot damn, I love watching the hogs work," said Holt.

Again and again, the gunships made strafing runs, firing their 2.75" rockets until each had expended their load of fourteen. When they were done, the buildings and barracks were leveled and in flames. The Cobras had begun their task of destroying the warehouses. The first helicopter fired six rockets in a spread along the buildings. As it flew over the destruction, it was engulfed in an enormous secondary explosion, which tipped the ship almost vertically. The pilot regained control and banked left over the town, firing its 40-millimeter grenade launcher into the buildings bordering the west side. The second Cobra followed, strafing the warehouse with rockets and grenades.

"Goddamn! Did you see that? What the fuck did they have in there? We never get secondary explosions like that," said an exuberant Dragon One.

"Fucking kill them! Kill them all," yelled Kelly.

The men cheered the helicopters and waved their hats.

The Huey supply ship returned and hovered over the center of the fort. With no opposing fire, the crew chief and door gunner kicked out wooden crates of ammunition and C-rations. Last out were four five-gallon plastic jugs of water, lowered on ropes.

"I hate to ask, but can you take out some of our wounded?" asked Holt.

"Sorry, we're not equipped for wounded. Ah, fuck it. Bring out your worst, and we'll take them."

The gunships prowled the streets, protecting the Huey, which landed in a swirl of dust. Camp and the two worst wounded were brought out and gently placed on the helicopter's floor.

Holt leaned toward the pilot and shoved an NVA flag through the window. "You guys are lifesavers. Hang the flag in your club, compliments of the Wolfhounds."

The pilot gave a stiff salute, and the Huey rose from the ground.

The next two hours were spent breaking open the crates and distributing the supplies. Two full medical packs were delivered to Doc, who went about putting clean bandages on the wounded. The first thing Holt did was boil water for coffee using his steel pot. He sat back with a cigarette and a fresh cup of coffee, feeling, for the first time in days, that they were no longer expendable and might just might survive.

Mercado gave him the radio handset. "It's the Colonel."

"Did you boys get your presents?"

"We did, sir. It was like Christmas day. Those helicopter guys were great. They laid waste to the gooks. Fucked them up, but good. Oh, sorry about the language."

"You're excused. Here is the artillery call sign. Based on the info supplied by the chopper pilots, they already have targets locked in. Just coordinate with them, and they will guide you through the basic procedures. Eighteen, maybe twenty-four hours, that's all I'm asking for. Can you hold on?"

"We will, sir. We'll be here waiting."

Chapter 32

The Final Day

Holt addressed the men. "If we hold out tonight, the relief column should be here tomorrow. Just one more night."

"Don, there's some artillery guy on the line. Call sign, Thunder One."

Holt identified himself and waited.

"I understand you've never called in artillery before."

"Correct."

"Don't worry. Your helicopter buddy, Dragon One, mapped out your situation for me and gave me firing coordinates. All you have to do is adjust our fire from set points. The buildings to your left are designated Point A. The building in front of you is Point B, and the buildings on the right are Point C. You got that?"

"Roger that. Points A, B and C."

"I'm going to fire a smoke round at point B, and you tell me where it lands. Shot out."

They waited several seconds until a round impacted in the middle of the buildings.

"Tell me where it hit. Say 'drop' to bring it in closer to you, or say 'add' to move the impact farther away. Give me the measurement in meters."

"Drop two hundred meters."

"You don't have to say 'meters'. Just remember that your adjustments are in meters. Drop two hundred. Shot out."

The white smoke round impacted dead center in the building. "Perfect."

"I've noted that on my drawing. Let's do Point A. Shot out."

"Move it over ten meters."

"Which way? Say left ten or right ten."

"Left ten."

"Left ten, shot out."

"Damn, you're good. Right on."

"I've made my adjustments. Dragon One said you may have visitors on Point A's street. How about I fire a high-explosive round down the street and see where it hits? Shot out."

"Add fifty and you'll be good."

"Noted. If you need us, we're set to go. Tonight, we'll fire some H and I fire to keep the gooks off-balance and let them know you're covered. Thunder One, out."

"Good news, guys. We got an artillery umbrella. They'll be firing Harassment and Interdiction fire tonight. So don't be surprised when you hear it."

"Mr. Freed, you have a piece of paper?"

"You can use my notebook."

"I just want to write everyone's name down. There's Kelly and Kimball on the M60. They both got shrapnel wounds and scrapes. Menendez will work the M79 grenade launcher. He's wounded, too. Kane and Wilson are alive, but can't fight. That leaves you, me and Nick. There are three guys from third squad, and Elderidge has himself and four guys on his side. And two wounded in the bunker. That's only seventeen. Who am I missing?"

"You forgot Doc, and don't count Kane and me out. I told you, we can fight," said Wilson.

"Speak for yourself," Kane said weakly.

"Eighteen. All accounted for."

"Do you mind if I take that list? I want to go around and put faces to those names and get pictures of everyone."

"Sure, Joe. I'm sorry. It's my fault. I should have known everyone's names."

It started to rain lightly around dusk, just enough to make everyone wet and miserable. At the back of the village, there were mechanical sounds of movement, but nothing they could observe.

"What do you make of that?" asked Mercado.

"It sounds like trucks. Maybe they're bringing in more supplies."

"Those Dragon guys really fucked up the gooks. Blew the shit out of the warehouse and leveled the barracks."

"That little shack I was in, that blew that up, too. The Lieutenant's body is still there along with his RTO's."

"Do you think there's anything left of it? The body, I mean."

"Wasn't much left to begin with. Just meat for the bugs by now."

"You think they'll hit us again?"

"They would have to be determined to want this place. They know we got artillery and air support. They paid a heavy price already. Just look out there, Nick. There's gotta be fifty or more bodies out there, not counting the ones we threw over the back wall."

"I counted sixty-one gooks out there."

"Why did you do that?"

"For once, I wanted an accurate body count. We paid for it and I wanted to get it right."

"You told the Major that?"

"Yeah."

"I bet he called in three hundred."

"What the fuck is that noise? It's getting louder. Even I can hear it, and I only got one ear."

"I was fucking with you about your ear. Doc did a good job sewing it back on. At first, he wanted to put it upside down and backward, but I said no. I told him, 'Nicky is too handsome to have a fucked-up ear.' But you're right; the noise is louder."

Kelly came over and bummed a cigarette. "Do you guys hear that? It's in the back, by the warehouse."

"Let's see if Thunder One wants to fire some rounds."

They stood and watched the shells impact. The noise was gone.

Later that night, at around two in the morning, they got mortared. The attack seemed halfhearted, at best. Thunder One responded with dozens of rounds fired in the warehouse area and in the jungle beyond. The explosions lit up the night, and the mortars stopped.

The morning arrived gray and damp. A light mist continued to fall. Holt brewed coffee and lit a cigarette. The men ate breakfast. The stench of death hung heavy in the air; it clung to everything like a wet rag. There was no word on the relief column.

At eleven, the sounds of men moving through the ruined buildings was undeniable. Two small trucks appeared with mounted guns, one on either street. They fired, and their first rounds went high.

"They got some sort of recoil-less rifle, like our 105s," Holt said.

The next rounds impacted the bunker, blowing large chunks of cement from the walls, showering them with dust and debris.

"Nicky, get Thunder on the phone and tell them what's happening."

The trucks wouldn't stay in one place for more then a few seconds, making the accurate placement of artillery impossible. Menendez fired a LAW. The Army's Light Antitank Weapon was notoriously ineffective. The round fired, cork screwed wildly, and skidded past the truck. From his side, Elderidge fired a second LAW, with the same effect. The trucks continued to fire. Each round impacted the fort, blowing the walls to pieces. Holt chased them with artillery fire, with no results. They moved continuously, stopping only to fire. Menendez sighted another LAW, but the impact from a shell knocked him to the ground, and the round shot harmlessly into the air. He got to his feet, dazed but unhurt. He used the final LAW; and this time, it hit in the engine compartment, blowing the truck in a circle. Holt blew it to pieces with some well-placed artillery.

"Thunder One, I don't know if you guys keep score, but chalk up a truck and a crew served weapons. A driver, plus three crew."

"You owe us a case of beer. Good beer. Not that shit you grunts drink. Where's the other truck?"

"He ran. How about hitting the buildings? Start with Point B and work your way left and right. I think the gooks are getting ready for a ground attack."

"We'll work our way back and forth. Shot out."

The men huddled behind the ruined walls while the big guns work. They methodically hit all the buildings, reducing them to piles of rubble.

"Add fifty in increments and resume firing," said Holt.

"Roger that," came the response.

"If they were massing in those buildings, they gotta be hurting."

"Joe, you look like a gopher popping up and down, taking pictures," said Mercado.

"I'm still a little nervous; I've never been this close to combat before. Usually, they let us in after all the fighting is done."

"That's because you're too good-looking and too valuable to be killed."

"What happens now?"

"Hopefully, our relief is on the way. Nick, get on the horn and see what's going on."

"They must know they'll pay dearly if they attack, now that we have artillery and helicopters."

"They have to get rid of us. They're supposed to reinforce their men in the valley. The only road they can take is right over there, the one we came in on. They gotta go right past us. As long as we're here, we can block them with the guns."

"They made a mistake in not securing the fort for themselves."

"If they see they can't hold out, they'll retreat right down the road and come past us to get into the jungle. Under our direction, the gunships and artillery will chew them up. So anyway you look at it, they got to get past us. We are a problem that has to be eliminated."

Mercado interrupted. "They'll be here, but not for a while. Three, maybe four hours."

"Everybody! Pass the word. We got to Alamo up and hunker down. We got plenty of ammo; if they come again, we'll make them pay for every fucking step they take."

They ate lunch and maintained fifty-percent alert. Holt was chain-smoking, and studying the village with the binoculars. Mercado turned on a transistor radio, and someone hollered to turn it down.

"Fuck that! Turn it up; we ain't hiding from these bitches. Blast it, Nicky!"

Mercado turned the radio to full volume; more static than music. The Armed Forces Radio Network was playing Steppenwolf's "Magic Carpet Ride", and everyone sang along. Next came John Denver's "Leaving on a Jet Plane", and the mood changed. The boys became quiet with thoughts of home and their last days on leave before Vietnam.

"Enough, Nick. We don't need everyone tearing up and getting sad."

Thunk! Thunk! Thunk!

"Incoming!" someone screamed as mortars impacted around the fort.

They walked the mortars onto the fort, forcing the men to seek cover behind the shattered walls. The air was filled with the whiz and sizzle of shrapnel. At the same time, under cover of the mortar barrage, six NVA sappers were packing the large crack in the boulder with explosives. They stuffed the crack with crates of Semtex and

Bangalore torpedoes. The mortar bombs changed to smoke rounds, and the field began to fill with rolling clouds of thick, acrid smoke. Concealed, the NVA poured from the ruins and advanced.

Holt grabbed the radio.

"Thunder One, we got gooks attacking directly to our front. Point B and drop one hundred. Fire for effect."

"Point B, drop one hundred. That's a big drop. Are you sure?"

"Fire, goddamn it, fire." Holt desperately calculated in his head. "Nicky, how wide is the field? About three hundred yards, right?"

"I guess. Yeah, three hundred yards."

"Thunder One, drop fifty and fire."

"Drop fifty and fire. Dude, that's getting awfully close. Please confirm."

"Right now, you're the only thing keeping them off of us. They're using smoke to hide themselves."

"At my discretion, I'm calling in the birds. Gunships will be up. You dickheads better hold on; we want our beer."

"Keep firing, and you can have our fucking club."

Above the explosions, Holt could hear a loud, grating sound to his rear. Holt pointed to a soldier from the third squad and screamed. "Check out what's happening back there, by that crack. I hear something."

The soldier ran to the rear of the fort, and was engulfed in a massive, fiery explosion. Bits of barbed wire, rock and shrapnel disintegrated his body into a bloody cloud.

The NVA sappers struggled to get through the opening, but were entangled in the remains of the barbed wire.

Holt whirled and shot the sappers as they came through the crack. Mercado joined in.

"Nicky, kill those motherfuckers. Don't let them in. Thunder One, drop another fifty and fire."

"That's Danger Close. You need to confirm."

"Drop fifty or it won't matter."

The artillery rounds were impacting within a hundred feet, and still the NVA ran through the smoke. The men returned fire on full automatic. Grenades were being thrown by both sides. Gooks were over the walls on the right side, and Elderidge and his remaining men fell back to the stub wall. Even with the intense fire, a dozen NVA had made it to the wall and were climbing over.

Kelly stood and fired his M60 until the barrel glowed red-hot. His gun jammed, and he threw it aside and began firing with his forty-five, point-blank, into the enemy. Two soldiers jumped on top of him, and he fell down. They pounded him with fists and rifle butts. He shrugged them off and stood up. He retrieved his pistol and forced it into the mouth of one soldier, and pulled the trigger until it was empty. The soldier's head exploded like a balloon. The second soldier stabbed him with his bayonet. Kelly ignored his wound and grabbed the soldier; and forced his thumbs into his eyes, deep into his skull, then dropped him. He screamed at Holt. "You got gooks behind you, on the bunker."

Holt fired at two gooks as they jumped from the bunker. He continued firing as they hit the ground. More soldiers were on top, throwing grenades into the men.

On the right, Elderidge's men were fighting hand-to-hand as NVA jumped the walls.

Kimball was locked in a death struggle with a soldier, their hands on each other's throats. Kimball kneed the soldier in the groin and fell on him. He picked up a large piece of concrete and brought it down on the enemy's head, shattering his skull like an egg.

Holt's rifle jammed; he tossed it to Wilson and grabbed his pistol, and continued firing. Wilson cleared the jam and shot two soldiers to Holt's rear.

Wilson was shot in the throat and Kane, in the upper thigh. Wilson killed the soldier who shot them. Kane covered Wilson's body with his own, and set about wrapping Wilson's throat. Wilson was looking into Kane's eyes as his face went a ghastly, ashen gray and he fell across Wilson's body. The bullet that had hit Kane in the leg severed his femoral artery, and he bled out in seconds. Wilson cradled Kane's lifeless body and cried.

A gook lunged at Holt with his bayonet. He stabbed him in his right side, above his hip; and Holt fell backward. The soldier lunged again, and Holt deflected the bayonet. But the blade entered his right cheek and came out above his ear. The soldier ripped the bayonet free and tore Holt's face from his ear to below his eye. The soldier went for the kill; two shots rang out. Mr. Freed had shot him in the back. The soldier fell, dead.

Magically, the smoke swirled aside as a Loach hovered above them. He leisurely drifted left, firing his mini-gun. Dozens of advancing NVA fell. He arched sharply to the left and up, and was replaced by two Huey gunships that set about clearing the enemy from the fort. As they retreated, they were pursued and slaughtered by the gunship's mini-guns.

From the road came the unmistakeable sound of armored tracked vehicles. First was an M551 Sheridan Light Reconnaissance Tank with its 152-millimeter cannon blazing. It was followed by a half-dozen M113 Armored Personnel Carriers. The APCs peeled off from the tank and began their pursuit of the enemy into the village.

The Sheridan tank pulled up to the bunker and turned its cannon toward the village. The turret hatch opened; and a sergeant with a huge, bushy mustache appeared. "Gentlemen, the cavalry has arrived. Consider yourselves saved."

"Bullshit," yelled Kelly. "We had everything under control. Who the fuck are you assholes?"

"L Troop, 11th Armored Cavalry."

"Well, goddamn it, you're fucking late!"

Chapter 33

Aftermath

The APCs and their dismounted infantry cleared the village and pursued the NVA into the jungle. Medivac helicopters were summoned. Additional infantrymen were brought in to secure the area and to retrieve the wounded and the dead.

The open area in front of the bunker was a bloody field of dead enemy bodies. The tracked vehicles tried to avoid running over the bodies not out of any sense of decency, but to minimize cleaning their treads of human flesh.

Medics from the 11th Cavalry attended the wounded, along with Mad Dog.

Holt slumped against a wall, holding a bloody bandage to his face and smoking a cigarette.

"Let me see that," said Doc as he gently removed the bandage.

The wound began to bleed again.

"How do I look?" asked Holt. "My whole face is numb; I can't feel it."

"It's... not that bad. Could be worse, I guess."

"At least you have your fucking ear," said Mercado.

"I should put in some staples to try and stop the bleeding."

"I guess I'll have a scar."

"Jesus, dude, you'll have more than a scar. That gook took half your face off."

"Nick, shut the fuck up," said Doc.

Mr. Freed, came by taking pictures.

"Thanks, Joe, for shooting that gook. You were right; you're a pretty good shot."

"I never fired a gun in anger before. I really don't feel a thing. Should I?"

"You saved my life; that's what you should feel."

"What a mess this was."

"Write it as you saw it. Don't try and make sense out of it. It's just another day."

Doc looked over at Wilson. "He won't let go of Kane. He just keeps holding him, and crying."

"Let him be for now. He'll be alright, won't he?"

"Physically, he'll recover."

"He's a tough kid. He'll be okay. How's Kelly?"

"He must have the luck of an Irish angel. Got stabbed, and the bayonet missed his heart by inches."

"He's a fucking monster, that's for sure."

"Let me tag you for your ride back to Cu Chi. I guess they'll start on your face first."

"I'll take the last chopper out. Get everybody else out first."

"You'll go when I tell you to go."

"Doc, you know you're bleeding?"

"Just some shrapnel, nothing serious. I'm going to check on the other guys."

Mr. Freed sat down and took an offered cigarette. "Well, your war is over. You'll be in the hospital for awhile. They'll probably send you home to recover."

Holt replied, "I am home. I'm not going anywhere."

"You say that now, but you don't mean it. You'll change your mind when you get back."

"There are guys over here who shouldn't go home. Kelly is one.

He's right when he said he was a killing machine. What's he going to do back home? He lives for this shit. He might not know it now, but he will at some point. If he's home, he'll wish he were back here. I did, and I won't make the same mistake again. This place and the things we've done will haunt us for the rest of our lives. We'll never be free of it, so why leave? This is what I'm good at. If they'll have me, I'll stay until the end."

"You'll feel different in a couple of days."

"I doubt it. Like I said: I am home. This is where I belong."

Made in the USA
Monee, IL
22 November 2019